Secrets Of Hellharth

TALES OF ARCADEA: BOOK 1

GENESIS BATISTA

Warning

Secrets of Hellharth has some themes that may be triggering for readers. Sexual activities, violence, cursing, drug and alcohol use, and graphic deaths are shown on page.

For Mama, Nyssa, and Bee.
For the ones that stayed.
For fifteen-year-old me.

Northern Baltic Sea
Mountain of Tartis
The Witches of Highland
Weis Highlands
Pentaros
Tempest River
Tendis
Baltic Fork River
Iron Forge
Aslan Deserts
Delvi Plains
Goblin Country
Aslan Foothills
Hildfree
Morning Song
Desmon Forest
Damoi River
Calisan
Alpine River
Middle Islses
Sarasol Gulf
Alcheart
Tarn Stead
Mountains of Frey
Mountain Tail
Idris
Calisan Capital
Hansian Gulf
Direfell
Arcadia
Bristbane Sea
Hellharth
Desmouth
Idris Sea

HELLHARTH
Villages
Anaferi Mountains
Freiza River
Feri Lake
Irefana City
Bris Forest
Anti Lighthouse
The Shires
Hylycyn Castle
Hylyncynia City
Anvil
The Grotto
Townsend
Visil Lighthouse
CITY
VILLAGES
SHIRES
FOREST
FARMLANDS
CAVES
WATERWAYS

Contents

1. Chapter 1   1

2. Chapter 2   18

3. Chapter 3   25

4. Chapter 4   40

5. Chapter 5   59

6. Chapter 6   75

7. Chapter 7   80

8. Chapter 8   93

9. Chapter 9   110

10. Chapter 10   114

11. Chapter 11   128

12. Chapter 12   136

13. Chapter 13   147

14. Chapter 14   156

15. Chapter 15   172

16. Chapter 16   183

17. Chapter 17   198

18. Chapter 18   207

19. Chapter 19   214

20. Chapter 20   220

21. Chapter 21   234

22. Chapter 22   241

23. Chapter 23   248

24. Chapter 24   255

25. Chapter 25   267

26. Chapter 26   276

27. Chapter 27   288

28. Chapter 28   293

29. Chapter 29   303

30. Chapter 30   315

31. Chapter 31   321

32. Chapter 32   330

33. Chapter 33   335

34. Chapter 34   347

35. Chapter 35   354

36. Chapter 36   364

37. Chapter 37   372

38. Chapter 38   378

39. Chapter 39   388

40. Chapter 40   393

41. Chapter 41   402

42. Chapter 42   416

43. Chapter 43   427

44. Chapter 44   435

45. Chapter 45   440

About the Author   445

CHAPTER ONE

Ella raised her bow, arrow notched, and pulled back to her pointed ear. Squinting with concentration, she watched as the Vilkri Ram stopped to graze. She felt Valla, the Pentarian feline, brush against her legs. Crouching at her feet, Valla's oversized ears honed in on the ram. As Ella released her arrow, it struck its target with a resounding thwack. Valla lunged forward, her pale body darting through the forest brambles and attacking the fallen ram's neck with precision.

"I think it's dead, Valla," Ella called out, amused. Her foot sank into the wet ground with a grunt. "I could have sent you out to hunt alone, but then you'd just eat everything—selfish beast."

Valla growled in annoyance, yellow eyes bright with intelligence, and long canines sinking into the ram's neck. Ella knelt to retrieve her arrow, wiping the blood on her leather pants. She didn't need to hunt; there were plenty of hunters in Hellharth for that.

Townsend was full of fruit and meat—hunting was just her escape from politics and Court.

She wasn't ready—at least that's what her mother kept saying. Not yet privy to Hellharth's secrets, despite eventually ruling it. How disappointing for a daughter who's a High Fae but refuses to fly. Maybe that was why she wasn't ready.

Night enveloped Hellharth, the moon looming overhead as thousands of stars lit up the forest. Solitude wrapped around her while fireflies danced nearby. Valla crunched on the ram's horn and Ella sighed.

"Impolite of you," she said.

Her black wings extended from her back, and she shook them, groaning in relief. Having her wings out during hunting didn't make sense; they would just drag on the ground or get caught in low-hanging branches. She had made that mistake plenty of times, removing thorns for weeks afterward. Valla, the cat, took interest immediately and swatted at the feathers playfully.

"Bad kitty," Ella murmured, plucking a black feather and twirling it before Valla. They stayed like that for a while, Valla alternating between playing and eating. Ella eventually rested on the grass, looking up at the sky when it happened again—the flicker. The moon shifted too quickly, and clouds appeared and vanished without warning. The temperature fluctuated rapidly, accompanied by distant horns blaring.

Valla growled, and Ella sprinted through the forest as the sky flickered between various shades of darkness: blues with hints of purple or orange. The city of Hylycyn—an illuminated white against a backdrop of stars—came into view. Thousands of twinkling lights radiated from homes and villages.

Ella's wings caught the wind as she hurried down the hills; she glided faster with her heart racing in panic. A few Queensguards halted to watch Ella's not-so-subtle ascent up the stone walls toward her bedroom balcony. As she grasped the vines and willed for her wings to retract into her back, Valla meowed angrily below.

She climbed up to her archway balcony using twisted vines and thrust open the doors—half-expecting Nattya or Highwing to be asleep in her bed uninvited—but her room was empty. Her ruffled blue quilt remained as she left it.

Ella knew her mother would disapprove of her sneaking out, but the castle felt overwhelming and suffocating. Surrounded by nagging and criticism, she longed for escape. The queen constantly berated Ella about her studies, which she refused to share with the other Lords and Ladies. At nineteen, she was the oldest Fae amongst her peers and frequently questioned her worthiness in the eyes of her mother, Queen Kahlisenya.

After a devastating war, Elves hoped for blessings of children from any gods still listening. Yet the gods did not favor Ella's mother, leaving her as an only child and a bastard. This legacy weighed heavily on Ella, wondering whether it played a role in her exclusion from court matters—questioning if the Queen considered her worthy at all.

She quickly rummaged through her wardrobe, selecting a dark blue nightgown and hurriedly putting it on. Ella knew her mother might not be easily convinced, due to her keen sense of smell. With that in mind, she sprayed herself with Hymanthian flower mist, hoping the scent would mask the forest odor. Ella approached the door, opened it, and nearly collided with Hamlet's chest.

"Sorry," she mumbled.

The Maji human male quizzically regarded her and raised a dark eyebrow. "Going somewhere, Ellarhyssa?" he inquired. He wore typical daytime clothing, indicating he hadn't even gone to bed yet. Golden trinkets were woven into his brown hair that cascaded down to his waist, creating a soft clinking sound whenever he moved. Ella wondered if Nattya had styled him on this occasion. She met his honey-brown eyes and straightened her posture.

"Off to see my mother," she replied briskly. Hamlet wasn't someone she had to worry about; he was kind but incredibly dangerous—beautiful and deadly, like most things in Hellharth.

Fortunately for Ella, that danger didn't involve her. He was her private tutor, as well as her mother's best friend and High Advisor in Court.

He waved a hand before his face, wrinkling his nose. "You need to try harder. You reek of the outdoors—and a cat." He sniffed, rubbing his nose and dislodging his spectacles. He was allergic to all types of felines, even magical ones. A glint of blue light shimmered when he waved his hand; her mother's Lifestone, responsible for preserving his youth.

The details surrounding how a human Maji acquired an Elven Queen's favor remained unclear since no one had ever fully explained it to her.

"I was bored," Ella said. "I have matters to discuss with her."

"I see..." he replied after a moment, stepping aside and allowing her to pass. "You won't fool her with all that perfume."

"Worth a shot," she called over her shoulder.

She walked past several Queensguards, who bowed their heads in respect as she made her way through the halls toward her mother's wing. Their eagle-like masks glinted from the moonlight streaming through the windows. With each step, she felt a growing sense of trepidation, questioning why she put herself through this repeatedly. She clung to the hope that maybe, this time, her mother would reveal more information—like why this flicker seemed to be a bad omen.

Kahlisenya awoke in terror, her white wings fluttering beneath her as tears spilled from her wide-open eyes. She had experienced the same nightmare for many nights, haunted by a pair of amber eyes filled with hurt and confusion. Sitting up in bed, she heard a soft mewl from Valla, Ella's long-tailed Pentarian beast who seemed aware of Kahlisenya's distress. The moon's pale light filtered through the open terrace, intensifying her sense of dread as she was reminded of the reality beyond her nightmares.

"Rough night for you? How'd you manage to get in here?" Valla responded by walking through the nearest wall. It seemed the cat had bypassed the wards, which didn't surprise Kahlisenya. The queen drifted to the terrace and stepped out into the chilly night air, an unusual occurrence for Hellharth. The typically warm weather had changed drastically overnight. Her breath materialized before her in small clouds as she gazed upon her kingdom—rolling hills, mountains, rivers—all encased in magical fog to keep her world safe.

Her long white hair danced in the breeze. She closed her eyes, feeling the familiar sense of loss that often crept in during the night. The wind cut through her thin nightgown mercilessly, leaving her heart aching and her shoulders weighed down by the burden of the world.

All of this happened because she loved a man who became consumed by vengeance. Her cerulean eyes shimmered with memories, which she quickly shook her head to dismiss. There was no use dwelling on it. She turned her gaze towards the darkness, where the remains of the tall lighthouse, Vilis, stood. One of only two lighthouses still standing at the foothills, despite their years of disuse. The light hadn't been lit in nearly twenty years. If the other lighthouse, Vanti, was lit, it would be visible across the kingdom and beyond the Anaferi Mountains. So bright, it once reached the shores of Calisan.

"Has it been so long?" Queen Kahlisenya murmured to herself. A deep ache swelled in her chest with longing. She dared not speak his name; she could never say it again. That was the price she had to pay.

A flicker of light caught her eye beyond the fog, and she squinted in confusion. A snowflake landed before her, causing her breath to catch in her throat. It must be her imagination; snow didn't exist in Hellharth.

But it did in Arcadea.

Gradually, more snowflakes began to fall from above, and she stifled a gasp. Twinkling lights appeared through the fog as it faded, revealing silhouettes of tall structures covered in snow and what looked like ships floating on an ocean.

"NO!" Queen Kahlisenya hissed. She clenched her eyes shut and pressed her palms together as she visualized the protective fog once more.

Disappear, she silently commanded Hellharth. *Away. Vanish from this place.* Her chest tightened with the effort it took to make Hellharth disappear from Arcadea once again. A lightning bolt of pain shot through her body, and she felt her world spin. She fell to the ground, her eyes tightly closed as the pain worsened. The pain was coming from somewhere inside her—her magical core cracking and breaking.

She turned on her side and retched.

After a long moment, the pain subsided and she finally opened her eyes. The sound of the ships faded into silence. Once again, the air returned to the familiar warmth she had known for years. She exhaled a shaky breath, placing a hand over her heart. She had almost failed—again. The abjuration protection magic she used to move Hellharth from Arcadea, combined with mutation, was meant to make the vanishing permanent.

But it didn't. The shift from Arcadea into the void should have lasted forever. Instead, it had only been stable for nineteen years.

A soft knock at her door pulled her from her thoughts. She spun around, composing herself with an expression of indifference. She crossed the marble floor of her chamber, seating herself on an ivory chaise as if she had been lounging there the entire time.

The golden filigree-decorated door opened slowly, and she noticed a dark silhouette darting inside from the corner of her eye.

"Ellarhyssa," Queen Kahlisenya greeted softly, looking up to meet her daughter's alarmed amber eyes. For a moment,

Kahlisenya held her breath, forcing herself to look away from those eyes.

Those perfect eyes held fire and danced in certain lights, framed by long dark lashes.

"Is something wrong?" Kahlisenya spoke gently, making room for her daughter to sit. They were a stark contrast in appearance. The Queen's white hair resembled Arcadea's foreboding snow; her antlers gracefully arched above her head and her eyes were blue depths like a clear river. Ellarhyssa's dark hair flowed down her back in waves and her eyes glowed like flames against golden skin. Dressed in a dark blue nightgown adorned with embroidered Haberneth lilies along the hem, Ella wore a disgruntled expression accentuated by the scent of blood and forest air clinging to her.

"I felt it," Ellarhyssa hissed. Queen Kahlisenya focused on the spot between her daughter's brows, deliberately avoiding Ella's eyes for several reasons.

"Felt what?" she asked, feigning confusion.

Ella bared her Elven fangs in annoyance. "I *saw*!" Ella's black wings flared behind her in agitation.

"Saw what?"

"I heard those big ships. I saw the sky. I saw it! Where were we?" Ella pressed. She grasped her mother's hands in hers. "Tell me."

Her mother sighed, running her hand down her face in exhaustion. "I believe it was the Calisan peninsula."

"How far is that from the original place that Hellharth was part of?"

"Not a long way."

"Last time we were in the middle of the Aslan Desert, right?" Ella asked.

"Yes."

"It is happening more frequently now," Ella exhaled somberly. "The flickering."

"Yes."

"Why?"

"I wish I had an answer to that. I'll have to reconvene with Hamlet," Kahlisenya answered.

"Does he know?" Ella asked doubtfully, thinking of her mother's Maji human best friend.

"No, I need to discuss certain matters with him."

"Regarding what?" Ella inquired.

"Why concern yourself with trivial matters?" The Queen sighed, knowing Ella wouldn't let it go.

"Your magic isn't holding up anymore. Hamlet mentioned that during his last visit to the Known World, people spoke of a mysterious floating island appearing randomly. The people of Arcadea might suspect it's Hellharth."

"Such rumors have circulated for years before the flickering," the Queen countered weakly. She bit her cheek and gently touched Ella's face with her claw-like nails.

"How beautiful you are," she whispered. "Consider Highwing as a spouse; he's handsome and a skilled shifter." Ella scoffed and moved away from her mother's touch.

"I haven't felt the mating pull yet. Besides, he's more in love with himself than anyone else. Don't change the subject," Ella snapped.

"You don't have to be mates now—starting as spouses could set a mating bond in place. Have you considered giving Nattya a bonding stone, then?"

"Of course I have. She's my best friend! But it must be her choice."

"Hmm, you have quite the attitude tonight," her mother observed playfully. "Didn't have a good time in the forest then?" Of course, her mother knew where she had been.

"You insist on keeping me from these important events. Do you not trust me?" Ella pouted in a rare form of vulnerability.

"It is not about trust, so much as it is about your safety. My magic was inherited from my mother, like her mother before her, and so on. No one has ever accomplished what I have. There is a very real possibility that the task will fall to you."

"I cannot alter things the way you can as it is. I can't make a protection barrier. There's no way I could disengage all of Hellharth from Arcadea," Ella stammered. She stood up and began pacing the room.

"Do not worry yourself over this. Get back in bed. I will be speaking to Hamlet in the morning, and we will go from there."

"I'm not a child, mother. You were just trying to convince me to get married, yet you put me back in a child's place when it comes to matters at hand!"

"Ellarhyssa," Queen Kahlisenya warned. "Do not question me. Go."

Ella stood there, baring her small fangs as the Elvish people did when expressing themselves. A subtle hiss escaped her throat, met with a cold stare from Kahlisenya. She hissed back, displaying more prominent fangs in dominance. Gradually, Ella's demeanor shifted to submission. "One day. When this all falls to me. I'll fail. Because you never taught me any better. I'll be alone," Ella whispered furiously, storming out of the room and slamming the door. Queen Kahlisenya swallowed hard, fixated on where Ella had been standing moments before. She knelt down, picked up one of Ella's fallen feathers, and twirled it in her hand.

"I won't let you fail. I will not let you be alone," she promised quietly, alone in her room with her racing thoughts and a broken heart.

⤙➤➤➤⟶

"The nerve of her!" Ella muttered to herself as she exited the castle gates and entered the heart of Townsend. The market area was lit by floating lanterns, and although it was late, a few guards and passersby remained. Curious onlookers peered from their porches while tavern patrons drunkenly nodded respectfully. Ella consciously retracted her wings, her nightgown trailing behind her.

With purposeful strides, she navigated the cobblestone streets until reaching her destination. At the town's center stood a magnificent statue of an Elven man, frozen in mid-swing with his sword. His presence emanated power and strength; Ella gazed up at him affectionately before seating herself on a nearby bench. Elven guards, clad in light blue armor that shimmered the lantern reflections, bowed briefly as they patrolled.

"Hi," she greeted the statue softly.

The statue of her father featured a permanent scowl; a testament to his battle-worn life. Though they had never met, this memorial connected Ella to him. With his hair tied up in a high ponytail and a fierce expression on his face, he looked like an eagle getting ready to swoop down on its target.

"She doesn't understand me," Ella whispered. "She sees me as a child. Perhaps if you were here, she wouldn't treat me like this."

She pursed her lips in amusement as she stood before the statue of her father, a reminder of his heroic sacrifice during the Purge War defending Hellharth against the Son of Bashet. Fond memories flooded her mind, stories about him and her mother—never married or officially mated, but secretly in love. Her birth was unplanned, yet spoken of warmly. With a teasing tone, she traced a delicate finger along the statue's base and said, "Oh? Nothing to say then?"

"The Bells rang, and you were born, though sadly, your father had been long lost during the battle. A statue was built in Townsend to honor his bravery," The Queen had said to her one night after Ellarhyssa had finally asked about her father. She was about six years old.

"What was his name?" Ella asked.

Her mother hesitated before finally answering, "Kai."

"Kai," Ella repeated. "You were in love?" she asked dreamily.

"Yes. Very much so."

"So, then he is in Olesa?"

"Yes. That is where the good people go in the afterlife," her mother answered. "And the bad ones go to Osmos."

"Does it make you sad that he died?" Ella had asked innocently.

Queen Kahlisenya was quiet for a long time. Ella was worried. Had she said something wrong?

"I was very sad when your father left," she answered carefully.

"I'm sad too," Ella pouted. "Gideon's father takes him hunting."

"Do you want to go hunting?" Her mother asked in surprise. "You could always ask Hamlet to take you."

"I don't want to go hunting...," said Ella.

"So, why are you upset?"

"I don't know..."

Ella knew that she wanted a father to take her hunting, but Hamlet wasn't the one. Initially hesitant, Gideon's father eventually agreed and took her on a hunting trip. He taught her archery, and by the age of ten, she had killed her first pig. She was skilled at it, yet Gideon's father didn't display the same pride he had for his son.

Now understanding why, her gaze shifted from the statue to the Vilis Lighthouse in the distance. Unlit for as long as Ella could remember, her feet guided her along the hill's path toward it. A shiver ran through her, unrelated to the cold.

She looked back at Townsend, and the castle silhouettes, teasing her from afar. Upon reaching the lighthouse's base, she noticed its overgrown vines from years of neglect. "Hi Gideon," she whispered into the night. "Sorry, it's been so long." She sighed regretfully.

The lighthouse entrance bore a rickety wooden door barely hanging on its hinges—a beast's mouth ready to engulf her. Its white paint was chipped away, revealing old brick. As the wind wailed, Ella felt a bittersweet recollection and found the courage to enter. Navigating up its wooden spiral staircase, she slipped a few times before she reached the top. It had been at least six months since her last visit.

Ella let out a shaky breath as she re-emerged into the outside air. This was the place that held so many memories, both lovely and tragic. From romantic moments to periods of turmoil, this lighthouse had seen it all. Her wings unfurled in the wind, and she grabbed onto the railing for a slight jump, letting out small laughs as she was picked up by the gusts. Staring out into the darkness, Ella looked across Hellharth—from Anvil farmlands to the Shires at its foot, Townsend near Hylycyn Castle, Vanti lighthouse to the North, and Irefana City lights—engulfed in fog but alive with sounds of waves crashing onshore. Feeling her wings catch the wind's current, she silently pretended she was flying again.

Her eyes pricked with tears, and her feet hit the floor with a clang. She fought hard not to let her mind wander to that night—but of course, it did, because this is where it all had happened. If she looked at the rocks below—where the sea crashed violently against them—she was sure she would see them painted red.

Ella ran her fingers through Gideon's short brown hair. She kissed him again and giggled against his lips—

"I thought I'd find you here," a male voice came, startling her out of her thoughts. She wiped her eyes and looked away.

"Highwing. I didn't hear you," she apologized. She fixed her windswept hair out of her face and turned to greet her visitor properly.

Highwing was a sight to behold, soaring in the air before gracefully landing by her side with a friendly smile showcasing perfect white teeth. His golden skin and steel-gray eyes glowed in the moonlight, accentuated by gold metal hoops draping from his pointy ears. Adorning his large arms were several black tattoos depicting vicious-looking Hyla cats—a decoration of strength and power. Standing over a foot taller than her, he gave her an astute look as he said, "You looked like you were having a good time until—you weren't."

"How long have you been standing there? Spying on me?" Her eyes snapped to the repaired railing, memories flooding back, before meeting his gaze with a mix of surprise and suspicion.

"I followed you out of Townsend. Quite the walk. I was a cat for a bit, but some of the other cats started acting dodgy because they could sense I wasn't one of them. Valla took a swipe at me, so I flew above you for a while."

"I didn't need an escort," said Ella. At the mention of her cat's name, she sighed. Valla was going to be particularly pissed when she got back. The cat hated being left behind.

Highwing rolled his eyes at her. "I'm trying to become part of the Queensguard. What better way to practice than with the Princess? Check out my new rune." he presented her with his palm, a small awkward semicircle in the center.

"Hopefully you can do more than shift into animals by then," said Ella. "This is the third rune you've gotten. I didn't think the pain would be worth that."

"I don't know if I could handle another one," he winced. "I don't know how some people get more than three. The pain gets more excruciating every time. This one is for strength—"

"Did you get her?" A female voice called up from the bottom. Ella rolled her eyes.

"You brought Nattya? Really? I'm *fine*. She worries more than my mother," Ella groaned. Her best friends habitually inserted themselves in matters that didn't concern them—out of the goodness of their hearts. Ella knew they meant well. Nattya would take any burden from Ella if she could.

"I heard that, you wench!" Natty called up. "I don't feel like walking up all these steps. It was tiresome enough walking over here. Come down."

"Go on, I'll meet you at the bottom," Ella said to Highwing. He hesitated before leaning down and disappearing out of her sight to join Nattya on the ground.

Nattya came from the opposite side of Hellharth, down in Anvil—the farmlands. She was an orphan brought up by a woman who housed cats and children. Her Brood mother bred hunting felines, and from two Pentarian cats she had gotten before Hellharth had been moved, came Valla.

On Ella's sixteenth birthday, Nattya and her Brood mother came to Hylycyn castle with gifts just like many others in Hellharth. Ella had been sitting on a smaller throne next to her mother, laden with gifts and jewels, her heart heavy and broken from Gideon's death just a few weeks before.

There had been nothing to celebrate.

Nattya had approached the throne, her hands clutching a small Pentarian kitten. This feisty and larger-than-usual kitten was the last of the litter. Ella had already been gifted fruits, cattle, and several marriage proposals for land and titles—including one from Highwing, who was being pressured by his unrelenting father. Valla, however, didn't take to Nattya's vice-like grip and decided to bite into her hand instead. Shocked at this sudden outburst of fury from the kitten, Nattya screamed which sent the cat flying beneath Queen Kahlisenya's dress causing an uproar of chaos in the room. Ella found it so amusing that she laughed uncontrollably until tears streamed down her face, relieving her from weeks of the trauma she'd kept hidden ever since Gideon's death. The laughter then turned into uncontrollable sobbing.

In mere seconds, Nattya had broken seven laws to reach her, wrapping her arms around Ella. Nattya's instinctive reaction to protect Ella was so powerful that Kahlisenya, moved by the display, became determined to keep Nattya close to Ella. Kahlisenya found herself taking dramatic measures to ensure they remained together; in effect, she kept Nattya a virtual prisoner for months with the hopes of preventing Ella from slipping into a deeper depression. It had been an extreme measure, but one that paid off in the end. Kahlisenya had paid a large sum to Nattya's Brood mother—effectively buying her.

It worked.

With each creaking step she took, she could smell the salt and moisture from the sea that had caused the steps to swell and rot, threatening their eventual collapse. Every time she ventured up or down them, it felt like something special—an emblem of a quickly fleeting chance to experience something old before it disappeared forever.

Nattya and Highwing met her with pinched faces. "You shouldn't have come out here by yourself," Nattya scolded, her sunkissed skin glowing in the moonlight.

"Sorry, Mom," Ella teased. "I didn't realize I was in immediate danger."

Nattya blushed. "We would have come with you," she argued. "Besides, what the ever-loving hell was all that before? We saw the fog disappear—the ships—and that white stuff falling from the sky."

"I believe it's called snow, though I've never seen it before. My mother says it snows in Arcadea," said Highwing.

"Yeah, well, this is Hellharth, and I've never seen that before in my life. Is everything alright?" Nattya asked. She looked rather disheveled—as if she had just rolled out of bed and run a few miles—which she probably did. Her crown of wild, honey-brown hair was in a lopsided bun, and she was wearing her white nightwear.

"My mother doesn't see fit to tell me anything, so I know as much as the both of you. I went and saw her after it happened, and she completely shut me down," Ella replied.

Nattya crossed her arms. "Whatever it is. It can't be good. People are starting to talk. Are we going to be integrated back into Arcadea?"

"Imagine? Twenty years go by and the Isle of Elves just pops back out," Highwing laughed.

"That's what it's starting to seem like, but she won't say anything to me. It keeps happening..."

"What about Hamlet?" Nattya asked. She blushed and tried to look inconspicuous. Ella pursed her lips. Hamlet had Nattya wrapped around his finger. Nattya was a Nomaji—a human without magic, and Hamlet was a Maji human—a wielder of magic.

"You need to let that man go. He's been alive for sixty-eight years and has never married. You're twenty-two. Find a nice man to settle down with," said Ella.

Hamlet was a rare "pet" as some Elves liked to call it; a term that wasn't widely used because of its *unique* nature. To extend the life of a human companion, Elves could transfer some of their life force into stones or gems, ensuring that the human would remain alive as long as they did. However, this only happened once and only while an Elf was mature. After their death, the human would resume aging at their natural rate. Hamlet was one of few people with such a Life Stone since the war, making it a rare occurrence indeed.

Before Gideon died, Ella had planned to give him hers. Though it hadn't occurred to her that he would die before she would reach maturity.

"Who says I'd marry him? He is just a good time!" exclaimed Nattya. "And you're one to talk, coming out here of all places. Your mother isn't bedding him, so what if I do?"

"I'm paying my respects to the dead, not swooning," Ella hissed.

"As titillating as this conversation is, I'm starting to lose interest," Highwing said in an attempt to diffuse the tension. "Am I, or am I not going to meet ladies in Arcadea? That is the question that I need answers to."

Ella swatted his arm. "If you do, perhaps my mother will stop trying to have us married. She'd love to see me with someone from Court."

"Am I such a disappointment?" He snatched her hand and kissed it. She rolled her eyes at him and wiped her hand on his blue tunic.

"Maybe I could get information out of Hamlet?" Nattya suggested.

"Sleeping with him for information? I like it. I wish I knew things," Highwing sighed.

"Good thing you're an idiot then," Nattya said. "We should get back. It's late and I have a mission in the morning," she said excitedly.

"She means missionary," Highwing whispered in Ella's ear. Ella snorted and slapped her hand over her mouth to keep from laughing.

"I heard that," Nattya snapped. They burst into a fit of laughter behind her.

When Ella finally made it to bed, after convincing her friends she didn't need the company, she found she didn't very much want to be alone with her thoughts. Gideon never got to see the flicker of Arcadea. She wondered how he would have reacted—would he have been excited? Of course, he would have. He had longed to know what the world was like outside of Hellharth, and instead, he died in the same place he had wanted to escape. She knew that if given the opportunity, Gideon's parents would leave their farmstead down in Anvil and run back to the Known World. She quietly wished for their freedom.

CHAPTER TWO

Highwing jumped up and down off the ground, tiring himself out. The sound of his heavy breathing echoed through his bedroom. Beads of salty sweat coated his body, and the thought of a shower was heavy on his mind. He had the terrace windows open, offering a cool breeze that he was thankful for. He loosened the ties in his hair, letting heavy silver braids fall down his back. Scrutinizing his hair, he realized some strands had come undone already.

Training day had been mentally exhausting, with everyone up in arms about what the flickering meant. It also meant the other Queensguards-in-training had set about nagging him for information, most likely due to fear that they were unprepared for war. The flickering to them was a sign of impending danger. Today had tested his patience.

Because of who his father was, many expected him to be abrasive or demanding. He preferred to believe he was kind instead. Althane was a general at heart, overseeing the training of the Queensguard and having a reputation for being a brute in both battle and wit. Despite Lord Althane's position over the Queensguard, he had hoped his son would continue a legacy in Court, rather than becoming just a guard. Highwing had hoped that showing an interest in the Queensguard would have made his father proud of him; instead, it created more self-doubt and feelings of inadequacy.

He almost wished he hadn't set about being the opposite of his father—then people would have left him alone.

A knock at his bedroom door took him out of his thoughts. "Enter!" he called out.

Upon seeing his mother enter, her large wings occupying most of the doorway, he groaned internally.

She always found the most ridiculous things to take up his time. The last time she showed up at his chamber, she made him go all the way to Irefana City for some ludicrous reason, the reason being "a new silk dress design only available there."

She made herself comfortable on his large black bed, analyzing his room with disdain.

"I hate all this black you put in," she said, motioning at his black sleigh bed and dressers. Ironically, that was exactly what she was wearing; a black corset dress that expanded at the waist, with slits that rose to her thighs. Her sleeves were short and laced, with a plunging neckline.

Nattya would kill for a dress like that, he thought to himself.

Her eyes fixated on a rather dark painting above the bed; two winged figures slicing through each other in the clouds as their blood rained down on people below them.

"Furia and Dalessa," she observed. "A dark story like that doesn't give you nightmares," she said sarcastically.

"I find it interesting," he said. "Two sisters fight on opposing sides, one marrying a dragon, the other a bird."

She scoffed, "A feud that is said to be the cause of the Five Hundred Years War."

"It's a fairy tale, Mother, hardly any truth to it," he laughed.

"All stories come from a line of truth," she said prophetically.

He pulled a towel from a shelf and began wiping himself off. "Was there something you needed? Let me rephrase... Can it wait until I've bathed?" He hated being sweat-slicked.

"I'll be quick, don't worry," she assured him. "The Queen plans to throw another ball."

Highwing blinked rapidly at his mother. An hour had already passed, and she hadn't stopped her squawking. He pinched the bridge of his nose, appalled at what he was hearing.

Finally, he said, "Ella doesn't desire me that way." His room had been filled with her heavy scent—lavender and Hymanthian flowers. She had been going on nonstop about how she and the queen had discussed the idea of a marriage between himself and Ella.

It sounded more like they were arranging something behind his back.

"You would be joining our bloodline once more since my grandfather, Aldwin, and your father's grandfather, Alaric, were brothers. You have more Anaferian blood than Tanyl's children." She ranted.

"That's because the Anaferians have a long history of marrying their brothers, sisters, and cousins," Highwing grumbled.

"Anaferi and Hylycyn *were* brothers. Your grandparents on both sides were siblings; your great aunt three times over is Ella's third grandmother. It all comes full circle. You and Ella share the same ancestry. It is a marriage that would benefit your children." She was making joining gestures with her hand excitedly.

Highwing refrained from rolling his eyes at her and fixed her with a cold gaze. "You didn't feel that father's marriage benefited anyone," he said.

Lady Rayne tilted her head, narrowing her sharp eyes and pulling her mouth down into a frown. "That's different, and you know it, Highwing. Your father already had me as his *mate*." She said the words pointedly. "Marrying Tanyl after me isn't the same as you marrying Ella. Tanyl doesn't even have royal blood!"

"The only difference is politics?" He snorted, fixated on turning his back on her, having no more of this discussion.

"You cannot tell me you do not find her attractive. Anyone with eyes can see it," she argued.

"Of course I do. But how can I live up to a ghost?" How could he deal with Ella's downtrodden spirit in a marriage?

She was silent for a moment. The girl's flavor did lean toward uselessness when it came to men. The boy's death had been a great tragedy, but Ellarhyssa was a princess—surely she understood that duty came above all else. Kahlisenya only had *one* blood heir. Ella was well into her childbearing years—well into the age of marriage.

"You have known the princess all your life. I seat you in Court. have given you countless opportunities. She will come around." Lady Rayne answered flippantly. "With your Grandsire's death last month, it should have really put things into perspective for you." Highwing turned to face her again.

"You're sounding more like father," he said in annoyance. He saw a flicker of something that passed along his mother's features, breaking her elegant facade. Her shoulders slumped, and her jaw clenched, feathering a muscle in her cheek.

"You've desired Ella for years. Are you going to be like Hamlet?" She dared to ask him.

Highwing sighed heavily. Hamlet was still the Queen's Lifestone partner, and he seemed happy enough.

Happy, he laughed to himself.

He shuffled around her to reach for a glass of water. "No. I won't be like Hamlet." He swallowed the water hastily, trying to find something else to do that would disengage him from this conversation. He could feel her eyes on him.

"I've been having relations with Dasyra," he said quietly.

The mention of Lord Cida's daughter caught Rayne's attention. "You wish to pursue a marriage with her?" she asked in disbelief.

Highwing sputtered and coughed, "Gods! No! It's just that Dasyra is expecting that I will ask her—"

"Why would she suspect it if you hadn't given her the idea?" she accused.

"I did not give her any impression that I would marry her," he started, "it's just sex."

Rayne grimaced at his words and turned a shade of pink. She cleared her throat, feeling slightly uncomfortable. "I am sure that Dasyra is quite adequate in bed, but as a wife, she would be severely lacking."

Becoming momentarily speechless, he made an undignified noise and said through gritted teeth, "I just told you I'm not interested in marrying her."

"So why bring it up?"

"There's always a possibility that I could find a mate," he answered timidly. He blushed. Admitting something like that to his mother was mortifying. He jutted his chin and crossed his arms over his chest.

To his chagrin, his mother smirked, until it cracked into a wide smile. "My son! A true romantic at heart!" She pinched his cheek and made mocking kissing noises, smacking her lips obnoxiously.

"Stop that!" He batted at her hands and jumped away from her. When her laughter finally died down, she took on a serious tone.

"Highwing, you realize that finding your mate is incredibly rare. It could take hundreds of years, and some don't even live long enough to see to it. Your mate could be generations from now. Or you could get lucky and have the bond snap into place at an unexpected time." She picked up a long braid of his, something intricate and artful that she knew the human girl, Nattya, had done.

She pulled her hand back and hissed. He jumped in surprise.

"It's not that human girl, is it? I know you two have been involved in the past," she said, waiting in horror as his face twisted from confusion to realization.

"Nattya? No, she's just... Nattya. I only say this because, well, I don't want to be like my father. A mate *and* a wife complicate things."

Relief flooded through her. She didn't have a problem with humans, she told herself, just that *that* human girl was every bit as wild as a boar. The amount of time it would take to make Nattya into a lady—she shuddered at the idea.

"You would not be like your father. Your father knew the repercussions of taking a spouse after me. That I wouldn't tolerate it."

"And if I find my mate and she rejects me because I'm already married?"

"Is that what you're afraid of? You are over-complicating things," she said dismissively.

"Am I? Look at what I've grown up witnessing. You and Father can't stand to be in the same room."

"The situation is different. Marrying Ella and producing would benefit Hellharth. You tell me, who else would be in her sights? Not your brothers," she scoffed at mentioning his half-brothers from Tanyl. "You needn't do more than that. Marriage is for titles and land; mating is for love."

"Ella is special to me. I do love her. She would be in good hands with me. With our friendship behind us, I can picture myself living my life with her. The same could be said for Nattya."

Two white dots appeared on Rayne's collarbone and she rubbed it roughly. "For Olesa's sake! I thought you said you didn't see the human girl that way?" His eyes latched onto her mating mark. It was glowing and causing her discomfort. Which meant something was troubling his father.

"What I meant was, I see Ella the same way I see Nattya—like family. Yes, it would be easy to see us married—I don't feel the dynamics would change in that sense. But what if I or Ella find love in someone else?"

"Then do your best to find your love in each other."

"Why do you act as if Father's marriage to Tanyl doesn't bother you?"

Taken aback by his bold questioning, she gasped at him. "It doesn't bother me," she lied thickly.

He quirked a silver eyebrow at her. "I often wondered who you are really hurting here. If you say marriage is all political, and mating is for love, why not forgive Father?"

Lady Rayne rose to her full height, a segment shorter than her son, but giving off an air of dominance. "Goodnight, Highwing," she managed.

Her scent had spiked and Highwing could tell that she was distressed. The air around her grew thick and he held back a sigh of relief when she finally left his room. He tossed his clothes onto the floor, meandering to his showers and placing the temperature to scorching.

Still, even with the water relieving some of his stress, his mother's words hung in the air.

CHAPTER THREE

"It is the same dream as the last. It is always the same. I am closing him into the mirror. I am with The Council. It is a memory of that night until it is not. The mirror cracks and breaks and he is freed. He is so angry, and I see the land burning, writhing in smoke." She lay on the grass, shaded by a tree that rustled in the wind, and gazed up at the blue sky. She fiddled with her green flowing skirt with anxiety, running a hand over her brown corset, trying to loosen it. The damn thing was making her sweat.

Hamlet sat and listened as the Queen recounted her nightmares to him. It was indeed the same dream she had relayed to him before. He adjusted his large-framed glasses on his hooked nose and ran a hand through his sleek brown hair. He still looked as if he were a man of twenty, in reality, he was well in his sixties. He was one of the few humans that still lived in the land of Hellharth. Born and raised.

"Do you suspect it is a vision?" Hamlet asked gently. He flicked at a blade of grass next to him. As of late, the grass had been drying out, taking on a straw color.

"I did not believe myself to have the gift of Divination. It has never manifested itself before. I have no markers of it in my lineage. That is usually an Anaferian trait." High Fae elves could trace back their roots right on a tree. Literally. The Tree of Ancestors resided in the Treasury at the heart of Hylycyn castle. The High Fae were marked by two Houses—though related. Hylycyn and Anaferi had been brothers with many wives and many powers. Anaferi was most known for his shifting abilities and married women who were said to be seers to try to outmatch his older brother, Hylycyn. They came upon the land more than a thousand years ago with their youngest sister, Safrina, long before the Five Hundred Years War. What remained of them was their bloodline, and the stronger of the Two houses would rule over the other.

It was always Hylycyn's line. Kahlisenya's ancestral grandfather was Hylycyn. The Court members were made up of Anaferi's and Safrina's kin.

"Power can appear at different stages in your life. Twenty years ago, I couldn't bend a spoon and only ever had an affinity for Rune magics. Things change my Queen. Power is not created, nor destroyed, it changes form." Hamlet was right. There had been instances where magic adapted to its need. It was also dangerous to use too much magic because it could kill you. "I believe the only reason you haven't died from using your magic for twenty years straight is directly a result of you siphoning magic from Hellharth itself." It was true. She had been doing that in order to keep herself from being drained. Magic was of equal give and take.

"The crops aren't yielding what they used to. The animals aren't as healthy," she agreed solemnly. If she kept this up, she was going to end up like her predecessors—withered to nothing. She was young in Elven terms at just over a hundred years old. She sighed heavily. "She is asking more questions. Questions I do not know the answers to."

"She is a young woman now. The questions become more serious as they get older, I am afraid."

"My powers are fading, Hamlet," Kahlisenya said gravely. "Or, as you said, they are changing to something else. The Gods must think it is time for something else."

He shifted himself to prop his head up, looking at her with reservations. "Permission to speak plainly?"

"Of course," she snorted and rolled her eyes.

"You have used your magic to move an entire place, keeping it guarded for twenty years. A feat that no one else can claim. You vanished us from the Known World— from Arcadea. Imagine what that kind of magic does to the caster. Your magic *is* waning, or it is giving birth to a *new* magic. This Divination. Your mind is warning you. You cannot keep this up."

"Perhaps..." she agreed sadly. "Which means I cannot protect her from them, Hamlet. They will hate her. They will persecute her for the mistakes of her—"

"There is no telling what the Nomaji and Maji humans of Arcadea will do. Speculating does not help the matter."

Queen Kahlisenya's hand shot forward, taking off Hamlet's glasses and placing them on her face. Hamlet did not seem surprised in the slightest at her antics. He tugged on her antler playfully.

"How do you see with these?" she teased.

"Well, I cannot see without them," he laughed.

"Will you visit Arcadea again?" she asked, her eyes slightly bigger through the lenses.

"If you request it, though, I am unsure if you should keep creating portals back through. We just had this conversation about the unnecessary expense of magic."

"I will be fine. I need you to go to Calisan Capital. That is where we were last night. I need to know what is being said about us. If we were seen." She could only hope that if they had been seen, there weren't already warships patrolling the waters to try and locate them. The last thing she needed was for Hellharth to flicker right into the middle of a Calisan fleet.

"Okay. I do hope you take into consideration that Ella is no longer a child. You cannot protect her from people's thoughts and opinions."

"Having that statue built in the name of her 'father' should have dissuaded people from such gossip," said the Queen. "The older generation looks upon her with reservations. They don't speak, but their children don't mind their ruddy business."

"There does not seem to be any residual damage from the Purge War in Hellharth. Humans do not act prejudicial here. You even have humans in Court…" He pointed to himself with a laugh.

"Oftentimes scars are not visible, Hamlet. Hatred is taught. There is probably a generation as old as Ella carrying the hatred of their parents and grandparents who were part of that war." She handed him back his glasses, no longer as amused with them as she once had been. "Not to mention the death of the Nomaji boy three years ago. Ella blames herself. His parents do too. They moved their home to the furthest point away from the castle in Anvil."

"Their tragedy should not be the burden of a nineteen-year-old girl," Hamlet argued. "She hasn't flown since."

"She hides her wings when she is in the town. She might as well scream her shame," Kahlisenya said bitterly. It wasn't her daughter's fault, but humans tend to find fault in the wrong places. Despite the peace in Hellharth with the Nomaji and the Maji humans, there was an undeniable tension that was residual from the Purge War.

They were lost in thought for a moment, not wanting to speak first. It was Kahlisenya who finally lost.

"I often wonder if there are still those out there with the same ideas and beliefs as him. Just quietly hanging about, waiting for their moment to strike again."

"There very well could be. Elves were not the only ones who were seduced by Idmodias. Orcs fought with him, goblins, the Banes of Tendal," he listed off. It was hard back then to tell who was a friend and who was foe. Which Elves fought for Kahlisenya and which fought for the Son of Bashet.

"Hn. And yet the elves are the ones who are hated because *he* was an elf."

The ones who fought alongside Idmodias, the Elves who believed that humans were inferior beings and deserved to be put beneath the boot, had been executed years ago. There were only so many places they could go in Hellharth, and around one hundred of his followers had been rounded up and killed. It was hard—those Elves had families as well. Families that were stuck with the darkness of their kin looming over their heads.

Sadly, it was an elf who brought The Dark Ones upon the world.

The Dark Ones appeared from the depths of Mount Tartis when the reign of Idmodias began. It started out as two; Sibba and Karkoff, who then made more. While Sibba and Karkoff could speak and resembled somewhat humanoid attributes, their creatures bore unmistakable traits—their skin as white as alabaster, eyes as dark as the abyss, and veins resembling obsidian rivers. Their bite alone turned other beings like them, creating an army. Their existence seemed to vanish as he was imprisoned, drawn into the Mirror of Shadows alongside him. They had been a harrowing sight back in the day.

"She is realizing that this is just a gilded cage. When will you tell her about her father?" Hamlet held his breath, waiting for her glare and exasperated sigh that usually came with such a question. It surprised him when she did the complete opposite.

She sighed in defeat, rather than defensively. "I know. I have to tell her. She will hate me for it."

"She mourns him you know," Hamlet said slowly. "Nattya visited me this morning. She told me that Ella was at Vilis again."

"I know. I wish she didn't... I know she grieves, but I wish she wouldn't. She mourns a lost father and a boy long gone. Highwing is such a nice young man. He's strong, and he has ties to the Court. His mother is a proper Lady, and it is a smart match."

"You can't keep pushing her to mate or marry. It will happen on its own." Hamlet wasn't against the idea of Ella being married, but if it was forced upon her it would only further the wedge that was between her and her mother.

"I'd be satisfied if she took up with a consort at this point—"

"Until she's drowning in men and has her own harem," Hamlet said.

"If it pleases her." Kahlisenya groaned and agreed begrudgingly. "She loved that boy. I don't want her to be like me, unable to move on. She has no escape—Hellharth is her cage as it is anyone's."

"It isn't too late for you to take up a consort," Hamlet said, glancing at her from the corner of his eye.

"Perhaps I should," she said. She knew what he was insinuating. It was like dangling a carrot. She knew Hamlet was in love with her, and while those feelings were reciprocated, she couldn't allow herself to feel happy with all that she had done.

They lay there quietly, watching the clouds in the sky that were illusioned to exist. For all they knew, they were in the middle of a storm somewhere at sea.

"That mirror will not hold for long. You will need to have that conversation. Soon." Hamlet said seriously.

"I'm going to speak to the Witches of Highland. Perhaps they can give me a clearer picture of what I am dealing with. Perhaps this is all just latent guilt for what I did."

He gaped at her. "Are you mad? The Witches of Highland?"

She knew he was going to have this reaction. The Witches of Highland were two women—once human maji—turned something else, more than three hundred years ago. They were outcasts living in the Highlands of Weis, West of the Northern Balic Sea. It was said that they had long ago been cursed by a man that they had rejected, and no men may look upon them now.

"I can make another portal and walk through."

"That is well beside the point! The Witches of Highland? No one knows how to reach them. You just expect to stumble across their living quarters?"

"I am sure I can find them just fine." *I have before*, she thought glumly.

"There are no current reports on them. The last one was made more than a century ago. How do you know they are still alive?"

"I don't, but it is worth a try." She rolled onto her side, facing away from him.

"So you are going to leave Hellharth? What happens if you leave?" Hamlet asked. He poked his pointer finger into the middle of her back and she jolted. "You're the beacon for the barrier surrounding Hellharth. With you gone, the barrier would be gone too."

"There is a barrier spell I've put in the Staff of Eresai. It's a protection spell I got from Lady Rayne... It should hold temporarily as a beacon, so long as the staff remains. I wouldn't be long." She spoke fondly of her great-grandmother's wooden staff that rested on a wall in her bed chambers.

"I have to insist that you do not go alone," Hamlet said sternly. His brows furrowed and he bit the inside of his cheek. He had known the Queen his whole life. He had been born in the land of Hellharth. A Maji human—a human born with magic in Elven lands. Even though he was in his sixties now, he aged at a snail's pace in comparison to the Nomaji—the non-magical humans. He had grown alongside Queen Kahlisenya when times had been simpler, and when times had been the most difficult. When she had just been a Crown Princess, and just Kahlisenya to him.

When he came of age, Kahlisenya gifted him a Lifestone. He had at first thought that meant they would be together, but then the complications of another lover and war got in the way. It had been over twenty years, and they never crossed that line.

He had been there to grieve the loss of her mother, Daliena. He had watched her fall in love, watched her grieve the loss of her lover. He had been there for the birth of Ellarhyssa—who had secretly been named after her father's sister.

He allowed himself to reach for her white hair, toying with the silk strands between his two fingers. Slowly, he twisted the strands in his chestnut brown hair, the way that she had done when they were younger. White hair weaved in the brown locks, and she turned to smile at him.

"I will be okay. I promise," she said gently.

Hamlet took a moment to gather himself. "If you are anything but okay, I'll be livid." He clasped her smaller hand in his, refusing to look at her. "You are not alone in this."

"I know Hamlet." She squeezed his hand. "I'll tell her. When I am sure. When the time is right. I trust her to you, should anything happen."

"I hate children!" He exclaimed in horror. "I wouldn't even know what to do with her!"

"She's your Goddaughter. Do what you always have."

"Walk the other way?"

"No, you fool!"

"Kiss her friends?"

"You are a foul brat. Those girls are hopelessly in love and if they find out about each other..." Kahlisenya shoved his shoulder with her finger.

"Are you going to tell on me, your Majesty?"

"Ella will be quite upset."

"I should be able to have my fun!" He protested.

"I fear I've put her in the wrong hands," Kahlisenya scoffed.

"Don't even joke," Hamlet said seriously. He squeezed her hand for reassurance. "She scares the shit out of me, though."

At this, she cackled. Her face contorted in a fit of laughter, and she released his hand to grab at her sides. "Me too!" she exclaimed. He met her mirth with a smile of his own. Only he dared to be so candid with her, and he was acutely aware of the Elven guards that stood watch near them, analyzing them. Human and Elven relationships were frowned upon, never going above the status of consort.

"So, it is settled then. I'm to be no father figure to your brat," He whispered close to her ear. She sucked at her teeth, her long, Elven ear twitching in response.

"Agreed, you certainly are not her father figure," she remarked happily.

⤜⤜⤜——————➤

The next morning, Ella, Highwing, and Nattya gathered in the castle gardens. They were somewhat shaded under large, willowing trees, pink blossom petals coating the ground.

"He wouldn't give up anything," Nattya sighed. "I tried everything! I do mean *everything*!"

"That's more information than I needed to know," said Ella with a disgusted face. She turned to Highwing, who was laying casually against a tree. "What about you? Did your mother say anything about a Court meeting?" she asked hopefully.

"She's either oblivious or really tight-lipped. The last Court meeting was a month ago, and that was for Grandsire Joanai's death," he said. He picked at his teeth with a clawed fingernail. Joanai had been an elder member of the Court, passing away at age three hundred and ninety-seven—a bit young for a High Fae. He was also the father of Lady Rayne. He possibly died so suddenly from constantly expelling magic—but it was just a theory.

Hellharth was not at risk for overpopulation, having been culled during the war so many years before. Still, an Elven death was jarring, because it was always *unexpected* when it came naturally.

"I did hear that your mother was planning on throwing another ball this week," he hummed.

Ella groaned and buried her face in her hands. "I don't suppose this is another attempt at trying to get me married." She rolled her eyes, already dreading the grandiose spectacle her mother was sure to make.

"Oh, most definitely. She's invited everyone," said Highwing.

"Sounds like a distraction to me," Nattya huffed.

"You're just saying that because Hamlet didn't mention the ball to you. Probably because he doesn't plan on taking you," he laughed. Her ears turned red, and she threw a rock at him. He caught it midair without even looking.

"At least I have someone!" She shot back.

"Nattya's right. Usually, a ball is announced at least a month or two in advance. This is sudden," Ella agreed. She was contemplating, her fingers tapping her chin. Nattya came up behind her and started braiding her long hair.

"Your mother has more secrets than anyone I've ever known," Nattya whispered in her ear, glancing at a handful of guards that were keeping watch over the Princess. They would elude them, as they often did.

Ella shrugged her shoulders at Nattya's statement but winced. Highwing noticed her pained expression and raised a brow at her. "You shouldn't keep them in for so long. It's not good for you and the pain will only get worse," he sighed. She glared at him.

"There's no reason for them to be out. I'm not using them," Ella said. She ignored the shared glance between him and Nattya. "If the flicker happens again, I think we should try to escape."

That caught their attention. "Are you insane?" Nattya shrieked. The guards looked in their direction and Ella slapped a hand over Nattya's mouth.

"Say it any louder, would you?" Ella hissed.

"Ella, your mother would kill you. And forget about *you*—she would kill us," Highwing scoffed. He gave a sideways glance towards the guards, who had gone back to talking among themselves. "We don't know what's on the other side of that fog."

"And if we don't try, we will never know. I'm tired of being kept in the dark about everything. If she isn't going to tell me, then I'll figure it out for myself."

"We are just expected to go along with this plan of yours? We don't even know when a flicker will happen." He looked to Nattya for help.

"It happens at night from what I have witnessed. Last time she told me we were in Calisan. Before that, the Aslan Desert—" Ella was cut off by Nattya's hand over her mouth.

"A desert sounds like the perfect place to jump ship," Nattya said sarcastically. "What if we flickered into Tendis? Goblin Country? Mount Tartis? Or Direfell of all places. Gods what if we end up going out there and getting *trapped*."

Ella's shoulders slumped. "I'm not going to find answers here. Whatever is happening—whatever is causing the flickering—it has to be bad. My mother was talking about the responsibility of keeping Hellharth segregated from Arcadea falling to me. I have *never* shown signs of being able to harness mutation. What if I can't? What if something happens, and I can't?"

Highwing tucked her into his wing, bringing the other around Nattya. "Whatever happens, happens."

"How helpful," Nattya snorted. She rested her head on his shoulder. "He's right, Ella. If it comes down to it, Hellharth will just have to be part of Arcadea again. If that happens, then we can go out there. I don't think it's wise to do it while Hellharth flickers back and forth. We don't know what is out there."

"Or what we will be greeted by," Highwing added, "The humans out there have to have some resentment for our kind."

"I'm tired of balls and lies," Ella grumbled.

"As your future husband, I apologize, as that is all I can provide you with," Highwing said.

"Absolutely crude," Ella laughed.

One of the guards that had been lingering at the edge of the castle walls announced his approach. "Princess. Master Highwing," he turned to Nattya with contempt. "Girl." Nattya matched the guard's sneer with her own.

"Something you need?" Ella snapped at him. The guard straightened himself, yellow eyes drifting back to Nattya.

"Master Hamlet is looking for you," he answered. "He asked for your audience in the trophy room. He asked that I remind you of your lesson planning." Ella rolled her eyes.

Highwing snickered from her side, "He wouldn't insist on teaching you himself if you only went and learned with the rest of us."

"I can't even *conjure,* and runic magic is so blah," Ella groaned. The guard stood there, waiting.

"Was there something else?" Nattya huffed. He ignored her and held out his hand for Ella to take. Reluctantly, Ella stood, giving her friends an exasperated glance over her shoulder.

"I am to escort you there. Master Hamlet's orders."

"So, he can take orders from humans but only if they are Maji—got it," Nattya goaded. The guard turned to her and bared his less-than-impressive fangs at her.

"Majorn. Bare your teeth at her again and I will have them filed down," Ella threatened, her wings jutting out and shielding Nattya from the guard called Majorn. Majorn made a face, lowering his gaze, and nodded.

"Forgive me, Princess," he said. "Master Hamlet waits."

"I'll see the two of you later," Ella called behind her.

"You aren't concentrating!" Hamlet reprimanded. He swatted his hand at Ella's outstretched palms. She hissed at him and swatted him back.

"I'm trying! This isn't my natural affinity," she argued. They had been at it for over an hour now with Hamlet's private tutoring, both of them clearly annoyed with one another. Hamlet was not a teacher— he did not have patience for children whatsoever. Ella knew he did this out of favoritism. Elven children were taught by Elven teachers, and Maji humans taught Maji humans. It was just how things were. But Ella didn't like the false praises she received from her Elven teachers and peers because of her status in Court.

"I can't do it. It isn't meant for me," Ella said in defeat. Her brow had broken into a sweat, and she was panting. "You wouldn't try to force anyone else to Transmute. I can't." She threw herself into a chair and poked at a stuffed boar's head nailed to the wall.

"The last three generations of women in your line were capable."

"Things change!" Ella cried. "Perhaps I am more like my father than I am my mother. So sorry to disappoint you!"

Hamlet's eyes flashed with something that Ella wasn't used to: shame. He swallowed hard, adjusting his stance and resting his spectacles on the top of his head. She rubbed at her nose, a familiar burning sensation creeping over her.

"Moving on. What is the difference between a halfling and a mixie?" Hamlet asked.

She raised a delicate eyebrow at him. "Really? Punishing me with younglings studies?"

"We can always go back to trying to turn the spoon into a fork?"

"Halflings are a result of breeding Fae to a human *with* magic abilities—a human *maji*. Mixies are beings with one Nomaji parent and one Fae parent." Ella recited everything perfectly.

"What is the largest civilization in the world of Arcadea?"

"Calisan Capital..."

"What are the eight branches of magic?" He conjured a vision of a tree before them, wisps of light spanning over eight branches, each a different color.

"Abjuration; protection, conjuration; bring forth, divination; the sight, enchantment; bewitchment, evocation; summons, illusion; trickery, necromancy; communal with death, and mutation; alteration."

"The difference between illusion and mutation?"

Ella faltered for a moment; her brows furrowed in thought. "Illusion is changing something on the surface. You can make a cup *look* like a plate, but it is still a plate in its base form. Mutation is changing something at its core. You alter the reality of the object—it wouldn't just *look* like something else; it becomes something else entirely. It can also be done with places, like transmuting Hellharth into a different world with nothing beyond it. It works so long as the caster can keep up with the expulsion of magic."

"At least you listen when I talk," Hamlet said with a smirk. "Now if only I could get you to read the human language—"

"Not this again! The humans here don't even write in that language, they write in Elvish."

"Knowledge is power. Tell me, who were the Original Arcadean Council Members during the Purge War?"

"Jarvis Orva, maji human. Froafna The Stout, goblin. Wenda Ased, halfling. Barnabas Crook, halfling. Sifrrod Whitefish, siren. Mira Halt, maji human, and Queen Lelot of Direfell, Dracaenean. Then my mother. Why can't we practice with fire? *That* I can actually do. Or I could try lifting some—"

"And ruin your mother's trophy room? She'd kill us." He took a seat in the chair next to her and rubbed his eyes.

"Something's going on. All this pressure to learn magic I have no affinity for. Asking me youngling questions and pressuring me to learn how to read human lettering—"

"Your mother is grilling me because you're behind in your studies. There is no ulterior motive behind this."

She glared at him then. "So, look at me," she challenged. "Look me in the eyes."

Hamlet scoffed and jumped out of his seat at her request. "You will not be mind—drifting me, young lady!"

"Why not?" She asked innocently, fluttering her lashes at him.

"Because I have things in my head that I don't want you looking at."

"Like Nattya naked in bed with you this morning?"

He went stiff at her question and grumbled something under his breath before speaking loudly. "Sending in the spies, are you? You'd have to do better than that."

"Trust me, I didn't send her to do any of that. I'm thankless. Highwing let it slip that you and Mother planned a ball? Nattya wasn't too thrilled by that information coming to her so late."

Hamlet blushed at the ears and sniffed. "I hope there hasn't been some miscommunication that I am attending said ball as anything other than an employee?"

"Seriously? We don't need another one." It felt forced and drained the fun out of it.

"It keeps Hellharth's morale up. Gets the people going," Hamlet mused. They sat there in comfortable silence, Ella thinking over the conversation she had with her friends prior. She glanced at Hamlet from the corner of her eyes, certain that he was lying about something. If the flicker happened again during the ball, the people would be too busy inside the castle grounds, enjoying themselves. Not that they would make a spectacle of such an event, since everyone chose to keep quiet about it. Ella suspected people talked about it in privacy, the way she did.

But, if the opportunity were to present itself, where she could escape, she was going to take it.

CHAPTER FOUR

Nattya had been on edge all day, her mood souring more and more as the ball drew nearer; it had been days since Highwing disclosed the news of an unexpected soiree. Highwing seemed to share in none of Nattya's anxiety though, lounging indolently atop Ella's bed with a deep blue cushion beneath his head, appearing quite content.

"I don't know why you girls get so bent up out of shape over these things," he sighed for the hundredth time. Nattya had gone through every piece of wardrobe Ella owned and was now circling back through it.

"I want him to see me and get slack-jawed!" Nattya growled, throwing a sage green tulle dress over her shoulder. "Ella! Why don't you own anything sexy?"

Ella picked up the dress and held it to herself. It had a see-through underbust corset and heart-shaped neckline, the skirts long and flowing. "I think this is sexy," she proclaimed in an offended tone.

"Don't be funny Ella! No one's going to want to lift all that tulle," Nattya huffed, examining a short and sheer blue dress. "This one is nice," she said with a tilt of her head.

"That's an undergarment!" Ella squealed in laughter. "It's for sleeping!"

Highwing perked up in the bed, leaning on his elbow. "You'll have to show us what that looks like—you know, so we can tell you yay or nay." His steel eyes were dancing with mischief.

"Ugh! What about this?" She held up a red sleeveless A-line dress, the neckline pointing at the top and dipping to the waist.

"It's supposed to be worn with a blouse, so your breasts don't show," Ella pointed out, holding up a silk puff-sleeved garment. Nattya wrinkled her nose at Ella's offering.

"I think not. This will do just fine. Are you wearing the sage one?" she asked Ella, beginning to strip out of her day tunic and leather pants. At her movement, Highwing turned his body away, staring at the wall.

"It will do. I'm not as excited as you are, Nat."

"That's because you get to dress like *this* whenever you want," Nattya grunted as she stepped into the red dress. "Thank Gods you and I are the same size." Her brown hair was tousled over her shoulders in soft waves, and she shook her fingers through to make it wilder. Her face had a pretty splatter of freckles, unique to humans, and her lightly tanned skin was doused in a glittering oil.

"Are you two done changing?" Highwing sighed. "I can only count so many specks on the wall before my attention goes elsewhere."

"For someone who always has perverted comments, you sure are the gentleman," Ella muttered, pulling the puffy sage sleeves off her shoulders. "You can look now."

Highwing looked over his shoulder, looking at them both up and down. He flashed his teeth at Ella, ruffling his gray feathers about him. "Aren't you something to look at?" Ella's face flushed, and she rolled her eyes.

"If I bend over, do you think I'll pop out?" Nattya asked. She leaned forward experimentally and shimmied.

"Absolutely," Highwing said, putting a hand over his eyes.

"Good. Hamlet should feel jealous, right?" Nattya giggled, her eyes gleaming.

"What is it about Ham that gets you all bunched up? I don't see it," Ella stuck her tongue out in disgust.

"That's because the man is practically your uncle. I'm glad you don't see it." Nattya twirled in the mirror, examining herself. "What's your mother wearing? I bet something white." She proceeded to paint her eyelids with shimmering oil.

Ella nudged Highwing over and sat next to him on the bed, his hands rubbing at the spot her wings were under her shoulders. "No idea. I haven't spoken to her in three days. She is always in meetings. They are saying Anvil's crops weren't doing well this year."

Highwing turned to Ella and said, "My mother said the people down in Anvil want to plow a part of Bris Forest down for new soil. It had some of the other Court members riled up. Hamlet is for it, my mother, Cida... But Petra, who took Joanai's place last month, Tanyl, and Althane are all opposed. A lot of the humans from Anvil are coming to tonight's ball to plead their case." Highwing eyed her when he finished.

"Gideon's parents?" she pressed, a stone settling in her stomach. She knew without him saying it.

"Likely," he answered carefully, shifting his eyes between Nattya and Ella. "We can hang out in the gardens if they come," he suggested.

Ella snapped her head to glare at him. "I'm not going to hide from them like a coward. I-I'll be fine. It will all be fine," she said unconvincingly. She hadn't seen Gideon's parents in years.

Highwing moved to a sitting position, throwing his arm over her shoulder and resting her head under his.

"I could use a lady's touch with my hair. What do you say?" He wiggled his eyebrows at the two of them and they scoffed. His hair was coarse and easy to manipulate, so whenever he offered, the girls took him up on it.

"Come here," Nattya commanded, pulling a comb from Ella's vanity drawer. "I'm thinking trinkets and braids."

⤜⟶

Queen Kahlisenya brought her long silvery-white hair into a braid around her head and looped an obsidian dagger onto her hip. She wore a breastplate under her leather tunic made of Bris whalebone, making her look somewhat clunky. She was just about ready to depart for the Highlands. Two female soldiers stood vigilantly in the corner of the Throne room, waiting for their commands. They wore sage-colored tunics, made of goblin metals and leathers, and eagle-like helmets that rested on their heads, covering their faces. Their arms were encased with bone plates that ended at their elbows.

Kahlisenya had chosen only two to come with her on her trip to the Highlands, a fact that Hamlet insisted on arguing about.

"Are you sure this will hold?" Hamlet asked with uncertainty. He held the end of the long wooden staff of Eresai in his palms, the wood a mass of twisted sticks that curved at the end. Kahlisenya raised her white eyebrow at him, then rolled her eyes. She had just finished imbuing the staff with some of her magic and it glowed a faint blue hue. Eresai was said to have used this staff as a conduit for her own magic—a staff made from the great God Tree. It was Kahlisenya's hope that it being from the God Tee would help to amplify what little magic she had left.

"Are you doubting me now, Hamlet?" she asked teasingly. He rolled his eyes at her and snatched the staff away from her. "It will hold as long as I need it to."

"I just don't need us crash landing on top of Calisan Capital once you leave here," He shot back. "You won't be gone long?"

"I'm a portal jump away. And when I get back, I'll send you through to Arcadea. You can tell me how the world is fairing."

"I can't imagine Ella is thrilled with your leaving," said Hamlet. Kahlisenya averted her gaze, and he narrowed his eyes. "You *did* tell her, right?" At her silence, he circled her. "Kahl—My Queen—I must insist that you tell her of your departure. She will notice your absence at this ball."

"I rarely go to those things. If I tell her, she will insist on coming with me. No," Kahlisenya said affirmatively. "It's better for her to remain. Keep her distracted with dancing."

"She hates these balls just as much as you do! You cannot keep doing this," Hamlet said exasperatedly. "How is she to grow into a ruler when you keep her wrapped in a bubble?"

"I do not remember you asking my permission to speak plainly," Kahlisenya said without any real bite. "These are the Witches of Highland. Ella's powers are... they are growing, but they are not polished."

"Does my opinion not matter? I have been by your side for *years*. Since I was small. I have been your friend and your advisor. I am advising you now. You should at the very least tell Ella you are leaving. If something were to happen to you—"

"Nothing will happen to me, Hamlet," she answered softly. "Your opinion does matter, and it was taken into consideration. However—"

"You've already made up your mind," he grumbled. He fixed his spectacles on the bridge of his nose, holding the Staff of Eresai more closely to his chest. "Understood."

Kahlisenya sighed, not looking at him. She smoothed her hands over her traveling frock and pants, more suitable for men than a high lady. She understood Hamlet's point. But she needed to be certain of her dreams, and she felt she had to do this alone. She looked at the staff in Hamlet's grasp. His knuckles had gone white. Gently, she placed her hands over his.

"I'm going to come back, Ham," she chuckled at his nickname.

"Don't call me that, you wench," he snarled. She laughed, grabbing at her sides.

"I have to go. Why don't you keep Ella busy? Make sure she's dancing."

"You're joking? Now I must babysit on top of watching Hellharth? You don't pay me enough."

"I don't pay you at all."

In their mirth, a moment passed between them where they fell silent. Kahlisenya smirked, and Hamlet cleared his throat. "You look ridiculous in men's clothing," he said.

"So do you," she quipped without missing a beat. "Be well. I'll see you shortly." She called out to the two soldiers and walked to the center of the room. The air had shifted slightly, suddenly becoming colder. She held her arms out, palms up, slowly raising them before swiping them down—her eyes a bright white.

The air crackled and sparked, a swirl of light emitting from nowhere until it turned into an opened door. Snow trickled in from the other side, a low wailing as the wind whipped through the throne room. Hamlet peered over to look through, seeing nothing but blizzard snow and rocky mountains in the distance.

"Are you sure about this?" he asked skeptically, the chill biting through his tunic.

"Go about your day Hamlet," she said, stepping through the portal with the soldiers following her.

Hamlet stared at the spot she had disappeared from, tapping his forehead with the wooden staff with indignation. Everyone was going to look to him tonight. The people of Anvil were coming to ask for more land to plant on, and the only other person who could make a final decision without the Queen's approval would be *Ella*.

"The girl didn't ask for this," he groaned loudly in the empty throne room.

The portal had closed behind them, the wind snapping at them angrily. Kahlisenya pointed a finger towards some mountain peaks in the distance. "There. We have some daylight left. We should be able to cover the distance if we move quickly." Her two female companions did not look at all thrilled by the prospect of traveling through the snowy weather, but they marched along with Kahlisenya leading them.

"My Queen, the Witches of Highland are said to be monstrous," one of her guards said. The Queen could hear the uneasiness in her voice and turned to give her a contemplative glance. The female guard, Orvis, was unremarkable, just as the other, Tsu, was. It was why the Queen picked them. They weren't conventionally beautiful, nor High Fae. They did not have wings; they had no families and grew up inside the castle with servants. They would not be missed.

"Are you afraid, Orvis?" Kahlisenya questioned. She tilted her head in a way that looked endearing, but really, she was detaching herself.

Orvis looked embarrassed, looking between Tsu and the Queen, red-faced. "N-no," she answered pathetically.

"Good. Let us keep going," her voice came out harsher than she had meant it to.

They are scared, she thought solemnly. *They have every reason to be.* She swallowed hard, determined not to feel anything. *This is for Ella*, she reasoned quietly. *For Ella.*

Kahlisenya and her companions had been trekking through the snow for some time now, their only light source being the torches that lined their path. Evidence of animals that had once resided in the arca could be seen in skeleton form to either side of them as they continued onward, a reminder that they were nearing their destination. The day was quickly coming to an end, and the sun hid beyond the trees, its rays obscured by dusk's arrival. Despite having gotten lost in conversation multiple times prior, not a single word was spoken between them as they walked; all that filled the air was the soft crunch of footsteps against the snow beneath them.

The ball is beginning about now, she thought to herself. She could smell the salt in the sea air being carried by the wind and hear the crashing waves of distant shores.

"My Queen," Tsu started, "How do we even know these Witches exist? We have been out here for hours."

"Have faith, Tsu. I have it on good authority that they reside here," Kahlisenya answered. "Did you know that the God Tree is just west of here? Right in the Northern Balic Sea," she said, changing the tone of the evening.

"Have you ever seen it?" Tsu asked excitedly. Orvis elbowed her in the side and raised her eyebrows. "My Queen," Tsu added hastily.

"No, I have not. But my grandmother wrote stories about seeing it when she was a girl. Perhaps one day I will..."

Finally, Kahlisenya and her companion came across a forlorn cave; its exterior was an unkempt pile of rocks and wood, with small decorative stone rabbits and birds nestled on the sides. Kahlisenya paused in their approach, unease settling in as she unconsciously put her hand over her mouth. The mysterious atmosphere emanating from the cave seemed to beckon them to explore, yet there was something unsettling lurking within.

"Don't worry, my Queen. We will protect you," Tsu said with determination. Kahlisenya stopped the painful noise from escaping her throat at Tsu's declaration and lumbered into the cave's open mouth.

Ask them your questions, she reminded herself. *Don't look into their eyes.*

The Cave was damp and cold, just as Kahlisenya remembered, the air ripe with a sweet, fermented smell of death. Her boots crunched over bones and trudged through remnants of clothing, the grim reminder of all that had once been left to succumb in this desolate place. It was not the same type of odor one would come across if they happened upon a forgotten animal carcass...it seemed almost ritualistic, like an offering to some unknown entity lurking within the depths of darkness.

Orvis stopped in front of a suspicious-looking rock, kneeling and picking up the large stone. "It looks like a woman's face. A sculpture," she said to Kahlisenya. "It's quite good. Looks almost real." She held it out for Tsu to examine, and Tsu twisted about in her hands.

Kahlisenya swallowed and resolutely looked at the ground.

"There's more," Tsu whispered. She stood in front of a feminine figure, the woman's mouth hanging open. "The Witches are artistic. I've never seen such sculptures before. They are all over the place."

Orvis meandered toward a fallen statue; the torso split in half. "This one looks like a Direwolf. Incredible."

Kahlisenya's head snapped toward where Orvis stood. A recognizable mass of stone lay at her feet. Kahlisenya reached down, her fingers grazing over the stone muzzle of the beast.

Jaspen, Kahlisenya thought. Her heart lumped into her throat, and she swallowed hard. His once vibrant mottled brown fur was a dull stone gray. Her hands ran over his neck, trying to remember its softness beneath the hard surface. Her nose and eyes burned, and she cleared her throat.

"Yes. They are... very talented," she forced out hoarsely. She heard something coming from the darkest point in the cave and the three of them stood to face the noise together. Out of the darkness, a woman with dark brown hair emerged, her naked breasts covered with black scales that reached from her exposed torso up to her neck. Her eyes were covered with a ragged cloth. The rest of her body slid to the front of her, coiling around her, and Kahlisenya's guards gasped.

From the waist up, she possessed the elegance and allure of a human woman. Her face, exquisitely crafted, bore features of ethereal beauty. A symphony of delicate curves and lips that were full and pink. Her brown hair cascaded like liquid silk, flowing in lustrous waves, framing her serpentine form.

But from the waist down, her body transitioned into a sleek, undulating serpent, sinuous and scaly. Her lower half, covered in resplendent scales, shimmered with a myriad of enchanting hues—iridescent greens, blues, and purples. With every sinewy movement, the rocks broke away from her weight.

The serpent-woman bobbed her head from side to side, her hair flaring out and then connecting to her neck like a hood. Another woman appeared from behind her, legs long and lithe; her hands tapping along the wall and taking her steps carefully. Kahlisenya recognized the women immediately; the second woman had unnaturally white eyes.

She was blind.

The snake-woman curled protectively around the blind woman. Kahlisenya could tell that, although this woman could not see with her physical eyes, there was still something uncanny in the way she seemed to be searching for something beyond what was normally perceived.

"Who seeks us out?" The blind woman called out.

"I do," Kahlisenya answered bravely.

"I am Kiandall," the snake-woman one said, touching Kahlisenya's shoulder tauntingly. Kahlisenya heard the familiar sound of swords unsheathing.

"I am Amaris," the blind one said, "We are The Witches of Highland."

"You brought us friendsss," Kiandall smiled, fangs protruding from her mouth like a viper, circling the three visitors. Tsu was the first to pull her rank, sizing up her opponents. Orvis following suit. They took a guarded stance at Kahlisenya's side.

"My Queen, stand back!" Tsu commanded, taking a valiant step forward toward the writhing creature. Kiandall stretched to her full height, her tongue flickering out to taste the air and her neck expanding into a flat hood that attached itself to the top of her head. Her hands then reached for the cloth covering her face. Kahlisenya recoiled at the motion with wide-eyed terror before shutting her eyes tightly. An eerie crackling filled the air, followed by an astonished gasp before the room was overcome by a deafening silence.

"NO! NO!" Orvis screamed. "They weren't statues! THEY WERE NEVER STATUES!"

Kahlisenya could hear Orvis frantically swinging a sword and then the clang of it hitting the ground. One final screech from Orvis and it was over. There was a rumbling of rock, and a tail tipped Kahlisenya's chin up.

"You paid your price to see, you may look," Kiandall said.

Kahlisenya's heart was in her throat, the screams of her guards echoing in her ears. Slowly, she opened her eyes, careful to look around. Tsu was on the left of Kahlisenya, her arms raised above her head to strike, her body transformed into stone. Kahlisenya took an unconscious step towards Tsu, her eyes feeling hot. She stared mindlessly, paralyzed at what she had caused. Her foot made contact with a rock, and it rolled a bit, glaring up at Kahlisenya. Orvis' head rested a few feet from her body, the rock having cracked as her body fell.

She felt sick.

Amaris felt about the cave, arms outstretched and searching. Her foot kicked Orvis' head, and she knelt to pick it up before it rolled away from her. Carefully, her fingers danced over Orvis' features. "This one had a crooked nose," she said.

"You have been here before, woman," said Kiandall. "A long time ago. With a man, a wolf, and a beggar woman. Though I have seen you many more times."

"Oh, a man!" Amaris said in a sing-song voice, wrapping her fingers around one of Kahlisenya's calves.

"I came here twenty-two years ago," Kahlisenya remarked, "and only that once.

"Before The Son was born," Kiandall answered. "I remember. You were there with him when he asked *his* questions. I *know* you."

"Yes," Kahlisenya confirmed. "I have come with my own questions. I gave you your sacrifices."

"What will you give us in return for this knowledge that you seek?" she hissed, her snakelike tail caressing Kahlisenya's legs.

"I've just given you my two soldiers. I was under the impression that would be all I needed. You told me I was safe to look at you." She hesitantly turned away.

Kiandall tsked. Her large body swirled around Tsu's frozen form, a clawed finger tapping the eagle-like mask. Even with Tsu's helmet on, Kahlisenya could see the fear that marred her face in her final moments.

"What is it that you want?" Kahlisenya asked calmly. Kiandall craned her neck in front of Kahlisenya's face, and the woman smiled at her.

"We only ask for something of equal ssstature," Kiandall hissed, her forked tongue licking Kahlisenya's cheek. "You want to know thingsss, we know thingsss. Tell usss a secret. Do not attempt to lie. I can taste liesss.".

"I thought you knew things," snarked Kahlisenya. Her patience was wearing thin with these witches.

"You want us to use our power to find out information for you, but you don't want to play by our rules?" Kiandall asked incredulously, her lip curling up in disdain.

"Turn her to stone! Amaris huffed, nudging in front of Kiandall to bare her teeth.

"Wait!" Kahlisenya yelled. "I have a secret."

"Tell usss!" They begged in unison.

"I am losing my power," Kahlisenya said quickly. She felt threatened by admitting this to them. To her dismay, they sighed heavily, clearly annoyed.

"Boring."

"Lame."

"That is a secret!" Kahlisenya replied angrily.

"It is not a sssecret so much as a *lie*. You aren't *losing* your power, it isss just changing. We could already sssense that. You already presumed that."

"I have a secret..." she started. "No one knows. No one knows!"

The women were quiet, the sound of bodies sliding over the ground, and Kahlisenya could feel them breathing on her.

"I could have killed the Son of Bashet. I had the power and the resources to do away with him, yet I chose to wait...hoping that one day he would realize what he was doing was wrong. My hesitation, however, came too late as the Council got involved, resulting in my inability to take matters into my own hands. It wasn't a sense of justice or an oath that kept me from killing him, though; it was an unwillingness. I ended up having no other choice than to imprison him instead and presented it as the only feasible solution for everyone involved. I asked Princess Lelot of Direfell for assistance but did so knowing that she couldn't comply due to her Treaty between our people. This drove her to resign from The Council altogether. I did it all on purpose"

"Why?" One of them pressed.

"I was only required to tell you a secret, not explain myself." Kahlisenya moved her hand to the dagger at her hip, her fingers flexing. Amaris' hand sprung out and twisted around the dagger's hilt. Kahlisenya's eyes flew open, and she whirled about.

"You do not need that," Amaris warned, licking her lips.

"I gave you my secret!" Kahlisenya shouted angrily. There was no telling how strong these women were. She wasn't as powerful as she had been the last time she had encountered them.

"You did," Kiandall agreed with a sigh. "I sssupose we have to keep our end of the deal."

"Tell us what plagues you," Amaris said gently.

"I have come here to ask questions about the future," Kahlisenya said with uncertainty.

"Ugh. That's not exciting. Fortune telling is the least bit of fun. What about forcing someone to love you? Or, how about bringing someone back from—" Amaris was disrupted by a tail over her mouth.

"She doesn't have the means for *that*," Kiandall said, moving her tail from Amaris' mouth.

"You brought only two sacrifices. We will answer two questions in the way that we *can*," Kiandall explained. "There are rules even we must abide by. You may ask any question—though, if answering the questions disrupts cosmic design in any way, we *cannot* answer."

"No refunds," snickered Amaris.

Kahlisenya thought carefully, feeling the weight of what was at stake. She had been prepared to ask her questions and now that the opportunity was here, her mind raced to figure out the best way to phrase them. Although she feared what their answers might be, they had inadvertently confirmed that Idmodias would rise again—because her dreams were real. They had already answered that question without needing to make a sacrifice.

"Tell me everything you can about The Son of Bashet rising again," Kahlisenya said. She swallowed hard, hoping she had asked the right question. She watched the serpent woman open her mouth, forked tongue flickering toward her. They turned towards each other as if they could see one another beyond the cloth rag that covered her eyes and Amaris' blindness.

There was a reverberating sound of hissing and cracking all around her. *You have been here before. This is nothing new,* Kahlisenya reasoned to herself.

Their heads tilted back, their jaws unhinging and opening wide. They made a low groaning noise, and glowing white orbs emanated from their stomachs, lurching from their throats and forming one large orb.

The orb floated above them before bursting into a blinding light. Their voices rang out in a ghostly hiss.

"The child born of a fallen Star,
A bridge between realms,
Though, never far.
No home but not lost,
Safe inside a morning song,
To first make right,
you must do wrong.
Answers found right near his heart,
Blackened stone,
And She shall part.
Blood of The Lady,
The Traitor and Daughter,
A Cosmic battle of Will and Power.
Son of Bashet rises once more,
War upon us
As twice before.
Family Legacies
Two women of the same side
Past promises made
and Royal lies.
Their choice alone may break or bend
To raise Arcadea
Or bring its End."

Her sight came back, and the light faded away, the two witches laying in a heap on the ground, breathing heavily. Kahlisenya nudged the tail with her boot, and it wriggled away from her. "What does that mean?" She interrogated them breathlessly. "WHAT DOES THAT MEAN?" She shrieked. Her heart hammered in her chest, and her mind became foggy with apprehension.

Kiandall used her slender arms to push herself up from the ground, gripping the cave wall for support. She helped Amaris up next, clearly exhausted. Amaris dragged herself away.

"We gave you what you asked for," Amaris groaned in pain.

"You gave me a riddle!" Kahlisenya exclaimed. "You gave me a half bit of a children's rhyme!"

"No," Kiandall hissed. "We gave you more than what you asked for! We gave you a prophecy."

"What good does a prophecy do for me if I cannot understand it?" Kahlisenya shot back.

"Sounds like you have some problems," Amaris giggled slyly. She rolled on the ground lazily.

"So, my next question is, what does this mean?"

"Prophecies are meant to be fulfilled. We cannot divulge cosmic design—because it is meant to happen. Those are the rules," Kiandall answered glumly.

"All I have been given are more questions than answers! You didn't answer my question, so that means one is still on the table."

Kiandall nodded her head. "Ssso it seems."

"Be done with her, darling. We need to rest," Amaris said.

"Ask your question, Elven Queen," Kiandall urged.

"How will we be able to defeat him?" Kahlisenya asked with a strained voice. Kiandall cocked her head to the side, her long dark hair grazing the floor now. She hissed, and she and Amaris again twisted together. They brought forth another orb, though not from their mouths, but with their hands. There was a mist inside the orb, swirling into a small twister.

"He will meet his demise when your daughter meets hers, inside the belly of Mount Tartis. It is clear…"

Kahlisenya fell to her knees at Kiandall's words. "There has to be some mistake—"

"The vision is clear! It happens! It does not change!" Amaris yelled harshly. Kahlisenya flinched at her words.

"Your divination has not peaked. Perhaps if you can harness your magic, you will be able to have the answers you seek," Kiandall suggested. She reached her hand for Kahlisenya and rested it gently on her shoulder. "I understand your pain."

"Then give me more! I beg of you! Give me something useful!" Kahlisenya pleaded tearfully.

Kiandall cocked her head in thought. A loud hiss rang out and Amaris looked disgruntled.

"No—" Amaris started. She recoiled, clearly agitated. "Kiandall—" Kiandall raised her hand, silencing her.

"What would you do for a power like ours? To be able to see what others cannot. Your power may be strong alone, but… with others… it is even more so. We combine those abilities together, to bring about the purest form of truth that is possible. We have done an immeasurable amount of magic, even with our limitations." Kiandall lowered her face to Kahlisenya's. "What would you do for that?"

Kahlisenya was taken aback by Kiandall's question. "I would give anything to know what is to come, so I could protect her—"

"We told you already, it is clear! Your daughter is dead by the end!" Amaris shouted viciously.

Kahlisenya lunged for the blind woman with a snarl, her hands just barely grazing the woman's neck before she was held in place by Kiandall's heavy tail.

"Do you want this power? Yes, or no?"

Kahlisenya looked up, her resolve breaking. "Y-yes."

"She doesn't know what she is asking for!" Amaris yelled. She turned her attention to Kahlisenya. "You would forfeit *everything*.

That man you love, the home you know. Eventually, you will be alone."

"She becomes one of us. I have seen it," Kiandall responded. "The choice is yours, the ending is the same," she said cryptically.

"This is not the life you want. You will be cursed," Amaris urged. Kiandall made a pained noise. "Have I cursed you, Amaris?" she asked sadly. Amaris gazed up, her eyes unseeing. "No, Kiandall," she sighed. "I have you, but she has them…"

"If I do become one of you, I'll be able to see what you see?" Kahlisenya asked.

"Yesss," Kiandall hissed. "But we are bound by rules. Some thingsss are meant to play out. Some people are meant to ssstay dead. It is not always pleasant." Her tail came to caress Kahlisenya's cheek.

"The sacrifices?" Kahlisenya asked.

"A necessary deterrent," Amaris answered. If people could gain what they wanted without consequences, then they would be flooded constantly. They needed some sort of exchange to keep themselves from expelling all their magic. A life.

Kahlisenya's mind was swimming with anxiety as she realized the commitment she was about to make. She needed to know for herself the meaning of the prophecy that she had been given, even if it meant that she could not share her insight with others. Knowing this, Kahlisenya nodded and allowed Kiandall to take one of her hands into hers. The sharp sensation of Kiandall's fangs piercing her skin made Kahlisenya gasp, yet she was determined to see through her decision and become one of the Witches of Highland. As Kiandall moved away from Kahlisenya's hand, Amaris flinched at the coppery smell of blood that wafted to her.

"My gift to you. You'll have less than a year's time to get your affairs in order. My venom will act as a booster, and you will see things as they are meant to happen. Should you try to levy out of our deal, my venom will overtake you and you will die." Kiandall shifted her weight off Kahlisenya and lifted her up. "Be gone now," she dismissed, turning her back to her and rolling into a ball.

The bite itself was small. Two puncture marks were inflamed against her alabaster skin. Kahlisenya looked at her hand in mortification. *Less than a year*, she thought in dismay, *what have I done?*

CHAPTER FIVE

As far as Ella was concerned, this was just another typical party, only she was riddled with anxiety and anticipation. Her eyes kept scanning the mass of people that gathered in the ballroom. It had been decorated in gold ribbons that cascaded down from a gilded ceiling. Four large crystal chandeliers that had been enchanted to twinkle hung above their heads. The archways had been opened, letting in a cool breeze from the terraces that overlooked the gardens. The walls had been painted with lilies and violets, spiraling in a mess of gold swirls.

Nattya had been chatting up two Elven men, who Ella recognized as Ruvane and Elmon, half-brothers to Highwing, and sons to Lady Tanyl and Lord Althane of Court. They were strikingly handsome with their coppery hair in high ponytails and chestnut eyes. It looked like they both had garnered new tattoos on their necks, as they had their heads tilted upward slightly, showing

Nattya their matching crescent moons. Ella watched as the boys were enthralled with Nattya—she had that way about her, where men flocked to her because she was radiant. She was always freely herself—didn't care about being judged... and she did look stunning in that red dress.

"Hamlet hasn't even looked at her," Highwing said from her left. Nattya had fixed his hair into a bunch of twists about his head, held in place by six gold pins that had dangling tassels. He wore a forest green garb with gold trim and matching breeches. He handed her a cup of Elven firewater. "Those boys have no idea that she's a shark and they are fish," he muttered with amusement at his younger brothers doing their best strut. Their mottled brown wings shook in a way he found comical. Nattya was tilting her head and laughing, twirling about.

"I almost feel bad for them," Ella simpered, taking a sip of the warm liquid. He scoffed at her comment, "I don't. Should have seen them when they were trying to impress her last week during the Meacorpa Games. Ran and slipped right off the oiled pole into the lake."

Ella giggled at this. The Meacorpa Games was a tournament held every two years, in which the males competed in a variety of athletic events—without magic or any other advantage. The winner got bragging rights and was celebrated. Ella had skipped watching them this year.

"Your mother hasn't shown up yet," he said. "Some of the humans are waiting for an audience. My mother's gathering the Court to hear them out." In reference to his mother, Lady Rayne, Ella caught a glimpse of the dark woman prowling out to the terrace, her long skirts and large gray wings obnoxiously swiping along unsuspecting faces. Her silver hair disappeared with her out of sight.

"It's quite informal to do this during a ball," Ella said. "Are his parents here?" She almost didn't want to know. Almost.

"Yes. They are out by the gardens. Haven't walked in yet. Where is your mother?" Highwing weaved away from her, pushing through a few oblivious partygoers, and Ella watched with mild trepidation when he tapped on Hamlet's shoulder. She wasn't any good at reading lips, but Hamlet looked shifty and uncomfortable, looking around until his eyes caught hers. She cocked her head and raised her cup.

"I came. I'm here," she mouthed to him from across the room. He pointed his finger at her, signaling for her to wait there. Highwing looked uneasy. "That can't be good," she muttered. She whirled around, ready to make a run for it, when Hamlet caught her by the arm.

"I'd love to know how you're that fast," she grumbled.

"Nice to see you too. I hate to do this to you, but I really need you on the terrace." He sounded apologetic, which made her take pause.

"Why do I need to go out there? Isn't that where the humans are meeting the Court?" Ella queried.

He nodded. "That's exactly what I mean." He tugged her not so gently through the crowd of people, laughing and dancing. Highwing manifested at her side, and she looked at him with wide eyes, feeling herself drift into his thoughts.

She's about to have a fit. She's not ready for this sort of thing. Too much pressure, she heard him think. She yanked her eyes away from his, feeling downtrodden at his blatant lack of faith in her.

She was nudged onto the terrace; the doors closing behind them, the people in the ballroom unaware as they drank and danced. She greeted the people in front of her—people of the Court who had an air of indifference—like this meeting was beneath them. She wasn't used to being alone with them, usually, she was to avoid them. The only one who smiled at her beyond a gracious greeting was Lady Rayne, who motioned for Highwing to stand next to her. Reluctantly, he went to her side.

"Princess Ellaryhssa," Lady Tanyl said. "It seems we have met an impasse." Lady Tanyl's striking red hair waved down to her ankles, her black ensemble of a dress making her look like burning embers. She was intimidating, as she was beautiful. Her arms were laced in gold bracelets that wired around to her elbows, and her nose was pierced with two small jewels on either nostril.

"Oh?" Ellarhyssa said dumbly. She cleared her throat, waiting for someone to elaborate. Lady Tanyl waved her hand down below, where a flock of humans had gathered in the gardens beneath the terrace balcony. "Oh," Ella breathed.

"Queen Kahlisenya had other matters to see to, and has left the conclusion up to you," Hamlet said pointedly. "Princess," he added with effect.

Ella leaned over the terrace railing, the humans bowing their heads respectfully. A couple of handfuls of elves were present, whom Ella assumed were from some parts of Anvil.

"The matter at hand; the humans seek more land to plow on. They want to cut down some of the Bris Forest. Bris Forest is where most of our wildlife live, but the soil is good and would yield better crops," Hamlet explained.

"Oh," Ella said again. She heard someone tsk—Lord Althane—and she straightened her back. Highwing's doubts rang in her thoughts, and she took a shuddering breath to calm herself. She knew Gideon's parents were down there.

"I would like for them to plead their case to me," she said with her chin held higher.

"Princess, we have already heard their case and just need a deciding vote," Lord Althane insisted. He was a tall man—taller than Highwing—with the same chiseled jaw and steel-gray eyes. His beard was trimmed close to the skin, casting a slight shadow along his jaw. He had mottled wings, the same as his twin sons, that had seen better days. He was scar riddled—the sign that he'd gone up against cursed blades and lived.

"How am I to decide where my vote should be cast when I have not heard it myself?" Ella challenged. She could play this game. She would show them.

"Hamlet had already—" Althane started.

"That's Master Hamlet," Ella corrected him. "He gave me a summarized reason; I want to hear from the people." Ella placed her hands on the railing and turned to the people below her, thoroughly dismissing Lord Althane. She had seen her mother do this hundreds of times and had studied the way she walked, talked, and moved when she was around people—when she disregarded them. Ella was sure that her mother's absence was some test for her, and if she passed, perhaps Ella would finally have earned her mother's grace.

"Hello," she called below with a steady voice. "I would like those of you who are in favor of cutting through Bris Forest to stand on your left. Those opposing on your right." She waited as the crowd separated into two groups. She studied them, the familiar faces of Gideon's mother and father on her right giving her tunnel vision. She stared at them, her heart stalling. Gideon had been such a perfect blend of his parents, favoring his mother with his curly brown hair and wide brown eyes. They shifted uncomfortably under her gaze, and she righted herself, forcing her eyes to look elsewhere.

"Choose two from each group to represent you in your case," she said. They talked amongst themselves about the elves choosing theirs, and her cheeks burned when the humans turned to Gideon's parents and shoved them to the front. "Miriam and Joffrey Cast," Ella greeted stiffly. They bowed their heads to her. They were not wearing their best clothing, as they had not come to join in the festivities. Ella could see the dirt on their hands, their breeches stained from working in the fields.

"El—Princess," Joffrey started. At the sound of his voice, she gulped, fighting back tears. "My wife and I are among the hundreds who live in Anvil. We tend to the crops that go to the tables of everyone in Hellharth. This past year, the soil has been temperamental; the crops are feeble compared to last. There is soil in the Bris Forest that would be useful in tendering crops for next year."

"We ask the Court to consider letting us cut a part of Bris Forest down, to make room for new land. We plead with the Court, not just for the people of Anvil but for all of Hellharth." He finished by bowing his head, and it made her eye twitch.

Ella listened intently, her grip on the railing vice-like as she struggled to hold her composure at hearing his familiar voice. Miriam had not even lifted her eyes from the ground. Ella wanted Miriam to look at her desperately. She wanted to see Gideon's eyes again.

There was a commotion below as several of the elves began to argue with the humans. Ella held up her hand, and they quieted. She turned her attention to the two elves that had been chosen to stand for the opposition,

"Graydal and Yelisil," Graydal introduced with a gruff voice. He looked older than most elves, with a graying beard and crooked nose. "Bris forest is a monumental part of our wildlife's natural system. Cutting down the forest would leave much of the game exposed and without homes. It would be devastating to the plant life that is already there. The crops are short this year, but the fish are plenty, and the hunting is still good." People nodded in agreement, and Lady Tanyl clapped lightly at his speech.

Lord Cida, Hamlet, and Lady Rayne all stood at one end, while Lady Tanyl, Lord Althane, and Lady Petra stood at another—clearly divided. Ella took a few deep breaths, her gaze falling over Miriam's downtrodden face. She thought for a moment, thinking of a solution that would not leave either side feeling snubbed. Lady Tanyl flicked open a fan and waved it under her neck rather dramatically, emphasizing her impatience.

"I have an understanding that the humans in Anvil are expert metal workers, and you have a mastery in carpentry," she addressed Miriam. Miriam nodded; her head still lowered.

"The Princess has addressed you!" Lord Cida shouted, causing Miriam to jolt her head up. Ella hissed at Cida, his dark eyes closing into slits as he stepped back.

"Yes, Princess," Miriam said in a shaky voice. Ella hated it. She hated the way Miriam couldn't look at her, but she expected it because had Ella not been seized to oversee this meeting, she would have avoided them too.

"You may not cut down the forest," Ella stated, and an eruption of hoots and cusses came from both parties. She raised her hand. "However, you may cultivate the soil in the forest and the ponds. You will have raised soil beds in the place where you originally farmed your crops. Mixing the original soil and the new soil should garner you more than enough to start over."

"Princess, that could take ages," Joffrey pleaded. "We would have to travel back and forth repeatedly. There are no working animals in Hellharth."

"I know. That is why they will help you," Ella pointed her finger to the group of elves below. Few looked surprised, some seemed to have already resigned to the idea. "Your work as farmers is important to us, just as our ecosystems are important."

Graydal took a few steps into the crowd that he had been opposing, halting in front of Joffrey. Slowly, he held out his hand, the way that humans did in greeting. Ella clapped when Joffrey shook Graydal's hand, and they patted each other's backs.

"Well done!" Lady Rayne cheered. Hamlet rested a hand on her shoulder and nodded his agreement. Lord Althane shoved past them and opened the terrace doors, disappearing into the sea of drunken dancers.

"That was excellent. I'm so proud," he beamed. At his words, Ella felt a lump in her throat, her eyes threateningly hot. She turned away from them, suddenly feeling exposed. Highwing was at her side in an instant.

"Don't mind my father. He's an ass. Doesn't look like Tanyl's been putting out," he joked. Lady Tanyl heard him, and she did not hide her disgust.

"So unfortunate your father's bloodline is tainted—" Lady Tanyl started. A large gray wing shot out in front of her face, obstructing her view.

"Care to finish that sentence, Tanyl?" Lady Rayne addressed informally; her eyes predatory. "Let us not forget that you only have Lord Althane because I didn't want him."

"My Lord has outgrown your tryst," Tanyl said.

"Really? I shall have to ask him," Lady Rayne threatened. "I was born a Lady. You had to marry to earn that title. Remember that."

Highwing coughed at his mother's venomous words, earning a final sneer from Lady Tanyl. She turned on her heels, whipping her red hair about her like a cape and following her husband.

"What a witch," Lady Rayne muttered. "You'd think the two of them would be happy that this didn't turn into a riot."

"They are only acting in the best interests of Hellharth," Lady Petra piped in. Her brown hair stopped just below her ears, slicked back, showcasing her prominent widow's peak. Her brown wings were wrapped in gold ribbons, making her look like she belonged as part of the decor. She remained respectful during the meeting, unlike her partners.

"The best interest of Hellharth should mean for *all* the people in it," Hamlet said. "Princess Ellaryhssa managed to do that."

"That she did," Highwing smirked.

"I just need some air," Ella said stupidly. "You know what I mean." She waved her hand at them dismissively, rushing through the terrace doors and making for the exit. People bumped into her, apologizing profusely. This party was a mess of people, even the children looked like they got into the drinks. She heard her name being called and she started running, her heels clicking against the marble floor. She swerved through people and launched herself towards an exit. People surrounded her and she felt like she was on a raft in the middle of the ocean, the waves threatening to overtake her.

"Princess? You alright?" Lord Cida's youngest daughter—Arysta asked tentatively. Ella lowered her gaze to the pretty young blonde girl, her eyes a striking violet. Ella forced a smile at her.

"I'm alright, just needed to get out of there."

"My father looks pleased. I hope the meeting went well?" Arysta asked. Ella began to walk, and Arysta wordlessly followed her. Of all four of Lord Cida's children, Arysta was the nicest.

"I really fucking hope so—" Ella slapped a hand over her mouth and gave an apologetic side glance at the twelve-year-old girl. Arysta giggled.

"I've heard worse. Dasyra and Highwing have a colorful vocabulary."

Ella arched a brow at the mention of the eldest sister. "Dasyra and Highwing?"

"I think she likes him. They were spending a lot of time together, but it suddenly stopped," Arysta answered.

Ella refrained from rolling her eyes. Probably had something to do with her mother and his parents wanting them to be mates. She knew it wasn't just the parents' doing—she knew that Highwing had held a candle for her ever since they were small.

He never pursued her outright—not even after Gideon died. He was just *there*. How long would that last? What if he did end up with Dasyra? She chuckled to herself.

"We'd end up like Tanyl and Rayne," she grumbled under her breath with amusement.

"Sorry?" Arysta said from her side. Her head snapped down, and she shook her head.

"Nothing. I was just going to take a private moment, if you don't mind?"

Arysta bowed her head, doing a formal curtsy. "Of course! Thank you for walking with me."

She's so pleasant, Ella thought, staring at the girl's retreating form. *A princess without even trying. A lady in training.* She sighed to herself.

Why? Why did Hamlet's words evoke such a reaction from her? It had to have been Gideon's parents' being there, on top of everything else. The gravity of what just transpired gutted her.

It was her first real act of authority as Princess. This was something she had longed for from her mother. To trust her to be able to do the hard things, and her mother wasn't even there to witness it. But Hamlet was, and he was *proud*. Members of the Court bore no faith in her, and she showed them. She ground her teeth together, running at full force until the sound of laughter and merrymaking was distant. She didn't go to Townsend, to the statue of her father. No, she went straight for Gideon's lighthouse—their lighthouse.

She stood at the bottom, the lighthouse looming over her. Lightning had started flashing about, igniting the darkness around her. It did nothing beyond the veil that held them all captive in Hellharth.

She slumped to the mossy floor, the sage dress a mass of tulle. "Nattya was right," she laughed. "No one wants to lift this much tulle."

The last time she had seen Miriam, Miriam had been screaming in her face, hauled off by Elven guards, and away from Gideon's burial.

She rested there, alone with her thoughts of Joffrey, Miriam, and Gideon.

"Good one!" She imagined Gideon saying with the same pride that Hamlet had shown her.

"I saw your parents tonight..." she whispered to no one.

"Where the hell is she running off to?" Hamlet called out to High-wing as they both set out to chase her.

"Either to Townsend or Vilis. She wouldn't go to the gardens—not with so many people here."

"I didn't think she'd get so overwhelmed. I thought she did things so well—not like a Princess, but like a Queen," Hamlet sighed. He shoved a drunk man who stumbled about, breaking into a run once they got beyond the castle walls.

To say Hamlet was worried was an understatement. He thought of the staff hidden under his bed, willing it to hold. Kahlisenya had been gone for the whole day and he was trying not to panic. If anything happened to her, the protective barrier would fall and Hellharth would be exposed.

"Are you looking for the Princess?" a small voice said. Both men turned to see young Arysta, twirling a periwinkle ribbon from her dress.

Highwing stepped forward, giving the girl a boyish grin. "Hey, Arys. You've seen Ella?"

Arysta narrowed her eyes at him. "The *Princess* went that way," she said, pointing a small finger in the general direction of Townsend. "She wanted to be left alone."

"It would be faster if you flew ahead," he instructed Highwing. He felt the gust of air and one of Highwing's feathers flitted into his view.

"No one listens to girls," Arysta mumbled, stalking off back to the castle party.

When the statue of the Elven warrior came into view, Hamlet was disappointed to not find her there. He looked up at the statue, feelings of guilt and hate for what it stood for.

"All these damn lies," he grumbled to himself. If she wasn't here, that meant she was at Vilis, and Highwing was closer to her than he was.

She sat there for a while, her eyes half-lidded, letting the bitterness consume her. She almost didn't catch it—that light in the distance over the seas and impossibly far for Hellharth. She shot to her feet, her wings jutting from their cage and spread wide.

There.

The flicker. The shadow of something beyond. She felt a jolt of adrenaline surge through her veins as ships blew their horns and shot fire into the night, igniting the skies. Without hesitation, she took off, her wings flapping vigorously against the wind currents as she raced forward, fearlessly running towards her escape. Her feet sank into the wet sands of the shores, and she let out a gasp as cold ocean waves crashed against her body. Soon enough she was gliding through the air, feeling an unknown freedom. But then suddenly something hard slammed into her with tremendous force; a momentary airlessness that threw off her balance and sent her skidding across sand and rock until it all eventually came to rest.

"The hell are you doing!" Highwing howled, throwing himself on top of Ella. She struggled against him, thrashing and clawing at the air. Her claws met his cheek, and she felt his skin rip beneath her fingers.

"Let me go!" she demanded. "LET ME GO!"

"Ella!" Hamlet hollered. "Not now! No! Stay still! Please!" Hamlet was next to use his body as an anchor and, to Ella's dismay, she couldn't move. She lay there, her hair riddled with sand and her tulle dress thrown about, completely defeated. She locked eyes with Highwing, radiating her betrayal.

"I couldn't let you just go," he answered her. He grimaced at her bared teeth and rested his head on her collarbone. "I couldn't let you go."

The veil set back in place, the lights that danced along the sea surface disappearing beyond the fog. He lifted himself off of her and she smacked him across the face, his head jerking to the side with the force of it.

"Ella!" Hamlet chastised. "What has gotten into you? What were you planning on doing out there?"

Her hand stung. She immediately regretted it. Ignoring Hamlet, she grabbed Highwing's face and held it in her hands. "I'm so sorry," she stuttered. He wouldn't look her in the eyes, his tongue darting to the inside of his cheek. "Highwing—I didn't mean it," she tried. He pulled her hands away from his face and stood.

"It's fine," he said monotonously. "I was just doing my duty as a trainee of the Queensguard."

"Gods! Your mother is going to have a conniption fit when she finds out about this!" Hamlet groaned, slapping a hand over his eyes. "Couldn't just have this one day without a hitch, could we? I didn't think I needed to keep you on a leash!" His pristine white tunic was stained with sand and seawater.

"I just want to know what is out there. I feel like I'm suffocating here!" Ella tugged at her hair and hid her face. She felt childish. She knew any pride Hamlet had felt for her in the last hour had quickly disappeared now.

"You take it upon yourself to endanger the lives of those around you? Can you not help yourself? We give you the responsibility you seek and then you run off like a toddler! How am I supposed to have faith in you? How is your mother? How are the people of Hellharth!" Hamlet was practically spitting now, his face red from fury and frustration. Ella had never been on the receiving end of such anger, and she recoiled from him. Highwing hissed and bared his fangs at Hamlet in warning, who pinched the bridge of his nose.

"No one else saw the little stunt you pulled. I really don't want to have to tell your mother about it. She has enough to worry about. You will stay away from the shores from now on—"

"What? You can't just—"

"I just did! If I find out you've run off to the shores, I will tell your mother. Any hope you have of being treated like an adult by her will be *ruined*. Do you understand me?" Hamlet waved a finger in Ella's face, and even Highwing didn't try to stop him.

She wiped at the few tears that fell. "Yes. I understand," she gritted out. Hamlet looked her up and down, noting her disheveled appearance. Her wings and hair were coated in sand. He waved a hand in the air dismissively, and the sand vanished from her.

"Take her to her room. Don't let anyone see her," he ordered Highwing.

Even though Highwing was technically a Lord by birthright, he was under Hamlet due to seniority, and he wasn't stationed in Court—yet.

Highwing nodded his head, taking hold of Ella's arms and holding her to him tightly. Her head was cradled against his hard chest, and he hugged her as his wings thrashed about to accommodate her weight. When they were airborne, she took in the feel of it. It had been a long time since she had been in the sky, and Hellharth looked different from what she remembered. She noticed he had taken a few extra laps around Hylycyn castle.

Highwing landed on her balcony gracefully, releasing her immediately, and she stumbled forward. She turned to him; his green garb now dirtied with wet sand. Hamlet hadn't cleaned him.

"I *am* sorry," she insisted. She reached for him, but he stepped back. "Please," she said gently. She took another step towards him, her fingers ghosting over his cheek. She stood on her tiptoes and kissed him lightly on the cheek, sniffling. She rubbed her nose along his jawline—an act of submission.

He inhaled deeply through his nose, the warm air tickling her neck. It made her shiver. "You were going to leave," he said accusingly, eyes narrowed. She still stood on her toes, his words making her head turn. She kissed the corner of his mouth, feeling him stiffen. She kissed him fully on the lips, lingering there for a few moments. When he didn't respond, she pulled away, feeling dejected.

He clutched the back of her head, fingers lacing in her hair, and kissed her hard on the mouth. Their noses smashed together painfully, but neither one of them pulled back. Their teeth clicked together, Ella biting down on his lip hard. He winced and stopped, touching his forefinger to his lip. He was bleeding and breathing hard. He furrowed his brows at her.

"Gods, you'd think you were a Dark One the way you're so violent," he glowered. It sobered her, and when he went to kiss her again, she turned her head, her cheek catching his lips.

"I should get to bed," she muttered. She pecked his cheek, hoping to pacify him. He cocked his head, running his bloodied finger over her lip.

"Sure. I'll see you tomorrow?" he asked cheerfully. She nodded vigorously, swallowing her anxiety as he flew from her balcony.

It wasn't that Ella didn't consider Highwing attractive. He possessed strength and handsomeness, a jawline resembling a finely honed blade. In all honesty, there was nothing amiss with Highwing. However, she couldn't feel the essential pull deep within her gut for him, as lore had described—the elusive mate connection. All she experienced was lust.

She found herself reflecting on Lady Rayne, who had snubbed her mating bond with Althane despite bearing his child. Eventually, he wed Tanyl, but their union lacked the true essence of a mated couple. It was merely a spousal agreement in name only. Could that be the future awaiting her, Dasyra, and Highwing if she hesitated too long? Each of them could have only one destined mate. What if her choice turned out wrong?

Highwing embodied everything anyone would desire in a life partner. As Ella's gaze lingered on the spot where he had just stood, she nervously licked her lips. His blood tasted unusually salty and left her feeling somehow incomplete, unable to pinpoint how or why.

Within her stirred an unquenchable ache that tormented her even more as thoughts of kissing Highwing invaded her. That night, Ella lay wide awake in bed, hands fisted in her sheets.

Chapter Six

Kahlisenya stumbled through the portal in the early hours of the morning, the party long over. Hamlet was seated in a chair, a single candle floating about his head to illuminate the dark throne room. He meandered over to her, lifting her to her feet. She carefully hid her wounded hand in her sleeve.

"What the *fuck*," he seethed. "You've been gone almost an entire day!" he hissed. Had Kahlisenya not known any better, she would have thought him to be elvish, the way he bared his perfectly squared teeth at her. He noticed that she had come back alone, her appearance disheveled.

"Apologies, I hadn't realized I was on your time," she scoffed. "You waited for me?" His eyes were roaming over her, examining her.

"What happened to the guards?" he asked gruffly. She averted his gaze, and he sucked in a breath. "You should have brought more. Are you hurt?"

"No," she answered swiftly, her fingers flexing. "How was the ball? Ella decided on the farming problem in Anvil?"

"She did." His arms were folded across his chest and he wasn't looking at her now.

"And?" she asked with a bite of annoyance in her voice. She was exhausted.

"And you should have been here for it," he answered, articulating every word.

"She didn't do well?" Kahlisenya asked. She saw his eyes flicker towards her bloodied sleeve, and she hid it behind her back. "What happened?"

His eyes bore into hers until it became unbearable for her, and she cleared her throat. "She did amazingly. She found a solution that satisfied both parties, and neither was neglected," he answered.

Kahlisenya let out a sigh of relief. "Good. I knew she would."

"Did you?" Hamlet asked. "Because I didn't. It would have been nice had you not sprung this on her." It was like beating a dead horse, having the same conversation over and over. He was supposed to be her High Advisor, yet she never took his advice.

"I didn't spring it on her," Kahlisenya argued, dusting off her leather pants. "If I did not think she was ready, I would not have left her to do it."

"You did. You insist on her not being part of Court matters, and then suddenly she is making final decisions. It threw everyone for a loop! Including her."

"Who is everyone?" Kahlisenya snickered. "Althane? His feelings hardly matter." She could picture his face—scornful and confused, as Ella took the podium and ordered him around.

"And what about Ella's? Gideon's parents were there."

At this, she stopped. "Ella... she was alright?"

"She did better than expected. But to put her in that position, Kahl, it wasn't fair."

"I didn't think they would," she said finally.

"Of course they would. They are the ones that have the best chance of winning Ella over."

"Did they cloud her judgment?"

"No. She was more than fair. For someone that had never been a part of Court matters, she handles it like she has been doing it her whole life."

"That's what I need from her. I need her to be the best when I am not around."

Hamlet shuffled his feet, conjuring a pitcher of water and pouring a tall glass for her. "Did you find what you were looking for?"

She took the water from him with her unmarked hand, thanking him silently. "I found more questions than I did answers. I was given something unexpected, and I do not know what to make of it. But, after the events of today, I have to admit that I was wrong, and you were right."

Hamlet's eyes shot up in surprise. "I was right?"

"Yes. She should never have been kept in the dark for so long. And after hearing what the Witches had to say, I don't know how I can fix this." Kahlisenya laughed mechanically, dumping the water onto the floor. "I messed up, Ham."

Hamlet had sat in silence while Kahlisenya relayed the Witches' prophecy. He brought his fingers together, clasping them at his lips. When she was finished, she was on her back, sprawled out on the floor of the throne room, still hiding her hand.

"Safe inside a morning song?" He mused quietly. "That's the name of one of the arcane schools in Arcadea. From younglings to college-level mages."

"How do you know?" Kahlisenya pressed.

"I had a friend I met in Calisan in my teen years who had been a teacher there before the Purge. I remember the name. Morning Song."

"And he is in Arcadea?" she asked, sitting up on her elbows.

"I don't know if he still is, but he was…" Hamlet did not like where this was going.

"I need you to find out."

He threw his hands up. "Ella deserves to know—"

"She will! When I am certain." She turned on her side, propping herself up on an elbow. He was looking down at her, hands on his hips.

"You have never been certain! You keep putting it off!" he snapped.

"Ham, this is all I need from you right now—"

"And what else will you need from me, My *Queen*? What else will you have me lie to her about?" He threw his hands up again in defeat and stalked about the empty room, leather boots clopping against the tiles.

"You promised you would do this for me. I need you to go to Arcadea. Go to Calisan Capital. I need you to gather information. I need you to gauge the outside world before I have to put her in it!" She crawled to her feet, wincing. "Ask your teacher friend. Bring her to him. Safe inside a Morning Song! That's what the prophecy said. You have to ask. Please."

He darted forward, shaking her shoulders. "Have I not done everything you have ever asked? I have done everything. With a smile on my face. This is our Ella—"

"Our Ella?" Kahlisenya questioned with a cock of her head. Hamlet's ears turned red.

"Don't," he warned. The crease between his eyes deepened, shifting his weight. "The staff held, but we flickered again… I'll have to be quick about it."

"Hm," she hummed. She clasped her hands together and slowly pulled them apart. The air shifted, a bustle of noise coming from behind him. "Do be quick about it," she said stiffly. Her eyes drifted to his lips and back up again.

He swallowed and shook his head, releasing his hold on her shoulders. "Remember what I said," he sighed, disappearing into the portal. It snapped closed and Kahlisenya sank to the floor, bringing her punctured hand to her face.

Less than a year, she thought sadly.

Chapter Seven

Hamlet was transported into a deserted alleyway, the smell of horses smacking him in the face. "Gods," he groaned, bringing a handkerchief to his nose. Daylight had already begun to peak over the spires of the tall buildings in Calisan Capital, the sound of vendors already settling themselves for the day's work.

It had been about four or five years since his last visit to Arcadea. Kahlisenya had been less than pleased with his tavern hopping and he reminded himself to stay away from Liveman's alley. He wouldn't want to get "lost" in a brothel—*again*.

"Candied apples here!"

"Chickens?" An elderly human woman asked him, holding a sharp knife and an upside-down flailing chicken.

"Hair tonics! We have a tonic for everything!" A man asked him, cutting him off. He had jutting lower canines and pale green skin. An Orc.

"No, thank you—"

"We have tonics that would keep you harder than a rock! Live it up in Liveman's Alley!" He made a vulgar gesture, grabbing around his crotch for emphasis.

"Gods—no. I'm good," Hamlet insisted. The man eyed him down, flashing a gold tooth fang.

"Wife's got you by the balls, eh?" He laughed.

"Something like that," Hamlet answered, shuffling away from him and crossing the busy road.

"Calisan news and announcements! One silver piece!" A small goblin man called out. His black eyes met Hamlet's, and he smiled a toothy grin. "Would you like a paper?"

Hamlet dug into his coat pocket, pulled out one silver coin, and dropped it into the goblin's awaiting palm. The goblin ruffled through his stack of papers, handing Hamlet a newspaper. "Pleasure doing business with you," the goblin said.

Hamlet tucked the paper under his arm, finding a tavern with outside tables and chairs. After ordering some tea and a pastry, he opened the newspaper, glancing around the front page.

MASS HYSTERIA OR HELLHARTH?

Calisan Capital has had a surplus of sightings of an island in the middle of the Idris Sea. Reports say that it appears in the location where Hellharth—Isle of Elves—had disappeared twenty years ago. Reports around Arcadea speak of the same phenomenon. A sighting of a floating island appeared over the dunes of the Aslan Desert.

Speculators believe it is Hellharth. An effort to gather intel has been underway by the Calisan Capital, grouping with The Council.

Twenty years ago, the original Council had gone through great efforts to protect the world of Arcadea from The Son of Bashet—a man of Elven descent, who brought the world under siege by the Dark Ones. Sifrrod Whitefish—one of the surviving members of the original Council—made a statement yesterday in light of the recent sightings.

"We do not know from where this moving island originally hails. If it is Hellharth, we hope to be able to integrate them back into a society that would greet them with open arms."

On the contrary, newer members of the Council, Aiden Mormant, Ivy Denford, and Hesta the Brave believe the appearance of the island to be an omen.

"If the Elven Queen believed her people to be innocent, why did they all disappear?" Ivy Denford commented.

"The elves that stood by The Son of Bashet were many and held the same values as he. While we have been able to capture and eradicate those criminals over the years—there is no telling how many escaped to Hellharth," Aiden Mormant commented.

Hesta the Brave has not been shy in her distrust for the elves. "They need to be interrogated. We will be working with great effort to make sure that any radical elves that are hiding will never see the light of day again!"

While many have agreed in their statements, others have reminded Calisan of the great lengths which Queen Kahlisenya took to ensure the safety of both Nomaji and maji humans during the Purge.

"We have all been deeply affected by the aftermath of the Purge War, but calling for such brazen actions to be taken against Hellharth should be seen as an act of war which is what the people of Arcadea do not want," Deacon Gregor, Highmaster of Morning Song voiced just last week. Deacon Gregor gained his reputation twenty years ago—during the war, he took in many refugees. He has been Highmaster of Morning Song, School of the Arcane, for the last fifteen years.

"While the sightings are no definitive proof that Hellharth has returned, it would be a welcomed event with me. It would be great to see elf younglings walking the halls of Morning Song, among the rest of the world," he stated.

The Elven Queen Kahlisenya helped to defeat the evil that was wrought against Arcadea. She, along with her homeland, disap-

peared without a trace. Is this the precipice of war? The Known World holds its breath.

Hamlet lowered the newspaper, taking a sip of his tea. Just a bunch of undecided people. But the name that caught his eye was the one he had been hoping to find.

Deacon Gregor, Hamlet mused. "Highmaster of Morning Song now?"

"Can you believe the shit they are spewing?" A woman with a pitcher came out to him, nodding her head at the paper laid out on the table. "Elves. Back here. They know better."

"Do they?" Hamlet asked, holding out his cup for her to refill.

"They'd have to be pretty stupid to show themselves again after all these years. Best to stay gone. Arcadea remembers," she said proudly. Hamlet lowered his gaze and looked back at the paper.

"You have some ink and paper? I need to write a missive," Hamlet said. The woman's forehead creased.

"Sure," she said, digging into an apron pocket. She pulled out a silver pen and a paper pad. "I'll be back in a moment for it."

It took Hamlet a moment to realize he had been writing in Elvish and quickly crumpled the paper, dropped it into his tea, and began to start over.

Deacon Gregor. It has been too long, hasn't it? You may be surprised to be getting such a letter from me, given how much time has passed since we last spoke. I hope that time has not swayed you into believing I am no longer a friend.

For a friend I am, and I am in need. It is not like me to beg, but I must beg of you this instant. I need to speak with you, urgently, and in the safety of Morning Song's haven.

I have someone I need you to meet. I trust that you understand the importance of secrecy that I am asking for. I await your response.

Sincerely, Hamlet Marks.

Hamlet nervously folded the paper and whispered the name of the person he intended to send the letter to. As his silent words escaped him, the paper began evaporating before his eyes and his heart pounded with anticipation. He looked up and noticed the old woman waddling over to ask if he was finished. He silently nodded, stood from his chair, and handed her one silver coin for her troubles. She gave him a warm smile and wished him well as he left.

⤜⟶

Two days. That's how long it had been since Hamlet had first sent the letter. He lay in bed, the Inn he had decided on discrete and quiet. He wondered what Kahlisenya was thinking with his absence.

"Probably thinks I'm at the whorehouse again," he laughed to himself. Something flitted into his vision on his nightstand, and he scrambled for his eyeglasses, his naked body thumping to the floor. "Damn!" he howled.

There it was, perfectly placed on his nightstand, the wax seal depicting a golden sun next to the small white stone Kahlisenya had given him to reopen the portal. He hadn't realized his fingers were shaking until he cut himself on the edge of the paper. He unrolled the parchment, sucking in a breath.

Hamlet Marks, how wonderful it is to hear from you. It has been a long time, has it not? I must say, I am surprised to receive such a letter of urgency from you after all these years. While it is surprising, it is not unwelcome.

The urgency of your letter is worrisome. There are a great many things happening in Arcadea. You wish for me to meet someone... and need to do so in secrecy...

But Morning Song?

My friend, I must remind you that Morning Song is a great and powerful place. It is safe for all. I would be happy to receive you and your friend. Please, use this letter to gain access through the Keeper. They will show you the way.

Please, do follow the roads.

I will await your arrival in the days to come.

Sincerely, D. Gregor, Highmaster of Morning Song.

Hamlet jumped up and waved the letter in his hand.

Kahlisenya paced the throne room, her white and blue gown whirling about her at every turn. Three days. It had been three days since Hamlet had left and she anxiously thought the worst. Ella had been unusually quiet the last couple of days, even with Kahlisenya praising her for her decisions with Anvil. She wriggled her gloved fingers and winced again. The pain in her hand was still there, but the bite mark had started to fade.

"My Queen, the Princess has had an incident with Lord Cida's daughter, Dasyra," a male guard announced to her. He was accompanied by four others, and they all smelled of smoke.

"What is it?" She sighed heavily.

So much for the quiet.

"Do the dare or tell the truth. If you do not, you have to take a drink," Nattya explained, holding up a fresh bottle of wine. Highwing and Ella exchanged glances. Nattya was adamant about them playing this human game and was determined to get drunk during the middle of the day. She had been on a tirade that Hamlet hadn't bothered to see or speak to her in the last couple of days.

"We don't have any Truth Syrup," Ella said in confusion.

"You've already had two glasses of Elven wine. You'd do anything," Highwing declared. He fiddled with a lock of his silver hair with disinterest.

"You don't need Truth Syrup. It's a game," Nattya grinned. "And there are no losers in this game! So, Highwing. Truth or dare?"

"Okay," he said through gritted teeth. "Dare."

Nattya shoves the bottle in his face. "I dare you to drink."

"I thought the premise of this game was to avoid drinking?" He took a swig and made a face. "Couldn't have gotten a mead?"

"Since when did you start drinking mead?" Ella asked with a knowing smirk. Dasyra drank mead. Lots of it.

"It's not his turn anymore. You can't ask him questions," Nattya said sternly. "Highwing gets to ask you." She waved a finger at Ella, her eyes crossing.

He smirked and lifted the bottle up in a salute. "Truth or Dare?"

Ella chewed on her bottom lip in thought. "If I do dare, it's just going to be to drink—so truth?"

Highwing leaned forward, so close that his breath blew into her face, and she breathed it in accidentally. Unconsciously, she moved closer.

"Why won't you marry me?" He exhaled.

She withdrew her face, her cheeks burning. Nattya swooned and clapped her hands together excitedly, until Ella snatched the wine bottle and tipped it back, taking two large gulps and sputtering. Highwing laughed while Nattya looked disappointed.

Ella turned to Nattya, "Truth or Dare?"

"Dare."

Ella was stumped. "What—do I make you do something? Like, anything?"

Nattya nodded expectantly.

"I dare you... to kiss Majorn," Ella's eyes flickered across the garden lawn, where the guard that had a clear dislike for Nattya stood at attention, watching them.

"HA!" Highwing cackled. "Do it!"

"I could always drink—" Nattya reached for the bottle, but Highwing stopped her.

"Chicken shit," he declared, pointing a finger at her. Nattya's face was already red from her drinking, but she blushed furiously.

"I'll get you back for this," she promised to both of them. Ella swatted Highwing's arm as they both watched in amused excitement when Nattya marched right up to Majorn.

Nattya stood there, pointing a finger at his face, her mouth flying about, and Majorn looked like he was getting angrier by the second. Suddenly, Nattya grabbed his face in both of her hands and crashed her mouth against his. Majorn's yellow eyes rounded, and he clutched at her shoulders but didn't shove her away. Eventually, he tilted his head and closed his eyes, earning a quiet squeal from Ella and Highwing.

"The man's loving it!" Ella gasped.

"She's using entirely too much tongue," Highwing said in mild disgust. Nattya slowly pulled away and stumbled backward, muttering something to the shocked guard. She sashayed back to them, triumph evident on her face as she sat down.

"Not a bad kisser," she preened.

"Did I see what I think I just saw?" A sultry feminine voice said, startling them out of their excitement.

Ella's head snapped up, seeing Dasyra standing there. Her long, flowing hair cascaded like liquid gold down her back, shimmering with every step she took, framing her delicately pointed ears, The tips of her ears are adorned with three small, intricate silver piercings. Her mesmerizing green eyes, like the emerald depths of a hidden glade, were scanning over the three of them on the grass.

Ella could understand how Dasyra had ended up catching Highwing's eye. She quickly glanced at him to take in his reaction, but he was preoccupied with playing with a blade of grass between his fingers. Dasyra then proceeded to settle herself between Ella and Highwing, adjusting her light dress so that it came above her knees. For a moment, Ella had an impulse to reach out and swipe a finger along her skin.

It looked soft and smooth, and impossibly shiny.

Despite the tension in the air, Dasyra seemed almost unaware of the unease created by her presence.

"Dasyra," Nattya greeted politely. "We were just playing a game."

"Oh, I do love games," Dasyra said. Her green eyes sparkled at Ella with something akin to predatory. "Might I join?"

Nattya was enthusiastic, Highwing shrugged, and Ella just smiled. There was no reason for her not to allow Dasyra to join. She had no real animosity towards her. She took another sip of the wine, her head feeling pleasantly fuzzy. After Nattya explained the details of the game, she asked her, "Truth or Dare?"

"Truth," Dasyra said shyly. Nattya scrunched her eyes. There was nothing that she had wanted to ask her.

But Ella was teeming with the question that was at the tip of her tongue— the one that scratched at the back of her brain for the last few days since the ball. Her impulse control long forgotten, she blurted out, "Is it true you and Highwing spend a lot of time together?"

Dasyra blinked and Highwing cleared his throat.

"We did... For a bit.... Has been a while though," Dasyra said flippantly. "I get to ask Highwing a question now. Truth or Dare?" she asked.

Highwing looked uncomfortable. "...Truth?"

"Who is the better kisser, me or Ella?" she asked, smirking at Ella's surprised expression. Highwing looked between the two women he was in the middle of and held out his hand for the bottle. Nattya held the bottle to her chest, slowly raising her middle finger at him.

"I've only kissed Ella once—" he started to say.

"Once is enough to know," Dasyra challenged.

"You don't have to answer. It's fine. Dasyra obviously has more experience than I—"

"And what's that supposed to mean, princess?" Dasyra snapped at her.

Ella's nose wrinkled at the confrontation, not understanding the sudden shift in the atmosphere. "I only meant that he obviously enjoys kissing you more...?"

Dasyra was clearly not satisfied with that. "If he enjoyed it so much, why'd he stop?"

"Maybe that's the question you should have asked him," Ella shot back, agitated. Dasyra bared her teeth at Ella and hissed. Ella's pupils expanded at the threatening gesture and she slowly crept closer to Highwing. Not taking her eyes off Dasyra, she slid her tongue up Highwing's neck, over his cheek, and sucked on the corner of his lip. It was petty and Ella knew it, not knowing what had come over her. When Highwing didn't protest, Dasyra shot to her feet, looming over them.

"Highwing would be better off married to *me*. You're too busy crying over your dead human to pay him any mind. His father *begged* mine to make us a proper match! If you were worth anything, your mother would have had you married by now!"

Nattya stood, the bottle clinking to the ground. "You don't get to say that to her! Ella! I *dare* you to punch her in the face!"

Dasyra smiled maliciously, her pretty mouth contorting. "Why? It's the truth. Friends with humans—fucks the humans—and kills them."

Ella sat on the grass; her head lowered as she began to understand the gravity of her circumstances. Suddenly, the ground around her burst into flames, smoking and twirling until it seared Dasyra's skin. Dasyra released a loud screech as she tried to put out the fire that engulfed her body and incinerated her dress and feathers in an instant. In what felt like an eternity, Ella realized whatever it was that held her back had been jolted loose. As the fire continued to spread, she could feel herself coming unhinged—finally free from whatever had previously bound her.

With a small laugh, Ella realized it was her incessant need to prove everyone wrong.

"HER WINGS—OH GODS!" she heard someone screaming. Highwing threw himself over Dasyra, his wings catching flame, and he let out a yelp as it flicked up his shoulders.

When Ella heard his yell, she snapped out of it, her pupils dilating and the fire vanquished, leaving nothing but wisps of smoke.

Dasyra lay naked on the grass, surrounded by horrified guards and servants alike. Her legs and wings were charred, bleeding, and unrecognizable. She let out a shaky gasp, her hand reaching for Highwing. Nattya was ranting to the guards about how Dasyra had instigated the whole thing.

His right wing had been burned at the tips, his arm an angry red. He looked down at Dasyra, his mouth hanging open. Slowly, he turned to Ella and held out his hand to her instead.

"I feel nothing," she whispered to Highwing, grasping his outstretched hand.

The Queen sat with her legs crossed on the throne, the oversize golden chair flashing with every movement from the spectators. She listened with rapt attention as everyone relayed their side of the event. Highwing stood by his mother, Lady Rayne, and Nattya, who was pale as a ghost. Ella was in the middle of the throne room, her eyes scanning everyone's faces.

"My daughter's wings! Where is the justice in that?" Lord Cida bellowed. He pointed to his crying mate, Lady Gielda, who had been a distraction through most of the meeting with her wailing.

"The healers have said your daughter will fly again," Kahlisenya said. "They expect her to make a full recovery."

"She was nearly killed!" Lord Cida argued.

Kahlisenya's gaze drifted to Ella, whose head wasn't even lowered in shame. There was a blank look on her face—one that worried Kahlisenya.

"Your daughter antagonized someone who was out of her magical capabilities. She not only insulted the Princess, but she also insulted me," Kahlisenya snapped. She rose from the throne and stood in front of Lord Cida, who backed up several paces.

"Your daughter was offered a healer by my daughter. I would not have been so gracious. I hope Dasyra has learned a valuable lesson here. Her jealousy of Princess Ellarhyssa's and Lord Highwing's relationship clouded her judgment. She made a very grave mistake."

"And what relationship is that?" Lord Althane barked from the dark corner of the throne room. "Young Dasyra was just laying claim to my son!"

"Are they to be mated? Are they fated mates? They have a bond?" Kahlisenya asked. She turned her attention to Highwing. "Did you, or do you have a bond with Dasyra?"

"No, my Queen. I did not," he answered swiftly. "I do not."

Kahlisenya raised her hands in a shrug. "So, then Dasyra has no claim. She bared her teeth at the crown and got hurt. Unfortunate as it is, it was deserved. I don't expect to see the two of you in Court for a month," Kahlisenya directed to Althane and Cida, to their dismay.

"Wha—"

"You speak out of turn, Althane. Until you learn your place, you do not have one. And Cida. Consider this my warning; Your daughter disrupts mine again, and I'll put her wings on the back of my chair and use the leftovers to dust my trophies." Gielda abruptly stopped her wailing at this.

"Yes, my Queen," they said in unison.

"Highwing, escort the princess back to her rooms. Madam Nattya, you too," Kahlisenya gave a pointed look to Nattya, who hiccuped and swayed in response.

CHAPTER EIGHT

Highwing stroked Ella's back, her wings flailing out around her as he tickled her spine with his fingertips. Nattya had busily helped herself to Ella's wardrobe, as per usual, wearing an odd hat that Ella didn't even know she owned.

"Your mother grounded my father," Highwing snorted in disbelief. His smile broke into a wide grin. If anyone was going to put Althane in his place, he was glad it was the Queen.

"Did you see the look on Cida's face when she said Dasyra got what she deserved?" Nattya guffawed drunkenly.

Ella grunted and turned to Highwing. "I almost killed your lover."

"She isn't my lover—anymore..."

"She could be."

"I ended things with Dasyra before all this happened because I didn't want to marry her." He wasn't about to tell her it was because his mother insisted on him pursuing Ella. It was only a small part. Dasyra was demanding, and truthfully, wouldn't know how to love anyone. He had seen it firsthand.

"You two just need to get it over with," Nattya scoffed, smearing lip paint on her lips. "I don't see why the two of you don't just marry already." Highwing stilled. "You would make the cutest babies," Nattya added.

He made an undignified noise and Ella flushed.

Ella pondered her words. It hadn't angered her at all when Dasyra had started becoming possessive of Highwing. It only angered her when Dasyra accused her of what everyone else had thought.

I killed Gideon.

Highwing had always been there. Always took her side. Always. Even when Dasyra had reached her burned hand towards him, he took Ella's instead. He was loyal above anything else.

Like Hamlet, Ella thought bitterly. So many broken relationships surrounded her. Hamlet had spent his entire life head over heels in love with her mother, and still, her mother never chose him, despite her feeling the same. It was obvious to anyone with eyes.

Highwing's mother, Lady Rayne, refused to marry Althane, even though they were *mates*. She still bore him a son. After years of pining, he married Tanyl, though that was never who he truly wanted. Tanyl made a show of it, trying to make Rayne feel beneath her, and Rayne rejected his advances thereafter. It was incredibly rare to find your fated mate, and it was devastating to Althane when Rayne began rejecting their mating bond. She never seemed phased by it, choosing to ignore him at every turn.

Ella chewed on her bottom lip while Nattya and Highwing bickered back and forth.

She could do it. She could take the steps to be with him. Perhaps that would calm her mother and the Court down. Perhaps that was her ticket to finally moving on and settling her place in Hellharth since they were so determined to keep her there. It would keep their families together.

It was a means to an end.

"We should," she whispered.

Highwing stopped stroking her back. "I didn't catch that. Nattya keeps making this obnoxious sound." He made a motion with his hand, mocking her.

"I was *talking*!" Nattya huffed, throwing a shoe at him.

"I said, we should," Ella repeated louder. "Should what?" Highwing asked, catching the shoe in midair with a grin.

"Court to marry."

Nattya's mouth pinched tightly, her eyebrows raised. Highwing said nothing, the bed shifting. Ella turned to look at him, and he was scrutinizing her with narrowed eyes. "Or not," she said flatly.

"You would let me court you?" he asked, his tone unsure. He looked fragile to her, as if he were about to break. Ella chewed on her lip. He was so kind, so gentle.

And she was a brute.

"I would," she answered with a small smile. It wasn't hard to think about—he was the best-case scenario for her. It was better than her mother arranging it and forcing it upon her, at least.

"Did I just witness a proposal?" Nattya screeched, jumping to her feet and throwing herself drunkenly on top of them. Ella and Highwing exchanged a nervous glance, neither wanting to be the one to answer first.

"Your mothers are going to absolutely swoon. Talk about the wedding of the century! Matter of fact this would be the first royal wedding since your grandparents, Ella!"

"No pressure," Highwing exhaled with a shaky laugh. He knocked Nattya off of him and she tumbled to the floor. "You're serious? I can start courting you?" It was just as his mother had said—that Ella would come around eventually. There was so much that they needed to discuss—in private.

"I said yes," Ella huffed in annoyance. Was it really so hard to believe?

"Can I be there when you tell your father?" Nattya asked from the floor. "I have to see the look on Althane's face when he hears his son finally nabbed the princess."

"I didn't nab anyone—yet. I doubt he will be happy that his son will surpass him in Court," Highwing said, his jaw twitching. He sat up, pulling Ella to a sitting position. "I am flirtatious, and a bastard—"

"So am I," Ella chuckled.

"Me too," Nattya quipped.

"Shut up. What I am trying to say is; I'll be a good husband to you. I'll do my best to make you happy."

Nattya cooed and sniffled. "You guys! I'm officially going to be a spinster. Ella you were supposed to get old and gray with me. Ugh." She rested her head at the edge of the bed, her brown eyes shining.

Highwing plucked one of his large gray feathers from his wing, twirling it in his fingers before presenting it to Ella. "My first of three gifts," he said quietly. Ella stared at the feather before doing the same, her ebony feather catching the light and turning a dark shade of blue.

Slowly, they took each other's feathers, as if any sudden movement would startle them. Ella let out a breath and smiled, teeth flashing. His feathers were impossibly large compared to her thin, dainty ones.

"I need to find a man," Nattya grumbled, rummaging under the bed. There was the sound of glass clinking and huffing when Nattya lifted a half-empty bottle of mead in the air. "Ha! Found it!"

"Where in the hell did you get that?" Ella scoffed, taking the proffered bottle in her hands and examining it.

"I hid it here the last time we drank in here. You didn't think I'd finished it?" Nattya answered.

Highwing pulled the stopper on the top and sniffed, grimacing. "That was a month ago. This smells like piss."

"Did you pee in the mead?" Nattya shouted at him.

"Why am I getting accused?" he asked, offended.

"Last I checked, we didn't have the equipment to pull off a stunt like that," said Ella. "You either did and don't remember, or it's gone bad. Try it and find out."

Highwing blanched. "Like hell I would. You go first."

"You would have me drink swill?" Ella gasped dramatically. He rolled his eyes at her, a smile playing on his lips. It was strange how comfortable Ella felt, as if nothing had changed between them in the last few minutes.

Because nothing was different for her. Yet.

"How romantic," he said, tipping the canter back and swallowing the remains of the mead. He raised his eyebrows, coughing a bit.

"Well?" Nattya asked.

"It was perfectly fine," Highwing said with a lopsided grin, tossing her back the empty bottle.

"You drank it all!" she protested, turning the bottle upside down and shaking it. A few drops spilled out onto Ella's pristine blue quilt.

"That was the plan."

"We have nothing to toast with now, you big bird!"

"Nattya, you can always toast with some *water*. You've been on a binge for three days," Highwing said pointedly.

"Last I checked, all three of us were bastards and had no fathers," Nattya snapped. "Don't tell me what to do."

Ella moved to her study table, a pitcher of water and some goblets coming into her hands. She swirled the water at Nattya, who took it begrudgingly.

"Already so boring," she mumbled.

Ella handed a goblet to Highwing, their fingers lacing over the glass. He pressed it to her lips, water dribbling ungracefully out of the corner of her mouth. She went to wipe it with her sleeve, but Highwing took the liberty of bending low, his tongue moving up her cheek and over her bottom lip.

"That's payback for licking my face earlier," he hissed in her ear. Ella's cheeks flared and Nattya coughed loudly.

"I am standing right here," she announced, waving her arms obnoxiously.

For the first time that day, Ella was able to forget about Dasyra's charred flesh scorching itself into her nostrils.

After a few hours, Nattya left Highwing and Ella to themselves, letting them mull over a few questions they were afraid to ask one another. It had turned to mid-morning, and while Nattya was nursing a hangover, the two of them snuck off to the Hylycyn Treasury and Library. They perched themselves at the foot of a large glass cabinet, a large, petrified egg floating over a golden podium. Beneath it, a long parchment with a mess of a script. The shimmer of magic that encased the items glinted every so often, reminding everyone that it was heavily guarded—if the twenty Silent soldiers didn't remind them enough.

The Silent soldiers: perfect assassins, a mix of Anaferian and Hylycynian descent dressed in black garbs and covered their faces with silver masks. Frozen faces that all looked the same, frightening and twisted. They were trained from a young age, never showing emotion or hesitation.

Nattya would make a game of trying to get them to react, going to the extreme, and walking around the Treasury naked. That stunt had earned Nattya a week in the Hylycyn prison, which she said was like a luxury spa—being the Princess's best friend had its perks.

"Do you think it would have hatched if they took care of it?" Highwing mused from her side.

"The Highborns of Direfell knew what they were doing, giving an egg that wouldn't hatch. They say the Highborns could shift into dragons themselves."

"Imagine one of them had laid this egg? It would have been like taking a massive shi—"

"That's disgusting," Ella blanched, unable to get the image of Dracaenean squatting.

"In classes, we were taught that the Highborns gifted three things. Direwolves, this egg, and peace."

"All we gifted them was a Princess who died in childbirth. Some gift," Ella scoffed.

"The whole war started with a Princess, to begin with."

"Men fight over stupid things," she sighed.

"I think it was romantic."

"War isn't romantic," she countered.

"No. Not war. The willingness to die for someone or something. It's the ultimate sacrifice."

"Dying doesn't sound romantic either," she chortled.

"I'd die for you," Highwing said confidently.

She blanched. "That's not a romantic gesture, Highwing! Living for someone is better. I'd rather you live your life," she nudged him, then placed a hand on the cheek she had struck the night she tried to flee. He swallowed, leaning into her touch.

"You don't have to do that, you know," he said.

"Do what?" She shuffled over to him, wrapping his massive wing around her like a blanket and pulling hers into her back.

"Pity me. You said you were sorry."

"I don't pity you," she said while rubbing his side. She smirked at him and leaned in closer. "If Nattya were here..."

"She would suggest something that would get us all put in prison for a decade. Have you decided on giving her the Life Stone?"

"Of course. You sound like my mother."

"What's the hold-up? If you aren't going to ask her, I will," Highwing said.

"What if she says no? I'm asking her to share a life with me. I'm asking a lot of her. What if she were to marry a Nomaji? She would outlive them. Any children she produces…"

"Nattya would never settle for a mundane life. None of her other friends are Nomaji. Besides, our Nattya is vain. She would hate to grow old."

"And if she says no, then I'm faced with the reality I'll outlive her." She didn't want to think of that.

"Have you thought perhaps you would give your Lifestone to another human male?" Highwing asked carefully. He was preparing himself for her answer.

She bit the inside of her cheek. "No. Never."

"Then ask. It won't kill you."

"What if she thinks I'm trying to… partner with her?" A blush crept over her cheeks.

"Your mother asked Hamlet and nothing sexual happened between them as far as I know… Would you want to?" His mouth pinched together, eyes shifting.

"Be in a-a- *partnership* with Nattya? I've never thought of it that way." She contemplated the idea in her head. Ella associated sex with love, and not just pleasure the way that Nattya and Highwing seemed to. She assumed they treated sex like a transaction. She knew the two of them had romped a few times—even in her own bed.

Would that change because Highwing and she would marry? Did she care?

"Please say yes, so I can have one good thing in my life," Highwing said.

"How did this become about you?"

"The prospect of a threesome should always be about me." He flicked her nose.

"Ha. You're getting demoted to consort instead of a spouse." She was a bit unnerved by how accurate his statement was—as if he had been inside her head.

He eyed her quietly, moving a few strands of her black hair behind her ear. "I wouldn't mind…"

"Mind what?" she asked curiously, her nose nuzzling into his neck. She inhaled his scent—pine, and wood smoke.

He blushed. "I don't expect you to be like your mother—never taking consorts or indulging in male company… you are the future Queen—"

"I'm not as adventurous as you would think. I've never been with a man or woman. Is this your way of asking for a-a pass?" She narrowed her eyes suspiciously. Perhaps he still wanted to sleep around with Nattya and Dasyra.

"A pass for what?"

"To be with others?"

"I wasn't—"

"I don't think I'd be jealous if you did," she answered truthfully. The thought of Highwing being with someone else wasn't as jarring as she thought it should be.

Perhaps she would feel differently if she were in love with him. After all, this was a marriage of convenience on both sides.

He was silent for a moment, and she chanced a glance at him. His eyebrows were scrunched in thought.

"What are you thinking about? You look constipated."

He snapped out of it and cleared his throat. "What if we find our mates?"

The question took her aback. "Do you feel the mate pull?"

He almost seemed afraid to answer. "No." She stood then, holding her hand out to him. "Come on, I'll show you something."

She led him down a corridor with a dozen glass cases, each holding some artifact or another. They came to a door—a door that only an heir to the throne could open. The door was solid stone, a twisting tree that grew and grew, branches winding out.

"The Ancestor Tree?" Highwing asked incredulously. Ella nodded her head, placing her hand on the door. It released and opened with a waning creak.

The room was impossibly large, a warm light emanating from the ceiling, illuminating the broad tree that curved about.

Highwing was afraid to get any closer, but Ella insisted, pulling him by his wrist.

The Elder scribes watched them quietly behind desks, books floating above their heads as they wrote down things that would be added to the library.

The Carver sat at the foot of the tree, so old and spindly that he looked as if he had merged with the tree roots.

"Hello," Ella greeted with a bow of her head. The Carver turned his head ever so slowly, small cracking sounds as he did so. He said nothing, looked at nothing—his eyes were gone.

Highwing swallowed hard.

Ella circled the base of the tree, found a place for her footing, and began to climb. The Carver let out a moan of disapproval.

"Ella, I don't think you should be doing that," Highwing called out to her. She wasn't listening. Her face inches from the tree and her hands moving along its surface.

"Here! Come here Highwing," she shouted.

He thought it best not to touch the tree, the Carver following him with empty sockets. He jumped and spread his wings, keeping himself level with Ella high in the tree's branches.

She was pointing to something, and he leaned in closer for inspection.

There were hundreds of thousands of names inscribed in the tree bark, names overlapping and having symbols across them.

Ella pointed to a name. Dyamora. Then another name that was connected to it, and another connected to that one.

"Dyamora had a husband, a Lifestone partner, and a Mate—all of which were found at different times in her life."

"So, I should expect you to have three people in your life?" he scoffed.

"Don't be crass. I'm showing you that these things happen."

"And what if our mates don't like the arrangement?" It was the conversation he had had with his mother previously.

Ella was quiet for a moment. "Your mother denied her mating bond with Althane... Why?"

Highwing latched onto the tree then, letting his wings rest. "A mating bond is a mingling of souls, when it came down to it, my father was irrevocably in love with my mother. She loved him too. But when they became mates, Joanai had her initiated into Court, and my father along with her. Tanyl took my father's eye because my mother was always too busy.

"My mother says it wasn't that my father strayed away. She would have accepted that. It was when Tanyl started to treat my mother as beneath her. Tanyl said my father would take her for a spouse, and my mother said she would deny him if he did.

"He said he never had plans to take a spouse since he had a mate and name for himself already. My mother wasn't buying it. He took Tanyl as his wife to gain lands in The Shire—a supposed gift to my mother—and my mother never looked back."

"I see the way he looks at her still. The same way Hamlet looks at your mother. If my mother said she would be with him again if he revoked Tanyl's title, he absolutely would."

"If your mate wanted you, and did not accept me?" she asked carefully.

He knew what she was asking. "I cannot be my father." Silence enveloped them—an awkwardness that they didn't know how to come out of.

"Then we should come to an agreement. If not for our love for one another... for our friendship. If it comes to that—if we find our fated mates and they are displeased with our marriage... then we do what we must in name only."

"You're saying..."

"We join our houses once again, maybe have an heir or two. Should calm down our families. I suspect my mother wants me barefoot and pregnant sooner rather than later."

"Are you truly alright with this?" he asked incredulously.

"Yes."

"I love you," he sighed quietly, a weight lifted from his shoulders. She beamed at him. "I love you too."

"Did you find your name on this yet?" Highwing inquired, shifting out of the serious topic.

She scoffed. "Yes, I did. Seems all worn out." She signaled for him to accompany her, guiding him to a different twisting branch. She indicated her name and the connected names. Kahlisenya's name was interwoven with hers, and Ella traced the line to where it read Hamlet as her mother's Lifestone companion.

"Your father's name is obscured...and another name nearby," Highwing observed. "Nevertheless, your father's line goes right back to Hylycyn's name."

"I attempted to find everything possible about Kai. The carvers remain silent. They're forbidden from discussing the history; they can only inscribe the names."

"It makes you curious about what hidden secrets lie within these names," Highwing playfully remarked. His hand glided up her spine, applying pressure on the sweet spot between her shoulder blades. A shiver ran down her spine as she arched her back and turned to face him. Their eyes locked for a moment before he closed the distance, brushing his lips tenderly against hers.

The sensation inside her swelled, and she pressed against him, back to chest. He encircled her with his strong arms and teasingly traced her lower lip with his tongue, sending pulses down her body. She gasped in surprise when his fingertips grazed the tender junction of her thighs, giving him an opening to deepen the kiss further. As their tongues danced, she tightened her thighs, turning up the intensity of his touch. In response, the claws of his other hand dug into the tree bark behind them with an audible scrape.

She pressed herself more firmly against his eager hand, and he nibbled on her lip with fervor. A soft whimper escaped her lips, followed by a throaty moan. It was unlike anything she had experienced before; stolen kisses with Gideon paled in comparison to this electrifying encounter. With each expert stroke of his hand, the anticipation continued to mount within her. Her thighs clenched and her insides fluttered. "Highwing," she panted. The sound of his name seemed to take him out of the trance. He pulled away from her reluctantly, breaking the kiss. He looked her in the eye, slowing his pace into small circles, his face a mask of uncertainty. She bit her bottom lip to keep from being too loud as the feeling finally reached its peak. She bit so hard on her lip, she bled and pressed her forehead against the tree. The scent of his arousal invaded her nostrils, and she was suddenly aware of the pooling wetness between her thighs. She blushed and looked away. He swallowed and cleared his throat, taking his hand back. "I'm pretty sure if we continue, we would be breaking several laws," he said in a hushed tone.

She was mortified, to say the least.

Dasyra grimaced, tossing restlessly on her stomach as various healers tended to her severely burnt skin. Her mother had been fussing nonstop for over an hour, making her wish to simply bury her head into the pillow and remain asleep indefinitely. She had been transported back to Irefana City, where expert healers from the Anaferi Mountains were summoned. Among them was Healer Eros, who meticulously treated the wounds on her back. At any other time, she would have enjoyed his pleasant appearance, if only she hadn't looked so dreadful.

"Tell me, what went through your mind to provoke the Princess like that?" Healer Eros scolded as he worked. He was a strikingly handsome man, sporting an assortment of gold jewelry on his ears and intricate black vine tattoos that meandered around his chiseled arms. His captivating eyes were mesmerizing patterns of green and yellow-orange, resembling miniature eclipses. Luxurious black hair cascaded down his back freely, framing his face, contrasting against the pristine white healer garments he wore.

Squinting with pain, Dasyra replied, "I didn't anticipate being set ablaze." Her once blonde hair had been charred nearly to the roots. "You can restore all this hair, can't you? I can't bear looking like this forever," she implored with desperate hope.

Upon meeting his intriguing gaze, Dasyra felt her heart race—for a moment—before quickly hiding her flustered face in the pillow.

Highwing was undeniably enchanting. Alluring, striking, and compassionate, but Eros had the appeal of a refreshing drink on a scorching summer day. She couldn't help but ponder what he would be like between the sheets.

"Be grateful she didn't yearn to slice you apart with a cursed sword. Don't worry, I can remedy this situation. Your wings will require time to heal, and I recommend keeping your hair short," Eros said as he applied a soothing paste onto her burnt skin, providing immediate relief.

Dasyra gasped in horror. "I'll resemble a boy!"

Her mother shared her distress. "Isn't there a magical way to mend it?" Gielda pleaded.

Eros scoffed at the suggestion. "Magic can't conjure something from nothing. An equal exchange would be necessary. Do you anticipate someone taking on these wounds for you?"

Dasyra retorted, "There's no need for such rudeness!"

Gielda continued her dramatic display, exclaiming, "This is unacceptable! Whether she's royalty or not! Our family holds high status in Irefana City!"

Healer Eros interjected, "And bear in mind that the Princess is destined to be Hellharth's future Queen. As Anaferians, we remain under Hylycynian rule—all of us."

"They removed my husband from Court! And Lord Althane too!" Gielda couldn't contain her despair.

Eros ushered Gielda out of the room firmly, announcing, "Enough lamenting; your daughter needs her rest."

When they were alone, Dasyra asked him, "Would you consider staying and keeping me company?"

He looked at her quizzically. "Do you require assistance with personal hygiene? If you need to use the restroom, Lyra is here to help."

Indignant, Dasyra squawked as her cheeks flushed, "No! I don't need to relieve myself!"

"Then, perhaps you're hungry?" He inquired.

Exasperated, she sighed and replied, "No."

After a brief pause, he asked gently, "What on earth did you do to incite such fury from the princess?"

Caught off guard, she felt a mix of surprise and embarrassment wash over her. She averted her gaze, asking defensively, "Why? Are you trying to gauge if I really deserved it?"

"No," he replied calmly, "it's just that I'm curious."

She hadn't meant for her sudden outburst. Casually strolling through the luscious gardens, the sound of Highwing's boisterous laughter unexpectedly graced her ears, instantly dampening her spirits. He had ended their relationship, claiming he had no interest in taking her hand in marriage.

Yet, his declarations rang hollow given how passionately entwined they had been just days earlier. She couldn't fathom what had made him change his mind.

That was until she saw them. Three joyful figures relishing a picturesque day in the garden, appearing utterly content and whole...as though they were parts of one harmonious puzzle. She couldn't help but feel an ache of envy, recognizing that she didn't complement their perfect dynamic. Though she knew of Highwing's sporadic flings with the human girl—his and Ellarhyssa's mischievous pet—she didn't believe that to be the reason for relinquishing nightly visits to her bed chamber. No, the actual reason had to be Ellarhyssa herself.

If Highwing were to wed the princess, he'd amass a great deal more prestige and influence than if he married her.

So, when she witnessed their easy camaraderie and unabashed happiness together, an overwhelming desire to sully it consumed her.

"I... I said something I shouldn't have," she admitted reluctantly.

"What did you say?" He probed with genuine interest. He had such interesting eyes and a captivating smile—sharper fangs than what she was used to seeing.

"I mentioned her deceased friend." She said it aloud and felt shame.

He paused for a moment, mouth agape in disbelief. "What on earth possessed you to bring that up?"

Dasyra clenched her fist, pounding it into her pillow. "I can't understand why everyone idolizes her so much! She doesn't study like the rest of us, she never strays from her clique, and she sorely lacks the refinement and poise befitting a princess!"

"Ah, I see," he mused thoughtfully. "You're consumed by jealousy."

"I am not!" she protested vehemently.

He continued, slightly amused. "Jealousy can be the root of hatred, you know."

"Fine!" she huffed, exasperated. "I've changed my mind. I don't want your company anymore."

Unfazed, he said, "Apply the burn paste twice daily," before turning to leave. As he approached the door, a young boy burst into the infirmary, his tousled brown hair and peculiar wings flailing wildly as he ran in.

"Stop running in here!" he barked at the boy, who couldn't be more than fourteen.

"Bastian, you've come to see me," Dasyra beamed, her smile lighting up the room. Eros couldn't help but roll his eyes as the boy named Bastian eagerly revealed a handful of wilted yellow flowers in his small grasp and offered them to her.

"I heard you were injured. I came all this way just for you. Even had to ride atop a Hyla cat!" Bastian exclaimed proudly.

Eros couldn't help but study the boy's wings—they seemed familiar somehow. He recalled delivering this child years ago, born to the Court woman Petra—a difficult and unusual birth where Bastian's delicate wings had snapped due to their awkward positioning. They had healed, albeit with an abnormal shape.

"Your kindness touches my heart," Dasyra said softly, her eyes shimmering with gratitude. Eros found himself taken aback by her tender reaction toward the boy. Perhaps he had misjudged her.

"It appears you have all the company you could ever need," he remarked, feigning nonchalance. "I must say, I'm rather envious," he added with a playful smirk dancing on his lips. "If you'll excuse me, I have a baby to deliver."

As Dasyra observed him slowly withdraw from the room, her stomach did a flip. Enthusiastically, Bastian engaged her in conversation and tenderly positioned the slightly drooping blossoms behind her ear.

CHAPTER NINE

Four days and Hamlet had finally come back through the pre-made portal set for him by Kahlisenya. He presented her with both the newspaper and the letter from Deacon Gregor. He relayed the details of his travels and encounters, while she relayed to him the near-death experience Dasyra had.

"She said *what?*" Hamlet asked in disbelief.

Kahlisenya nodded her head. "Healer Eros says her feathers are finally growing back."

At the mention of the healer's name, he raised his eyebrow at her. "How has Eros been doing?" he asked.

Kahlisenya met his gaze then. "He is doing quite well. His parents raised a fine young man." Her voice didn't falter at the memory of the young healer. Far from the small child she had known.

"And Cida and Althane aren't in Court—as of this moment? For the next month?" He whirled around, making his way to the arch doors to leave.

"No—where the hell are you running off to?" she called after him.

Hamlet turned sharply to her, tripping over his feet in his excitement. "I have to go tell Cida he's a fat, pompous—" He stopped in his tracks when he realized Kahlisenya was holding her finger up for silence.

"Hamlet, come now. Don't take cheap shots. Ella nearly killed the girl," Kahlisenya scolded, even though her amusement was evident. He nodded his head, his eyes downcast, but he did not apologize. He was missing his chance to tell them off without repercussion.

"She has always been well controlled with her fire," he said, his gaze still on the ground. Kahlisenya nodded her head and walked over to stand beside him.

"Which tells me she really desired to hurt Dasyra," she said, her voice quiet. She placed her hand on his shoulder.

He looked up at her. "Can you blame her? After what she said? I've seen people put to death for less," Hamlet said.

Kahlisenya glowered at his words. "I try not to be that person anymore." She remembered the start of her pregnancy when some of the former Court members openly disapproved of her unwed, unpredictable status with an unclaimed father for the child. Only Lord Joanai and Hamlet survived *that* meeting. At Lord Joanai's insistence, his daughter Lady Rayne and her consort, Lord Althane, joined the Court.

Althane had his moments. He loved Rayne, but Rayne loved politics more. Her time was consumed with Court matters and never favored him. When he had pledged himself to Tanyl, who had been a mere shire woman with some land at the time, he did so to get a reaction from Rayne.

He never got one. Lady Rayne let him go without so much as a second glance.

Kahlisenya envied her for that.

"Perhaps Ella was right on that front. We should have been teaching her how to handle her pyromancy," Hamlet said.

"Fire wielders aren't a common occurrence in Elves. This school could help her with that?" She was trying to tell herself this was best. That it would be beneficial to her.

Hamlet fixed his gaze on her. "I can't make any guarantee that Gregor will accept her as a refugee. And how do we explain her absence? What happens when Hellharth flickers back to Arcadea permanently? How do you explain a missing princess?"

"I'll think of something. Hamlet?"

"Yes?" he asked, his eyes on hers. He could feel the weight of his responsibilities pressing down on him. He took a deep breath. He was only one person. He couldn't do it all.

"It's time we had that talk with her."

Valla was pacing back and forth in the chamber, hissing and growling to get Ella's attention. Ella's gaze was fixed on her reflection in her vanity mirror. She wasn't even listening to Valla. Ella was too busy daydreaming about her impromptu date with Highwing. She could never have dreamed that she would act so audaciously. She could still feel the heat of his hand there—in her most private place. And he had kissed her, and she had kissed him back. It was a kiss of passion and of understanding. She had never been kissed like that before. She was tingling from it. Maybe she should ask Nattya how he was as a lover—what to expect—and then she could be prepared. The thought that Highwing would compare her to Nattya in bed crossed her mind briefly—what if she was lacking and her inexperience bored him?

Well, hadn't they agreed on taking other lovers…?

Valla yowled again, scratching at the door, wanting to be taken hunting. "I know, I know. But I can't come out tonight. I'm exhausted. I need to rest," she said. Valla huffed and chittered in irritation, her pale coat turning a dark shade of red. "Don't you take that tone with me," Ella scolded, squinting her eyes at Valla's display. At this, the cat huffed again, walking straight through the wall. Ella looked at the door and sighed. "Guess she's going solo." She turned her attention back to her reflection and picked up her brush.

She got ready for bed and was about to climb under the covers when a knock came from her door. Her heart thudded for a split second, hoping that it was Highwing. But she shook the thought out of her head—he would have used the balcony and not the door. She opened it to find Dilfree, a female Queensguard, standing there. Dilfree had a stern expression on her face.

"The Queen Mother has requested your presence in her chambers immediately," she said. Ella just stood there, frozen. Had her mother found out about her and Highwing? She braced herself for the scolding that would surely come. Dilfree took a step toward her, and Ella took a step back. "No time to dally, Princess," Dilfree said. Ella nodded and hurried out of her room, hoping that Highwing wouldn't be punished for what they did on top of the branches of the Ancestral Tree—coming undone atop the names of her grandsires—above the Carver and within earshot of scribes. She had never felt so nervous in her entire life.

CHAPTER TEN

Kahlisenya tapped her chin in thought. This was it. This was what she feared would come. Guilt and anxiety swelled within her. Ellarhyssa had struggled most of her life, Kahlisenya knew, feeling misplaced. Like a part of her was missing.

She was waiting for Ella to come to her bed chamber. It was late in the night, but she knew she would be awake.

"You're pacing," Hamlet called from her chaise behind her. She turned to him. He was looking at her with concern.

"How observant of you," she replied.

"It will be alright," he added. She knew he was trying to comfort her.

"Don't lie for my benefit. We already don't have the best relationship. She thinks I've been out to suppress her all these years—I can't even look in her eyes for long." She fiddled with a tea set, setting about reheating it repeatedly. Hamlet took it from her hands and placed it on the table, pouring her a cup of tea. She took it from him and sipped it, then began pacing again.

»»»———————▸

Ella knocked timidly on the door. It wasn't like her mother to send for her in the middle of the night. The guard that escorted her waited for her dismissal with a bow of her head. "Thank you, Dilfree." The female guard bowed and turned her back from her as she went inside. When she opened the door, she was greeted by her mother's apprehensive gaze and Hamlet with his back turned to her. He was staring at a painting of the royal family.

"Mother," Ella said in greeting. "You sent for me?" Her mother stood up and motioned for a snack tray lined with all her favorite fruits. Ella looked at the fruit tray and back to her mother. "A little late to be eating, don't you think?" she asked, her voice wavering.

She knows about the Tree incident, Ella thought anxiously, *that has to be it.*

"It's never too late to enjoy things," Kahlisenya said with a forced laugh. Hamlet turned to her with a grimace.

He looked at Ella with concern and she felt her face burn. If he knew what she did, he would be as angry as her mother—more so even.

"Did I do something?" Ella asked. Of course, she had. She tried escaping Hellharth, almost killed someone, got engaged, and defiled their sacred tree. All in a span of a few days. Her eyes shifted over to Hamlet.

He said he wasn't going to tell about the escape part, she scoffed to herself.

Hamlet rubbed his top lip with his forefinger, an action that Ella associated with when he was nervous and trying to avoid something. Either Dasyra died, which was unlikely, or Hamlet knew about the tree incident, or—

"You haven't arranged a marriage already for me, have you?" Ella asked, her heart seizing in her chest. Her mother's face contorted into a mix of grief and surprise and Ella put a hand to her mouth. "No!" she gasped, "Highwing—"

"I didn't," her mother reassured her. "Just...damn it!" Kahlisenya exhaled. She grasped Ella's hand and pulled her to her body, hugging her. The act shocked Ella and made her more uneasy. Her mother was never the type to show physical affection. She could never even recall her doing this when she was small. Her mother squeezed her tighter and Ella held her breath.

"Ella. My sweet Ella. I have done many things so utterly wrong in my lifetime and I have regretted it. I wish I could have done better. For you." She touched Ella's cheek lightly, as she had done for many years in place of hugs and kisses.

"Why are you speaking like this?" Ella breathed, recoiling from her touch.

"There are things I have kept from you for so long. I thought I was keeping you safe by not telling you the truth. But all that has done is leave you confused and unprepared."

Ella looked to Hamlet for reassurance. Something about this conversation was making her nauseous. He stood still, looking at the floor.

"As you know, twenty years ago, there was an Elven man who was known as The Son of Bashet," Kahlisenya started hesitantly. "He caused great strife in all of Arcadea. He wanted to conquer the Known World. He believed humans were dangerous. He took some Elven warriors and enslaved many Nomaji and Maji human villages and cities."

"This is common knowledge... I don't understand. Why are you telling me this?" Ella shook her head, confused.

Kahlisenya took a breath and continued, "This was all brought up by the death of his beloved sister, Ellanna, who had been killed by humans. Her wings cut from her body. They violated her and bragged about it. It still is no excuse for what he had done. He wanted to conquer Arcadea. He needed more power, so he sought out the Dark Ones in the Mountain of Tartis. They came from the pits and worked in Bashet's name. Tartis is said to only appear to people who are fully committed to dark magic. He *wanted* it. He performed their rituals and drank the blood of the Demon Bashet. That's when he started killing. It wasn't enough to just enslave them anymore."

"His wrath was no longer aimed just toward the humans. It turned on anyone who did not stand by him. That time became known as the Purge War. So many died. The Council of Arcadea gathered to put a stop to him—"

"And you put him in The Mirror of Shadows," Ella finished. Kahlisenya nodded.

"Yes. I did that. Only seven of the eight Council members were present, including me."

"What happened to the eighth?"

"Princess Lelot had to bow out due to a Treaty from more than five hundred years ago. Her kind could not fell ours, or the treaty would be null. It angered many when she did not take her soldiers up against *his*."

"You're talking about the Treaty of Stagnation?" Ella concluded.

"Yes. We set a trap for The Son of Bashet, luring him to the shores of Hellharth. I-I created the Mirror, while the others used their magic to hold him in place. It took a great deal of magic—and some of the original Council members died from expelling all of it at once. It was a great sacrifice."

"I put him in the Mirror, and we set about rebuilding. The people of Arcadea were demanding reparations in blood. They started retaliating and many innocent Elves lost their lives. Arcadea became mistrustful, and I became afraid."

Kahlisenya stood up then, turning her back from Ella and gathering her nerves. "See, I found out that I was pregnant. With you. And I thought of all the hate in the world and all of the lives that had been lost. I had a lot to be afraid of. So, I did the only thing

I thought I could do at the time. I moved Hellharth, making it disappear from Arcadea, and created its own realm. All that is here is Hellharth. No war... I was protecting the people, as their Queen, and you, as your mother."

Ella appeared next to her side and tilted her head in an endearing way. "I know this..."

Kahlisenya met her daughter's amber eyes and was determined not to flinch. "Your father wasn't a soldier who died during the Purge."

Ella's face scrunched up in confusion. "What?" she asked incredulously. "There's a monument of him in the town. My father was a soldier named Kai. You told me so," she accused. When her mother didn't shy away from her gaze the way she usually did, her heart sank.

"That monument is of no one in particular. It was built to commemorate lost ones. It is not your father. He was not a soldier. I gave the statue that name. *Kai is not real.*" Kahlisenya stepped back, waiting for an outburst. Ella stared at her in disbelief. She was furious, hurt, and confused. She had been lied to her entire life, and now she was being told the truth?

Ella hissed, baring her teeth. Her wings blasted out and vibrated at her sides. Her eyes were pricked with tears. How long had she been mourning the loss of her father? How many nights had she snuck off to see the statue of him and told stories, hoping the wind would carry her words to him in the next life?

She hissed again, louder this time. Kahlisenya didn't hiss back or blink. She held her daughter's gaze—something she never did.

"Why?" Ella shouted. Her voice cracked, her heart torn.

Hamlet made his presence known and rested a hand on Ella's shoulder. Her head turned to him, and her eyes widened. "Don't tell me you're my father?" She blanched.

Hamlet sputtered and then composed himself. "No. No!"

She narrowed her eyes at him, and the realization hit her. "You've known. You've known all this time who my father is, haven't you?"

At his stunned silence, she turned back to her mother, who looked defeated.

"Your father... He was a radiant man, Ellarhyssa. Warm-hearted and kind. He loved completely and without restraint," she murmured gently. "Our love was a secret. My mother had just passed away after a three-century-long reign, leaving me vulnerable and suddenly queen. Your father belonged to one of the smaller villages in the Anaferi Mountains."

"Was? So-he's-he's gone?" Hope flickered within her, only to be snuffed out just as quickly. "His name is scratched out on the Tree of Ancestors. Did you do that?"

"You've been going down there?" Kahlisenya's voice bordered-lined on scolding and Hamlet cleared his throat.

Okay, so maybe they don't know about that part, Ella thought.

"Your father is still alive," Kahlisenya whispered so faintly that Ella almost missed it. Her keen ear twitched. She pulled away abruptly, staring at Kahlisenya with shock etched on her face. "My father's alive?"

Her mother winced at the excitement that flashed in Ella's eyes—eyes that were hauntingly like his. She couldn't help but think ruefully, *she has your eyes.*

"The man I knew and cherished is long gone. Only a stranger remains now—an unpredictable danger," Kahlisenya continued cautiously. "He's the reason behind Hellharth's instability. My magic has been strained for years trying to keep it in check... This level of power would've destroyed lesser beings."

"You mean he's attempting to break into Hellharth?" Ella asked, her voice quavering.

"I hoped that one day when my time came, you would inherit my abilities and become the guardian of Hellharth," Kahlisenya admitted regretfully. "But now I realize that burden shouldn't fall upon you. My betrayal of the truth all these years weighs heavily upon me. You don't possess my power. Instead, you've inherited his."

"What are you saying?" Ella implored, confusion and apprehension overtaking her. Her wings fluttered, and she felt a bit sickened. How could her mother have done this?

At that moment, Kahlisenya despised herself more than ever.

"Ella," she uttered cautiously, "Your father is the one who initiated the Purge War. The one they refer to as The Son of Bashet."

Ella gasped, stepping back in shock. Her gaze shifted between Hamlet, his face filled with worry, and her mother's sad eyes. Deep down, she knew it was true, but she couldn't bring herself to accept it.

"You lie!" she shrieked. "YOU LIE! YOU LIE! YOU LIE!" She hurled the fruit tray to the floor, its clash echoing through the room.

Kahlisenya reached for her daughter, but Ella violently swatted away her hands, baring her teeth.

"Gan-Na!" she cursed vehemently in Elvish. "Gan-Na!" Her hands' stripes began pulsating with dark energy—energy Kahlisenya had only witnessed in one other person.

"I understand you're upset—" Hamlet tried to reason; his voice shaky as he held up his palms in surrender.

Ella choked on a bitter laugh, darkness swirling around her like a malevolent storm. "Upset? Do you think I'm merely upset? I'm *overjoyed* that you both deceived me all these years! Did you laugh at me? Did you find amusement seeing me wander into town every day searching for a piece of my father?" She teetered at the edge of hysteria. Flames spiraled at her feet and blazed in her eyes—a firestorm beckoned from within, ready to consume everything around her. "Do the villagers know? Do they suspect anything? Is this why they tiptoe around me? No wonder Gideon's parents didn't want me near him!"

All this time—Gods! What am I? she thought to herself.

Kahlisenya retreated to a corner, her voice quivering as the flames danced around her daughter's feet. "I never spoke of it openly. Your birth was celebrated, but the enigma surrounding your conception was largely dismissed. There was no escape; I had already relocated Hellharth. What else could they do? The ones who questioned my pregnancy in the Court, they're all dead now. Every single one of them."

The other horrible things Kahlisenya had done... she prayed her daughter never knew.

"I don't think that will make her feel any better," Hamlet muttered.

Ella clutched at her chest. *My father is Idmodias,* she thought with a heavy heart. "What am I?" she whimpered, and the fire that had surrounded her finally diminished. "Were you taken...by him? By force?" Did her mother suffer at the hands of the man who was her father?

Kahlisenya was taken aback by her question. "You're Ella. You're good. Your parents do not define who you are. He never took me by force. I was willing."

"I'm not like the other Elves—the other Fae. I'm different... There's something *wrong* with me." Ella began to cry. She could feel that something was inside of her—something tainted.

It was *him* all along.

"Everyone is different," Hamlet answered gently. "You are still the same Ella you were two minutes ago. Nothing has changed."

"Everything has changed." Ella wiped at the tears. "How could you do this to me? Why are you telling me all of this now?" She asked, her voice hoarse.

Kahlisenya wearily trudged toward her large bed and sat down with a sigh. She patted the mattress gently, signaling for Ella to join her. Hesitantly, Ella sat down next to her mother and waited. Hamlet opted for the chaise instead. The three of them sat in silence for a moment.

"I went to consult the Witches of Highland," Kahlisenya began. "I left Hellharth for just one day and found myself back in Arcadea. Everything felt different...not like it used to be."

"Why didn't you take me with you?" Ella shot back spitefully, feeling a pang of hurt pierce her chest. "Was this during the day of the ball?"

"I-yes." Kahlisenya frowned slightly before continuing, "For the past three months, I've been tormented by recurring nightmares—all eerily similar. It wasn't until recently that I realized they might be a warning for something terrible."

"Divination? But I thought your powers were fading?" Ella asked incredulously.

"Well," Kahlisenya hesitated for a moment before continuing, "I needed definitive answers, so I sought out the witches' wisdom. They confirmed that my vision was indeed foretelling future events. A prophecy came of it, and now I realize that I haven't been honest with you...but that stops today."

Ella's mind raced as she tried to grasp the situation. "What was your vision? The prophecy?" she urged.

Glancing over at Hamlet for reassurance, Kahlisenya exhaled deeply. Drawing upon his strength, she repeated softly: "That ends here."

"I saw his face first," Kahlisenya's voice trembled. "He was trapped behind glass, screaming, yet utterly silent. Hellharth flickered in the background. Suddenly, the glass shattered, and his eyes were everywhere. Arcadea was swallowed by darkness as a black sphere appeared in the sky."

"He escapes..." Ella deduced quietly. She rose to her feet and walked to the mirror of her mother's vanity. Ella stared at her own reflection. She drew her hands to her face, touching her cheek, her lips, her hair. Her eyes.

Ella tried to quell the overwhelming mix of emotions welling up within her; betrayal, fear, and a longing for her unknown father, who she'd never known. Her heart ached for Gideon and the people of Hellharth.

"And the prophecy?" she asked, her voice barely a whisper.

Kahlisenya's dark blue eyes glistened wetly as she took a deep breath. As she opened her mouth to speak, an eerie hiss escaped from deep within her. The voice that followed was not entirely her own, and it sent chills down Ella's spine as she instinctively scooted away from her mother on the bed. The ghostly wail seemed to echo off every wall, the air heavy with foreboding.

"The child born of a fallen Star,
A bridge between realms,
Though, never far.
No home but not lost,
Safe inside a morning song,
To first make right,
you must do wrong.
Answers found right near his heart,
Blackened stone,
And She shall part.
Blood of The Lady,
The Traitor and Daughter,
A Cosmic battle of Will and Power.
Son of Bashet rises once more,
War upon us
As twice before.
Family Legacies
Two women of the same side
Past promises made
and Royal lies.
Their choice alone may break or bend
To raise Arcadea
Or bring its End."

The eerie whispers ceased, and Kahlisenya snapped back to reality. She swallowed hard, acutely aware of Ella's ragged breaths beside her.

"So, you sought out these witches for clarity, and all they gave you were cryptic riddles? What are we supposed to make of that?" Ella demanded.

Kahlisenya hesitated. "I can only offer my best interpretation for a portion of it. It corresponds with my visions. The Son of Bashet is destined to rise once more. Another war will ensue... And the loss of my magic..."

Ella's eyes widened. "It mentioned parting ways... Does that mean you're going to die?" Ella demanded. Kahlisenya hesitated.

"I don't know the answer to that," Kahlisenya admitted, her unease manifesting as an itch on her bitten palm. "In regard to royal lies, that must refer to me. Hamlet and I have been trying to decipher it, circling back around."

She paused before continuing. "But the first part seems certain. It's about you. A child born from a fallen star, without a home but never lost... I am convinced this speaks of your destiny. Sheltered within a morning song... There exists a place in Arcadea called Morning Song—an academy of the Arcane welcoming students of magical lineage from all corners of the realm. A friend Hamlet knew years ago now serves as Highmaster there; I believe it's where you truly belong."

Ella rubbed at her tired eyes before massaging her ears, mortified comprehension dawning on her face. "You're sending me away, aren't you?" Her hands clenched tightly around her white night robe. Memories of Highwing and their recent plans for betrothal flashed through her mind. Of Nattya laying in her bed while they spoke of wedding flowers and dresses. Things she would miss if she left. "I'm not going," she declared, shaking her head. "I won't."

Hamlet placed a gentle hand on her shoulder. "Think of it differently, Ella. Hellharth won't remain safe forever, and we have no way of determining the timeline for this prophecy."

Frustrated, Ella said, "Then why not find the mirror? Assemble The Council and warn everybody—"

Hamlet sighed, cutting her off. "Because we have no clue where the original Council might have hidden it. It could be at the deepest depths of the ocean for all we know."

Ella's voice trembled as she argued, "But to not warn anyone? To let them all live in ignorance?"

Kahlisenya interjected. "To do so would incite mass hysteria and turn people against us. They might even begin hunting down the Elves. Fear can make people commit terrible atrocities, Ella."

Ella scoffed bitterly. "You want to dispatch me to some school for Maji humans?"

Hamlet clarified: "Morning Song is open to all magical beings."

"And Elves?" Ella added pointedly.

"Deacon Gregor can be trusted. He always abhorred war and prejudice in his youth." Hamlet's voice carried certainty. Ella scrutinized him.

A fleeting thought crossed Ella's mind; *If only he were my father...*

She caught his eyes and held them, diving into Hamlet's thoughts. She caught a whispered affirmation: *She will be okay. She will be just fine.*

Noticing the slight intrusion, Hamlet's eyes narrowed, and he reprimanded her halfheartedly, "You know better than that."

"Sorry," she muttered dispassionately.

Hamlet continued, "Mind-drifting can be perilous at times, Ella. The mind is quite fragile. Some people's minds are dangerous... When you're at Morning Song, please avoid it."

Ella flushed with embarrassment, conscious of how effortlessly she'd always infiltrated his thoughts. Numerous times she'd been tempted to explore her mother's mind, but never managed to maintain eye contact for long enough. "I told you I wasn't going," she said hotly.

Hamlet answered her as if she hadn't been adamantly refusing, "You'll need gloves to conceal your distinctive markings; though fairly faint, they might give you away to anyone familiar with our traditions. And don't forget to hide your ears and wings," Hamlet warned, noticing the telltale signs that Ella had recognized his attire as suited for travel, not rest.

"I can't just go! Highwing... we... I just... We exchanged our first gifts mere *hours* ago. We're meant to marry," Ella pleaded. She wanted to scream, to give in to the part of her that said she would feel better with blood beneath her fingertips. It was a cruel twist of fate that, not long ago, she had been so desperate to leave Hellharth in search of answers, and now that she had them, she yearned to stay.

Hamlet and Kahlisenya regarded her with slow, deliberate blinks. "You accepted his proposal?" her mother asked gently, a melancholic smile dancing on her lips.

"I was the one who proposed," Ella corrected, her body trembling from the tumultuous mixture of anxiety and anger. "I can't just abandon him now. I'm not finished here."

"Ella, sometimes we must hurt others, not out of desire, but because it's the only way forward," Kahlisenya softly intoned. Ella recognized the deeper meaning hidden beneath her mother's words and felt an icy chill run down her spine.

"I won't hurt him! He's my best friend," Ella snapped back fiercely. Hamlet and Kahlisenya exchanged a knowing look—a tiny gesture that spoke volumes. "I have to tell him and Nattya. I can't do this to them!" They expected her to go quietly.

They had another thing coming.

Hamlet and her mother shook their heads solemnly, making Ella's heart race. She felt time slipping through her fingers. She unleashed a guttural growl, an attempt at intimidation that fell on deaf ears. "You've controlled everything in my life! When I finally make choices for myself, you tear them away? You only want me to leave so I won't reveal who—or what—I am to them!" Ella screamed. "My father—the one I mourned in Townsend—may have never been real, but he was real to *me*. My friendship with Highwing and Nattya is real. My courtship with Highwing is real!"

Hamlet's disbelieving gaze only fueled her desperation. "Don't do this," she whispered, tears streaming down her face as she threw herself at her mother's feet, clutching her night robes. She could feel Hamlet looming behind her, the atmosphere in the room heavy and suffocating. Kahlisenya gazed down at her daughter with a cold detachment, unmoved by Ella's pleas.

"NO!" Ella screamed, terror consuming her as she felt strong hands grasp her gown collar and begin to drag her away. She thrashed in helpless panic, scratching at the floor in a vain attempt to stay anchored to the ground. "NO! NO!" she wailed between heart-wrenching sobs, calling out for salvation. "MOTHER!"

Hamlet was wrenching her from the ground, the air swirling and crackling. She felt herself being pulled across the room, her body weightless, before being sucked into a vortex of darkness.

Chapter Eleven

The portal snapped shut behind them, and Ella instinctively reached for it, her stomach churning with anxiety. Hamlet quickly grasped her elbow, pulling her close and enfolding her in a protective embrace. "Everything will be alright," he whispered soothingly into her hair. She clung to him desperately, her fists pounding his chest as she cried out.

"YOU DID THIS! BOTH OF YOU! YOU!" Her bitter accusation echoed off the surrounding trees.

Time seemed to stretch on endlessly as Hamlet held her, their bodies pressed closely together while her tears soaked through his tunic. Overcome with guilt, he allowed each painful blow from her fists to remind him of the first time he had held Ella—a tiny baby wrapped in bloodstained blankets. His heart had swelled with both terror and love at that moment. Hadn't he sacrificed everything for this family?

"Ella," he murmured softly.

Her voice hitched as she gasped, "What if I never see her again? What about Nattya and Highwing? They can't possibly think I would abandon them like this. I didn't even have a chance to say goodbye!"

Hamlet tightened his embrace and pressed his lips to the top of her head. "There are greater forces at work here," he explained quietly. "We don't have the luxury of options right now, Ella. I need you to be strong. Not just for yourself, but for all of us. I know this isn't fair... it never was."

A shiver ran up Ella's body as cold night air pierced through her thin dress. Hamlet carefully draped a heavy fur cloak around her shoulders before handing her a pair of leather boots from his bag to protect her bare feet.

As she adjusted the cloak around herself, Ella's eyes slowly adapted to the darkness that enshrouded them. The haunting beauty of the surrounding forest and the sounds of rustling leaves and distant animals only heightened her feeling of unease.

"Where are we?" she inquired, surveying their barren surroundings under the vast blanket of stars above.

She began to notice her breath materializing as small clouds in the cold air, a sight that momentarily distracted her. Despite herself, she found the phenomenon oddly entertaining.

She truly was far from Hellharth now.

Unbelievable, she thought.

"Just north of the Calisan capital, in Desmon Forest," Hamlet said with an amused smirk. He had caught on to what she had been doing.

"I can't believe there's a school out here," Ella remarked, staring at the colossal trees with their thick trunks. If not for the cold that had stripped them of their foliage, she would have been submerged in impenetrable darkness. "Nattya would freak out in all this gloom."

"Not here, it's more towards the north," he reassured her. "You'll know when we're there. Stick close to me, and if you spot anyone—anything really—drop down and stay quiet."

"Is it unsafe here?" she asked, her voice wavering.

"I'm not certain. Fix your hair," he commanded, tossing her a leather tie with a stern look on his face. Ella frowned and touched the top of her head defensively. Seeing her confusion, he sighed and explained further. "Hide your ears. Quickly!"

"What happened to that understanding Hamlet from a moment ago?" she questioned, noticeably annoyed.

"That guy? He's freezing his hide and considering taking back his coat," he retorted playfully. Grabbing a few strands of her hair, he draped them over the tips of her ears to hide them. "Not the best way to disguise them, but it'll have to do. Let's get going."

As they stumbled through the pitch-black forest, their irritation levels rose steadily until it became unbearable. Following Hamlet's fourth trip that dragged Ella down with him, she reached her breaking point.

"Couldn't you have just brought a torch or some light? I can—" she started to protest while raising her hand to summon a fiery orange flicker from her palm but got interrupted abruptly by Hamlet slapping her hand back down.

"Are you crazy?" he hissed angrily. "Do you want us to get caught by someone? Or worse? Imagine if something saw that glowing ball in the woods! Use your brain!" He poked at her head for emphasis, making her scowl.

The sudden snap of a twig nearby made them both spin around, searching the darkness. Hamlet quickly whispered, "Get low," and pushed her down to the frosty grass, their hearts pounding wildly. Desperately scanning the gloom, they sensed the danger that now lay just beyond their sight. Hamlet grabbed his blade from its sheath as an ominous growl echoed through the trees.

Among the bushes, two luminous eyes flickered at them before being joined by a dozen more pairs in unison. It was then Ella heard Hamlet's urgent hiss through gritted teeth, "Light! Now!"

Ella raised her hand, palm out, and exhaled. A stream of fire launched from her palm, aimed at the multitude of eyes. The forest lit up briefly as the fire grazed past the trees in a semicircle. Ella had anticipated wolves but now realized with a stunned gasp that she would have much preferred them to this creature. Startled by the sudden burst of fire, it spread its massive gray wings, yellow eyes embedded in its feathers blinking rapidly. The beast had a wolf-like body that almost reached the treetops when fully extended. Its pale complexion was ghostly, with bat-like ears and bared teeth that snarled at them, pushing through trees that split with a resounding CRACK!

"RUN!" Hamlet yelled, energetically helping Ella to her feet. She darted forward into the darkness, her right hand stretched behind her left shoulder as she sent streams of fire at the creature to slow it down. It roared ferociously, shaking the ground while Hamlet's heavy breathing echoed beside her.

"ELLA! FLY!" Hamlet implored. "FLY AWAY!"

Ella halted suddenly at his command. She couldn't do it—she couldn't fly. And even if she could, there was no way she could carry Hamlet too. Grabbing his arm, they ducked under low-hanging branches while the monster's jaws snapped menacingly behind them.

"I'm not leaving you!" Ella exclaimed, launching another ball of fire at their pursuer. Ahead, she spotted an opening in the tree line leading to a meadow and a lake. Twigs snagged on her gown and hair while scraping against her skin. Her breathing grew labored as an ironic thought crossed her mind: I was safer in Hellharth.

As the creature flapped its wings, trees began swaying ominously. Ella was certain that once they reached an open area, it would capture them. Turning her body, she skidded to a stop in the meadow, hands raised, and unleashed a barrage of fire that illuminated the darkness. Flames licked the trees, but nothing caught fire. Exhausted, she collapsed to the ground.

"It stopped chasing us," he gasped, his glasses absent and hair disheveled.

Indeed, the winged wolf remained at the edge of the forest, pacing back and forth as if blocked by an invisible wall. It snapped its jaws and spread its wings angrily, the myriad eyes seething with rage. A low growl emanated from the beast, and it took flight, flying low over the trees and disappearing.

"What on earth is that thing?" Ella groaned. Her sides ached and her lungs burned. At least she wasn't cold anymore—her coat was long abandoned in the woods.

"His name is Grothorn. He guards the forest," came a female voice from behind them. Hamlet swiftly pushed Ella away and aimed his sword at the newcomer—a bald woman in flowing black robes with catlike eyes outlined in kohl and a nose adorned with gold hoops. She leaned forward, pressing her palm against the sword's tip. As it pierced her hand with ease, she withdrew it without any signs of injury.

"What are you?" Hamlet implored, lowering the blade.

"I am Elysium, Keeper of Grothorn and the Gates," she replied, her voice raspy.

"You're the Keeper?" he asked, rummaging through his trouser pockets. He produced a rolled parchment and handed it to her breathlessly. "I'm a guest," he explained as she took it between two delicate fingers. She unrolled the parchment, glancing at it dismissively.

"Guests use the road to enter, not Desmon Forest," she chided. Her head tilted, revealing a well-lit road that skirted the forest.

Ella slapped Hamlet's side. "Seriously? There's a road?"

"I was trying to be inconspicuous!" he defended.

"We caused quite a commotion, screaming through the forest and nearly setting it ablaze! We could've taken the road," Ella grumbled.

Elysium reassured them that the forest remained unharmed. "And we are just fine, thank you for asking," Ella retorted sarcastically.

Elysium incinerated the parchment. "Highmaster Gregor was expecting you," she stated flatly.

"As I said," Hamlet replied irritably, conjuring a new pair of glasses.

"Perhaps next time, use the road," Elysium suggested sweetly. "Follow me."

"This is in the middle of nowhere," Ella complained.

"It only appears so. You need to pass the Gates," Elysium said, moving toward the lakeshore. The air shifted as a mist rose from the ground, dissipating to reveal an imposing castle with spired towers and bright windows that reached into the clouds. It appeared to have a thousand eyes as light spilled from windows into the dark lake below. A wide stone bridge connected Morning Song's metal portcullis to its moat. Elysium stepped onto the bridge and held out her hand to help them. The bridge was covered in a thick layer of ice that creaked beneath their weight.

"Incredible," Ella whispered to Hamlet. "This is Abjuration magic?"

"Yes. There's an entire protective barrier," he confirmed.

Elysium led them across the bridge, explaining that Morning Song housed nearly 800 students, with dorms on the upper levels and staff quarters below. Hamlet heard her, but he only marveled at the immense castle.

The Highmaster's office was in the South Wing, and Elysium escorted them, preventing any chance for them to get lost. She opened the metal portcullis with a wave of her hand.

In the deserted courtyard stood a fountain crowned by a statue of Grothorn.

"So, the students know about him?" Ella asked.

"They adore him," Elysium replied, laughing. "I had to stop them from feeding him dinner scraps because he was getting fat."

"He didn't seem very friendly back there," Hamlet grumbled.

"You aren't a student. You were trespassing," Elysium argued. She jogged up some steps to her left, leading to a wooden door with a swirling circle on it.

"Is this his office?" Hamlet asked.

"No, this is a portal," she answered flatly.

Hamlet opened the door, and a few brooms fell at his feet with a clatter. "This is just a broom closet," he said, annoyed.

"These special doors are for students who are running late or want to get somewhere faster. They aren't always open to prevent students from misusing them at all hours, and they keep a log of everyone who goes in and out. Most students prefer the ten-minute break between classes and choose not to use them." She ushered them in and closed the door, plunging them into total darkness. For the first few seconds, nothing happened.

"Highmaster's Office," Elysium said. The broom closet was momentarily engulfed in blue light before returning to darkness. She opened the door, revealing a corridor lined with sconces and tapestries adorned with golden suns. She pointed ahead. "Go down there and take the left door. I'll watch you go in."

"What? Aren't you going to escort us?" Hamlet mocked.

"Not really," Elysium sighed. She turned to Ella and adjusted her hair to cover her ears better. "Hide those more effectively. They would startle anyone else," she said gently. Ella blushed, and Hamlet stepped between them.

"Thank you," he said curtly. Elysium glanced between the two of them before nodding, retreating into the broom closet, and closing the door behind her. A flash of blue light seeped through the cracks before disappearing.

"She knows," Ella whispered, her face turning pale.

"Yes, she does. That's one more person than I'd have liked. But there's nothing we can do about it." He gripped her arm and guided her towards the door Elysium had pointed out. He knocked softly. "This is it," he whispered to her.

Ella held her breath, beset by self-doubt.

"Enter," a male voice called from behind the door. Slowly, Hamlet turned the handle, and the door creaked open.

Chapter Twelve

"Hamlet, my goodness! You haven't aged a day!" The man was an awe-inspiring figure with long ash-blonde hair and curious violet eyes. His features were delicate, and his long blonde eyelashes framed his eyes—an effect that Ella found captivating. When Hamlet extended a hand in greeting, the man clasped it warmly without hesitation. It was evident that they were delighted to reunite, making Ella feel out of place amid their interaction—two old friends greeting each other. "Has it been—twenty years? Twenty-one?"

"Thank you for meeting with me, Highmaster Gregor. I know this is short notice," Hamlet said, bowing his head respectfully. He then greeted the imposing figure behind Master Gregor with less enthusiasm. "Hello."

"Master Moore," the brooding man replied. "You may call me Grayson." He was tall and handsome, sporting a long black braid over one shoulder and wavy bangs framing his face. His most striking feature, however, was a deep scar across his left brow, nose, and down to his right cheek. His voice was deep and slow as if speaking were a chore, but it did nothing to detract from his striking eyes—a shade reminiscent of the glowing Habbi plant found in Hellharth's forests. He was dressed in black robes, a color that seemed to match his cold demeanor. His ears were pierced, and two rings hung from his earlobes. His ears were slightly pointed—a trait that seemed to be common among halflings.

"Very well," Hamlet agreed. He motioned for Ellarhyssa to step forward in front of him, giving her lower back a gentle nudge.

Ella felt nervous as she observed the two strangers before her, her bright amber eyes darting between them. She timidly uttered "Hello," her breath catching at the sight of Grayson—whose piercing green eyes seemed to pierce through her. Grayson extended his hand towards her which she took uncertainly and shook firmly, causing Gregor to chuckle as Ella shifted uncomfortably in her nightdress.

"Miss...?" Highmaster Gregor inquired. He offered his hand to her next, which she stared at blankly before slowly grasping it. She shook it rather forcefully and let go abruptly, shooting Hamlet a pained glance despite Gregor's amused reaction.

"I didn't shake it right," she whispered not so subtly.

"That's quite alright," Hamlet mimicked her less-than-discreet whisper and smiled. "This is Ellarhyssa, the reason for our meeting today."

"Miss Ellarhyssa, your tattoos on your hands and neck...are you from Aslan?" Gregor asked, gesturing to his own bare neck.

"I—no, I'm not."

"Forgive me, your markings reminded me of a friend from the Aslan Desert. Please don't be offended."

"I'm not," Ella assured him.

"You were quite vague in your letters," Gregor mused to Hamlet. "Please, have a seat." He waved his hand effortlessly in the air, summoning two comfortable-looking chairs for them to sit in front of his large oak desk.

Ella fidgeted in her seat, accidentally catching Grayson's eyes once more. This time she held his gaze defiantly and narrowed her eyes in response to his stare. Grayson's lip curled into a sneer, revealing sharp canines before he looked away.

This man is something else, Ella thought to herself as she waited for Hamlet to settle down.

"I hate to start off like this, but I need your utmost secrecy. I need a blood vow," Hamlet said urgently. Moore and Gregor raised their eyebrows simultaneously. "It's a sensitive matter," Hamlet added.

"Are you asking us to use blood magic to bind a secret? Blood magic is typically used for wardings, like the school's," Gregor said cautiously. "Should we involve the Arcadean Council?"

Hamlet exhaled sharply. "No, they must not know. Nobody can."

"Are you sure you want him here?" Ella asked, pointing rudely at Moore.

Moore glared at her with surprising venom for someone who didn't know her. He radiated anger and coldness.

Master Gregor smiled gently at her, his violet eyes twinkling with amusement. "Master Moore is my trusted assistant. He teaches History and Advanced Magics to our college-level students."

"I insist on a blood vow," Hamlet urged. Gregor eyed them both with a mix of wariness and curiosity. After a long moment, he gestured to Master Moore, who conjured a glass goblet and a golden dagger from thin air.

"I hope you understand the implications of using such magic, Hamlet," Gregor advised softly.

"I do."

Master Moore placed the goblet on the oak desk, tapping its side three times with the golden dagger. Each pulse of sound echoed through the room, intensifying with each tap of metal on glass. He pricked his thumb with the blade and watched as droplets of blood fell into the cup. Gregor added his own offering next, carefully pricking his finger and dripping it into the goblet. Finally, Hamlet took the dagger in hand and hesitatingly cut across his palm. His blood joined that of Moore and Gregor in an eerie display of unity before he wordlessly passed back the dagger without so much as glancing at Ella. This was a bold move, indicative of the seriousness of the matter at hand.

"The girl," Master Moore drawled, pushing the dagger back and gesturing for Ella's hand.

Hamlet held up his hand. "That won't be necessary."

Gregor raised an eyebrow. "I thought we were all being sworn to secrecy."

"We are. I'll explain later."

"Do you expect me to trust that this child won't speak of witnessing an illegal blood vow?" Moore sneered.

"I'm nineteen!" Ella retorted, unconsciously hissing and baring her small fangs.

Moore looked down at her from his slightly crooked nose and sniffed, green eyes flashing.

What's his problem? Ella thought.

"That's enough, Grayson. If Hamlet says we can trust her, let's proceed. I'm eager to hear about this pressing issue." Gregor spoke, turning in his high-winged chair and tilting his head at his assistant.

Moore grunted and returned to the goblet. Holding his palm above it, he chanted a spell in an unfamiliar language: "Dloh ot esimorp a, wos uoy tahw paer." The goblet glowed, and the blood turned black.

"Nothing spoken in this room shall leave our company," Gregor began. Moore and Hamlet repeated the statement.

Moore turned to Ella expectantly. She said nothing but crossed her arms over her chest.

"Why don't you get us some tea, Grayson? Then we can begin," Gregor suggested. Master Moore nodded once, his expression unreadable, and disappeared behind a large opaque curtain. Ella watched him with concealed suspicion, but Hamlet appeared oblivious as Moore returned bearing a silver tray and an elaborately painted tea set. He distributed the tea, first to Gregor and then to Hamlet, before finally offering a cup to Ella. She took it cautiously and raised it to her lips.

Ella examined the men in front of her while sipping the bitter brew; she grimaced at its taste while trying to clear her throat. Hamlet emptied his cup in one gulp, setting it back onto the tray gratefully. "Thank you. That was just what I needed to calm my nerves," he said.

Ella observed Gregor and Grayson exchange a knowing glance. "I find it strange," she began, drawing their attention, "that Master Gregor, an esteemed conjurer—and you, Master Moore—didn't simply conjure up this tea set. Instead, you sent your assistant out of the room to make tea—a concoction that neither of you has touched." She smirked at Grayson Moore. "Not that I'm actually complaining; the truth serum adds quite a kick. I've had it before."

Turning to Hamlet beside her, she chuckled, "And you, you're an imbecile."

"You're a pompous brat," Hamlet sputtered defensively but quickly said, "I'm sorry." However, Ella laughed knowingly, "No, you're not sorry."

"No, I'm not," admitted Hamlet.

Grayson's eyes seemed to flash green as he glared at Ella who matched his intensity with her own defiant smirk.

"Your potions and your magic—they don't affect me as you'd expect," she revealed before prodding Hamlet's side. "But they do work on him..." She forced Hamlet to face her suddenly.

"Did I catch you and Nattya under the Whistling trees last year? Yes or no?" she asked eagerly, disregarding the stunned expressions of the other two men.

Hamlet's cheeks flared as he answered, "Yes."

"I knew it!" Ella exclaimed triumphantly.

"But you didn't catch me with Marrienna," Hamlet replied smugly, referring to one of her maidservants.

"What? Marrienna? You scoundrel!" Ella gasped in disbelief. "You've been seeing her and Nattya?"

"Yes."

"You're despicable!" Ella snapped furiously. "I'm telling everyone!"

"And you're a prude," he retorted.

Ella's mouth fell open. "I am not a prude."

"Are so."

Her head whipped back to the two astonished men before her. "Does this potion allow room for opinion?" she hissed.

Gregor slowly turned to Grayson, waiting for a response.

"No," Grayson sneered. "It doesn't."

"Told you," Hamlet declared proudly.

"I think we need to get back on track," Gregor finally spoke. "I apologize, Hamlet, but I had to take precautionary measures. You understand?"

"I understand. You drugged me. Swine," Hamlet mumbled. Ella crossed her arms, feeling a bit offended.

"Why doesn't the potion affect her?" Grayson inquired.

Hamlet shot him an angry glare. "Because...she's a very special High Elf."

"An Elf?" Gregor exclaimed in surprise. "There haven't been Elves in Arcadea for... twenty years. Not since Hellharth's disappearance."

"Yes. Well. There's one now," Hamlet snapped.

"Where are you from?" Gregor asked Ella.

She hesitated for a moment before answering with feigned defiance, "Oh, you're addressing me? Because I can still lie, you know." Gregor looked embarrassed at her remark.

"Your arrival is quite unsettling," Gregor admitted. "I hope we both can establish understanding, if not trust."

"I come from Hellharth," Ella finally revealed. She assessed their reactions—Hamlet twitching slightly in his seat, Gregor's eyes widening in surprise, and Grayson exhaling slowly.

Hamlet nodded. "It's true. For the past twenty years, I have been traveling to and from Hellharth, sworn to secrecy regarding its continued existence and whereabouts. The Queen herself has released me from my vow so I may share this story."

"The Queen... Kahlisenya?" Gregor whispered.

"Yes."

"And the Elves, they allowed a human among them all this time? Even after the Purge?" Grayson inquired skeptically.

"We don't hate the Nomaji or Maji people!" Ella exclaimed defensively.

"Idmodias would beg to differ," Grayson spat. At this, Ella shrank back in her chair, her fire rightfully extinguished.

"Many Nomaji and Maji humans still reside in Hellharth, living freely and happily under the Queen's rule," Hamlet reassured.

"Why have you been allowed such access, Hamlet?" Gregor questioned.

"To keep the Queen informed about current events in Arcadea. And to speak with you about what's to come."

"And what would that be?" Gregor asked, crestfallen.

"The rise of Idmodias once more."

"That's preposterous!" Grayson shouted. "He's in the Mirror of Shadows! There's no escape from that."

"Except he does. It has been prophesied."

"Idmodias... this is grave... and yet you bound me to a blood vow forbidding me to tell The Council. Why?"

"Roughly twenty years ago, there was a High Elf male. Strong and gifted; however, his sister's death led him to seek power from the Dark Ones. He drank Demon Bashet's blood inside the Mountain of Tartis—The Forbidden Place."

"You speak of Idmodias. We know his origin story," Moore interrupted bitterly. "A human killed his sister, and he unleashed his fury upon the world."

Hamlet ignored his comment and continued, "He started targeting humans, rallying similarly-minded elves. Yet all elves were ostracized—"

"Because they initiated it!" Grayson yelled. Hamlet silenced him with a glare.

"It became known as the Purge. It took The Council and the Elf Queen to imprison Idmodias within a conjured mirror—a mirror with deep-seated ties to Idmodias himself. It had belonged to his deceased sister, and using that bond, they trapped him in the Mirror of Shadows, leaving him only darkness for company.

"Out of wisdom and concern for her people, the Queen concealed Hellharth from Arcadea's population. Fearing continued retaliation and potential repetition of history, she made Hellharth vanish altogether from the Known World. As far as Hellharth is concerned, it might as well be in a completely different realm."

"She went to great lengths," Gregor admitted solemnly.

"You would too, for your child," Hamlet replied.

"The Queen had a child?" Gregor gasped.

"She was pregnant when she sealed Idmodias in his prison."

Ella, who had been sitting quietly during the story, shifted slightly in her chair.

Immediately, Grayson's gaze met hers, his expression unchanged, but his eyes flashed with unmistakable realization. "You. You're her daughter," he declared, nodding at her. Ella's cheeks flushed, and she looked away.

"She is," Hamlet confirmed.

"By gods, a princess," Gregor fumbled for his desk drawer and retrieved a large bottle of what appeared to be dark brandy. "Please excuse me. This is a lot to take in." He apologized, conjuring a few glasses and pouring generously into four of them. Handing one to everyone present, he settled back into his high-backed chair and downed the contents as if it were water. Ella gripped her glass tightly, observing the burgundy liquid swirl before cautiously taking a sip. It wasn't Elven Firewater but provided a pleasant burn, nonetheless.

"Please don't call me Princess," she cringed. "Ella is fine. Or Rhyssa, Rhys even. Anything but that."

"Apologies. This is… incredible. We all believed Hellharth vanished during the war. We had no idea your mother—By gods! To relocate an entire kingdom! The whole continent was missing! People speculated Idmodias took the entire place into the shadows! Then rumors of sightings of Hellharth reemerging—" Gregor rambled excitedly, his cheeks flushed from the drink.

"Yeah, well…" Ella mumbled, acutely aware of Grayson Moore's stare.

"Her extreme actions were necessary. Now with visions of Idmodias resurfacing, she fears Hellharth cannot protect Ella any longer. A prophecy has been spoken."

"The child born of a fallen Star,
A bridge between realms,
Though, never far.
No home but not lost,
Safe inside a morning song,
To first make right,
you must do wrong.
Answers found right near his heart,
Blackened stone,
And She shall part.
Blood of The Lady,
The Traitor and Daughter,
A Cosmic battle of Will and Power.
Son of Bashet rises once more,
War upon us
As twice before.

Family Legacies
Two women of the same side
Past promises made
and Royal lies.
Their choice alone may break or bend
To raise Arcadea
Or bring its End."

There was a lengthy silence before Grayson spoke up. "That's all? I thought prophecies were meant to be ominous," he said sarcastically.

"I'm conveying the prophecy as it was told," Hamlet said.

"And who created the prophecy?" Gregor asked.

"The Witches of Highland. After the Queen was tormented by visions and other occurrences, she consulted the Witches of Highland, who then delivered the prophecy."

"A child born from a fallen star..." Gregor solemnly repeated.

"This leads me to my next point. The Queen's magic is weakening. No one understands why, but the rumors about Hellharth are accurate; there have been sightings because the Queen can't maintain the magic needed to conceal it.

"Ella has spent her whole life in Hellharth; her status as Princess is common knowledge there but not here. The Queen is concerned that her inability to keep outsiders away implies she will be unable to keep insiders within. The Queen can no longer restrain Idmodias in his confinement, and The Council's power isn't sufficient to hold him without her assistance."

"What is our role in all this?" Gregor asked, refilling his glass. Ella sat silently, anticipating what would come next. "If Idmodias rises again, there's nothing I can do about it."

"The prophecy mentions safety within a morning song. This school is called Morning Song. The Queen believes Ella will be secure here."

"It also refers to a traitor," Grayson pointed out. He smoothed his buttoned frock and adjusted his deep purple cravat. "We're not accustomed to harboring refugees. So what if people learn about her existence?"

"Then they will suspect either The Queen or Ella of liberating Idmodias intentionally and accuse the Queen of treachery."

"Why?" Grayson huffed.

Ella grabbed the bottle from Highmaster Gregor's desk and chose to drink directly from it. Laughter erupted from her as she sputtered and cursed. Why did everything boil down to this?

"Because I'm the illegitimate child of Idmodias," she announced fiercely. Raising the bottle in the air, she said, "Cheers."

CHAPTER THIRTEEN

Grayson Moore was certain he hadn't heard her correctly. There was no way she could be the secret love child of the Elf Queen and the most notorious scoundrel in all of Arcadea. Who would confess that? Grayson questioned himself.

"I beg your pardon?" Highmaster Gregor asked incredulously. "What did you say?"

"Now do you understand why I requested it in blood?" Hamlet insisted.

Gregor rose from his chair, running a hand through his long blonde hair, and exhaled. "Kahlisenya cooperated with the Council twenty years ago to imprison Idmodias. To imply she had a child with him—"

"I'm not implying. I'm informing you. Their relationship began years before Idmodias became what he is now—"

Grayson observed the young woman named Ella with apprehension and anger. "She should not be here," he stated emphatically.

The Highmaster turned to him and shook his head. "Grayson, this matter goes beyond that," he told his assistant enigmatically.

"I didn't request to come here," Ella interjected. "Trust me, I'm just as bothered by this as you are." She placed the nearly empty bottle back on Gregor's desk. Nattya would undoubtedly find a way to ease the tension in the room. Ella bit her inner cheek, wishing those thoughts away.

Grayson sneered; his attractive face distorted. "I highly doubt that."

"The Queen relocated Hellharth entirely—its inhabitants along with her. The people are aware of Ella's existence but not her father's identity. It may have dissuaded some of them when she did help imprison him. Idmodias had numerous followers…most were executed. But some… some could still be out there."

"I believed all Elves returned to Hellharth? No one has seen any in all this time," Gregor said.

"We can't account for everyone. Hellharth appears to be devoid of his followers, but no one knows for certain."

"They've been living openly in Arcadea. All this time. Just as I've claimed!" Grayson laughed victoriously. "I knew there was no way they had all vanished from Arcadea. They likely own shops in Calisan!"

"Some elves may be innocent, unable to return to Hellharth before my mother moved it!" Ella argued. "That's probably why you haven't seen any. They'd be automatic targets. Humans live freely in Hellharth. I don't share your prejudice."

"Trapped, you mean," Grayson retorted angrily. Gregor sighed in exasperation.

"Now that the Queen's power weakens, and the prophecy has been revealed, she knows Idmodias' return will expose Ella. Hellharth's Elves face exposure. The prophecy warns of impending war—like twice before," Hamlet spoke softly.

"Many wars have happened," Grayson scoffed. "Take your pick."

"I think history is repeating itself, signaling another war between humans and Elves—" Ella began.

"That only occurred once, due to your father," Grayson hissed. Gregor elbowed him.

Ella stood defiantly. "You have no right to judge me!"

"I believe we're straying from the topic. Grayson, be quiet. Princess, I apologize. This is a lot to process."

"I was abruptly brought here in my nightgown, learning my father's identity just hours ago...leaving the only home I've ever known and those I love. I'm not here by choice." Ella said the last part while glaring at Grayson.

"When Hellharth returns permanently, we anticipate an invasion. The Known World will search for Ella upon learning of her existence," Hamlet said gravely.

"You want us to hide her in plain sight," Gregor concluded.

"It wouldn't be unusual for a student to start their term late, right?" Hamlet asked.

"No, college students come and go all the time. But we can't be expected to cater to a criminal—"

"GRAYSON!" Gregor thundered. Grayson merely crossed his arms without flinching.

Hamlet rose from his chair, gripping Ella's arm. "Clearly, this arrangement is unsuitable. We must depart."

Gregor raised his hand. "Hold on. Please." Ella hesitated, her shoulders drooping with weariness. Gregor went on, "Grayson doesn't represent me. As the Highmaster of this school, I strive to foster compassion in everyone. This situation transcends us all. I understand your desperation and am willing to help, provided the Princess conceals her identity and our agreement.

"Additionally, she must not use her magic against anyone here. She will join the junior and senior college classes as a student. We need to fabricate her paperwork, which should be ready soon. Perhaps we can give her a halfling origin and a human surname—Marks?"

"Deacon—you can't be serious—"

"My decision is final, Grayson. I'll inform the teachers shortly about the new student." He turned to Ella. "Grayson will escort you to your accommodations."

Defeated, Grayson threw his hands up in frustration, scowling.

Hamlet hesitated in astonishment. "Gregor—your generosity is immense."

"Deacon," he corrected amiably. "We're among friends here. You'll want to keep in touch, I presume? All mail for students passes through our mailroom for sorting before arriving in their dormitory mailboxes."

"I'm unaccustomed to being a student like this, as I always studied with Hamlet alone," Ella admitted sheepishly.

"I believe you'll excel, Miss Marks," Gregor assured her with a glimmer in his eye. "On visiting days, Hamlet Marks will sign in as your father."

Both Hamlet and Ella snickered at this notion; "Hi Daddy," she jested.

He grimaced; "Never call me that again."

"Do these terms suit you?" Gregor asked. They exchanged glances before both nodding.

"It seems this arrangement will suffice... Your mother will be relieved to hear," Hamlet whispered gently. "Please behave. I'll miss you," he added hurriedly.

"Truth Syrup still taking effect?" Ella quipped. He stooped down and pecked a kiss on her crown.

"Now, off with you," he murmured, pushing her toward Grayson, who caught her by the shoulders before leaping back as if scorched.

Hamlet respectfully bowed his head before leaving Ella without looking back, his cheek clenched between his teeth.

Alone for the first time, Ella gazed after him as the weight of their separation crashed down upon her. She would never have tried to leave home if she had known this is how it would feel.

"Miss Marks," Gregor called to her. She had to get used to that name – it was hers now. "I know you said magic doesn't work as we might expect, but we need to conceal your ears, eyes, and markings. If you could stand still for a moment, I'll use some enchantments that should last until Master Moore brings us a better solution."

He waved his hand over her face, a warm sensation tingling her skin. After a while, Grayson snorted, "She wasn't joking about magic not working..."

Gregor hummed in agreement. "I'll have to apply more magic." They worked on it for ten minutes until they were satisfied with the results.

"Master Moore will show you to your room. You have class in the morning," Gregor smiled, dismissing her.

Ella followed Master Moore, her heart racing with a mix of anxiety and excitement. She tried to take in every detail of the maze-like hallways and ornate plaster ceilings, which exuded an atmosphere of grandeur and warmth, much like Hellharth. Despite the silence, she found it difficult to keep up with the Master's purposeful strides as his black braid swung behind him.

Unable to contain her curiosity, Ella quietly asked, "Where is everyone?" It seemed strange that they hadn't encountered anyone in such a vast establishment as Morning Song. Master Moore muttered something she couldn't quite hear. "Pardon?" she asked again, causing him to stop suddenly and turn toward her.

"Everyone else is in their dormitories," he said with clear irritation. "Unfortunately, you'll be staying in the East Wing with me. As if I didn't have enough students to tend to already," he complained. Taken aback by his curt manner, Ella frowned and replied, "You don't seem very welcoming! How old are you anyway?" She had been wondering about his age since they met – he appeared only slightly older than Hamlet, but Hamlet's age was difficult to determine as a Maji and this enigmatic man was undeniably filled with magical energy. "What kind of Fae are you?" she asked.

"Don't expect special treatment from me, Princess," he snapped coldly before adding, "And my age is none of your concern—nor is anything else."

"I never expected special treatment, Master Moore," Ella said. His eyes met hers, suspicion evident in his gaze. Suddenly, he turned away, causing his vivid violet cloak to smack her face as he continued on.

"Ouch!" Ella exclaimed, wiping her face. He ignored her and continued walking, causing her to follow with growing frustration. The silence between them seemed to last for hours, their footsteps echoing on the flagstone floor.

"So, Highmaster Gregor mentioned you're a history teacher?" Ella tried, hoping to break the tension.

"It's one of my many subjects," he replied curtly. "Get ready; you're about to be the least popular girl in school."

"Why? I haven't done anything wrong!" Ella argued.

They stopped in a dimly lit hallway illuminated by flickering candles and ghostly floating lanterns. There were no doors or windows. Master Moore waved his hand, and twelve wooden arch-top doors appeared along the walls.

"Welcome to the East Dorm Wing for Juniors and Seniors," he declared. "Rooms are separated by gender, not species. Each houses five students, making twelve rooms before today. Today adds a thirteenth." He counted the doors as he walked along them.

At the end of the hall was a large stone archway with a lifelike resting dragon.

"This door leads to my chambers. Never knock unless it's an emergency," he warned seriously, his gaze piercing into her.

Ella glanced between him and the door, examining it closely. It looked almost alive, subtly pulsating as if breathing. The sculpted dragon suddenly moved its head down and cocked it to one side, startling her.

"What if someone else tries to enter?" She asked apprehensively.

The dragon seemed to understand her concern, raised its neck, opened its mouth wide, and produced a flickering flame from its throat. Ella stepped back in surprise, while Master Moore chuckled. "They won't get far."

"You said there are thirteen doors. Will I stay with you?" she inquired.

He stared at her incredulously. "I'd rather shit in my hands and clap," he replied sarcastically.

"It was just a question!" she defended herself.

"An idiotic one. My door isn't part of the student dormitory. Yours is here," he said gruffly, pointing at an empty wall.

She watched in amazement as a magnificent redwood door materialized before her, adorned with intricate vines stretching gracefully over the archway.

"Oh," she whispered in awe.

"Our Highmaster believes it's unwise for you to reside with others in the usual dorms, so he arranged separate accommodations for you, even though there are still three vacant beds," he stated disdainfully.

"So, I'll have my own room?"

"It appears that way." His eyes narrowed suspiciously. "The other students won't be pleased about this arrangement."

Her eyes widened in realization, and she nervously chewed her lower lip. "Is there absolutely no chance of me staying with the other students?"

As he scrutinized her appearance, it was evident that he held her in contempt. The spells and enchantments had been effective for now but required daily reapplication. Her captivating amber eyes had become a plain brown; her hair was slightly shorter than before. Thankfully, her wings remained unseen, securely tucked away from curious gazes. For now, she looked like an ordinary Maji or Nomaji human. But how long would that deception last?

Grayson shook his head. *Gregor and his harebrained schemes... She doesn't belong here.*

"I highly doubt it," he murmured before ordering, "Go!" He prodded her towards the door with an assertive shove as it swung open. He pushed her inside and slammed the door shut, leaving her alone in the transformed room.

"That man has some serious issues," she grumbled to herself.

Her eyes quickly adjusted to the darkness, taking in the four-poster bed with a floral canopy. The intimate room had dark green walls adorned with pink-painted flowers that moved enchantingly toward the high ceiling. The ceiling gave way to a dome-like skylight, which she suspected was magically introduced. Wooden dressers sat in the corner, and an open archway led to another part of the room—presumably the bathing quarters. She spun around, marveling at how her new room reminded her of Hellharth's botanical gardens.

Overwhelmed, she collapsed onto the mattress, her face buried in the pillows. It had taken her mother mere days to arrange all this—without her knowledge. Ella had only just learned about her father and the truth behind it all. She still didn't fully understand the Purge, but knew that her mother had been so afraid of the fallout that she moved Hellharth.

And now I'm here, Ella thought bitterly.

She was sent here because her mother believed one part of the prophecy was literal: "Safe inside a Morning Song," she repeated hoarsely.

How could she be safe here? When Hellharth finally fell back into place and her mother's magic faded, what would happen? Safe among Maji, Mixies, and Halfling children? Hadn't she resigned to her fate with Highwing? Was that not enough?

"Doubtful," she scoffed. Now she had to play the part of Ella Marks, a halfling with a Maji father—Hamlet for a father.

Her mind raced with questions. It was clear that some people—like Grayson Moore—didn't want her there, either. How cruel would others be if they discovered her heritage?

If Grayson's reaction was anything to go on, then she surely had a rough road ahead.

She was not going to think about who her father was—is. She could compartmentalize this information, just like she did with many things. Roll it up into one big ball and keep it inside of herself. There would be no tears—no screaming. She had to go about her life as if nothing was wrong.

With that thought looming over her and her head fuzzy from drinking, she turned to her side and drifted off to sleep.

Chapter Fourteen

She awoke hours later, the morning sun glaring down on her from the enchanted ceiling, showing no mercy. She groaned, rubbed her eyes, and stretched. Ella fumbled out of bed, her bare feet touching the soft woolen rug. She glanced around anxiously before making her way to the dresser and chest in the corner. Opening the drawers, she discovered dark blue pleated skirts, black robes, and matching dark collared shirts, each adorned with a golden sun emblem on the pocket. Another drawer contained footwear, long black stockings, socks, and undergarments. She blushed, wondering how they knew her size.

She grabbed the uniform sets, underwear, and socks, then made her way to the open archway she had noticed the night before. As she suspected, it was the washroom. It reminded her of her mother's bathroom with its gold-trimmed sink and large stone tub. A sizable oval vanity mirror hung above the sink, adorned with moss around its edge. Towels and toiletries were neatly stocked in the cabinets.

Ella held her breath when she saw herself in the mirror, her light Elven stripes back in place framing her arms and neck, amber eyes staring back at her. The enchantment had worn off. It was a face her mother never looked at for longer than a second.

When her mother looked at her, she didn't see Ella. She saw a monster. She saw a threat. She saw a shadow that would never be gone.

She punched the mirror with the heel of her hand. Spiderweb cracks spread across the surface, distorting her image. Those eyes.

The mirror slowly mended itself, the cracks vanishing. She scowled at her reflection and then looked around for a robe.

She arched her back, allowing her wings to slowly unfurl from her shoulders. Breathing a sigh of relief as the tension in her back subsided, she approached the bathtub and turned on the faucets, testing the water temperature with her fingertips. She removed the soiled nightgown from her body, grimacing at the idea of having slept in it, and discarded it on the floor.

She bathed herself slowly, contemplating the drastic changes in her life over the past few days. She had once longed not to be Elvish, keenly aware of the humans' uneasiness—those who were essentially trapped in Hellharth against their will. Now, she had to conceal her Elvish identity altogether.

A sudden *BANG* interrupted her thoughts, causing her to cover her bare chest. She listened intently; her pointed ears twitching to detect any sounds. Grasping the edge of the stone tub, she carefully lifted herself out to avoid making noise. Her wings retracted into her back as water dripped onto the tiled floor. Peeking around the archway, she scanned the room and spotted something new on her bed. Grabbing the closest towel, she wrapped herself in it and shuffled back to the four-poster bed.

A small glass vial rested on her pillow, accompanied by a note. The writing on it puzzled her, causing her to blanch. Though she could speak the human language fluently, necessary for living among humans in Hellharth, she struggled to read it. Hamlet had tried teaching her on several occasions, but she had never paid attention to him.

She picked up the vial and swirled it around. The liquid inside was thick, purple, and utterly uninviting. She removed the stopper and sniffed it, immediately gagging. The odor was repulsive!

"They can't expect me to drink this!" she exclaimed. She suspected that was exactly what they wanted her to do. "Probably a potion to make me appear more human," she mumbled to herself. The enchantments had already worn off; perhaps this solution would be more permanent and last longer?

She raised the stout to her lips, closed her eyes, and took a sip. The thick liquid coated her tongue, its taste matching its odor. She spat it out, catching the remains in her hands, and gagged. "Absolutely not!" she shrieked.

Rushing to the washroom, she prepared to cleanse the purple mess from her hands when she paused. The elven markings on her hands began to disappear where the potion had made contact, leaving smooth, unblemished skin.

"You've got to be kidding me. I just drank that!" She groaned. Applying the remnants of the vial to her face, she observed as her features gradually transformed back into her human appearance from the previous night. Even her eye color altered. Astonishingly, there was no odor once it touched her skin.

"Hello, Ella Marks," she remarked to her reflection. Another *BANG* and Ella shot out of the washroom, still wrapped in a towel.

"Let's go! Rise and shine, ladies and gents! Last call!" boomed Master Moore's deep, commanding voice. It echoed against the walls as if he had been in the room with her. She shook her head and hurriedly donned a uniform, puzzled by the lengthy row of buttons on the collared shirt, which felt uncomfortably tight around her neck. Fortunately, a pair of modest black boots awaited near her door, so she slipped them on and adjusted to their unfamiliar feel; they were nothing like the soft fabric footwear crafted by Elves. Lastly, she retrieved a black cloak adorned with a hood and elegant gold trim from its hanger by the door.

Already, she could hear the commotion outside her door, voices loud and animated.

"Is this a new dorm?" Someone asked.

"When did it show up?" Another chimed in.

"Is someone new inside?"

"Hey! Open up! Who's in here?" A few knocks began, escalating into a chorus of pounding.

"LINE UP, PEOPLE! CLASS STARTS IN TEN!" Master Moore bellowed from the other side of the door. "Miss Marks! GET OUT!" He shouted at her.

She opened the door and stepped out, conscious of everyone's gazes. Master Moore stood before her with crossed arms and an intimidating demeanor. "So glad you finally decided to join us," he sneered, his breath hitting her face. She blushed as some students snickered.

A lovely girl with auburn hair and a defined nose darted in front of her, entirely blocking her view of everyone else. "Hi! I'm Annabeth—my friends call me Beth—or Anna, or Annabeth! You're new here! What are you? A Maji? A Halfling? Are you a Mixie?" She spoke rapidly, her vivid pink eyes shimmering.

"I—" Ella began, unprepared for the barrage of questions.

"Enough of your chatter, Miss Dox," Master Moore snapped. "Get back in line. Take this one with you," he said, pushing Ella to follow Annabeth and proceeding to the front of the line down the hall.

"Why does she get her own room?" A few students murmured. Master Moore shot them a stern glance, and they fell silent.

"He seems to be in a better mood this morning," Annabeth whispered to Ella, with a serious tone.

"Is that considered a better mood?" Ella asked incredulously, as she found her place in the long line of students.

A boy turned to her and laughed, "You don't even know half of it. Ethan Isles, Halfling. Pleased to meet you." He extended his hand, and Ella shook it with less enthusiasm than she had with Highmaster Gregor. He was handsome, with iridescent yellow eyes, sharp canines, and dark skin. His light brown hair was twisted into braids around his head.

"Ella Marks. Maji…" she said cautiously, returning his friendly smile while feeling self-conscious about her appearance.

Darn, I'm supposed to be a halfling, not a Maji, she thought, wincing.

"Boo, that's no fun," Annabeth pouted. "I was hoping you were something interesting. Alas, I'm a Pixie."

"Sorry to disappoint," Ella chuckled. "You're rather large for a pixie…"

Annabeth shrank to the size of Ella's hand and waved up at her from the stone floor before returning to her normal size. "Magic. Cool, right?"

"So, another human? I swear this school is getting overrun. I should have gone to Desmouth," a brunette girl nearby scoffed. "At least they're more selective in their admissions."

Ella leaned forward, furrowing her brows at the girl who spoke, but Annabeth pulled her back. "That's Sienna Whitefish. She's a Siren—obviously—the name… Usually, Sirens attend Desmouth because it's in the middle of the Bristbane Sea."

Sienna was arguably the most stunning girl Ella had ever seen, with an angular face, high cheekbones, thin brows, ice-blue eyes, and long, dark hair that curled at her waist. Her shirt was unbuttoned rather low, revealing a glimpse of lace from her undergarment. Ella blushed and tugged at the tight buttons around her neck enviously. She wasn't as well-endowed as Sienna.

The girl named Sienna tossed her hair over her shoulder and crossed her arms. "The Pixie's right."

"So why not go to Desmouth?" Ella asked.

"Her mother is on The Council," Ethan replied as if that explained everything.

"Oh," Ella responded simply. The students shuffled along the corridor, following Master Grayson.

"All the Council kids attend Morning Star. It's the most prestigious school for the arcane," Annabeth chimed in cheerfully.

Sienna scoffed, "Sure, it's a great school if you're comfortable with humans constantly breathing down your neck."

"Originally, it was a school just for human Maji. As part of integration efforts, they invited other magical beings," Anna explained to Ella. "It's a kind of peace initiative."

Sienna scoffed again, "It's a trade tactic. They invite people like us to their school in exchange for knowledge. It's all an attempt to lower our defenses and learn about our weaknesses."

Ethan rolled his eyes. "Not all of us care about that, Sienna. You and your conspiracy theories."

"Says the human halfling," she retorted. "The humans didn't care about us until they started encroaching on our lands and seas, forcing us to fight back—"

"That was hundreds of years ago," Annabeth interjected.

"And what did we get in return? Human taxes and an invitation to 'learn with them.' They just want to learn more about us," Sienna gestured toward other Maji students who blushed. Several students nodded in agreement.

"Your mother is on the Council that united to stop the world's greatest villain and his followers," Ethan retorted. "She collaborates with Maji, Nomaji, and Fae beings."

"Being one of the few survivors isn't something to boast about–" Sienna began.

"Quiet, you're scaring the new girl," Annabeth whispered.

Ella winced at his words and swallowed, thinking about that villain with unease.

"My mother and I don't exactly have a close relationship. Don't forget, the Nomaji and Maji humans committed genocide for a long time," Sienna snapped back.

The students suddenly dispersed, some moving to opposite ends of the wall. Ella stood awkwardly in the middle.

Annabeth, Ethan, and Sienna leaned against the far-right wall.

"Miss Marks! As a Senior, you should be on this side of the hall. Are you confused?" Master Grayson inquired, tilting his head and pointing to his left.

"No sir," she stammered, quickly squeezing herself between Ethan and Annabeth, wishing she could vanish. They waited against the wall outside an empty classroom. Master Grayson continued with the Junior students, disappearing around a corner.

"Great. She's a dunce," Sienna hissed.

"She's new!" Annabeth defended.

"I don't care. I'm not letting her ruin our streak," Sienna retorted.

"Streak?" Ella inquired.

"Yes, the first class is Charms with Mistress Ased. She divides the class into two teams, and we were short a person, so you'll likely join ours," Annabeth explained cheerfully.

"Ased?" Ella asked.

"She's Wenda Ased's granddaughter."

"*The* Wenda Ased? Original Council Ased?" Ella's eyes widened.

"Do you live under a rock?" Sienna scoffed. "We don't need another person," she insisted to Annabeth.

"I don't think I'll be good at your game anyway," Ella mumbled sheepishly.

"See?" Sienna complained.

"Will you lay off?" Ethan snapped.

A woman appeared in the doorway suddenly, wearing an ostentatious, bright orange cloak that clashed with her long red hair. Her hair was pulled back into a high ponytail, and her sharp, angular face reminded Ella of Lady Tanyl. The woman's lips formed a tight line as she squinted at the line of students.

"Quite a commotion this morning!" she exclaimed, her eyes catching Ella's hidden form. Smiling, she continued, "Miss Marks! A pleasure to have you. I'm Mistress Ased, the Charms teacher. You've certainly caused a stir."

Ella's mouth opened and closed as she felt the overwhelming number of eyes on her. The whispering resumed. "Yes. Sorry," she stammered. This was the most interaction she'd had in a long time, apart from Nattya and Highwing. In Hellharth, people greeted her with respect and rarely spoke unless spoken to. Here, everyone seemed to lack those boundaries.

"That's not your fault. You're the talk of the town! Don't worry, dear; it'll die down in a week. Come on in - I'll have you sit with Annabeth, as long as she promises to be quiet," Mistress Ased said with a pointed look at Annabeth, who was already buzzing with excitement.

⟫⟫⟫⟶

Nattya was the first to notice Ella's absence in the morning. She barged into Hamlet's quarters, demanding to know Ella's whereabouts. Hamlet maintained his composure and said firmly, "She is not here, and I cannot disclose any further information."

"Dasyra started this whole mess! Ella better not be in jail because of her!" Nattya retorted.

Hamlet chuckled at the notion. "I assure you, she's not in jail."

Nattya's voice seethed with rage and desperation as she yelled, "If you don't tell me where Ella is!"

Hamlet collapsed onto his bed, pulling the covers over his head with a deep sigh. "Nattya, I'm exhausted. A Grothorn nearly killed me last night. All I can tell you is that Ella is safe."

Hearing this, Nattya's eyes filled with concern. She started smacking his covered figure multiple times until he suddenly pulled her close and cocooned her within the blankets beside him.

"If you promise to let me sleep, you can stay," he mumbled, his voice heavy with fatigue as it intertwined with her soft curls.

She remained silent for a while, and he began to drift off to sleep. However, he was suddenly jolted awake when she grabbed his manhood and asked incredulously, "What the hell is a Grothlewhore?"

Charms class was progressing as Ella had anticipated. Her team trailed by five points, largely due to her mistakes. Sienna, fuming at her desk, wore a sneer that reminded Ella of Master Grayson.

"Next two questions are for you, Ella. Five points each. What is the correct charm to make a Hymanthian Flower bloom?" Mistress Ased asked earnestly. Judging by her pronunciation and the expressions on the opposing team's faces, Ella deduced that this must be a simple question—perhaps one for younglings.

However, it wasn't simple for her. Biting her bottom lip and taking a deep breath, she knew what she was about to do was wrong. If caught, there would be severe consequences. She locked eyes with a girl across the room and felt herself subtly entering the girl's mind without detection.

"New girl doesn't even know it's a trick question. Hymanthian flowers only bloom at night. There's no charm for it," the girl's voice hissed in Ella's mind, prompting her to look away.

"That doesn't sound right," Ella began. "Hymanthians are nocturnal flowers. No charm can force their bloom." She searched Mistress Ased's face for confirmation.

"That's correct! Five points to your team!" Mistress Ased waved her hand, and bright red tally marks materialized with a shimmering haze. "Next question: All charms are spells, but not all spells are charms. Which charm would you use to change the appearance of, let's say—your hair?"

I have no idea, Ella thought. She dared not look at the girl again; it would be suspicious. Instead, she quickly scanned the opposing team and focused on a not-so-handsome boy who appeared annoyed that he hadn't been asked this trivia question.

"Capilamuta Charm!" his mind screamed at her.

"The Capilamuta Charm," Ella replied, struggling with the pronunciation.

"Yes! Well done! Another five points! Now, remember that while some charms can be cast nonverbally, others—like the Capilamuta Charm—require verbalization and inflection. And as with all spellcasting, some spells and charms come more easily to certain magical beings than others. Go ahead and try it on each other."

The group shuffled their feet, and a few girls voiced their objections.

"I assure you, I can easily reverse the charm," Mistress Ased said with a chuckle.

Annabeth grabbed Ella's wrist excitedly, her pink eyes sparkling. "I've always wanted to try this! Partner with me!"

Ella exhaled, amused by Annabeth's enthusiasm, and nodded. "Sure. Um. How— how do I do it?" Ella's studies at home had focused on history and basic spells like shields, moving objects, and mutations. She had seen her mentor cast charms, but never needed to use them herself—it was something more common among the Maji.

They hardly ever practiced her fire magic, either.

"Oh, just hold your hand above my hair and say the incantation."

Ella held her palm over Annabeth's head. "Capilamuta!" Nothing happened. Frustrated and embarrassed by her inability to perform such a simple spell, Ella patted Annabeth's head several times.

"Visualize the transformation in your mind," advised Mistress Ased to the class. "Then recite the spell."

"I want long white hair!" Annabeth implored. Ella flinched at her request, reminded of her mother.

"Very well." She placed her hand on Annabeth's head, imagining long white hair—like her mother's. "Capilamuta."

With that, Annabeth's hair shifted dramatically from auburn to white, beginning at the roots and spreading to the tips. "Show me!" she exclaimed excitedly, tugging at her tresses. Annabeth delved into a black satchel for a small mirror. "Incredible!" she declared. "Now it's your turn!"

Ella smiled warmly and shrugged her shoulders. "You can choose whatever you'd like."

Annabeth pressed her palms onto Ella's head. "Capilamuta." A moment later, Annabeth cocked her head in puzzlement.

"I don't think I did it correctly. Your hair is longer, but your eyes have changed color." She presented the small mirror to Ella, who instantly saw the issue.

Her striped skin began emerging around her hands and neck. In a panic, she drew her hood up over her head. "Oh no," she whispered softly.

"It's okay. Mistress Ased can fix it. I think it rather suits you, to be honest," Annabeth reassured. Just as she raised her hand to get their teacher's attention, Sienna let out a strangled cry.

"ETHAN! ARE YOU SERIOUS RIGHT NOW?" she squawked, flailing her arms toward her now bald head, the skin of her scalp shining.

Ethan, who was sitting smugly with a blonde bob haircut, smirked. "You started it!"

"Miss Whitefish! Mr. Isles! That's enough from both of you," Mistress Ased snapped. Bells chimed as she threw her hands up in the air. "Anyone who needs a reversal stays after class. Everyone else, off you go!" She snapped her fingers and waved her hand; books and papers flew to her desk and neatly stacked themselves.

Ella sprang from her seat, with Annabeth calling after her. "Hey! She said to wait!"

Ella spun around, pulling her hood down tighter. "It's fine, really! It's my first day, and I don't want to be late for the next class."

Annabeth cocked her head in thought and smiled. "We're allowed ten minutes to get to the next class—this place is huge. But this may take a while. Master Moore doesn't mind when we have an excuse. Better just move on then."

"Master Moore's our next class?" Ella asked in alarm.

Annabeth looped her arm in Ella's, saying, "Yes, he teaches History and Advanced Casting. He's one of the best—trained by Highmaster Gregor himself. Surprisingly, he isn't much older than us."

Ella took note of this information, thinking about his youth.

"Your hair is still white. Why not stay behind and get it fixed? I can go on ahead," Ella suggested, concealing her hope.

"Oh! I completely forgot! Master Moore would definitely be pissed," Annabeth frowned. "If you're okay with going alone? His History class is to the right, down a bit, then take a left—first door."

Ella nodded, replying, "Yes! Thank you, Anna."

Annabeth beamed. "My friends call me Anna," she said cheerfully.

"I know."

Ella hurried towards Master Grayson's chamber door, weaving through the lingering students in the hallways. She kept her hood low and her face hidden.

"Is that the new girl?" Ella overheard someone ask.

Not stopping to find out who asked, she dashed down the dormitory corridor. Doors appeared with a resounding *pop* as she ran past before finally reaching the large stone door of Master Moore's personal chambers.

The menacing stone dragon atop the archway sprang to life, rearing back its colossal head. She raised her hand and knocked furiously; the dragon lowering its neck to meet her gaze. It seemed as if it were genuinely scrutinizing her. She pulled back her hood and whispered frantically, "Help me!"

The stone dragon rumbled, baring its long, curved fangs, and growled irritably. It shook enormous stone wings that clattered with each motion. Master Moore's door creaked open slightly, the dragon appearing displeased.

"Thank you," she exhaled, slipping inside and closing the door behind her.

His chamber was rather dim—not at all reminiscent of Ella's enchanting botanical garden. It was faintly lit by a crackling fire in a stone pit. A cedar desk occupied the center, cluttered with papers—a bewitched pen scribbled furiously on parchment.

The floors were blanketed with books that towered high, magically kept from toppling as they twisted every which way. The shelves displayed hundreds of glass jars and vials—some glowing and others shimmering. There was no open ceiling like hers—merely candelabras dangling from metal chains and sconces adorning room corners.

She surmised his sleeping quarters lay beyond this room and felt a blush rising. What had he told her before? That she'd better be on the verge of death before ever venturing here?

Master Moore stomped past students, who anxiously moved out of his way. His door had informed him of a student's presence, briefly showing him through its eyes who was invading his personal space between classes.

"Of course, it would be her. Not even an hour," he muttered irritably.

He burst through his chamber door, slamming it behind him. The girl jumped and squeaked, her hands covering her face.

"You better have a good reason for being here, Miss Marks."

She winced and removed her hands, taking off her hood.

He recoiled and hissed, "Didn't you use the salve?"

"I did!"

"So what the hell is this?" he waved his hand at her face. Her markings had returned, and even her eye color had changed. He lifted her hair away from her ears. "Pointy," he confirmed.

"We were practicing hair charms with Mistress Ased. Annabeth took her turn on me, and this happened," she explained sheepishly.

"That salve should have lasted the entire day and not been trumped by a Capilamuta," he snapped. "You followed the instructions, right? Every drop on your skin?" His eyes narrowed at her.

She shuffled her feet, her neck flushing. She didn't want to admit she couldn't read the language. "I didn't see the directions at first. I thought I was meant to drink it. I drank some of it..."

His eyes widened at her confession, and he exhaled sharply several times. "You didn't. Tell me you didn't put that filth in your mouth. The instructions were clearly on the bottle!"

Ella gagged at his reaction and remembered the taste. "Oh, Gods! What was in it?"

Master Moore shook his head. "Bat guano, among some other things."

"YOU MEAN I DRANK BAT SHIT? Why is that even an ingredient in anything?" She dry-heaved several times, her face turning red.

"Why wouldn't you read the instructions, you fool? Serves you right—stop doing that! This instant! Stop—" He mimicked her gagging noise and turned away, searching a shelf for a vial. He uncorked one and inhaled deeply.

She continued to gag, her hand over her mouth and complexion turning pale green. Suddenly, he pushed the vial's neck into one of her nostrils and closed the other with his finger. She struggled against him, the scent stinging as she inhaled. Whatever it was, she no longer felt sick—the urge to retch vanished entirely. She stopped resisting.

"You," he hissed, "will use the salve again and leave my office immediately. It's bad enough I have to watch over you as it is." He removed the vial from her nose, reached into his cloak pocket, and thrust a familiar vial into her hands.

She looked down at her hands and pushed it back against him. "I think the hell not!"

He pinched the bridge of his nose, sensing a migraine approaching.

"Apply the salve. I have classes in a few minutes."

"I'd rather shit in my hands and clap," she echoed his words from the night before.

"DETENTION, MISS MARKS!" He sputtered, and she raised an eyebrow.

"What is detention?"

He let out a frustrated growl and massaged his temples. "This is the only solution I can offer right now. I can create illusions or use charms, but there's no telling how long it will take for your body to eliminate them. If you apply the salve correctly, it will last for exactly eight hours—as the instructions stated. If I have to restrain you and apply it myself—" he stopped and closed his eyes, searching for patience.

Ella remained silent, though defiant. "Fine," she finally conceded, grabbing the vial back and smearing the salve on her face and hands. The scent was as pungent as before.

He stepped back to ensure she applied it correctly. The bells chimed, signaling the start of the next class, and he let out an exasperated sigh.

"Five years of teaching, and I have never been late," he snorted. He grabbed her shoulder and hurried her out of his room. "Move it, Marks!"

"Why all the pushing?" she asked, swatting at his arm.

The halls were empty, and she was seated at the back of the class within five minutes. Curious eyes followed the pair.

His classroom was about as dreary and dark as his chambers. At the front of the classroom, there was a large wooden desk stacked high with parchment—glass pens scribbling across the surface. Behind the desk, was a massive blackboard displaying complex formulas, sigils, and illustrations of various alchemical processes. Work benches were covered with various spellbooks and grimoires. The walls were a deep, rich red, and the windows were covered with heavy black drapes. A large stone fireplace sat to the right of the room, and a large, brass-framed mirror hung above the mantle.

Master Moore opened a few window drapes, momentarily blinding everyone. He turned to face the class and glared directly at Ella, who had found a seat next to Annabeth—her hair now its original color.

"He seems to be in a foul mood," Annabeth whispered.

"Yes, he does," Ella agreed.

Then Moore's lips curled into a wicked smile. "Who can tell me about the Elvish Queen, Kahlisenya?" he asked contentedly, fixing his gaze on a furious princess.

Chapter Fifteen

I t wasn't that Ella was unaware of her mother. She knew about some of the questionable things her mother had done. What she didn't realize was how opinionated everyone else was about her mother. Fuming in silence, she listened as Master Grayson-Moore baited her by asking students for their thoughts on the Queen and her history.

"Queen Kahlisenya is—or was—is? Queen of Hellharth, an island continent once located south of Calisan Capital in the Idris Sea," a girl named Mira said.

"Good. What else?" Moore pressed. His gaze kept sweeping back to Ellarhyssa, who found a spot on her table more interesting. Annabeth raised her hand.

"Yes, Miss Dox," Grayson nodded for her to answer.

"She was said to be beautiful with wings like a thunderbird and incredibly powerful," Annabeth beamed. It dawned on Ella that perhaps Anna admired her mother.

"That's a matter of opinion, Miss Dox," Grayson coughed. He noticed a muscle twitch in Ella's jaw at his comment. "Tell me something else." He waited until several hands were raised.

"No one knows for certain what happened. The theory is that Queen Kahlisenya either destroyed Hellharth in a fit of rage or somehow made it move," Sienna explained. "Some believe she was so afraid of retaliation that she made the elves hide."

"Raise your hand next time, Miss Whitefish," he admonished. "What role did she play in the defeat of The Son of Bashet? Anyone?"

Ella tried her best not to look up.

"Miss Marks? Does my class bore you? Is there something on your desk so fascinating that it outweighs my teachings?" His voice was a gentle purr, concealing the condescending nature of his words.

She raised her head quickly, opening and closing her mouth several times, anger boiling within. "No, sir," she replied, biting down on her tongue.

Deep breaths, she told herself.

"What can you tell us about Queen Kahlisenya's part in ending the Purge War?" He puckered his lips, lifting an eyebrow. Ella recoiled at the thought of once considering him handsome; now she wanted nothing more than to add another scar to his face.

"She worked with the Original Council, comprising various Fae beings, and Maji humans to defeat him," Ella responded succinctly. It was a brief answer. Uncomplicated.

"I heard the elves were a menace. They ate people," said Droa, a boy with teeth jutting out at odd angles, likely an Orc halfling. His statement was ironic, given that Orcs were known for cannibalism.

"That's ridiculous," Ella scoffed, crossing her arms.

Master Moore's mouth twisted. "Oh? Is it? Records show that some followers of The Son of Bashet partook in eating the flesh of Nomaji and Maji humans." He observed the blush creeping up her neck and cheeks.

"The actions of some are not the actions of all. We all have free will—"

"And should the elves' actions be excused?" He cocked his head like a curious dog, but it wasn't endearing.

"You're generalizing them. There's good and bad, black and white." She held up her hands, mimicking a scale.

"What about gray? The Son of Bashet believed he was doing The Known World a favor by ridding Arcadea of humans." Grayson slowly approached her desk, peering down at her. That terrible scar marred his face, like a ruined masterpiece. "To some, he was doing good," he added pointedly.

Ella took a deep breath. "History has a tendency to repeat itself in wars. One side always believes they are right. Consider the Five Hundred Years War, for instance, when the Dracaeneans and Elves were locked in a battle for centuries—"

"We're not discussing the Dracaeneans!" he snapped, slamming both hands on her desk. This elicited murmurs and Ella's hair began to stand on end. Feeling threatened, she hissed at him, baring her teeth, and the class let out a series of low gasps. Grayson hissed back just as fiercely, his fangs lengthening and eyes flashing.

Overcome with anger and a desire to hurt him, Ella suddenly witnessed Grayson's left hand, which was resting on the desk, burst into flames. She recoiled as students screamed. Grayson frantically shook his hand and smothered the fire with his cloak.

"Settle down!" he roared at the agitated students before hesitating to rub his uninjured hand. The bell chimed overhead, signaling the end of class, but no one moved.

He continued: "I expect a three-page essay on the Purge War due by the end of the week. Front and back. Don't try to get away with large handwriting—Philips, I'm talking to you."

The class groaned in response. "You can thank our new student for your diminished free time," he announced cheerfully. "You're dismissed."

⤙⤙⤙⟶

"You lied to me!" Annabeth exclaimed. Ella was caught off guard and jumped slightly.

"What? Sorry?" She followed the other students, unsure of where to go.

"We all saw you and Master Moore hissing at each other! And the fire? Clearly, you have an affinity for it," she said. "He became agitated when you mentioned the Dracaeneans—I was surprised you did that. It was foolish. Then I realized you're a halfling like him! No wonder you said you were a Maji human. You're a Dracaenean halfling, like Master Moore!"

Moore's Dragon folk? She thought, concealing her surprise. *Great. More reason for him to hate me. We are practically natural enemies.*

"I—yes. Yes. Sorry."

"Two Dracaenean outcasts in this school now. You're a long way from Direfell," Sienna remarked sarcastically. "Don't your kind usually have horns? Or is your human blood interfering with that?"

"I don't have horns," Ella grumbled. "Do you just despise anyone who isn't a siren?"

Sienna's ears turned blue, and she haughtily raised her nose in the air.

"Bold move mentioning the Dracaenean and Elven war," Ethan interjected from behind her. "It's all anyone is discussing now. Get used to being stared at during breakfast."

"I'm starving," said Annabeth. "I miss being a junior. Seniors eat breakfast after the second period, then lunch any time after the fifth period—though most seniors are free for the rest of the day. We only have three classes today."

Ella's stomach twisted. She hadn't thought about food amid all the excitement and asked, "What's after breakfast?"

"Free period," Annabeth replied. "You'd better head to the library and start studying Master Moore's essay. He's quite irritable."

"He's a dragon. They breathe fire!" Ethan exclaimed, waving his cloak-like wings and baring his teeth to mimic a dragon. Annabeth elbowed him in the side.

"She might find that offensive," Annabeth whispered, not too subtly.

"No offense taken," Ella laughed. Her stomach growled, and they chuckled, but Sienna made a disgusted face and stalked off, joining a group of animatedly chatting girls.

"Why do you let her hang around? She seems so—"

"Bitchy?" Annabeth offered.

"Bitter?" Ethan suggested.

"I was going to say mean," Ella sighed, finding comfort in their presence and thinking of Highwing and Nattya.

They walked in sync towards the entrance of a spacious hall filled with rustic tables and benches. Students had already begun eating.

"Because we're not mean," Annabeth explained. "Some people are incredibly lonely and don't know how to ask for company."

"She seems popular to me," remarked Ella as she took her seat on a bench, glancing at Sienna's chiming laughter.

"When she first arrived here, she got a lot of unwanted attention because she was abrasive. People either swooned over her or teased her due to her mother, Sifrrod Whitefish, being one of the only surviving original Council members," Ethan said before biting into a pastry. "Her and Wenda Ased."

"I think Sienna likes us. Why else would she always linger around? Maybe she's jealous of you," Annabeth shrugged. "I share a dorm with her. She generally keeps to herself. Has a huge crush on Master Moore, but most girls do."

"Jealous of what?"

"Everyone's excited to meet you. You're making friends easily enough. It wasn't easy for her. Some of the students accused her of using her Siren Song to hypnotize them and gain popularity." Annabeth sipped her tea. "People are vicious; it was obviously a malicious rumor," she said sadly.

They ate together, with Ella indulging in an abundance of pastries. She would have been scolded at home for eating so much. Ethan had been right. Everyone was casting curious glances or outright staring at her, gathered in clusters and whispering.

The third period was a free period, and they spent it in the library. Ella felt daunted by the number of words she couldn't read. Annabeth had prepared notes and made copies for Ethan and her, but she held a parchment unknowingly upside down. If Ethan and Anna noticed, they didn't say anything. The library was mostly empty, except for a few younger students huddled between bookshelves. Books rose high, spiraling toward the ceiling when not placed on magically rotating shelves.

"How do you find anything in this place?" Ella asked as a book flapped past her like a bird. "It may look messy, but it's quite organized. Go to that wall, ask for a specific genre or title, and a list with a map will appear," he explained, pointing to a seemingly blank wall adorned with bricks and portraits.

Oh. More reading, Ella thought numbly. She hoped she could decipher the symbols, but had no luck.

Throughout the day, Sienna would linger, insult Ella, and then vanish again. By lunchtime, Ella was overwhelmed by everyone's gossip and stares. "Is it true you set Master Moore on fire?" A college junior inquired, wide-eyed. Ella awkwardly moved away.

A boy cornered her in a stairwell. "You bit off Master Moore's hand? He's been in the infirmary all morning!" he gaped.

"Wha–? No! My gods!" Ella protested as Ethan stepped in to end the interrogation.

"Can you believe this?" Annabeth laughed on their way to the final classes. "In just a few hours, you've become known for killing Master Moore."

"I'm so over today," Ella mumbled, resting her head in her hands.

"This will be an easy class—just Herbology. We might even grow some Frollstin grass," Ethan said. Upon reaching the classroom door, they noticed everyone else was already seated and waiting. Ethan rummaged through his backpack and pulled out a book, handing it to Ella. "Here, you can borrow my guide," he offered with a smile. Ella hesitated as she took the book, examining its plain green cover.

"Thank you, Ethan—" she began.

"Miss Marks," Highmaster Gregor's voice interrupted from behind her. Startled, Ella dropped the book and spun around, her heart pounding in her chest. Highmaster Gregor tilted his head, his strikingly handsome face revealing no emotion. Wearing his exquisite gold robes, he resembled the sun, with his flowing blonde hair cascading over his shoulders. "I'd like to have a word with you. Please, come with me."

Ella exchanged nervous glances with Annabeth and Ethan before stammering, "Alright." She bent down to retrieve the green book and handed it back to Ethan. "Thanks anyway," she said.

As they walked down the corridors, a few lingering students stopped and whispered among themselves.

"–In trouble."

"–Expelled."

With her Elven hearing, Ella caught their words and her ear twitched in annoyance. "Sir, if this is about the incident in Master Moore's class—"

He raised a hand to halt her, making her pause mid-step. Noticing she had fallen behind, he turned and gestured for her to catch up. His wrist jingled with numerous bangles as he moved.

They stopped before a door that Ella recognized as the same office where she and Hamlet had been greeted. Gregor held the door open as she hurried in, filled with apprehension. He pulled out a leather chair for her and then seated himself at the other side of his large desk. The distance between them felt immense.

"So, I hear there has been a lot happening on your first day," Gregor remarked. Ella blushed deeply.

He folded his hands under his chin. "There's something we should have addressed during our meeting last night. It was an oversight on my part—a grave lapse in judgment."

"I'm sorry?" Ella stammered.

"Your pyromancy. I hadn't anticipated... Was it an accident?"

"Yes! I would never have done something like that intentionally," she promised, avoiding any mention of the incident with Dasyra.

Gregor nodded and explained, "Our school for the Arcane hosts beings with various natural affinities for magic. For instance, a Siren's natural element would be water, making them adept at water-related magic. But they can still learn other types of magic.

"Your mother's altering-mutation ability is extremely rare. pyromancy is less unusual here, though your near immunity to spells and potions intrigued me. Thankfully, Grayson's salve worked well for you, despite this morning's hiccup.

"That said, pyromancy is an advanced-tier skill and should be practiced in appropriate settings. Your orange flames represent a tier three level. Still powerful and dangerous, despite being the lowest tier. Not all our teachers are fireproof, like Master Moore, the only one here who can perform a tier two pyromancy."

"Because he's a Dracaenean," she blurted out without thinking.

He regarded her for a moment, raising a thin, blond brow. "Yes. He is. You must forgive him for his behavior. I suppose even after all these years he is still worn down," Gregor said. He tapped his fingers against his chin in thought.

"Was it the war? He isn't much older than us, so it's strange to have someone so young teaching, especially with such a clear dislike for Elves." She shuffled in her seat, gaze fixating on a feathered quill that was scratching against floating parchment.

"He's highly skilled in his teachings. Unfortunately, his beliefs are his own, and it's not my place to share his story." His lips formed a thin line and he cleared his throat.

"Am I in trouble?" Ella asked hesitantly.

He raised an elegant eyebrow at her. "No. I just needed your understanding before explaining my solution. You possess immense power, Ellarhyssa, surpassing those who have studied for years in top Arcane schools. With your permission, I'd like to use Runes. It wouldn't diminish your magic, but rather attenuate it to a more manageable level." The quill and parchment suddenly appeared in front of him and he scanned it over with his eyes before waving it away.

"After some research, I learned that there were—and still are—Elves immune to specific spells and elixirs, like you. It's akin to abjuration—protection magic—that you unconsciously invoke. Think of it as internal armor. I read Elves with this ability remain vulnerable to Runic magic."

Ella started to protest, but he interrupted her. "I know you'll have concerns, but you admitted the incident was accidental. I also wanted to try using runes to avoid replacing enchantments and your need for that salve."

She couldn't help gagging at the mention of the salve, prompting him to chuckle.

"I had the same reaction," he laughed.

He opened one of his desk drawers, pulling out what appeared to be a black crystal, long and thin, with a pointed end. "This is a Runic pen. I'll be drawing the runes on you. The process can be painful, and hopefully, it won't need to be repeated. Runes can enhance spells, clothing—"

"People?" Ella interrupted.

"Yes. But simply being inscribed with runes isn't enough; one must be a strong enough vessel to contain the Runic magic." He rolled up his sleeve, revealing an array of etchings on his skin. Some markings were black, some raised, and others resembled liquid fire against his golden skin. Ella gasped. In Hellharth, runic work was a serious matter, with each new rune causing more pain than the last; it was warned against having more than four. She had never seen anyone with so many.

Twelve.

"Why do you have so many?" Ella asked as she unconsciously reached to touch one. He withdrew his arm, and she offered an apologetic look. "The pain—how did you endure twelve?"

"I received them during the Purge war while defending the Calisan Capital," he replied. "I'm surprised Hamlet didn't mention it. He's the one who inscribed mine, and I did his."

At this revelation, Ella sighed in exasperation. "I didn't know much about those around me," she admitted sadly. "Hamlet has as many as you?"

"Last I knew, he had thirteen. It caused him to have a seizure."

"Thirteen?" she gasped in disbelief.

"The known record is sixteen, but they died shortly after—their heart gave out. No one has ever achieved the full twenty-eight," he explained. Gregor gave her a thoughtful look, his fingers gripping the Runic Pen. "I need your consent."

"What Runes will you use?"

"I'll inscribe two runes: a shifting rune for controlling your appearance, and a constraint for your pyromancy to prevent accidents."

"How can I remove it later?"

"You can extinguish Runes by overlaying them with other runes," he replied, offering the pen.

"Can't we just place a Rune on jewelry or something?" she offered, eyes flicking to the sharp end of the Runic crystal pen.

"Strong runes require stronger vessels for better control. It's best on the skin."

She hesitated, glancing from the black crystal to him. "Where should we put them?"

He sighed and blushed slightly. "Somewhere hidden. How about the bottom of your feet?" He suggested hastily.

She removed her boots and socks, placing her feet awkwardly on his desk, trying not to wiggle her toes in embarrassment. He placed the crystal on her skin, and she gasped as it began to glow.

Gregor cleared his throat. "This will hurt. I apologize." She brushed off his apology, her eyes watching him intently.

Ella steeled herself for the searing pain. Nothing could have prepared her for it.

"THIRTEEN?" she screamed.

CHAPTER SIXTEEN

Ella winced with every step as if walking on shards of glass. She tried shifting her weight onto her heels, drawing curious looks from lingering students in the hallway. Classes had just ended, and she longed to reach her room as quickly as possible.

An ice bath would be perfect, she thought.

By chance, Ella spotted a door adorned with a swirling circle. Recognizing it as a portal door, she hurried through and slammed it shut behind her.

"Senior dorms."

Upon reopening the door, she found herself in the same hallway. A few girls snickered at her blunder. A male from Mistress Ased's class approached her, offering a warm smile. He was strikingly handsome, with sharp cheekbones and full lips. His brown eyes were highlighted by kohl liner, while an intricate swirl of tattoos extended from his face down to his neck.

"After hours on weekends, they shut some of those portals down," he explained. "The one by the Highmaster's office usually works."

"Figures," Ella sighed. The one she could have used. "Thank you, Armand."

"You remembered my name!" he exclaimed delightedly. "Do you need help getting somewhere? I know it's easy to get lost here."

"I just wanted to return to my dorm. There's been too much excitement on the first day."

"I noticed you limping. Would you like to go to the infirmary?" Armand asked.

"No, I just tripped earlier. Must have sprained my ankle."

"I can carry you," he offered, adjusting his position to lift her. She yelped as his arms cradled her legs. "It's really not a problem."

"I assure you, I'm fine. I can walk," she insisted. Ignoring her protest, he began taking long strides, passing snickering girls who gawked at them. "Armand!" she exclaimed as they sped through the corridors.

"The way you were limping, it would've taken ages. We're already here." He lowered her gently, her hair windswept.

"How did you do that?"

"I grew up in the Aslan Desert. You learn to be fast when everything wants to kill you," he laughed, tapping his ankles to reveal speed runes. She grimaced, reminded of her burning runes.

"Thank you," she managed through gritted teeth, pain shooting up her legs.

"No problem. I'll let Ethan and Anna know you're okay. They were ready to protest your expulsion."

Ella thought they were definitely like Nattya and Highwing. Her expression darkened as she wondered how long it would be before seeing them again and what Hamlet and her mother had told them about her absence.

A wave of bitterness stirred within her as she took a moment to collect herself. After thanking Armand once more, she stepped into her room. Her gaze was instantly drawn to the bed, where a neatly wrapped white box rested on the pillows. With anticipation, she picked it up, inhaling its delightful fragrance before carefully opening it. Inside, she found a large feather which she delicately twirled between her trembling fingers.

"Highwing," she whispered, her heart soaring. Although her feelings for Highwing were different from those she had for Gideon, she knew she loved him. Her love for Highwing was similar to her love for Nattya—and that was enough for now. Love could grow; it had to. She brought the feather to her nose, taking in his scent once more before glancing back into the box. There, she found a letter written in Nattya's familiar handwriting—thankfully in Elvish.

Ella, you have got to be fucking kidding me with this timing. I know it's only been a day, but it feels like forever. Highwing has gone absolutely batshit. Your mother and Hamlet decided that telling us at the crack of dawn of your departure was a good idea. Hamlet is on my shit list by the way—I don't care that he almost got eaten by a gropplethorn or whatever the beast's name is. I thought we were planning a wedding.

Tell me what the men are like out there—

The lines became scribbled midway.

Ella, don't listen to her. I'm sure you've had a long day. Hamlet told us that they sent you somewhere safe because they are afraid that Hellharth will be under siege any day. I fought with them. Told them they should have let us come with you. Your safety is a top priority. Everything happened so suddenly. Hamlet says he will be able to see you at the place they have you in. He says he can't tell us anything and that he is sorry. I hope when we see you again you can explain it to us.

Until then,

Yours, Highwing, **AND NATTY**

Ella laughed out loud until tears streamed down her face, eventually turning into an unbearable sob. The pain in her feet seemed to vanish. After her emotional outburst, she went to the washroom and was surprised by the plain brown-eyed girl staring back at her. She yearned for her amber eyes but remembered they were his, just like her black hair and wings. She undressed, stepped into the stone tub, and turned on the water. Her wings extended with a groan, aching from being hidden for so long.

How would Nattya and Highwing react upon learning she was Idmodias' daughter—public enemy number one? With no classes scheduled for tomorrow, she decided to take some time for herself and hopefully write back to them.

She was mistaken. In the morning, Anna and Ethan knocked persistently on her door, leaving Ella no choice but to entertain them as they bombarded her with questions.

"What did the Highmaster want?" Ethan inquired, fiddling with her lamp. He knocked it over and tried sticking the lampshade back on it—lopsided.

"Only some paperwork. Nothing thrilling," she fibbed. Spotting the box crumpled amidst her blankets, she swiftly pushed it under the bed.

"Armand carried you through school?" Anna probed. "You know he's Gertrude Rydelle's man."

"I have no clue who Gertrude Rydelle even is," responded Ella flatly.

"Think Sienna Whitefish but worse," explained Anna.

"Quite the character indeed," Ethan agreed.

"It was nothing. I tripped, hurt myself, and he saw me limping. He offered to help," clarified Ella.

"Good luck explaining that to Gertrude. Not that I can complain—I was her rebound after their last breakup," mentioned Ethan.

"I believe Sienna might be into you, though," Anna told Ethan as she rummaged through the room, opening drawers.

"For two years now, Sienna has been hopelessly infatuated with Master Moore," Ethan dismissed.

"Sienna likes Master Moore?" Ella asked incredulously. "How could anyone like him? He's so curt."

"Well, I can't blame her for appreciating his looks. There were rumors they were an item a while ago—before she was a student here, but I don't buy it," answered Anna. "On a related note, did you manage to finish any of Moore's essay?"

"No," Ella admitted sheepishly. "I planned on delivering an oral essay." They stared at her in disbelief.

"He'll flay you alive," Ethan chuckled. "Why do you seek punishment?"

"I think it's brilliant," encouraged Anna, her pink eyes gleaming. "No one has ever dared to defy him before."

"Honestly, I'm not trying to stand up to him. I'm just not that great at writing," Ella admitted.

"They say he went to an Idris prison—he killed a bunch of men in a tavern or something," Ethan explained. "Ran his hand through their hearts."

"And they let him teach? With his temper?" Ella asked incredulously.

"Highmaster Gregor has some pull with the Arcadean Council. I suspect that is why. Said to have paid a great deal of money to have him removed from prison." Ethan shrugged.

"Are your parents visiting at the end of the month?" Annabeth asked, changing the subject.

Ella furrowed her brow in confusion, and Anna explained further, "The last weekend of the month is visiting day—the wards go down. Students either meet their parents here or in Calisan Capital or Hildfree. Hildfree has lots of shopping options, while Calisan Capital can be quite busy for a weekend visit."

"Some students go home," Ethan chimed in. "Did you always live in Direfell? What's it like there?"

Ella hesitated before answering. "Not much different from anywhere else, I suppose." She carefully recalled what she knew about Direfell and added, "It's hot."

Anna nodded. "Yeah, all those volcanoes... Have you ever seen a dragon?"

"No," Ella replied.

"What a shame! Anyway, have you written home yet?" Annabeth asked as she picked some grapes from a fruit bowl.

"I haven't... Like I said, I'm not great at writing."

"We could help you write it," Ethan suggested, retrieving a book and writing materials from his satchel. "I have sloppy handwriting too. Anna makes it look like art."

That's not what I mean, she internally groaned. "That would be lovely, thank you."

An hour passed while Annabeth had made the letter look like something out of a textbook and Ethan entertained them with stories. Ella herself couldn't read it but she knew what was written, and she wondered what Highwing and Nattya would think getting such a letter from her.

Dear Nat and Highwing,

It's been interesting being here. I have made new friends and learned some new things. I miss you both as well. Father should be visiting me soon, as they allow visitors once a month. I am hoping to convince him to allow you to come with him next. It is cold here. I haven't seen snow yet. You would love Annabeth and Ethan; they remind me so much of you. It is busy here... I will keep you updated on my studies.

Love, Ella

"Highwing is an interesting name," Annabeth mused aloud.

"It's a nickname," Ella replied, lying. She hoped Nattya and Highwing could decipher her letter, that she had left enough hints for them to ask the right questions. She imagined them questioning Hamlet. She had used the word studies—which could be associated with school, and she mentioned it being cold, so she was somewhere in Arcadea.

"Is he your boyfriend?" Ethan teased.

"He's my-my beau," Ella responded. "We have feelings for each other." Despite her words, it still sounded too formal.

"How romantic!" Anna exclaimed. "I hope I get to meet him someday." She folded the letter and handed it to Ella. It was then that Ella realized she had no way of delivering it—Hellharth's veil would prevent her from doing so. All she could do now was wait for Hamlet to appear.

If he ever did.

Ella's eyes softened. "Me too."

⤜⟶

The days sped by in a haze. Ella coasted through her schoolwork, using the excuse that she was still new, and discreetly relied on other students for answers. Two weeks had passed since she first arrived. Gertrude Rydelle began making her presence felt, constantly shoving Ella against the stone walls or tripping her when they were alone. Even Sienna showed sympathy towards Ella.

Ella's shoulder collided painfully with the stonework as the pretty blonde shoved her. "Sorry," Gertrude snickered. Despite being slightly shorter than Ella, her bullying persisted.

Gertrude had her arms crossed over her chest, tilting her head, her shaggy haircut framing her heart-shaped face.

"I already told you I'm not interested in Armand," Ella snapped impatiently. She could hurt this Maji human, just like Dasyra, but the sharp pinch of the rune on her foot reminded her why she shouldn't. However, after two weeks of enduring this torment, she was tired of playing nice.

Gertrude laughed. Lowly. bringing up a slender finger and poking her hard in the chest.

In a sudden burst of anger, Ella pulled back and punched Gertrude in the face, causing her head to snap back with force. Shock registered on Gertrude's face as she wiped the blood from her nose. Ella raised both arms with clenched fists and landed another blow to Gertrude's cheek. "What's the matter, Gertie? Don't like it when I fight back?" she taunted.

Gertrude held her cheek, seething.

People began to gather around them, cheering and encouraging the fight. Gertrude lunged for Ella's braided hair, but Ella ducked, spinning and striking her with her left hand. For a brief moment, Gertrude's image was replaced by Dasyra in Ella's mind, causing her to hesitate as the scent of burning flesh filled the air.

"Ella!" Anna called out. This distraction allowed Gertrude to raise her palm, unleashing a bright blast of light toward Ella. Reacting quickly, Ella crossed her arms and shielded herself just as the teachers began to intervene.

"Miss Rydelle!" Mistress Devoro, the divination teacher, exclaimed. "What is the meaning of this?"

"She started it!" Gertrude accused, pointing a slender finger at Ella. Ella's eyes flicked to the polished red paint of her nails and then back up to her freckled face, her lip curling.

"No, she didn't!" Annabeth retorted, stepping in front of Gertrude. Anna's pink eyes glowed brightly while her hands crackled with energy.

"Miss Dox, calm down! You are all College seniors! Adults! You should not behave like savages!" Mistress Devoro scolded.

"She's been tormenting Ella for weeks now! All because she's jealous—"

"I am not jealous!" Gertrude interjected.

"Oh, she definitely is," Sienna chimed in from the sidelines, nonchalantly leaning against a wall while picking at imaginary dirt beneath her fingernails.

"Miss Marks?" The hall fell silent as Ella sighed inwardly. She turned to face Highmaster Gregor with his hands clasped behind his back.

"Is everything alright?" he asked.

At least I didn't set her on fire, Ella thought to herself. "Everything is fine."

"Hmm. Miss Rydelle, please visit the infirmary for your nose. Miss Marks... I'll be assigning you extra lessons with Master Moore in the coming weeks."

Everyone around her erupted.

"Fuck, that sucks.

"I saw the whole thing! Ella didn't do anything wrong."

"Extra assignments with the dragon—"

"—harshest punishment—"

"Be quiet," Highmaster Gregor snapped. "Everyone, back to what they were doing." He leaned in and whispered in Ella's ear. "There are better ways to let your anger out."

⋙———⟶

Grayson Moore was in quite the mood. The school's bells had rung, and he only had a small free period in between classes. He ran into students, shoulder-checking them and glaring at them from his height. The students scurried in opposite directions, afraid of the man that gave out detentions just for breathing. He had clocked Ella chasing after him out of Mistress Ased's class.

He was unhappy with Ella's presence, swerving between students in a failed attempt to try to lose her. His deep violet cloak billowed behind him menacingly, and his strides were wide, almost breaking into a jog. He grimaced when he heard Ella's voice calling after him.

"Master Moore! Master Moore!" she cried out, desperately trying to keep up with him amidst the bustling crowd. Ignoring her plea, he took a sharp left turn and ascended the flagstone steps leading to a rooftop. Grayson was aware of her recent altercation with Gertrude Rydelle and secretly commended her for finally taking a stand. He wondered how long it would have taken for her to reach that breaking point.

Finally, he broke through the door to the rooftop, stepping into the snow with the crunch of his dragon hide boots. He dug through his cloak pocket, whipping his black braided hair over his shoulder angrily. His hands finally clasped over a small rectangular silver tin that kept his few rolled smoking herbs. Just as he brought one to his lips, his finger ignited with flame, he heard her barreling through the door and onto the rooftop.

He groaned out loud and turned to the thorn at his side. El-larhyssa was on her knees, a look of shock on her face as she held clumps of snow in her hands. Her black wings had flared out from her back violently, causing the loose snow to drift off.

"Miss Marks," He acknowledged grumpily, lighting his smoking stick and inhaling deeply.

"Master Moore," Ella whispered, not moving from her spot on the ground as she held the snow with pure fascination.

"You don't need to follow me everywhere," he snapped at her. She paid him no attention. He puffed on his smoking stick, wisps of smoke drifting before him, and to his surprise, she remained silent. "Make sure you hide those *things* before anyone sees you," he said, nodding at her ruffled wings.

He heard her rise and stand behind him, rolling his eyes. "Your free time doesn't involve mine," he spat out. Yet she still said nothing. Ella joined him, holding the snow in her hand and crumbling it between her fingers. "So that's what it feels like," she murmured, a smile tugging at her lips.

"Have you never seen snow before?" he asked curtly, glancing at her sideways. She appeared incredibly happy. She shook out her wings, their sheer size momentarily catching his attention before he regained his composure.

Ella turned to respond, but he abruptly turned away. "I wasn't asking because I was interested, Miss Marks."

"Then why ask at all?" She retorted angrily, staring at his back with a heated gaze, noting how he hunched over like a hawk protecting its meal. "What are you smoking?"

"Lavender root," he replied absentmindedly. He shuffled some snow with his boots and wrapped his violet cloak around himself for warmth against the winter chill. After finishing his smoke, he flicked the remnants away and conjured a soft magical swirl from his mouth. Small bluebell flames danced between his palms to keep him warm.

He had labored for hours grading essays the night before and still felt the effects of sleep deprivation. His usual morning tea failed to prevent the migraine that now plagued him. Every time he blinked, he saw the disappointing, repetitive nonsense his students had written. Although they were senior and junior-level students, they wrote like novices. He suspected that half of them had copied from each other since it seemed impossible that they were all this stupid.

He lowly growled, closing his eyes in response to another sharp pain in the back of his head.

Unaware of his situation, Ella observed him from a distance before approaching the inviting flames. A shiver ran up her spine as her body struggled to adjust to the cold; her hands and legs started to ache where the snow had touched her.

He'll be furious with you for invading his personal space again, she thought. Nonetheless, her curiosity prevailed, and she inched closer. Tentatively reaching for the flames in his hands, their eyes met—his green ones locked with her captivating brown ones—and he visibly flinched, curling his lip and raising an eyebrow in displeasure.

"So warm. I can't control mine like this," she said with a satisfied sigh. Her feathers ruffled from the chilly exposure, and she wrapped her wings around herself for protection. He held his palms out closer to her, and she snuggled further into his space. She shivered again, her nose and cheeks flushed from the winter air. She smiled at him, his gaze fixated on her small canine fangs, as he stood up straighter.

"You're cold?" he asked incredulously. "Aren't your kind supposed to be, I don't know, indestructible?"

Her hands cupped around his without touching him, and she looked a bit disgruntled. "Indestructible? No. It hasn't snowed in Hellharth for twenty years. I'm not used to cold like this."

"Why didn't you say anything?" he asked with annoyance. "Or better yet—you're a pyromancer."

"You seem to hate when I say anything, sir, and I can't do that," she retorted, stepping away from the warmth. The flames abruptly disappeared, and he glared at her, rolling his eyes and pinching the bridge of his scarred nose with his fingers.

He tugged at his neck, pulling roughly until the snaps of his cloak came apart. He tossed it at her without grace and turned away from her again, mumbling something under his breath.

She held the cloak in her hands, the velvet and heavyweight surprising her. She gaped at him, looking from the cloak to his turned back in shock. When it became apparent that he was resolute to not look back at her again, she brought the cloak around herself, her wings disappearing into her back.

An uneasy silence ensued before she finally spoke. "Thank you."

"Don't. You brought this upon yourself by following me," he snapped, spinning to face her as his long braid whipped through the air. He was prepared to scold her once more, to express his immense displeasure with her presence.

"I—" she began, chewing her lower lip while her eyes darted around uneasily. She drew the cloak tight around herself.

He paused for a moment and clicked his tongue. "You're quite disappointing in my class. Other teachers say you perform well when questioned, but it's been a week and you haven't submitted a single assignment. Being new won't excuse your lax approach for much longer."

"I know—I just—" she stammered before stopping abruptly.

"So used to everyone catering to your whims, Princess?" he sneered, causing her to flinch at the mockery.

"I don't even want to be here!" she yelled, tearing the cloak from herself and shoving it forcefully against his chest. "You're not the only one unhappy with my presence!" She hissed and bared her fangs. The rune on her left foot burned faintly as her appearance momentarily shifted, revealing bright amber eyes, pointed Elven ears, and pale skin-toned stripes. Seconds later, her brown eyes returned and her ears regained their rounded shape.

He looked down at her condescendingly. "You're fortunate no one else witnessed your little transformation."

"I did that intentionally!" she protested.

"Of course you did," he said sarcastically.

She pushed his shoulders repeatedly, eventually forcing him against the rooftop door with a strength that shook the wood. She was fuming. Everything about him enraged her—his haughty, self-righteous demeanor and air of superiority.

He glared down at her from his nose, his breath whispering out his nostrils in the cold air.

"Just when I start to think you might be tolerable, you open that offensive mouth of yours and prove me wrong! If your goal is for me to loathe you, then well done. I cannot stand you!"

He smirked at her menacingly, towering over her by a full two feet. "Yet here you are, following me—"

"I have no one else!" she yelled in his face with a hint of desperation. Her hands gripped the front of his royal blue frock, the cloak crumpled between them. Realizing what she had just blurted out, she released him as if her hands had been scorched.

"Is lousy company better than none at all? I don't wish to be friends, Miss Marks."

"That isn't even my name!" she retorted, clenching her fist.

"As long as you're at Morning Song, it is. Why not bother Mr. Isles and Miss Dox?" he asked with a weary sigh, his tone annoyed.

"I've been trying to tell you that Highmaster Gregor assigned me to you—for pyromancy. I don't want your company any more than you want mine."

"He placed a Rune on you for pyromancy but expects me to teach you while you're limited?" he scoffed.

"Perhaps he's concerned for your safety," she said.

"Please. You can't even create a small fire to keep yourself warm," he snorted.

"I never had to before," she huffed.

His migraine was now blurring his vision. "I need to know the extent of the Rune's effect. Show me what you can still do." He gestured for her to step back, and she complied.

"Right here?" she inquired, glancing around the rooftop.

"No, in the Grand Hall during dinner—of course right here, you fool."

Ella rolled her eyes and took her stance, hands steady in front of her. She aimed for the air and exhaled, orange flames spiraling out of her palm but stopping short. She glared at her hand, and then her foot.

Grayson snorted, "He expects me to teach you with your magic in handcuffs."

"My foot just started hurting," she explained.

"Form a fire barrier. It's basic enough for your level," he instructed.

With a swift movement of her hands, she directed flames before her, creating a towering wall of fire. The flames crackled and roared, sending sparks and embers into the air.

Pain from her foot coursed through her legs and overwhelmed her. The fire ceased abruptly.

"These stupid runes—" she began, pain radiating from her foot.

"It's not the runes. It's you. You're barely in control."

"I'm in control just fine!" she protested.

"The rune is burning to prevent you from losing control completely. That's its purpose." He sighed, feeling his migraine intensify. "Training will start after lunch next week."

CHAPTER SEVENTEEN

"Eros, Dasyra is here again," Healer Lyra said with exasperation. "It's like she's a cat in heat." She pushed her white hair behind her ears and rolled up her robe sleeves.

Eros sighed. "Let her in, but stay in the room with me." This marked the sixth time Dasyra visited the infirmary in the past two weeks. The first three times, she sought more salve; the remainder, complaints about pains for which Eros diligently concocted tonics. Nothing seemed to satisfy her.

Lyra washed her hands in a water basin, her blue healer robes stained with blood from tending to a Queensguard's wounds during training. Thankfully, nothing major—merely routine. Nonetheless, the blood always appeared brighter and more sinister against her pale skin, accentuating her dark blue veins—a stark reminder that she was born a sleeping child who stole life from her mother upon birth. Now a pariah, she lived among the remote villages in the Anaferi mountains.

"I really don't see the point," Lyra scoffed with characteristic snark whenever Dasyra emerged. "It's obviously driven by lust."

Eros sighed inwardly. "I maintain professional relationships only. Furthermore, we can't turn her away; she's a Court member's daughter."

Lyra tossed a soiled rag into the basin, splattering water onto the rickety table they used for their work. Its wooden surface was marred by countless water stains. They could have replaced it, but it held sentimental value from their early days in the healing profession. The room still contained the same old shelves and glass jars from years gone by.

Lyra had run out of patience and burn paste. With her mouth pursed into a tight line, her dark eyes locked onto Eros' distinctive green-and-gold pair. "She's after more than just your healing skills."

Eros smirked. "You sound jealous." His disarming charisma often left women breathless, and Lyra wasn't entirely immune to it herself. However, she had been around him long enough to resist its sway. While not conventionally attractive—her crooked nose and dark eyes made others uneasy. Eros had always regarded Lyra solely as a colleague and friend. Besides, she preferred the company of women in her bed.

"Hardly," she said, preparing another tonic with ginger root and assorted greens. A slow drip came from the corner ceiling, water landing in a small bowl to catch the leak. The Healer's Hut needed extensive repairs, so Lyra worked through the night to concoct elixirs and brews for sale in nearby cities and towns.

"Merely looking out for my well-being?" he teased. She blushed deeply. "You laugh, but you know what she said to the princess."

"We must remain unbiased when treating patients, even if we disagree with their actions," he said in a patronizing tone that made her feel insignificant.

She stopped pounding the herbs. "I had to retrieve the boy's body from those rocks. You didn't see the princess or what I saw. Despite the tide threatening to sweep them away, she clung to the rocks, holding him. In my opinion, Dasyra should've had her tongue removed." Lyra knew others might have overheard her harsh words, yet she spoke her mind without fear.

"You're taking it too personally. That's why I'm treating her and you aren't," Eros remarked firmly. "Send her in." He assumed his professional healer demeanor, leaving Lyra feeling dismissed.

Eros knew that Lyra wasn't the only one with mixed feelings about Dasyra. Others had also complained about her frequent visits. Eros tried to be fair, assuring himself that he was merely treating her. However, if there was nothing to treat, he would send her on her way. He wasn't oblivious to the fact that Dasyra's visits had taken on a more suggestive tone as her dresses became tighter and shorter. He half expected her to be laying on the table, legs spread wide and already glistening.

"Your scent has changed," Lyra muttered through gritted teeth. "So much for professionalism."

"I have no interest in her," Eros responded honestly. "Just let her in."

Lyra left the room and called for Dasyra, returning with a smug grin.

"What's with that face?" Eros asked.

"You'll see," Lyra replied cryptically.

When Dasyra entered, she wore a chest plate made of bones and leaves —a traditional outfit from the remote villages of the Anaferi Mountains. Lyra struggled to maintain a forced smile.

"Dasyra, it's good to see you. I trust you're doing well?" Eros inquired, keeping his gaze steady with hers. He couldn't fathom why she chose this attire; even he didn't dress like that despite living in the village.

"I am doing better," she said softly. She blinked rapidly at him, her long thick eyelashes fluttering.

Lyra made a low noise, her dark eyes fixed on the back of Dasyra's head. "So, what brings you in?" she asked sharply.

Dasyra didn't look away from him, instead running her hands down her breastplate. "I thought I'd come to express my gratitude for your patience with me."

Eros' eye twitched slightly. The room was heavy with the scent of desire, but Lyra's presence soured it. He detected a familiar undertone—Fara Lilies woven between the bones and leaves on her breastplate. Their powerful aroma was meant to act as an aphrodisiac. If he were a lesser man, it might have worked. During spring, the lilies were used to encourage elves to procreate. Women had tried using these flowers on him before, but they never succeeded.

"Your recovery is thanks enough," he responded tersely. "I have other matters to attend to. Is there anything else?"

Dasyra looked affronted. "I was hoping to have more of your time. Outside of the healer setting."

Lyra snorted from behind, crossing her arms and glaring at Eros. Dasyra was all but throwing herself at him and couldn't understand why he wasn't biting. The lilies always worked on Highwing—or any other man for that matter.

"I am preoccupied at the moment," he explained. "Lyra? Could you tend to Lady Dasyra for me? I just remembered I have to check on a baby today." Lyra's face dropped at this, her mouth agape. He tried not to laugh as Dasyra and she had the same expression and he slipped out of the hut.

He breathed in the outside air anxiously. Dasyra was as relentless as Lyra had said, resorting to herbs to try to get her way. Had she not been so blatantly cruel to the Princess, he may have considered entertaining her. But she was clearly a woman who wanted to settle down, and he was not about to father children just yet.

He was the one to make the women's brews for their cycle pains and to prevent unnecessary pregnancies. Lyra had given the brews to all but the youngest of Lord Cida's daughters. They were quick to bed and quicker to anger. Any children that came from that brood would surely be just as sour.

As he made his way down the dirt paths of the villages, he greeted his neighbors with curt nods. Coming upon his own home, he pulled back the drape to the entrance and walked in, feeling his wards accept him. He half expected Dasyra to one day show up at his hut. He peeled his healer garbs off, having lied about needing to deal with some village baby, and threw himself onto his bed. The bed groaned under his weight—he had grown larger over the years—his feet now hung off the edge. He was supposed to have dinner with his parents tonight and was dreading it. Surely, they were going to start spewing the same nonsense they had been in recent months. That it was time for him to find a woman.

Not yet. He wasn't ready. Gods help him if they found out that Lady Dasyra had shown an interest in him. He would never hear the end of it. He pulled his leather gloves off and flexed his hand. A small birthmark in the shape of a semicircle on the back of the left one. He knew they meant well. They had gone most of their lives childless and then were blessed by being gifted a small boy who had lost his birth parents. The story of his birth was shady, and he remembered nothing of his childhood, except a braid of black hair and a soft-sung tune that scratched at his mind. He hummed the tune aloud.

He wasn't like the other elves, and he knew it. There was something different about him, and his parents knew it too. When Eros had first started showing signs of his magic, his adoptive parents; Vrisa and Macan, told him that he was better off keeping it to himself. So he did. As years went on, he befriended many of the villagers and knew them all by name. When he had met Lyra, she had been a frail thing, lanky and starved and unloved. When he had brought her home, his parents had been wary, explaining that a sleeping child was a curse at birth. He never saw Lyra as such, and eventually, neither did his parents.

"If she says anything about Dasyra tonight, I'll kill her," he groaned, running a hand down his face. Lyra would absolutely tell his mother and father about Dasyra's interest.

Just as he thought. Dinner time had amassed into an intervention in his love life. His mother had guffawed as Lyra casually mentioned Dasyra wearing a breastplate of Fara lilies between bites of her potatoes. His father was staring at him with a look of disappointment.

"The girl all but invited you inside and you shut her out," he said gruffly, forking violently at his slab of meat. "You want to be a bachelor your whole life? I want to be a Grandsire!"

"There's plenty of time for that. I am only twenty-six winters old," Eros argued. He was glaring daggers at Lyra, who was staring into her mug.

"I'm ninety-two!" his mother complained. "Don't be so selfish."

"How am I being selfish by not wanting children yet?" Eros asked. He pushed his plate away and crossed his arms. His mother went tight-lipped. He knew that one thing that annoyed her the most was when he didn't eat. It was her favorite thing—to feed him. She poured her love into her cooking. She looked from his plate to him and slowly pushed it back toward him. "Eat," she commanded in that tone that he was all too familiar with. She wasn't amused.

"Besides that," he said while eating a vegetable, "Dasyra isn't the kind of woman I'd want as the mother of my children."

"What's not to like? She has great birthing hips, and her dowry could feed all the villages," Macan reasoned. He avoided looking at his wife, who narrowed her magenta eyes at him at the mention of Dasyra's birthing hips. Vrisa was a willowy thing, with brown waves of hair and skin that was taught around her bones, while Macan was a tall man, with a wide build, and no hair.

"The girl is a bore. She's mean and callous. She pretends to be one of us but has never struggled in her life," Lyra added. "Being a descendant of Anaferi doesn't make her better than others."

The room grew quiet as Vrisa considered the situation. "You could always be the mother of his children, Lyra," she said, glancing between her and Eros.

Lyra, in the middle of taking a drink, coughed and sputtered in surprise. "No!" she slammed down her mug in embarrassment.

Macan didn't hide his distaste. Tolerating Lyra was one thing; wanting her to have children with his son was another.

"Let's change the subject," Eros suggested cheerfully.

Dasyra stomped through Anaferi Castle, hissing at guards and unsuspecting maidservants. Men turned their attention to her, and she realized she was still wearing the breastplate adorned with lilies. She tore it off once she reached her room, feeling utterly humiliated. He hadn't shown any interest at all! Her older sisters, Mysera and Oryann, stopped their idle chatter on her bed and looked at her up and down quizzically.

"What in the Gods' name is that?" Mysera asked, pointing to the ruined breastplate on the floor. The leaves and bones had crumbled onto the shaggy sheep rug.

"I thought if I dressed up like one of his village women, he would notice me," Dasyra huffed. She walked over to the mirror that the girls had silently agreed to cover with a blanket and pulled it off. Her reflection made her wince. She was still pretty, as always, but her hair was slicked back and ended at her ears. If it weren't for her delicate features and breasts, she would look like a man.

"We can enhance your appearance—perhaps wear a circlet on your head. I bet it would look lovely!" Oryann suggested dreamily. They had all inherited their mother's golden locks, but Oryann was blessed with an impressive figure.

"You don't have to try so hard," Dasyra muttered to her, glaring at her sister's large breasts and thick hips.

"Is this about the Healer? Eros?" Mysera inquired, rifling through her closet and pulling out their best dresses. If there was one thing that made Dasyra happy, it was dressing up.

"I've never had to work this hard for a man's attention," Dasyra scoffed. "I could have been touching myself on his table, and he wouldn't have even had the decency to notice."

"He might prefer the company of other men," Oryann suggested. "Cousin Torin does."

"I hadn't considered that possibility," Dasyra admitted. If Eros did prefer the company of men, then perhaps the issue wasn't her but rather her equipment. She sighed in defeat. "Why is it so difficult to find a suitable husband?" She yearned for the connection that marriage promised.

"Bastian will come of age soon. He's been trailing you for years now," Mysera said as she tossed a red dress at her and snapped her fingers. "Put this on. It will complement your hair."

"What hair?" Dasyra retorted, fingers curling around her short locks.

Arysta entered and climbed atop the bed. "Are we dressing up?" she asked with enthusiasm.

"Yes," Oryann replied cheerfully, rummaging through her own clothes. Soon, heaps of garments littered the room while bursts of laughter filled the air. They dressed Dasyra in the red dress, adorning her with a circlet of golden leaves and jewels. Mysera lent her some bangles, and they ornamented her forearms. The snug dress accentuated her figure, with an open back that dipped just above her backside. They gathered around the mirror to admire her.

Despite Dasyra's short hair, she finally recognized her feminine allure once more. Mysera and Oryann rested their heads on each of her shoulders.

"You don't need men's attention to know that you're stunning," Mysera stated, smiling at their reflection.

"Your worth depends on how you perceive yourself," Oryann added wistfully.

"Boys are gross," Arysta interjected with a grimace, sticking out her tongue. The room burst into laughter once more.

CHAPTER EIGHTEEN

By the time the second week arrived, Anna and Ethan pulled Ella aside—more like cornered her. They were in the library, discussing the essay and how Ella hadn't written anything for any class.

"When you said you can't write, you really meant it," Ethan said gently. "And I suspect you can't read either."

Ella's face turned red with embarrassment. What adult couldn't read and write? She couldn't tell them the truth—that she could only read and write in Elvish.

"It's because she's from Direfell. Arcadean is usually everyone else's second language—except for humans. I speak Ruid—it's my first language since I'm a Pixie. You could have told us. There are many students in this school who learned to read and write Arcadean late. I learned just last year, and you see how I write," Annabeth said, smiling.

"You could have gotten a translator from the library—a Direfell Draca to Arcadean translator. They would have set it up for you," Ethan added with a chuckle. "We wouldn't have laughed at you."

Ella snorted. Of course, there would be translators. A school initially meant for Maji humans that later accommodated Fae beings would have translators. However, Ella couldn't read or write Draca either.

"I just didn't want to seem so... I don't know..." Ella stumbled over her words. "They placed me with seniors, and I felt stupid."

"Well, they weren't going to put you with younglings. Honestly, your parents should have arranged for translators," Anna said with a sigh. She pulled a book from her satchel and handed it to Ella. The Arcadean storybook contained basic words and accompanying pictures.

Ethan handed her a pen and paper. "We are going to teach you Arcadean. You'll get it down in no time!"

Ella glanced around the library. People were busy in their work, writing or reading, and in their own world. Ethan and Anna were practically bouncing in their seats waiting for Ella to agree.

Ella groaned inwardly but complied, nonetheless. She began slowly, tracing the letter 'A' on the paper, then moving on to 'B', then 'C'. But after a few more letters, Ella started to get the hang of it. She began writing faster and more confidently.

"Now read this word. Sound it out," Ethan prompted, as he showed Ella a word on a piece of paper.

"Wa-tear," Ella sounded out hesitantly.

"No, no, no," Ethan shook his head. "It's wa-ter, not 'wa-tear'. Try again."

"Wa-ter," Ella corrected herself. "Water."

"Good job," Ethan grinned.

"You're a natural at this, Ella," Anna said, patting her on the back.

Ella smiled weakly, feeling slightly encouraged. But then Anna showed her another word, and Ethan pulled out a new letter, and the process started all over again.

As the night dragged on, Ella began to feel more and more exhausted. But Anna and Ethan were relentless in their pursuit of teaching her the Arcadean language. Finally, after what seemed like an eternity, Anna checked the clock.

"It's almost midnight, guys," she announced. "Time to call it a night."

Ella had never felt more relieved in her life. But she also realized, with a sense of pride, that she had come a long way in just one evening. She may not have mastered the language, but she had certainly made progress.

As they gathered their things and prepared to leave, Ella turned to her friends and said, "Thanks, guys. I couldn't have done it without you." She handed Anna a small, handwritten note she wrote their names on.

"See? Look at you!" Annabeth exclaimed happily. It reminded Ella how the younglings would draw horrid pictures and get praised by their mothers. She cringed inwardly and smiled back.

"I don't think I am anywhere near ready to start writing whole essays," she grumbled.

"Just take the weekend and practice. I have the outlines for you in the journal," Ethan said.

"I really can't thank you guys enough. Seriously, what would I do without you?"

"Fall down a flight of steps—" Anna laughed.

"Again," Ethan added. "Never turn in an assignment."

"Ever," Anna finished.

"Okay, Okay, I get it!" Ella laughed.

She submitted her first written assignment just a few days later, no longer relying on mind-drifting into other people's thoughts. Master Moore had been less than thrilled with her script, calling it a monstrosity.

It was supposed to be her first day of Moore's tutoring, and as she wandered about the halls looking for the room, she ran into Armand's chest. His arms shot out to steady her.

"Sorry," she apologized stiffly. They stood there awkwardly for a moment before Ella moved to go around him. He grabbed her by her wrist gently to stop her.

"Hey, I've been meaning to talk to you about what happened with you and Gertie," he said. "I know it's my fault—I wanted to apologize. She tends to get really... intense over me."

"By intense, you mean psychotic?" Ella huffed angrily.

He gave her a sheepish look, a hand coming up to scratch the back of his head. "Yeah. That." Silence filled the air as they stood there, not sure where to go from there. She broke it after a while, unable to handle the awkwardness anymore.

"So, what now?" she asked, hoping for some sort of resolution.

His eyes flickered, and he shuffled his feet. "I don't know. I mean, I didn't expect to see you here and—"

"Well, if it is all the same to you, I really should get going. Don't need her planning my assassination for bumping into you," she grumbled, quickly cutting him off.

"Right, of course," he said, understanding her need to distance herself from him. "I don't want to cause any problems for you."

"Thanks," she replied, her voice laced with bitterness. "I'm sure I'll see you around."

He nodded, not wanting to cause any more tension between them. "Yeah, take care." He went to walk away and halted. "You look lost," he tried.

She sighed in exasperation and said, "Because I *am* lost. I can't find the stupid training room I'm supposed to be in."

"Which training room? Who's the teacher?"

"Moore."

"That would be in the Southern Tower. You're just about there. Go up the steps down the hall, the door on the right—left is Mistress Devoro's meditation class," he said.

"Thank you so much. I was getting frustrated," she said, relieved.

"No worries, happy to help," he said as he walked away.

She suddenly felt terrible about how she treated him. He hadn't exactly done anything wrong to her and had been apologetic. She made a mental note to apologize to him later—she was already late.

When she arrived in his training room, she was disappointed to see that she was the only one besides him who was there. He wasn't wearing his usual cloak, a black and silver uniform with symbols etched on the front. He looked more like a soldier than a master.

"You're late," he snipped.

"I got lost," she offered apologetically. Upon entering the large room, she was amazed by its open space and high ceilings. Minimal furniture filled the area, with only a wooden table and a few chairs to break up the emptiness. The walls were artfully decorated with paintings and calligraphy, as well as a small altar tucked away in the corner. The centerpiece of the room was a raised platform in its center, while mirrors dominated one wall. Sword and spear racks ran along other walls, providing metal or wooden weapons depending on preference. Finally, her gaze fell upon the black tile floor, which resembled an endless abyss of seawater.

"I didn't ask for your excuse," he snapped dismissively. "Let's go."

⟫⟫——⟶

Grayson was merciless. "I bet you won't be late again," he said smugly. Ella had run eight laps around the training room. He told her she could stop when she managed to reach the end of the room.

What he hadn't told her was the room was enchanted to expand, so she was running endlessly and hopelessly.

"Can I stop yet? I won't be late again," she huffed tiredly.

"Doubtful," he scoffed. "Get on the platform," he commanded. At his words, Ella threw herself up onto the platform unceremoniously. She lay there, panting.

"If you are already exhausted, it's no wonder your powers lack finesse and control," he said.

He gave her a quizzical look after she managed to lift her head and showed him a brash finger gesture. "Am I supposed to understand that?" he asked. She blushed and fell back onto the platform, grumbling, "It doesn't have the same effect if I have to explain it."

He raised his eyebrow and motioned for her to stand up. "I want you to concentrate on the feeling of when you are about to release the fire from inside of you."

She visibly shivered, and he wondered for a moment if the chill in the air was getting to her.

"Don't go beyond what you can control. Start with creating a perfect sphere," he instructed.

"There's no such thing as perfection," she said automatically, echoing what Hamlet had always told her. Grayson scoffed at her.

"If you truly believe that, teaching you would be pointless."

Ella bravely tried to create the perfect sphere of fire, but despite her best efforts and concentration, she couldn't achieve the desired shape. Each failed attempt prompted Grayson to snort and pace around the room like a predator watching its prey. After two hours, Ella's stomach began to rumble.

"Miss Marks, take a break," Grayson finally said.

He motioned for her to sit at the wooden table with chairs on opposite sides. Ella sat down with a sigh of relief while Grayson conjured a jug of water and a tray of fruits and cheeses. Without waiting for his offer, Ella grabbed apple slices, stuffing her cheeks like a chipmunk as juice dribbled from her mouth.

Grayson observed her in astonishment, tilting his head and wrinkling his nose as she breathed heavily between bites.

"Attractive," he drawled.

She stopped chewing and blushed. "Sowwy—arn you goving ter veat?" she said with a mouthful of food.

He almost laughed. Almost. "I doubt there will be any left when you get through."

She looked at him in disbelief and swallowed. "Was that a *joke*? You're making jokes now?"

He gave her his best scowl and opted for a piece of cheese. He felt a bit of nostalgia, watching her attempt the sphere that Gregor had him endlessly practicing when he was younger. He knew she was starving. Magic depletion was a real thing and it zapped your energy quickly.

When he was satisfied with how much she ate, he dismissed her. She seemed a bit confused but complied. He was left alone in the training room and a small chuckle escaped him.

He brought forth a ball of fire, not perfectly spherical, and in the empty room said aloud, "There's no such thing as perfect.

CHAPTER NINETEEN

Kahlisenya adjusted the sleeves on her white gown, allowing them to gracefully fall at her feet. She had chosen a modest gown of gossamer and silks, prioritizing comfort over extravagance, with the dress's trumpet skirt trailing behind her. Taking a deep breath, she emerged from her room, and the guards in the hallway stopped their whispers. Outside, a crowd eagerly awaited her address.

As Kahlisenya slowly navigated the hallways of Hylycyn Castle, her heart raced and she became increasingly aware of the heavy crown adorning her head. The golden starburst design symbolized both strength and courage—exactly what she needed for today's daunting task of explaining Ellarhyssa's absence to the people of Hellharth. As she drew near the doors to the throne room, their whispers ceased, leaving a deafening silence that Kahlisenya could feel even behind closed doors. Taking another deep breath, she entered the room and assumed her authoritative posture. She was ready for this—it was for the greater good.

That's what she told herself to fall asleep at night, but it hadn't worked at all. The Lords and Ladies of the Court welcomed her with heads bowed in respect. Hamlet stood with his arms crossed over his chest, appearing as if he hadn't slept in weeks. Things were not right between them, and she knew that after this meeting, nothing would ever be the same. Highwing remained by his mother's side, yet bravely met her gaze. A pang of guilt tightened her chest.

Oh, the many mistakes she had made.

The balcony doors opened, and the Court and Queen stepped out in unison, as the morning sun shone brightly upon them. The people had gathered in the gardens, encircled the castle grounds, and filled Townsend, leaving little space untouched. Hamlet presented her with a magical horn, amplifying her voice for the entire crowd.

"Welcome, my Hellharth family. I have invited you all today to address the rumors about Hellharth's continued presence in Arcadea and my daughter's absence." Kahlisenya held her head high and continued.

"It is true. The world you are seeing beyond the veil is Arcadea."

There was an explosion in the crowd, and Kahlisenya's hiss echoed through the horn. The people quieted down, but she could feel their scrutiny.

"Hellharth will become part of Arcadea again. My daughter, Ellarhyssa, no longer belongs to this place."

The murmurs persisted as she continued.

"I renounce my daughter's claim to the throne and her status as my heir. I have chosen a successor, unrelated to me, who will become Queen when I pass."

Hamlet appeared at her side immediately. "What the—"

"I appoint Lady Rayne of Anaferi House as my successor when I pass."

Beside her, Lady Rayne sputtered and clung to Highwing's arm for support. Lady Tanyl and Lord Althane stared in disbelief at the announcement, while Lord Cida's pudgy face turned several shades darker. Lady Petra maintained an impassive expression.

"Where is the princess?" someone shouted.

"Are we at war again?"

"What does this mean for us?"

"Thank you for your time," Kahlisenya said, turning away from the inquiries and guiding the bewildered group behind her. The outside world dimmed as the guards closed the doors.

"You can't do this!" Hamlet shouted as the balcony doors closed.

"Last I checked, she could do as she pleased," Althane retorted.

"Oh, fuck off! Just because your child's mother is named the Queen's successor, doesn't make you special!"

"It would make our son a prince," Althane argued. Lady Tanyl frowned at his words, evidently thinking about their twin sons.

"So kind of you to notice me now, Father," Highwing remarked sarcastically. Althane grunted indignantly at his comment.

"Ella is the rightful heir to the throne!" Hamlet spat. "You can't just take her claim!"

"I just did," Kahlisenya replied emotionlessly. Hamlet yanked the sash symbolizing his role as Advisor from his chest.

"You have no honor," he whispered, throwing the sash at her feet. Eight guards encircled him, spears aimed menacingly in his direction. He swatted one aside, his hand glowing ominously.

"Hamlet," Kahlisenya said gently. Her soft voice dissipated his rage, and he lowered his hand, revealing a face etched with betrayal. He strode out of the room without a backward glance.

"My Queen, though I'm honored by your consideration for this position, I must express my concerns. It's all so sudden. You said that Ella is no longer part of this world? Is she...?" Lady Rayne let the question linger.

"Ella is of no consequence. I've stripped her of her titles. She's no longer a princess or in Hellharth and will never return."

"You've banished her?" Highwing asked disbelievingly. "Hamlet mentioned—"

"I know what Hamlet said. Young Lord Highwing, I believe it'd be in your best interest to marry Dasyra," Kahlisenya stated coolly.

"I'm courting the princess—"

"*Ella* is no longer here," Althane interrupted.

"My Queen, I implore you. Highwing and Ella have intentions for each other. It's unfair to deny them the chance to explore their relationship. Who can say they won't marry?" Lady Rayne protested.

"With all due respect, the Queen has made her decision clear. Highwing cannot court someone who isn't present," Lord Cida retorted. He was clearly pleased with the prospect of his daughter taking the lead as the prince's partner in court.

"I have no interest in Dasyra. I want Ella," Highwing declared, frustration evident in his voice. "I'll go to her if I have to."

Kahlisenya regarded Highwing thoughtfully, her gaze traveling from his feet to his face slowly. He was a tall, striking figure even among elves, his wings seemingly too large for his body. A handsome countenance, a boyish grin, and steel-gray eyes that could captivate any girl.

But he was not right for Ella. Despite numerous conversations with her daughter trying to convince her of Highwing's merits, Kahlisenya knew in her heart that he was too gentle for her bold child. A sensible match? Certainly. That much was clear.

Yet he didn't challenge Ella or question her actions, of which there were many missteps. Highwing had always sought her affection as a loyal dog yearns for its master's love.

She understood her daughter—she recognized herself in Ella.

Ella was Kahlisenya, and Highwing was Hamlet. There would be someone darker and mysterious who would entice Ella and be her Idmodias. And while Hamlet embodied everything Kahlisenya desired in a man and she loved him deeply, she would forever ponder about the one she felt a soulful connection with.

With that thought in mind, she leveled her gaze at Highwing, raising her chin assertively. "You were just a means for her to find solace in her gilded cage." With that, she turned and walked away, convinced that her metaphorical knife was doing him a favor.

In the days that followed, unrest spread throughout Hellharth. People began constructing boats to leave the shores while others fortified their homes with wooden spikes and dug trenches in the sand. Lord Althane and Lady Rayne worried this would send the wrong message to those in Arcadea: that Hellharth was preparing for war.

Kahlisenya reclined on her chaise, the heavy crown discarded on the ground. Her room's brightness and cheerfulness countered her mood with its golden curtains and marble floors. The filigree-decorated door remained closed as she longed for her raven-haired child to walk through it.

Her palm itched.

"Do you think she's alright?" Nattya whispered to Highwing. They lay in Ella's bed, faces buried in her pillows, as they had been for the past few weeks. Nattya appeared thinner, her hair duller. Highwing noticed she had been eating less and struggled to get her to consume anything other than mead and wine.

"I don't know," he replied honestly. They had the same conversation every night, ending with Nattya in tears.

"That jerk won't tell me anything!" she growled, referring to Hamlet, who had been scarce lately.

Highwing questioned everyone. He pressed his mother, who claimed ignorance about Ella's whereabouts. He brought it up at every Court meeting without fail. The Queen sighed, and either his father or mother corrected him; Ella was no longer a princess according to the law.

"This isn't how things were supposed to go," Nattya sobbed. Highwing gently rubbed her back.

"They keep reassuring us that she's safe somewhere else. But how is any place but home safe?" he scoffed. "And they've discredited her as the rightful heir."

Valla, the cat, jumped onto the bed, causing the mattress to shift under her weight. She perched on Nattya's back, purring loudly.

"Valla misses her too," Highwing observed; the cat appeared just as unhappy as Nattya.

"Do you suppose Ella had the right idea of trying to escape the veil?" Nattya asked softly.

"I'm not sure. But something is happening, and I have a feeling it won't be good." Highwing replied, his voice barely above a whisper.

Chapter Twenty

Grayson snarled, "For fucks sake!" yet again, and Ella collapsed to her knees, chest heaving as she tried desperately to catch her breath. She shouted accusingly that it wasn't fair—Hamlet had neglected to teach her pyromancy, and she felt bitter for not taking his advice on improving herself in any way.

This was the third time Grayson had asked her to conjure flames into shapes. He had already created a flaming dragon that circled above them like an agitated sentinel. He clarified that it wasn't as hard as creating a creature, that all Ella needed was control from the runes drawn on her foot—but it was lost on her. Grayson rolled his eyes at her next failed attempt—a circle that died around her in a puff of smoke.

"What happened to the fire show when you first arrived here?" He mocked, "Don't tell me your skill ends with lighting campfires."

Out of anger and frustration, she dove over a table. "That's it! You and me—hands up!" She swung at him and he ducked, rolling over and tackling her legs.

Grayson and Ella wrestled on the ground, with Ella fiercely grasping Grayson's braid and pulling it harshly. He yelped, then changed their positions, pinning her beneath him. He released a bright blue flame aimed at her face, attempting to blind her.

She clawed at him, and he bit down on her shoulder—not enough to break the skin—but enough that she froze in place for a moment before she kicked him off her and stood.

"You really thought you could beat me?" Grayson taunted confidently. In response, Ella stepped back and hurled a massive fireball toward him. It connected forcefully, striking him squarely in the chest, giving Grayson no opportunity to react before the impact sent him flying backward.

"Take that, fire-breather!" Ella yelled triumphantly.

Grayson stood, giving her a menacing look before shifting his attention to the fire dragon above and then back to her again. As their eyes met, Ella's heart skipped a beat, causing her to stumble back nervously. Suddenly, the creature roared and dove at her, jaws open wide. Instinctively, she raised her arms and spread her wings for protection. Instead of searing heat, vibrant blue flames enveloped her. A look of disbelief passed over her face as the flames burned around her, and she laughed loudly—halfway of joy and mockery.

Grayson observed Ella's expression change from anger to excitement. He knew fire wouldn't hurt her. If he had wanted to actually hurt her, he would have used any other manner of spell—or claws and teeth. He felt awkward, as if witnessing something intimate, but couldn't tear his gaze away from her. She was in her own world.

When she turned to face him, flushed red with embarrassment, he knew the spell was broken and cleared his throat. She asked how long it had taken him to master such a skill, and he shrugged.

"I first did it at six winters old," he replied coolly.

Her eyes widened in shock. "How can someone who creates such beauty be so hateful and mean?" she asked. Her sudden question surprised him.

"Mind your business," he answered tersely.

She exhaled heavily and asked, "I guess that means training is over for today, right?" He eyed her carefully; her eyes were downcast, seemingly saddened by the end of their training. He raised an eyebrow, puzzled by her inconsistent behavior. One moment she tried to strangle him with his own braid, the next she begged for more practice. It appeared she couldn't decide how to feel about the situation. Neither could he.

"I suppose we could try one more time," he said cautiously. Her face lit up at his words, a wide smile spreading across her features. She nodded eagerly and quickly returned to the center of the training room. Grayson raised his hand, moving gracefully in a circular motion as if dancing, his footwork smooth. She followed suit with renewed passion, occasionally glancing at the swirling dragon. They repeated the motions in perfect unison a dozen more times, their bodies reflecting each other's movements seamlessly.

It was the final week of the month, and Ella was incessantly biting her nails down to the skin again.

She hadn't received a letter since Highwing and Nattya had sent her one. All around the school, students were packing for the weekend, readying themselves for family visits.

As people gathered in the meadow and along the bridge, Ella leaned against a window, scanning the ground below. Grothorn lazily flicked his hundred-eyed gaze around while standing guard at the forest's edge. With everyone passing through the wards, he was on high alert. Ella had anticipated this day for weeks and tried not to get her hopes up.

"Waiting for your parents?" Annabeth asked smirkingly. "You're practically jumping."

Ella hesitated. Had she ever insinuated she had a mother? Had she mentioned Hamlet's name? What was the story again? Would Hamlet even come? Did he know about this event?

"I hope my father isn't too busy," Ella responded tentatively.

"Do you want to come wait with me and meet my parents? They would love to meet you," Anna offered cheerfully.

Ella smiled and nodded, grateful for Anna's kindness and eager to meet her parents. The two girls walked together to a portal door and used it to reach the ground floor. They entered the Courtyard, where Grothorn's statue attracted significant attention.

"The parents are usually too afraid to get near the real Grothorn," Anna explained.

A table was set up at the entrance to the Courtyard, where Master Moore and Mistress Devoro counted attendees and recorded names as a line formed before them. Anna and Ella took their place in line.

When it was their turn, Master Moore motioned for Ella to step on his side of the line. She stared at him nervously, and he returned a stern glance.

"They're in the Highmaster's office," he stated dismissively.

Her eyes widened. "They?" she echoed. He rolled his eyes at her and waved her away.

Ella turned to Anna, who had been giving her parents' names. "I'm sorry, I have to go," Ella apologized quickly, running back to the door. Anna called after her, but Ella was closing the portal door behind her.

⟫⟫⟩——————▶

Hamlet and Nattya stood uneasily in the Highmaster's office. Sensing their anxiety, Gregor offered them tea. Hamlet declined, remembering their last encounter with tea. "Nice try, but I won't be duped again," he quipped. Nattya looked at him suspiciously, but he dismissed it, claiming tea upset his stomach. Gregor chuckled from his corner desk.

"Ella has made progress, although there have been hiccups," Gregor said with a hint of frustration. "It would've helped to know she couldn't read Arcadean and had a penchant for fire."

Hamlet blushed and assured him that the fire issue was under control, though Gregor remained skeptical.

"Where is she?" Nattya groaned. She had been anticipating this day since Hamlet invited her a week prior on the condition that she behaved herself. Highwing had been envious as Nattya prepared to see Ella, and he couldn't.

Hamlet had argued it was too dangerous for Highwing to go, adding another elf would cause too much attention. Nattya carried a satchel filled with gifts for Ella from Highwing.

The door slammed open, and Ella appeared, gasping for air. Nattya squealed and embraced her best friend. Ella buried her face in Nattya's neck, smelling of strongly of Highwing—of her bed, of Valla, of home. Nattya held her close, and Ella cried. Gregor looked at Hamlet with a glare of disappointment.

Ella released a shuddering breath. Both girls were clinging to each other. "I've missed you so much," she whispered. Gregor cleared his throat, and his eyes twinkled.

"Of course you did! Just look at this outfit—what the hell do they have you wearing?" Nattya scoffed. Ella noticed Nattya was wearing a floral dress with puffy sleeves and recognized it immediately.

"Raiding my things while I'm gone?" she teased.

"Always," Nattya retorted. Ella kissed Nattya on the cheek, running her nose along her jaw in greeting. Nattya reciprocated, pressing her nose against Ella's cheek.

When they finally pulled apart, she turned her attention to Hamlet and strode over, her face impassive, before slapping him on the arm repeatedly. "YOU FATHER-LESS-NO-GOOD-TRASH-RODENT—"

"Ow! C'mon, Ella!" Hamlet yelped under her onslaught.

"You just left me here with no way to communicate with you! The veil wasn't going to let my letters through! I didn't even know if you were going to show up!"

"Perhaps, it would be best if you did your continuous screaming with the door closed," Grayson suggested from behind them. Ella promptly ceased her attack on Hamlet and swept her hair away from her face.

Nattya stared in awe at Grayson, then at Ella. "Why on earth would you complain when you have the pleasure of gazing upon *that* all day?" Nattya whispered to Ella.

Grayson chose not to acknowledge the remark, but Ella knew he'd heard it. He extended his hand to Nattya and engaged in swift introductions.

"Master Moore," Hamlet acknowledged. "Gregor shared some tales about Ella's studies under your guidance."

"Hm," Grayson muttered. "She has ample opportunities for growth. It's a pity no one thought to assist her in refining her talents earlier."

"I mentioned to Hamlet that—" Gregor interjected.

"So, Gregor, you informed him of the runes?" Grayson interrupted him.

Gregor crinkled his nose and shook his head vigorously.

"What runes? What are you referring to, Gregor?" Hamlet implored.

Gregor sighed, "On the first day, Ella accidentally set Master Moore's hand on fire, and it was clear that enchantment spells and potions couldn't maintain her ordinary appearance."

"You didn't really," Hamlet gasped.

Ella removed her shoe and sock, wiggled her toes, and revealed her heel. "It hurt quite a bit. Now, it allows me to control my appearance at will and prevents me from using magic beyond my abilities."

"I cannot wait to share this story with Highwing," Nattya snickered.

Anger boiled within Hamlet. "You cannot simply etch runes onto a child!"

"I'm not a child! I'm grown! Besides, you were barely older than I am when you got yours—"

"Who told you that?" Hamlet's piercing gaze fell on Nattya, who raised her hands defensively.

"I said nothing," she insisted.

Hamlet's fiery glare turned to Gregor. "You shouldn't have mentioned it. And you shouldn't have inscribed runes on her."

"I don't see the big deal. It's like a magical tattoo–" Ella was silenced by Hamlet's finger wagging in her face.

"A mere tattoo would've been better! Runes cause pain. You'll need more to reverse their effects," he argued.

"I find them intriguing. Maybe I'll get more," Ella countered, arms crossed.

"If I knew I'd walk into a father-daughter dispute, I'd have stayed outside," Grayson remarked. "Do you bring news from Hellharth?"

Suddenly, the atmosphere grew tense, and everyone went on high alert. Nattya and Hamlet shared uneasy glances that didn't go unnoticed by Ella.

"What happened?" She frowned.

"She did *WHAT*?" Ella's voice pierced the air, anger and disbelief surging through every syllable. Hamlet and Nattya recoiled, the fury of her words hitting them like a wave. Grayson remained unflinching, his stoic visage unwavering. Meanwhile, Gregor reached for another drink, seeking solace in the glass.

"I attempted to dissuade her from doing it," Hamlet interjected, his voice laced with frustration. "But lately, she has not been receptive to my counsel."

"She's disowned me!" thundered Ella, her voice vibrating with pain and rage. "Never meeting her lofty expectations, so she sends me away in exile while snatching away my crown!"

"Highwing still wants to marry you if that offers any comfort," Nattya offered weakly.

"Dasyra must be keening in delight right now!" Ella fumed. "I ought to have torn her wings to shreds!" Flames danced between her fingers as resentment heated every nerve in her body.

"Many things have been occurring behind closed doors that even I'm oblivious to," Hamlet said cautiously. "Your mother's thoughts are an enigma."

"That's how it feels to be left in the dark," Ella retorted smugly. Her gaze shifted over his and for a moment, she wanted to dive right into his mind and not give a damn about his *feelings* about it.

"Perhaps your mother is attempting to shield you from potential harm," Gregor slurred drunkenly. "When Hellharth emerges permanently, who would concern themselves with a banished princess?"

Nattya stared at him, incredulous, and pointed with her thumb. "This intoxicated man is the Highmaster of your school?" she asked with a raised brow.

"It's my day off!" Gregor defended himself adamantly. "In addition to your ceaseless chatter occupying my space and consuming my thoughts—my existence–" He paused for a moment, furiously rubbing his face. "Waiting is our only option now—there must be a reason behind your mother's actions. In the meantime, you three are free to leave the grounds and explore, if you will."

"We can't stay," Hamlet said. He turned and walked away.

"What?" the girls said simultaneously.

"The veil is unpredictable. Anything can happen at any moment," Hamlet replied.

"But you only just got here!" Ella protested. "It's a visiting weekend..." she added lamely. She knew she sounded like a spoiled child.

"Might I suggest all three of you stay in Ella's room for a bit? I could have supper sent to her room," Grayson suggested. Gregor was surprised at his kind gesture. He was ashamed to say that he had not thought of it.

"Please!" Ella begged Hamlet. "Just stay for supper."

Seeing both Ella and Nattya start their wide-eyed stares, Hamlet conceded. "Just for supper."

The evening stretched on as Nattya insisted on taking a bath in Ella's stone tub and trying on her uniforms. Meanwhile, Ella sifted through the satchel of gifts Nattya had brought, and Hamlet fumed in a corner.

"It would have been lovely to have Valla here too," Ella commented wistfully.

Hamlet rolled his eyes with a huff. "I had enough trouble stopping your winged creature from joining us. Besides, that cat is nothing but trouble." He fidgeted with his lapels, a hand searching his pocket.

"She most certainly is not!" Nattya interjected defensively from her spot at the vanity. "She's just... choosy." She returned to braiding her hair.

Hamlet held out a small box to Ella, barely the size of a coin.

"What is it?" she asked.

He smirked at her, cocked his head, and said, "You didn't really think I would leave her behind, did you?"

The box inflated in his palm, and he tossed it onto her bed. It grew and shook violently, angry yowls and hissing coming from the box.

"You just left her in there this whole time!" Ella screeched, pulling the lid off to reveal a very disgruntled Pentarian cat. "Valla!" she cried, picking up the large feline and hauling her to her chest. She buried her face in Valla's fur, which had turned a vibrant shade of red, large ears flat against her head in agitation.

"Be grateful I brought that thing," Hamlet said with a sniff. He scratched at his eyes as his allergies started acting up. Nattya was grinning from the vanity.

Valla made it perfectly clear she had no interest in being held. "I'm sorry. You can't go wandering the halls here. Someone will see you, and I don't know the policies about pets," Ella said. Valla answered her with a low growl and bristled fur. Valla squirmed out of her grasp and began exploring the room, sniffing and hissing at everything.

"Mongrel," Hamlet scoffed.

⇉⟶

"Why didn't my mother come?" Ella asked, trying her best to avoid Hamlet's gaze. She perused Highwing's letter, which had arrived with Nattya, for what felt like the tenth time. "She could have changed her appearance." Valla had made herself at home, stealing a pillow from the bed and making herself comfortable in a corner.

"Considering the current chaos, I assume her absence would leave Hellharth vulnerable," Hamlet deduced.

"Or perhaps she simply can't face me after disowning me," Ella uttered bitterly. "Coward. Am I really surprised though? She has deceived me my entire life. She should have given me away as an infant." For once, Hamlet offered no retort. Eventually, Ella swallowed hard and turned to him. "I need you to do something for me."

Hamlet sighed deeply, visibly frustrated. "Why are the women in this family so demanding? What do you need now?"

"I require your help in crafting a small stone suitable for embedding in a piece of jewelry." She averted his gaze.

Hamlet scrunched up his nose in confusion. "A stone for jewelry? What could you possibly... Oh. I see." He glanced at Nattya with sudden understanding, pointing at her as Ella nodded. He raised an eyebrow and smirked.

"Alright, here's what you need to do." Hamlet closed his eyes and clenched his fist before presenting it to her. "Place your hand over mine and envision the stone you desire. Imagine that it is strong, unbreakable."

"I've visualized it," she confirmed. Hamlet cautiously opened his hand to reveal a shimmering blue sphere nestled within it. She carefully picked it up with trembling hands.

"Now picture your magic flowing out of you. Put it into the stone," he instructed.

Ella's fingers tingled at first, then her hands, then they swirled with light and vanished into the stone. There was a small white tornado that swirled inside before settling. "How exactly did my mother give you her stone?"

Laughing, Hamlet replied, "She threw it straight at my head and ordered me around. Hurt actually."

Overwhelmed with anxiety, Ella called out hesitantly, "Nattya, please come over here." She felt more confident propositioning Highwing than she did requesting Nattya's lifelong companionship—especially against the backdrop of a war on the horizon.

Nattya flung herself haphazardly onto the bed, making them both bounce slightly. "What's up?" she asked curiously. Ella held out her hand, exposing the small blue stone resting on her palm. Nattya's breath caught in her throat as realization hit her. "Is this... does this mean...?"

With a straight face, Ella said, "If you say no, I'll just throw it at your head."

Nattya laughed a full-body laugh. Laughed until tears gathered in the corners of her eyes. "Of course. Gods! Is this what it feels like to be proposed to?" She took the stone from Ella tentatively, and the splash of freckles on her cheeks lit up. "Wow," Nattya squealed and threw her arms around them. "I know exactly how I want it set!" She placed it lovingly into her satchel, not taking her eyes off it.

Just then, a knock echoed through the room, and Nattya leaped from the bed. Valla flashed red and made a chattering noise with her teeth.

"Ella? Are you in there?" Annabeth's voice floated through the door.

Ella sighed with relief. "She's a friend of mine. Completely harmless." As she opened the door, Annabeth and Ethan practically tumbled in. Valla quickly blended in with the background of the green and pink petaled wall, slinking under the bed.

"You just vanished out of nowhere and I was so worried–" Anna suddenly halted mid-sentence, and Ethan collided with her back. "Oh! I didn't realize you had visitors."

As Ethan caught sight of Nattya, his grin widened. "Well, hello there," he greeted smoothly, and Ella cringed inwardly.

"You can't just hit on her mom," Annabeth said, slapping the back of Ethan's head.

Nattya looked affronted. "I'm not her mother—"

"She's my sister. Na—Nan..." Ella offered. Hamlet ran a hand down his face in exasperation.

"Na-Nan..." Annabeth said. "It's nice to meet you. I'm Anna. This pervert here is Ethan." Ethan squinted his gold eyes at her.

Hamlet cleared his throat with a loud, exaggerated noise, causing Anna to jump in surprise.

"Goodness, I didn't see you there! You must be her... brother?"

"Father," Ella said, her voice trembling with a mix of amusement and embarrassment. She felt her cheeks burning.

"Mister Marks! Oh, Ethan, we're totally interrupting something here," Annabeth said, her eyes widening with realization.

"No, no, not at all," Hamlet reassured them with an easy smile. "We were actually just getting ready to leave."

"But do you really have to go?" Ella asked earnestly, her gaze shifting nervously between Nattya and Hamlet, disappointment evident on her face. "Nattya, you would love Anna and Ethan—"

"Especially me," Ethan said, not-so-subtly. His yellow eyes flashed and he gave Nattya a toothy grin, flashing fangs at her. Ella always wondered just what kind of halfling he was, but never asked.

Nattya cocked her head at him, looking from his feet up with a creeping smile. Ella, knowing that look, knew that Nattya saw him as a toy—something to play with.

"I'm sure I would," she said with her tongue in her cheek. Ethan's eyes fluttered, and he looked dazed. Ella almost laughed at his expression. She looked at Hamlet, who was not amused.

"In front of me, boy?" Hamlet scoffed. "Really. No respect."

"Sorry," Ethan spluttered.

"I'm sure we will see each other again, and we will have more time," Nattya said reassuringly.

When Anna and Ethan gave their goodbyes and left, Hamlet tried to usher Valla into the box but couldn't find her.

A glimmer of the cat appeared in the corner of Ella's eye, and she shrugged. "She probably snuck out when Anna and Ethan came in."

"We can't leave that beast—" Hamlet started.

"We should. Didn't you say we were in a rush?" Nattya hummed. She flashed Ella a knowing smile.

After a ten-minute debate about whether or not leaving Valla behind was a good idea, Hamlet finally gave in begrudgingly. "Your cat, your problem," he snapped.

As Ella watched them leave, her heart was heavy, wondering if this was the last time. She felt Valla brush against her legs and let out a sigh of relief.

Chapter Twenty-One

"Focus, ground yourself!" Grayson demanded firmly.

"I'm trying my best!" Ella retorted, her voice strained with frustration. Her brow creased and her fingers shook as she furiously tried to concentrate on the spell.

"You need to put in more effort!" Grayson insisted.

"Your yelling isn't exactly helping, you know!" Ella snapped back.

"Well, maybe if someone had pushed you harder before, you'd have mastered this by now!" Grayson shot back, his tone sharp.

Feeling defeated, Ella dropped her arms to her sides. "I can't do it."

Grayson scoffed and crossed his arms. "I should've known you'd give up."

"What's that supposed to mean? I've been at this for two hours straight! It's not like creating a sentient being out of fire is easy," she argued.

"You're supposed to be training. That rune on your foot will only stop what you can't control. Be in control of your magic."

"I am in control—"

"Doesn't seem like it. Seems to me your mother knew that too."

She whirled on him. "What did you just say?" she demanded, her temper flaring.

"I said—"

In a split second, he found himself flat on his back, skidding across the sleek tiles and through the room. Panting, he leaped to his feet and glared icily at her. "Struck a chord, have I? Can't handle talking about dear ol' mum?" he taunted. Ella's eyes flashed with anger and her cheeks burned with embarrassment. She felt an undeniable surge beneath her skin as though a tempest was churning inside her. It was as if her veins writhed restlessly below the surface. An intense heat burned within her eyes, and she exhaled heavily, tendrils of magical energy lacing the surrounding air.

⟫⟫——————▸

Grayson observed intently as Ella's entire disposition transformed before him. Her eyes blazed with a dangerous glint before abruptly settling into a frigid gaze. Veins crept beneath her skin, taking on a darker hue. She slowly raised her hands, seemingly against her own will, while her lips curled into a snarl.

"Miss Marks," Grayson cautioned urgently as Ella's Elven features snapped back into place, the stripes on her hands radiating sinister energy.

"Snap out of it!" Grayson shouted, desperation creeping into his voice. The surrounding air crackled with magical energy as tendrils of smoke slithered from Ella's fingertips, steadily encroaching upon him.

"Stop it!" Grayson shouted. The shadows enveloped the room, suffocating and blinding. He lost all senses. It was as if he had died. His mouth opened to scream, but his chest wouldn't fill with air.

Suddenly, he was surrounded by fire, the wooden floorboards beneath him were hot and crackling. But there shouldn't have been wooden floors. It should have been the black tiles of the training room. Grayson heaved himself off the ground, the screams of people around him growing louder.

Trapped within the crumbling remnants of a building, he was surrounded by a suffocating inferno consuming the caved-in ceiling above. Scorched rugs lay strewn across the floor, and in the corner, an undersized bed barely fit for a child clinging to existence. The walls were adorned with similar paintings of dragons and a mysterious woman, their eyes seeming to follow his every move. A solitary music box played a hauntingly soft melody, eerily contrasting with the surrounding pandemonium.

Desperation clawed at his throat as he screamed for help, each call shredding his vocal cords. Suddenly, a low creaking emanated from the splintered floorboards behind him. Fear gripped his heart as a monstrous figure emerged from the shadows of the ruined bedroom. Deathly pale skin stretched over a grotesquely misshapen spine and unnaturally elongated arms. The creature was devoid of any clothing, its malformed genitals exposed to view, its gaze seeming to go through him.

But the true terror lay within its maw — row upon row of jagged black fangs nestled in gore-stained pink gums. This nightmare before him could be nothing else but a Dark One.

Grayson took a defensive stance, blue flames swirling to life in his palms and bursting forth, creating a protective ring around him.

The Dark One didn't notice at all. Its focus was solely on something under the bed.

No, Grayson thought. *No. NO!*

In the farthest recesses of his mind, a memory stirred—a place shrouded in the darkness where his most damning thoughts churned beneath a deceivingly serene facade. He was painfully aware of what lay beneath the bed, what the Dark One was approaching with malicious hunger.

"Stay away from him!" bellowed a sturdy voice just beyond the bedroom's entrance. The Dark One crumpled onto its gnarled knees within seconds, a sharp blade embedded in its temple. It screeched and scraped at its injury, black eyes wide and frantic as it tumbled backward.

A figure appeared before Grayson, who gripped his head tightly in disbelief. "This can't be real! It isn't real!" he muttered.

The man who stood before him bore an uncanny similarity to Grayson himself, save for the fierce tattoos adorning half of his face in jagged streaks. With gentler blue eyes and a more prominent nose, there was no mistaking his identity.

It was his father.

As his father lowered himself to the floorboards and embers rained down from the sky above, Grayson reached out wildly, desperate for any chance to save him—to preserve a fragment of his past he could hold close.

Something tangible.

Alfreid Moore gently extracted young Grayson from under the bed and enveloped the sobbing toddler in a comforting embrace.

"I'm here. Don't fret, little man. I'm right here."

He didn't notice the two Elves that had crept up behind him. He didn't notice when they slipped out their cursed daggers and raised them above their heads.

But Grayson had. The child version and the adult version made similar sounds of profound horror and Alfreid shoved his little body away. The Elves were on him in an instant. He conjured a sword, swinging wildly and hitting one in the chest. The other was too quick, bringing the knife repeatedly into his stomach and twisting.

Small little Grayson wailed, and the Elf turned to him, blood splattered across his face.

"Gray...son... run," Alfreid pleaded, his head lolled to the side, and he let out a final whispering breath.

"Papa! Papa!" Little Grayson sobbed. The older Grayson crumpled to the ground, clutching his nose as vivid sensations erupted within him: the sharp sting of a blade slicing through his cheek and across his nose bridge; the warmth of gushing blood; and the scorching scream that left his throat raw.

He felt it all over again.

"I'm here! I'm here!" Ella's voice pierced through his own agonized cries, and he felt her hands yank him back from the edge of darkness.

Eyes wide open, he found himself staring at the stark white ceiling of the training room. Ella's concerned face hovered above him as the pain disappeared, along with the putrid scent of burning and muffled death cries.

"What in blazes did you do to me?" he demanded hoarsely.

She stared at him in horror. "I—I didn't expect that at all! One moment you were upright, then—Gods!" She shook her head, tears falling down her face. Grayson felt his face. He was whole, his scar long healed.

His heart pounded with fear as he made a chilling realization. "You invaded my mind, dragged me into a realm of shadows. A waking nightmare."

He shoved her back, scurrying to his feet. He hated her. He hated her with every fiber of his being. If he could have killed her, he would have. Would have run his claws through her rib cage.

"I don't know what you're talking about," Ella insisted. She had to be lying. He felt like he was losing his mind.

"You malevolent little wretch," he seethed. She flinched at his words and took a step back.

"I don't know what you're talking about! I didn't do it on purpose!" She had been glowering at his words about her mother being disappointed, and then suddenly felt like she had been underwater. When she finally broke the surface, Grayson's eyes were rolled in the back of his head and he was screaming.

He brought his arm up, an invisible force pummeling Ella and smacking her against the wall. She felt the breath get knocked out of her lungs and her head slam against the wall.

"We are done here," he said coolly, his face taking on that impassive mask as he looked at her crumpled form.

She moaned, eyes pricking with tears. Getting to her feet, she had a mounted boar's head fly across the room and knock him off his feet.

He picked up a spear from the weapons rack—something polished and unused. With a swift movement, it was soaring through the air, the point whizzing by Ella's face and piercing the floor.

"You missed!" She mocked, facing away from him for just a second. She heard the pounding of footsteps and then her back hit the tile.

He pinned both her arms above her head, legs on either side of her waist to hold her in place. He was panting hard, green eyes cold and furious.

"Filthy elf," he hissed.

"Ugly halfling," she shot back.

There was a heavy silence that fell over them, and Ella became aware of his weight on her. "Get off of me," she glowered.

He rolled away from her, picking off the debris and smacking away dust from his person. "We are done with training. For good." Gregor could teach her himself if he wanted.

"Good! Do me a favor. I won't speak to you, and you don't speak to me!"

"You wouldn't believe what I witnessed! It felt like something possessed her," Grayson exclaimed, taking a sip of his wine. He had been trying to stress the danger that Ella posed to everyone around her.

Gregor absentmindedly twirled a golden lock of his hair and hummed, "Seems like she's brimming with hidden secrets."

"How can you be so casual about this, you cow! It was a horrifying experience. She invaded my mind, forcing me to relive my worst memory. What if her lineage from —"

"Idmodias was merely a mortal before becoming anything else. Maybe placing the runes on her wasn't the brightest idea, as Hamlet had warned. Should I arrange a meeting with him?"

"What's the point? He failed to inform us about her pyromancy. There's no telling what else they're concealing," Grayson retorted. "What if she does that to a student? The rune was supposed to dull down her magic to keep her in control—but it was—I can't explain it."

"Do you recall when you accidentally demolished the house? You were only fourteen and furious at me," Gregor reminisced. "You discovered your potential only when anger consumed you. I can't help but think you subconsciously provoked Ellarhyssa to see the extent of her abilities."

"That's absurd! She and I bear no resemblance!" Grayson protested.

Gregor raised an eyebrow, violet eyes sparkling mischievously. "Are you certain?"

"Get fucked," Grayson snapped.

CHAPTER TWENTY-TWO

Grayson was enjoying his book, carefully flipping through the pages. He sighed, looking at the cover. A fairy tale about a girl and a dragon. If anyone knew he had a love for fairy tales, they would be shocked. He placed the book on the table next to him and stood up. His clothes were starting to feel tight. He stretched his arms out, trying to get rid of the stiffness. He glanced at the clock on the wall. It was half-past three in the morning.

Stripping his clothes off, he tossed them on the floor. He pulled on a pair of shorts and a cotton shirt, shrugging his arms into the sleeves. Yawning, he headed for the archway leading to his bedroom.

His windows were dressed in heavy, floor-length curtains made of deep green, velvety fabric lined with golden thread. The walls are painted in a soft, earthy green hue, and adorned with forest-themed wallpaper featuring intricately designed trees, leaves, and woodland creatures that came alive with the touch of a finger.

A grand, custom-made bed crafted from rustic, reclaimed wood, resembling a cozy tree house was nestled in the middle of the room. The bed frame was carved with branches and leaves and draped with a gold comforter. Overhead, a dreamy canopy made of sheer, flowing fabric cascaded from the ceiling, like a willow tree.

He hated his room.

Every time he had tried to decorate it, the enchantments would go haywire and the room would become a mess. Gregor's doing.

He climbed into bed, pulling the covers up to his chin. He stared up at the ceiling; the moonlight casting a hazy glow through the sheer canopy. His eyes began to close...

Something fuzzy and warm brushed against his leg. He jolted upright, letting out a loud, startled yell, falling to the floor. Pulling the covers back, a large cat with gleaming green eyes stared at him, her tail lashing back and forth.

"The hell are you doing in here?" he asked, scowling. She meowed in response, her eyes narrowing. She was a beautiful cat, with soft pale fur and oversized ears, like a bat. "Which one of those heathens do you belong to?" he growled. She meowed again, stretching her full length across his pillows and making herself comfortable. He pointed to the ground.

"Down," he ordered, glaring at her. She slowly dropped her head and curled up in a ball, her ears flattened against her head. "You're joking with me. Get out of my bed this instant!" he yelled, but she didn't move. She stared at him with those piercing green eyes. Glancing at the clock, he groaned. In a couple of hours, he would have to get up and get ready for classes.

"Move over," he grumbled, pulling the covers back and crawling into bed. He would worry about the cat later. From behind him, she purred loudly.

>>>————➤

"Valla," Ella whispered harshly. Class was about to start and she couldn't find the damned cat anywhere. "Come here, you lousy brat!" she hissed, slapping her hand on a table. If someone else spotted Valla, she was sure to get in trouble—or worse—they would probably send Valla away.

"Please, Valla!" Ella pleaded, hearing the first chime of the morning bells. Her eyes flickered toward the door, watching as Valla walked right through it with a shimmer of magic. "Where did you go!" Ella yelled, stomping over to the door and picking the cat up. She carried Valla to the bathroom, muttering about her as she went. "If they catch you here, it's over," she scolded. "Stay out of sight."

Valla meowed loudly. Ella sniffed her, burying her face in the fur, and her eyes widened in surprise. "You smell like—"

Banging on the door made her jump. Master Moore's voice floated through her room. "GET OUT!"

Valla meowed again and her ears perked up at the noise.

"You literally could not have picked the worst person to run into," Ella groaned. "Master Moore will kill you if you aren't careful. Stay here," she instructed, waving a finger at Valla.

>>>————➤

"There's a cat roaming Morning Song," Grayson said to Gregor during dinner. He had been staring intently at the sea of students, eyeing them down. "I'm not sure who it belongs to."

"A cat? Strange. Where is it?" Gregor asked between a bite of chicken. Grayson shrugged, taking a sip of his water. "It was gone when I got up this morning. It was in my room. Can't figure out how it got in."

He had gone over his door guardian's sight and didn't see any trace of the cat coming in or out of anyone's rooms. "It belongs to one of these heathens," Grayson said, gesturing toward the students.

"Perhaps you dreamed it," Gregor suggested. Grayson rolled his eyes.

After a while, his eyes narrowed as he noticed a girl walking down the table aisles. She was merrily laughing with her friends. He watched her closely, waiting for her to look at him. She didn't.

A cold flush of magic encased his body, telling him that Gregor cast a spell over them. The voices drowned away, and he realized it was a silencing charm so no one could hear them talking.

"Training going alright with Miss Marks?" Gregor asked him, noticing Grayson glaring at her with disdain.

"You already know the answer to that, old man," Grayson replied. "Keep the little chit away from me."

"I've never known you to shy away from a challenge, Grayson. Why are you so afraid of this one?" Gregor asked, putting down his fork.

"I'm not afraid of her," Grayson answered, his tone cold and gruff. Gregor raised an eyebrow.

"Don't let your pride get the best of you. We need to train her. She has a lot of potential." Gregor said.

"When you say we—you mean *me*," Grayson said, pointing at his chest. "If you desire to train her so much, then *you* do it."

"Grayson, if I had the ounce of pyromancy capabilities that you have, I would do it myself. I don't. You can handle her." His tone took on an icy edge.

"Maybe if you sat in on our training sessions, you would understand why I simply don't want to!" Grayson spat, slamming his chair back and stomping out of the Grand Hall. The cold flush of the spell left him and he straightened his lapels, walking past whispering students and by Miss Marks. He was not going to let her ruin his day.

As Grayson settled into his favorite armchair, he immersed himself in the pages of another captivating novel. The soft glow of a reading lamp cast a warm light on the pages. He huffed on his smoking stick, letting the herbs burn and releasing a plume of smoke.

Just as he began to lose himself in the tale, he felt a gentle nudge against his leg. Looking down, he discovered a visitor—the sleek and curious cat with bright, inquisitive eyes. The cat approached him with graceful strides, its tail swaying gently from side to side.

His attention shifted momentarily from his book to his unexpected guest. He placed a bookmark between the pages and leaned forward, extending his hand to offer a gentle caress. The cat responded with a satisfied purr, pressing her head against his palm repeatedly.

"Back again?" he asked, stroking the cat gently. She meowed in response, then took the liberty to explore the surroundings, gracefully maneuvering through the stacks of books and perching on a nearby bookshelf. Her amber eyes glistened with intrigue as they watched him.

"You knock anything off there, and I'll skin you," he warned before he resumed his book.

Every so often, the cat would venture closer, carefully inspecting the book cover or playfully batting at the dangling bookmark. He caught himself reading a passage aloud, sharing the words, and the cat would respond with a flick of its tail or an affectionate nuzzle. Eventually, Grayson allowed the cat to sit on his lap, her large frame taking up most of the space.

As the evening waned and he reached the end of his chapter, he closed the book with a contented sigh. The cat, sensing the conclusion, gracefully leaped down from his lap and padded over to the wall, giving him a long, lingering look before walking straight through the wall.

"So that's how you got in here," he said to himself.

He awoke hours later, disoriented and confused. He smelled something faint—something familiar. Of forests and rain and—

His eyes snapped open, and he jerked away from the cat who had snuggled into his side. He blinked, trying to focus his eyes.

"You're her cat," he whispered to himself. "Of course. You would be. Go back to your mistress," he added, gently pushing the cat away. The cat hissed and turned away, her tail swishing through the air as she settled back against his pillow.

"Fine. Do what you want. Everyone else already does," he mumbled as he rolled over and closed his eyes.

"Valla! You witch! Where the hell are you?" Ella whispered down the hall. It was late, well past curfew. The halls were dark, quiet, and empty. The only light came from the moon filtering through the windows, illuminating the dust particles in the air.

"I told you to stay in the room!" Ella whined.

Gods, what if Moore killed her? She thought anxiously.

Suddenly, a meow came from her right. She spun around, her heart in her throat. Moore was standing in his doorway down the hall, a lit candle in his hand. Valla was at his feet, rubbing herself against his legs, purring loudly. Ella glanced at her, then looked back at Moore. He didn't notice her, and she slowly sank into the shadows, her back pressed to the wall.

"I don't know what you want, cat. You keep pawing at me when you can just walk out the door," Moore's voice drifted through the air. He was talking to Valla with surprising gentleness, his tone soft and calm. Valla's tail vibrated, and she flashed a shade of gold.

She wants to go hunting, Ella mused to herself. Moore wouldn't know that she was asking for company. Valla could go hunting alone, but she wanted to go with him—not her. Ella felt a pang of jealousy. "Traitor," she whispered. Valla's ear twitched, and she looked down the hall where Ella stood, hiding.

"Go back to your mistress," he said with a yawn, his voice deep and sleepy. He motioned with his hand at Ella's door, and her heart sank. He knew the cat was hers.

"Get," he said, motioning with his hand again. Valla meowed and walked through Ella's door, disappearing. Ella felt a hot flush of embarrassment and waited for Moore to close his door before she crept out. She walked down the hall, her feet silent on the cold, hard floor. She reached her door and opened it, finding Valla curled up in the corner, as if she had been waiting for her.

Ella placed her hands on her hips and scowled. "You've made a friend out of the worst possible person," she hissed. Valla purred, rolling onto her back and exposing her spotted belly.

⤷⟶

Grayson watched through the stone dragon's eyes as Ella silently crept down the hall and retreated to her room. She had no idea he knew she was there the whole time. He wanted her to know that he knew—he knew whose cat it was.

He would let her sit on this without confronting her—make her sweat it out.

CHAPTER TWENTY-THREE

Anna, Ethan, Ella, and Sienna huddled together, their laughter and hushed voices echoing off the stone walls. It was the last night of the weekend, so they were all free to enjoy the break. Anna had shown Ella a small alcove, hidden behind a tapestry that hung from the wall on the third floor. It was a small area that Ethan had spelled to include a small wooden table, a few chairs, and a creme-colored, plush carpet. Potted plants hung from decorated ropes on the ceiling, and candles floated delicately by, casting dancing shadows in the small room. An enchanted fiddle played in one corner, plucking on its strings softly.

"No one comes here. Everyone is out enjoying themselves in Hildfree or Calisan," Anna said, taking a spot on the floor.

Sienna had invited them to hang out—which to Ella, was a bit out of character. Anna had nudged her and said that Sienna was secretly lonely. Despite Sienna's knack for attention, and making friends, she didn't seem bonded to any group or person.

"Her mother doesn't want her going through the ocean. She's essentially stuck here, " Anna had whispered. Ella knew what that was like, and reluctantly had accepted the invitation.

Unbeknownst to them, their evening was about to take an unexpected turn.

As the group passed around a bottle of wine—a gracious gift from Sienna, they were becoming increasingly loud and rowdy. Sienna had taken to dancing with Ethan, and as he spun her around, she pulled him closer to her and kissed him. Ella smiled at the two, then turned to Anna.

"They seem to be having a good time," she said to Anna. Anna had an odd look on her face as she stared at the two. She shook her head and looked away.

"You alright?" Ella asked.

"I'm fine," Anna replied, but her voice was flat and emotionless. It dawned on Ella that perhaps Anna was feeling more than just a little jealous.

Ella's head was swimming, her vision blurred as she leaned in close and whispered in Anna's ear. "You like Ethan?"

Anna's pink eyes widened, and she let out a laugh. "No. I—" she began. A sudden creaking sound echoed through the alcove. The tapestry swung open, revealing Master Moore standing there, his expression cold. The room fell into an abrupt silence, broken only by the sound of the bottle dropping to the floor, its contents spilling onto the carpet.

Moore's eyes scanned the room, taking in the sight of the startled seniors frozen in their places, guilt etched across their faces. He cleared his throat, his voice a blend of ice and steel.

"What do you think you are doing?" he asked. "Is this what you think is appropriate behavior? You know *unsupervised* drinking is prohibited on school grounds."

"We were just talking, sir," Sienna slurred. Moore narrowed his eyes and turned to Anna. She flinched.

They fumbled for words, their voices barely audible as they tried to come up with an explanation. They knew they had been caught red-handed.

Ella was staring resolutely at a spot on his pant leg. A hair shined against the black fabric.

Valla's fur.

"You will have plenty of time to drink and be merry during the winter formal. Under the watchful eyes of the staff." He said. "And if you don't want to be watched—don't do it here. I expected better from all of you," he said firmly. "You should have gone to Calisan. This isn't a tavern." He eyed Sienna and Ethan, who were standing together, their faces red.

The room was filled with an uncomfortable silence, broken only by the sound of Master Moore's footsteps as he approached them. He knelt down, picked up the fallen bottle, and set it aside on the table. Then, he turned his attention back to them, his gaze unwavering.

"You are all of age, but there are rules that must be obeyed," he said. Ella winced when his eyes met hers. "Drinking can make one lose... *control* if they are not careful." She understood his hidden warning.

Sienna hiccuped.

"Wouldn't want any accidents," he continued, with a sneer. "Unfortunately for me, I cannot give out punishment on *free* days."

They let out a sigh of relief—too quickly. The bells chimed, signaling midnight. Moore smiled at them.

"Looks like it's the start of a new day. You will be spending the morning cleaning cauldrons and helping Elysium sweep up Grothorn's shit. He's left quite the pile on the lawn." A flash of parchment and a glass pen appeared in front of him, writing furiously in red ink. The group stood frozen in their places, staring at the parchment.

With those final words, Master Moore snatched the bottle off the table, turned, and walked out of the alcove, leaving them stunned and drunk.

"He's such a miserable cow," Ethan muttered. Ella nodded her head in agreement, her lips pressed together in a thin line.

»»»———————➤

"Where did you get this?" Gregor asked with a raised brow, examining the bottle.

"Sienna Whitefish, Ethan Isles, Annabeth Dox, and Ella Marks," Grayson listed off. He paused for a moment, eyes watching as light orbs drifted overhead in the office. Gregor's desk was a mess of papers, books, and spilled ink. He sighed, waving a hand and clearing the mess off the desk. The books neatly stacked themselves on the shelf, and the papers were sorted into piles on the desk. The ink formed a ball and dripped itself back into the inkwell.

"Oh? Are they alright?" Gregor asked, taking the stopper off of the bottle and sniffing it.

"They'll be fine. I assigned them to clean cauldrons and sweep up the mess that Grothorn made in the morning."

"Why did you do that?" Gregor asked with a frown. He took a tentative swig of the wine, before pouring himself a glass. "It's a free day."

"Do you not care for your own rules? They were drinking, unsupervised on school grounds."

"Nothing nefarious, Grayson. They are just a few young adults, who made a mistake. I do not see the harm in it." He took another sip of the wine. "It seems you were more out to punish them than anything. How did you know they were doing this?"

Grayson pursed his lips together and looked at the bottle, his eyes narrowing. "I may have followed them, but that is beside the point—"

"So, you followed them, waited for them to get drunk, and then, as you said, punished them for it," Gregor finished for him. Gregor sighed. Grayson never was one for parties, or breaking the rules. Dracaeneans were known for being harsh—the second most hated kind of Fae. Childhood was not kind to Grayson.

Nor were humans.

"What are you getting at?" Grayson snapped, grabbing the glass away from Gregor's grasp. "I did my job!"

Gregor eyed Grayson for a moment, his thin fingers coming up to his lips in thought. "This is more about you punishing Marks."

"She broke the rules—she gets punished. That's how things work around here." Grayson said, his hands tightening into fists.

"What has the girl ever done to you, that you haven't instigated yourself?" Gregor asked with a tilt of his head.

Grayson got up from his seat and went to the door. He opened it and turned around, his hands balled into his fists. "She isn't above anyone else!" he said with a snarl.

"I seem to recall an entire country of people shouting the same thing about you when you were released from prison," Gregor said with a slight smile.

Grayson blanched, his face turning red before he turned and stormed out of the room. Gregor laughed.

In a quiet corner of the school grounds, Ella, Ethan, Sienna, and Anna stood together, their faces reflecting a mixture of embarrassment, annoyance, and resignation.

"This is bullshit," Ethan said with a shake of his head. He had a hand to his head, obviously fighting a hangover. Sienna was rubbing her eyes with her thumb and forefinger.

Ella felt nauseous.

"No. This is Grothorn's shit. Here's a shovel," Elysium said, handing one to each of them. They reluctantly grabbed their shovels and gloves, the pungent scent of the task ahead already hanging heavy in the air. They eyed the piles of manure scattered across the field, wondering how they had ended up in this predicament.

"Moore is a tyrant!" Annabeth seethed. She was fighting back tears of frustration. Her hair was pulled back in a tight ponytail and she discarded her outer robes onto the grass.

"Remind me never to hang out with you three again, " Sienna grumbled. Her opalescent skin was shining under the rising light.

"Don't act like this is our fault! Little Miss come-get-drunk-and-dance-with-me, " Anna snapped back uncharacteristically.

As they approached the first pile, a collective sigh escaped their lips, and they gingerly began their work. With every scoop and shovel of manure, they couldn't help but exchange occasional glances, sharing a mix of frustration and disbelief at their current situation.

"What the hell have you been feeding him!" Ella cried out indignantly after the tenth pile.

Ethan leaned over her shoulder, nose scrunched up. "Is that corn?"

Ella gagged—a hand over her mouth, her eyes watering. Annabeth gagged as well, and they both began to retch. Ella turned to Annabeth, her eyes wide.

"This is hell," she said, shivering.

A few passersby raised their eyebrows in surprise, observing their unusual punishment. Some snickered or offered sympathetic smiles.

"Can't we just use magic?" Ella begged. Elysium shook her head, arms crossed over her chest.

"I was told if either of you were to use magic, to send the pile straight to your room," she said.

Ella groaned. She was never going to get the smell out of her clothes. No amount of magic could fix that.

As the last of the piles were cleared, Master Moore approached them. Ella's eyes were downcast. Valla hadn't been in her room all that night, which meant she had been in Moore's room.

Ella didn't want him to know that she knew.

"I've seen you all managed to clean this up in a timely manner. See to it that you clean yourselves up and make it back in time for lunch."

Ethan threw the shovel down, letting out a sigh of relief. "Thank Gods, I'm starved!"

Moore turned to him and said, "Good. We have corn on the menu."

CHAPTER TWENTY-FOUR

Weeks had passed since the incident in the training room with Moore's freak-out. True to her promise, she hadn't spoken to Moore in all that time, unless addressed during class. He was especially harsh on her during those times, but she never reacted. He seemed to become more and more irate at this.

Tonight was supposed to be the school's winter dance. Armand had been lurking about for days, and Ella had a suspicious feeling he was trying to ask her to be his date. She avoided him like the plague, settling on going without a date. Gertrude continued to eye her with disdain throughout the day but stayed clear of her. Every time they were in the same hall, everyone would get quiet—anticipating. Waiting.

Everyone was to dress up and have a good time, but Ella couldn't help but think about the grandeur balls her mother would throw back home.

"This isn't my home," she muttered resentfully. It was the closest thing to a ball she would experience for now. Ella's heart raced, thudding against her ribs. All those giggles and excited chatter about the winter formal hadn't made sense to her until this moment. Nervously, she gazed at her reflection, struggling to recognize her face beneath the magical façade cast by the runes that controlled her appearance.

Earlier in the day, she had ventured to Annabeth's dorm—against her will, really. Annabeth insisted on doing Ella's hair and painting her face. She had diligently put in the laborious hours, subjecting Ella to a tiresome styling session for her hair and makeup. The result was a stranger staring back at her. Her typically long, wavy locks were magically curled and pinned atop her head, with delicate tendrils cascading down to her shoulders and braided tinsel through the curls. Dark kohl accentuated her eyes, making her bewitching brown gaze appear more intense. The transformation was something Nattya would've effortlessly achieved.

A fleeting thought crossed Ella's mind: maybe she should skip this event altogether instead of facing everyone downstairs. She was weary of feeling out of place. Sienna told her that everyone would attend, which only added to Ella's apprehension. Amongst all students, she was probably the oldest one there secretly, and none of the adults seemed eager about the dance either. Instead, they prowled the hallways with anxious expressions etched on their faces—even Moore seemed grumpier than usual.

Valla was nowhere to be seen, though in recent weeks she had been getting plumper. Ella wondered what Moore had been feeding her.

"I shouldn't be this excited," she said to herself. She hadn't many flashy clothes with her, but Gregor had apparently informed Hamlet the last time he had visited with Nattya of the school's scheduled events. He had a garment sent to her with a note that said "Don't thank me. Really. I'm never shopping for dresses again. Hope it fits."

"Is he insane?" she asked herself as she lifted the emerald-green dress from its velvet-lined box. She was apprehensive. The dress was beautiful, with a sweetheart neckline, lace appliques, and a mass amount of long, flowing tulle.

She thought of how Nattya said no one would want to lift all that tulle—and suspected that was for Highwing's benefit. She chuckled.

He even added little emerald earrings and an obnoxiously expensive gem necklace that she absolutely would not wear.

Ella straightened her shoulders, taking a deep breath. It wasn't the apocalypse, after all. She could handle this. It was merely a dance—a simple waltz or two. She loved dancing, so what was there to fear? If she didn't show up, Annabeth or Ethan would undoubtedly come looking for her, anyway. Slipping into the dress, she shimmied it up over her hips and carefully adjusted it to cover her chest. As soon as it settled into place, she immediately realized how risqué and revealing it truly was—clearly Nattya's influence at work.

"I'm going to murder that man!" she growled under her breath, envisioning Hamlet's arrogant expression. She could practically hear his voice taunting her, calling her uptight while cackling in delight. Her cheeks flushed with embarrassment and anger, but she couldn't deny that the dress looked striking on her. She spent a long moment examining herself in the mirror, her trembling fingertips brushing against her lips as anxiety bubbled within.

"You've done this before, Ella. Snap out of it!" she chided herself sternly. How she longed for Nattya's unwavering confidence—that sense of belonging in every setting without a care in the world. With a last glance and a forced smile at her reflection, Ella turned toward the bedroom door and vanished into the eerily quiet hallway.

Naturally, the Grand Hall was already bustling with excitement, making her late arrival even more conspicuous. Anxiety swelled as she imagined the inevitable stares that would follow. She tried to ignore the echo of her silver heels on the cold flagstone floor, their sharp clatter bouncing off ancient walls.

Drawing nearer to the Grand Hall, a cacophony of laughter and chatter greeted her ears. Entering further, she caught sight of students from her Divination class. Several boys gaped at her transformation, much to their dates' annoyance.

"Is that really you, Marks?" Ivan Ilgrid queried, astonishment in his voice.

"Yes," she replied, ever so steadily.

"Wow! You clean up quite well!" chimed in Ajor, as he whistled appreciatively.

"Thanks…" She glanced at the boys and then at their dates, who were seething at their sides.

Ella's face turned red as she rushed past the crowd, suddenly enveloped by a cacophony of music and voices. Seeking refuge from the overwhelming sensations, she glanced at Master Moore lurking in a shadowy corner. Leaning against the wall with arms folded, he appraised her with a raised eyebrow and a hint of a smirk. Choosing not to engage after their recent argument in the training room, Ella rolled her eyes defiantly and turned away.

Feeling out of place near the entrance, Ella observed the floating lanterns casting a magical glow on immaculate white tablecloths. The walls, draped in flowing white silk, glimmered under the soft illumination of crystal chandeliers, casting a gentle, iridescent light across the space. White roses, delicate and pristine, graced every corner. In the center of the room, was a large dance floor of white marble, surrounded by a colonnade of white marble columns.

Crowds of dancers moved to the lively melody, while the scent of roses mingled with the aroma of polished wood. Her hands shook as her heart pounded. She hesitated, unwilling to move forward. Catching the sight of Annabeth, Ella desperately waved at her friend. Despite their apparent eye contact, Annabeth's gaze seemed to flit right past her.

"I swear she looked right at me," Ella murmured in disbelief. Approaching a busy table filled with animated students, she hesitantly asked, "Hello, would you mind if I joined you?" The two girls didn't even glance in her direction.

Muttering an apology under her breath, Ella strode away with a furrowed brow as several people bumped into her thoughtlessly.

"Hey! Watch it!" she snapped, irritation lacing her voice. But no one seemed to care. Feeling utterly disregarded, she became engulfed by dancers lost in the electrifying rhythm of the music. Panic surged within her, sending shivers down her spine and through her limbs. With great effort, she fought against the suffocating crowd as flailing arms and sharp elbows assailed her.

Catching the sight of Annabeth's auburn hair whipping through the air, Ella shot forward and seized her friend's shoulder.

"Thank gods! What's up with these people?" Ella shouted over the music, relief washing over her. However, confusion clouded her face when Annabeth continued dancing wildly, laughing and coaxing a blonde boy closer.

"Anna!" Ella shouted again while tapping Annabeth's shoulder, only to be met by cold indifference.

"Did I do something wrong?" Her voice wavered with uncertainty—Annabeth was among the few she could genuinely consider a friend.

Despite Ella's efforts for attention, wallflower status clung to her like a second skin. Her fragile confidence shattered as fellow students danced and collided with her, paying no mind. She meekly tried to blend in with the throng of fervent dancers.

Unexpectedly, Ivan Ilgrid and his date, Maxene Carpenter, stumbled into her. Relief surged through her and she smiled brightly at Ivan, but his gaze breezed past her while he danced with Maxene. In a last-ditch attempt, Ella tapped Ivan's shoulder and asked, "Have you completed Mistress Devoro's Divination assignment?" The words sounded pitiful even to her own ears. She hoped for a response from either him or Maxene, however petty it might have been. Nothing came.

Overwhelmed by rejection, Ella withdrew from the lively crowd, feeling more insignificant than ever. It was painfully evident she didn't belong there; her presence had gone unnoticed. Annabeth wouldn't have come looking for her. Maybe she was upset about something. She couldn't make a fresh impression on anyone; it all seemed futile. Suppressing a choked cry as another person bumped into her, she hurried away and halted at the entrance of the Grand Hall.

She searched for the one individual who couldn't possibly ignore her. And there he was, occupying his usual corner with the familiar arrogant expression on his face. His stance was relaxed, yet there was an underlying alertness to his posture as if he were always attuned to his surroundings.
Nonchalantly swirling a drink in his hand, he strolled toward her, sporting a sly grin.

Fantastic, she mused bitterly to herself, *unable to keep away from me.* She examined him from the feet up, making sure to wrinkle her nose in disgust.

He was wearing his regular school garments—a deep purple cravat that matched the insane amount of buttons that went down his black frock. His bangs framed his face messily, and his eyes were lined with kohl.

She hated that he looked beautiful.

"Enjoying yourself, Miss Marks?" he asked, his voice oozing false concern. His voice was like silk.

She hated how it sent a jolt through her.

Her seething anger bubbled below the surface as sharp breaths escaped her chest. "Actually, I'm just about to leave."

"You've only just arrived," he noted bemusedly while taking a swig of what appeared to be wine.

"Well, now I'm leaving," she retorted sharply and shoved past him with her shoulder.

"Wait!" he barked and clasped her wrist firmly, spinning her around to face him once more. Loose strands of hair tumbled free from their pins and her eyes filled with unshed tears.

Determined not to cry in front of him or anyone else, she strained out through gritted teeth, "Release me."

With a disdainful sneer that distorted his facial scar further, he replied simply, "No." His claws pricked her hand.

With all her might, she yanked her wrist from his grasp. "Never touch me again!"

"Don't get ahead of yourself," he scoffed. "I'm just making sure all students are where they're supposed to be. Can't have anyone sneaking off and causing trouble or ending up pregnant." His condescending leer made her breath hitch in her throat.

Sarcastically, she replied, "Looks like you'll have your hands full!" She felt her concealed power pulsating beneath her skin as she struggled to stay in control. Her foot ached with searing pain.

Suddenly, someone bumped into her, sending her off balance and onto the sleek floor. Glaring at Sienna, who stepped over her without even bothering to look back, her fury overflowed. She felt herself change into her Elven form—a sensation that left her exposed and utterly afraid. She braced herself for screams of terror or pointing fingers at her transformation. Meanwhile, the unbearable pain in her foot worsened.

Slowly, she locked eyes with Master Moore's steady gaze. His expression remained stoic, betraying no hint of emotion. As she glanced around the room, she noticed that nobody else seemed to be aware of her existence. Master Moore observed her closely, his head tilted slightly and eyebrows furrowed as if assessing her.

"Did you... did you do this?" She asked through her angry sniffles.

"Did I do what?" Grayson Moore asked nonchalantly, tilting his head curiously.

"You made me invisible, didn't you? Because I wasn't until I saw you!" Her accusation was fierce as she gathered herself, clutching her dress with frustration. "You're despicable."

"All I did was cast an illusion. To them, you hold the same interest as a teacup," he retorted coldly.

Tears streaked down her face, smudging her makeup as she tried to wipe them away. "Why? Why are you so cruel?" Her voice was barely audible by the end of her question.

Grayson's jaw clenched involuntarily; he had anticipated an outburst, not a genuine plea for understanding. Much to his dismay, he saw her trying to suppress more tears.

"Enough of this sniveling!" He commanded firmly, jabbing a finger into her shoulder while maintaining his intense countenance.

Swiping away his hand with defiance, her wings flared outward, making her appear larger and more imposing. In an instant, she thrust her palms forward with all her strength, sending him flying across the room. As Master Moore hurtled through the air, his expression of shock was undoubtedly the highlight of her evening.

CRASH! The sound of shattering glass and splintering wood filled the Grand Hall as he collided with the refreshment table. All eyes in the room focused on him as he awkwardly freed himself from a punch bowl, soaked and dripping with various sticky sweets and drinks. His face contorted in pure rage—an image that was both comical and imposing.

"Overindulged a bit tonight, have we, Grayson?" Highmaster Gregor asked cheerfully, patting him on the back. Mistress Opaline and Mistress Ased shared disapproving glances at his behavior.

"No worries, Highmaster. Just lost my footing," Grayson replied, his voice tense as he clenched his teeth. His menacing glare fell upon Ella, who sported a triumphant grin. Tauntingly, she raised her middle finger at him before repeating the action with her other hand.

Grayson's face turned red with anger as he advanced toward her, his footsteps echoing through the hall while the crowd watched his every move. Picking up speed, he launched into a sprint just as Ella unleashed a string of curses that cut through the air like daggers.

Her heart racing, she dashed up the flagstone steps in an attempt to escape his fury.

He was certain that the girl would be his downfall. Ellarhyssa seemed intent on tormenting him. As Grayson paced the silent halls of Morning Song, he knew everyone was tucked away safely in their dorms. The dance had ended long ago, but there was no sign of her.

"Where did you disappear to?" Grayson muttered in frustration, his voice echoing through the shadows. The dimly lit sconces barely illuminated the walls. With a flash of his emerald eyes, the darkness retreated, and his surroundings brightened.

Grayson had searched every corner of the school, or so he thought. The twisting corridors were more familiar to him than anyone else. Agitation swelled within him as he checked behind each tapestry and hidden nook, a deep growl escaping his throat.

Muttering under his breath, he walked down the hallway and passed his history classroom for the fourth time that night. On the verge of giving up and turning around, a sudden realization hit him like a splash of icy water. Suppressing a frustrated yell, he sprinted down the hall with renewed determination, took a left, and bounded up the steps leading to the rooftop. He burst through the wooden door forcefully, causing it to rebound against the stone wall.

"Aha!" Grayson declared triumphantly, pointing at Ella's back. She didn't even bother to look his way.

Ella sat motionless on the frost-covered ground, her ebony wings wrapped tightly around her shivering body as her head lolled to one side and her eyes remained closed.

An icy knot clenched in Grayson's stomach as he called out sharply, "Miss Marks!" She neither flinched nor awoke from her seemingly peaceful slumber.

"Damn," he cursed under his breath, rushing forward and touching her face with trembling fingers—she was as cold as ice.

"SHIT!" He exclaimed.

He hastily removed his cloak and wrapped it around both of them, pulling her close for warmth. Cupping his hands, he exhaled sharply to ignite bluebell flames within his grasp. "Wake up, Marks!" he urged, his voice tinged with alarm as he held the flames near her stiff body.

Her wings remained frozen, her lips a lifeless shade of blue. As he pulled the cloak above them, delicate bluebell flames flickered on her skin like ghostly fireflies. Anxiously, he awaited any indication that she was escaping the icy hold on her life.

All he had intended was to tease her – be an annoyance during what was supposed to be an enjoyable night at their chaos-laden school.

Her claim of him being mean had taken him by surprise; he was all too aware of his brusque and unwelcoming demeanor. Everyone knew it – that's why they steered clear of him. But why wouldn't this girl just avoid him? And what made it so aggravating when she entered the Grand Hall with her nose upturned at him, acting as though she was superior? Did she honestly believe donning a fancy dress and earning admiring glances from boys made her better than him?

By the time she made her entrance—fashionably late—he had already downed his third glass of wine. He observed with disdain as she arrived timidly, seemingly oblivious to the gazes that followed her. She had opted for a green dress and an unconventional hairstyle, which admittedly suited her well.

He liked green. He caught himself gazing unabashedly before she finally made eye contact, arching an eyebrow in response, and sauntered away without acknowledging or greeting him.

Why did this affect him so deeply? Maybe it was because she had been so persistent in seeking his company in the past just to suddenly treat him as if invisible.

She *had* said they wouldn't speak again.

He thought drunkenly, "We'll see how you like being ignored then." With a flick of his fingers, he cast a discrete illusion.

And now here they were huddled under his cloak, all because she had ventured out into the brutal cold just to escape his presence. All due to his deplorable behavior.

"Alright, Marks, enough with the theatrics," he said in a slow drawl. "There's no need to play the damsel in distress."

Gradually, color returned to her lips, and her breathing steadied. Despite the heat radiating beneath the cloak, he continued to maintain the flames even as sweat beaded on his forehead. Thankfully, her eyelids began fluttering, and she weakly stirred.

"Come on, you ruddy bird," he murmured. How he wished she could hear and appreciate the insult!

Ella slowly awakened, disoriented by the unusual warmth that enveloped her. Was she back in Hellharth? She remembered it was winter in Arcadea, and they had been at Morning Song.

"So warm," she mumbled sleepily, nestling further into the warmth. Her head moved forward, resting on something hard. Her eyes opened slightly, blue flames dancing in front of her. Master Moore came into her vision suddenly. His face looked worried, scrunched up in a way that she had never seen before. She was dreaming, she was sure of it. He would never look at her with anything more than a sneer.

Her fingers grazed his cheek with a feather-like touch. She traced over the scar that marred his cheek and nose, slowly following the straight slope of his nose. His eyebrows furrowed together, his mouth in a straight line.

Why did this man hate her so much? Because she was Elvish?

Her thumb touched his lips, lightly pulling them down, and his eyes became brighter. She liked his eyes. She was jealous of his long, dark lashes. Her palm tickled from his stubble along his jaw.

"You're so pretty, you don't even have to try," she mumbled lightly. He didn't say anything. Dream Moore would let her call him pretty.

Boldly moving closer, the tips of their noses brushed against one another, causing him to flinch, almost making her withdraw. Ignoring the urge and breathing against him instead, she asked in a near-whisper, "Why do you hate me so much?" Their lips hovered tantalizingly close, feeling the warm breath that fell upon each of their mouths.

CHAPTER TWENTY-FIVE

Grayson was certain that the girl had lost her sanity. There was no possible way she could be in her right mind, acting this way towards him. She leaned into his personal space, murmuring words that should never have escaped her lips. Now, she was practically perched on his lap, her fingers tracing his face and daring to graze his scar—a place no one else had ever touched. He instinctively flinched, causing her to pull back slightly; her warm amber eyes brimming with sorrow. She was dangerously close.

"Why do you hate me?" she whispered, her breath dancing against his lips. Their mouths didn't quite meet, but it felt as if she were gently brushing them with each word.

His heart pounded in his chest while he held his breath, anxiously waiting for her next move.

Put a stop to this now, he scolded himself. *You need to end this before it goes too far*. He inhaled, nostrils flaring, breathing in her scent. She smelled of a fresh storm. His mind was ringing in alarm.

"Grayson," she sighed dreamily. He snapped to attention. She had never said his name before, and it made his stomach do a strange flip. He pulled back suddenly, and her eyes came into focus. He shook her rather violently.

It took a moment for her to gather her bearings, but when she did, she all but yelped.

"Detention Miss Marks," he seethed. "For accosting my person."

"What—?"

"You didn't think the little stunt you pulled was just going to go unpunished?" He pulled the cloak from them, breathing in a sigh of relief at the cool, fresh air.

"You deserved it! You beastly little—!"

"Is this how you thank me for saving your life?"

Ella stared at him blankly, moving away from him with a groan. Her body hurt and felt stiff. She looked around in confusion. She was still on the rooftop.

"I fell asleep," she stated lamely.

Grayson guffawed. "Stupid girl. Have you no instincts of self-preservation?"

"I've had quite enough of your bullying!" She stood on her feet and shook her wings out with a wince.

"If I were capable, believe me, I would see to it that you were expelled."

"Don't threaten me with a good time," she snarled. "I've expressed to you how deeply I hate it here. And I hate *you*."

His left eye twitched at her words, and he almost laughed. "Oh really? I thought you found me pretty?"

"The hell are you going on about?" She shivered, now fully exposed to the cold air.

Grayson noticed her shivering and sucked his teeth. "Get inside. Go to bed. You're about to have a shitty morning."

"I'm not doing your detentions," she said. "I'm not even a real student. This is all utter Vilkri crap."

"You are only saying this to me because I know you aren't. Who said your detentions would be with me? I'll just assign them over to Mistress Ased. What are you going to tell her? Besides," he smirked. "If you're studying here, practicing magic like everyone else—then you are, in fact, a student."

"Have you made it your own personal mission to make my life hell? What is your deal? I leave you alone and you *still* manage to find a way to harass me. I'll stay out of your way! Just leave me be!" She swiped angrily at her nose. She would not cry! "Is it because I'm an Elf? Is that why you are like this? I see you engage with other people, and you are standoffish and rude. But to me, you are cruel. I try so hard. I did your training—" She halted, her breathing became erratic, and she swiped furiously at her eyes.

Damnit. Not in front of him. Not in front of him!

Grayson stood in shock, witnessing Ella's emotional breakdown before him, her gasping sobs slicing through the air. He had always made it a point to steer clear of weeping students. If they weren't nursing broken bones, they weren't his concern. He recalled an unpleasant incident when he found himself trapped in the staff room with Mistress Devoro, who was sobbing about her boyfriend's infidelity that she'd seen in a vision.

Against all odds, Grayson blurted out, "I don't hate you," taking himself by surprise because, until this very moment, he was quite sure he did. He had wanted to kill her not too long ago, and try as he might, he could not find that feeling again.

Ella's quivering shoulders stilled, and she slowly lifted her tear-streaked face from her hands.

"What?" she asked hesitantly.

"I hate your father," he confessed, "and I find your crying pathetic."

Ella's expression soured as she crossed her arms defensively. "I've never even met the man! You've been treating me like garbage, and that's exactly what my mother fears will happen when people find out about me—that they'll treat me just as you have."

He countered with an attempt at levity, "To be fair, I treat everyone the same."

"But you didn't make Sienna Whitefish invisible," she pointed out.

Grayson admitted without thinking, "People would notice her absence." In response, Ella threw her hands up in frustration.

"You're impossible," she said.

He pinched the bridge of his nose in irritation. He reached into his pocket and pulled out a sleek, silver tin filled with fragrant rolled herbs for smoking. Placing one between his lips, he ignited it with a fiery touch of his fingertip.

"I don't make a habit of repeating myself, Miss Marks."

"Quit calling me that," she muttered. In a quick motion, she snatched the smoldering herbal stick from his grasp. He lunged for it, but she teasingly held it just out of reach.

"Hand it back—"

Driven by curiosity, Ella pursed her lips around the roll and inhaled deeply, imitating Grayson's earlier action. Immediately, she broke into a harsh coughing fit. "It's awful!"

Grayson stared at Ella in disbelief. "I've never encountered someone so incapable of controlling her emotions, her magic, and utterly devoid of survival instincts. You're like a moth drawn to a flame." He swiftly retrieved the smoldering stick from her grasp, observing as her eyes gradually glazed over and her lips curled into a delighted grin. The rich aroma of the smoke lingered in the air, and she burst into a fit of giggling.

"Terrific. A nap is in order for you," he exhaled with a hint of annoyance. At his words and his mildly disgruntled expression, her laughter only intensified.

"What was in that blend?" she asked between giggles.

"Meraroot," he replied, "And before any fingers are pointed, you drugged yourself. Time for bed." As he seized her arm to guide her down the steps, she erupted into uncontrollable cackles. "Lightweight," he uttered under his breath.

At one point, he had to slap a hand over her mouth because she had progressively gotten louder, and she found it hilarious.

When they came upon his door with the stone dragon, it peered down at them curiously. "Don't ask," Grayson muttered to it. He needed to get a sobering tonic in the idiot before she completely lost herself.

"Have you never had Meraroot before? Can you hold still!" he demanded, pinching her chin in his hands and trying to tilt back a red liquid into her mouth. He wrestled her down onto a pile of pillows by his fireplace until she calmed.

"Remember that time I drank—bat poo—" she said in a fit. "I couldn't read Arcadean! Anna and Ethan had to teach me!" She kept cackling at her own joke. He let go of her chin and she sat up, slapping her hands on her thighs.

As much as he tried to resist, Grayson could not help the smirk that tugged insistently at the corners of his mouth.

He confessed, "I knew you couldn't read." The effects of the tonic engulfed her as she gradually stopped laughing. Her mood shifted, turning solemn and serious.

"You knew?" she questioned with a tinge of disbelief in her voice.

"The missing assignments and all the classic signs of a Fae struggling to read Arcadean were there. At least you speak it well. But I had no idea you could read minds," he stated cautiously.

Her reaction gave him all the confirmation he needed. Mind-drifting was a dangerous gift. Forbidden to use—unless sanctioned by The Council for interrogation purposes. He pointed at her sternly. "If you do it again, I'll have no choice but to report you."

"Why not just tell on me now? You wanted me gone anyway." Her eyes darted to the floor and back to his face.

His eyes narrowed as he began listing off, "You summoned waking nightmares without effort; a rune had to be etched into your foot to prevent your elemental magic from spiraling out of control; you meddle with substances you have no business touching." He silently wondered how they managed to get to this point, as if the incident in the training room had never happened. "Keeping you here would be in the best interest of everyone out there." He paused to let the words sink in.

"You think I'm dangerous," she yawned heavily, the exhaustion evident on her face. "I didn't mean to hurt you."

"Couldn't you have just flown off the rooftop instead of waiting until you were unconscious? It seems to me that you're a hazard to yourself. If you don't care about yourself, how do you care about those around you?" Grayson reasoned. "Your behavior is erratic and you frequently display self-destructive behavior."

Valla padded out of his bedroom and stretched, her large canines snapping up in the air with a yawn. She flopped down next to Ella and swished her tail.

Ella chanced a glance at Moore, whose mouth was pressed in a thin line.

"Valla," she said sleepily. Valla's ear twitched at the sound of her name.

"Pardon?" Grayson asked.

"That's her name," Ella yawned, rolling over and scratching the cat's head. Valla's eyes shifted from green to yellow.

"I didn't ask," he said curtly, and Ella shrugged.

She nestled into the enormous pile of cushions he had tossed her onto. Her eyelids fluttered halfway closed as she sleepily announced, "I can't fly."

Grayson wanted her to clarify. How could a being with wings not possess the ability to fly? Perhaps she was hurt. Although he had glimpsed her wings several times before without seeing any signs of damage. He turned to ask her, only to find her snoring. Sighing and rolling his eyes, he nudged her gently with a foot. Valla didn't even budge. "This isn't some kind of sleepover, wench. Return to your own chamber. Take the cat with you."

"It isn't fair that I cannot see her, and you can!" Highwing shouted at Nattya.

Nattya slumped. "I have only seen her once."

"Once more than I have. I could shift into you—"

"Hamlet would know instantly," she scoffed dismissively.

"What? You don't believe I can accomplish it?" Highwing asked. Nattya crossed her arms defensively, gracefully lifting her breasts.

"Prove it," she dared him.

Highwing's gaze shifted from her face to her chest and back again before he let out a resigned sigh. "There's no way to replicate *those*. Besides, if Hamlet even tried to touch me, I'd be mortified."

Nattya's eyebrow rose, her cinnamon eyes drifting in thought. Highwing gasped and jabbed her with a finger. "You were just thinking about me getting molested by Hamlet, weren't you?"

Her face was stoic as she replied, "No, I was actually picturing the two of you violating me."

Highwing bit his lip nervously, making steady eye contact with her. "Ella wouldn't object," he whispered as he fidgeted with the Lifestone adorning Nattya's wrist, a golden bracelet coiled like a vine around it. The gem pulsed and shimmered as he caressed it. This was as close to Ella as he could be. Nattya had been eating more, drinking wine less, and seemed happier now.

She inclined forward to plant a tender kiss on his chin. "While that might be true, it feels…wrong when she is not here to voice her consent. You are to be her husband."

"We're not in love—"

"Do you anticipate me to act as a shared plaything for you both? I miss her too, Highwing. However, I refuse to play your games. To fuck you, just so you can experience some sort of connection to her," Nattya countered, her voice firm.

Highwing looked ashamed. "I didn't mean to sound like I was using you. I'm just tired. The Queen disowned her. Is there even going to be a wedding? She was set on me moving on from Ella like she didn't approve. I can't help but feel like she wants to keep Ella far away from here. If we married, then Ella would be a Queen beside me."

"I have all these thoughts racing through me. I told my mother that I love Ella in the same capacity that I do you. Ella and I agreed to marry for duty and indulge elsewhere if we wanted or needed. I don't know what the right answer is," Highwing admitted. "I don't know if after all of this, Ella will still want to be with me."

Nattya swallowed hard, the weight of his words settling around them. "What's that saying? Climb that mountain when we get there? All we can do is wait and see what happens."

Anna and Ethan were eyeing her curiously from across the breakfast table. Anna had her head in her hands, and Ethan was chewing slowly on an apple.

"I didn't see you at the dance," Anna huffed. "Then I went looking for you, and your room was empty."

Ethan pursed his lips and tilted his head at her. "Who's bed did you end up in last night?"

Ella spewed her water across the table and coughed. "I—I didn't up in anyone's bed," she guffawed.

"A stairwell then? Or did you feel daring and try for the forest?" Anna teased.

"I wasn't doing anything nefarious. I just couldn't bring myself to come," Ella said.

"So where did you go?" Ethan asked between mouthfuls.

Ella blushed, remembering waking up in her own bed and wondering how she got there. "I fell asleep in the library," she lied.

"Boo. You going on a tyrannical sex frenzy was more interesting to me," Anna pouted.

"A sex frenzy?" Sienna said suddenly from beside them. "Did I miss something?"

"No. There was no sex frenzy," Anna mumbled.

"You and me both. It's been forever," Sienna sighed. Her eyes drifted over to the staff table and lingered on the empty seat. Moore's seat. "The dance was fun. What the hell was up with Moore last night? He was completely wasted."

"I don't know. I heard the crash, then saw him peeling himself off the food table," Ethan laughed. "He was getting loose."

"I'd like to see more of that," Sienna admitted wistfully. Anna rolled her eyes and turned to Ella, who had stayed unusually quiet.

"You missed quite the event last night. Master Moore disappeared after falling onto a table. He's probably nursing a hangover now," Anna nodded to the empty chair.

"I wish I had been there," Ella smirked.

CHAPTER TWENTY-SIX

Among all the subjects, Ella found Herbology to be the most fascinating. The myriad varieties of plants and their applications amazed her. The classroom was bathed in soft, natural light streaming through large, stained glass windows, casting gentle rays upon the botanical treasures that adorned the space. Lush, leafy plants of various shapes and sizes thrived in every corner. Books hovered and glided through the air above their heads. Shelves lined the walls, housing an extensive collection of jars, vials, and containers holding magical herbs, rare seeds, and mystical components. Each container was carefully labeled, displaying the names of the plant specimens and their unique properties. The shelves themselves seemed to extend beyond the limitations of physical space, accommodating an ever-growing collection of plants and magical artifacts.

Master Sevoy, a charming stout man with boundless energy, caught her attention. With his scattered beard resembling a spider's legs, wide-set brown eyes, and a beak-like curved nose, Ella was intrigued and surmised that he could be a Halfling Goblin.

Today's lesson focused on the remarkable Virida Lily, a flower with vibrant orange petals that served as an antidote to its own toxic sap. Ella was partnered with Armand, whose enthusiasm was palpable.

"I've seen a similar plant in Aslan; the Yuvak Tywi," he mentioned. Ella attempted to mimic his pronunciation but stumbled on the words, eliciting laughter from Armand.

Curious about his homeland, Ella asked while trimming the flower's stem, "What's Aslan like?"

"Well," Armand replied, "It's mostly scorching heat and endless sand. We have giant snakes, scorpions, and spiders." As he mixed petals into a bowl, he continued, "The desert's real thrill lies in surviving its deadly inhabitants." When he was satisfied with the color of his paste he added a black powder to it.

"And those Runes help you with speed?" Ella asked, her eyes drifting down to his ankle.

"Yes," he answered. "We receive them when we learn to walk." Noticing her shocked expression, Armand added reassuringly, "At that young age, you barely remember any pain." She internally winced at the thought of a baby having to endure pain like that. She had barely handled the pain of hers.

He chopped and stirred, then prompted, "And what about Direfell? What's it like there?" Ella's knife slipped, slicing her finger. She gasped and held up her bleeding digit. Armand quickly took her hand, gently wrapping his lips around her forefinger to suck out any toxins. Ella squeaked in protest but couldn't budge from his grip.

"You must remove the toxins first," he clarified before spitting into a nearby bowl. He then took some of the petal paste they had been crushing moments before and applied it around her wounded finger. With a smile, he offered her a taste of the mixture.

She hesitantly opened her mouth and sampled the mashed petals, finding them oddly sweet. "Thank you," she uttered between bites.

"Excellent work, Mister Tyren!" Master Sevoy praised, drawing everyone's eyes to the pair. "An exemplary demonstration of the plant's properties!" He started ranting about the levels of toxins in the plant and how it could kill you within days.

Ella subconsciously met Gertrude's glaring stare and sighed inwardly. She withdrew her hand from Armand's grasp. "Thanks again," she mumbled reluctantly. Someone made a noise behind her and she caught sight of Anna and Ethan holding their thumbs up at her, pointing between her and Armand. Ethan made a crude motion with his fingers, making a circle and plunging a finger into the opening repeatedly. Ella swiftly shook her head, a blush creeping up her cheeks.

Once the room had settled, Armand launched another round of unexpected questions. "Do you have someone special in your life?"

She raised her eyebrow, slightly puzzled. "There are many special people in my life." Was she to name them all?

"I mean, the one who is your *canitema*—your other half," he clarified, his accent heavy.

Caught off guard, she hesitated before replying, "Yes, I guess I do," thinking of Highwing. Unsure of their future together and not wanting Armand to know any details, she changed the subject. His face fell upon hearing her response.

"What about you? Is Gertrude your canitema?" She avoided turning around—sure that Gertrude had her eyes glued to them at this very moment.

He snorted and sighed. "Not at all. I believe in showing kindness to all creatures and Fae. Gertrude only seeks to possess, not love. She's no canitema."

"Is canitema another word for love?"

"No, Aslanic doesn't have a word for love. *Canitema* means something like *wholeness*. It's derived from the tale of Giada and Hantimel."

"I'm not familiar with that story," she admitted apologetically. Another thing she was kicking herself for—not learning the history of the world outside of Hellharth.

"In our culture, we have a God called Yuriba," he began, drawing her attention. "Long ago, Yuriba was the sole deity. Feeling lonely, he created Giada, the first woman, and Hantimel, the first man. They lived in harmony, exploring the world together while Yuriba ventured into other realms."

Pausing for a moment, he gave her a sly grin. "During Yuriba's absence, Giada and Hantimel created life—a child with four legs, four arms, and two heads. They named these two sides Cani and Tema. Cani radiated love and kindness, while Tema embodied malice and cruelty. Naturally, their parents favored Cani."

As he continued preparing the petal paste to put in small mason jars, he went on. "Distraught, Giada, and Hantimel begged Yuriba to separate their children. Obliging their plea, he split them into two with a sword at the Temple of Pias." Ella gasped in horror but was quickly reassured by his chuckle. "Remember, it's just a story."

He carried on narrating. "From then on, Cani was treated kindly while Tema suffered neglect from her parents. Noticing her twin's suffering, Cani secretly shared food and water with Tema in the Aslan Desert. Eventually, they devised a plan to switch places—Cani took on her sister's role and endured the hunger. Eventually, their parents caught on, asking why they had done such a thing. Cani said, 'Who am I without my sister? We were one. We were happy. It was you who did not like us as we were.'"

"You can't truly love someone if you don't embrace all of them," Ella whispered softly. "What became of them?"

"Yuriba created more beings, and they eventually had offspring of their own. But they always longed for the lost parts of themselves, their Canitema. You see, unlike other cultures that focus on fated mates, soulmates, or spouses, Aslanic culture perceives this bond as independent of one's sexual orientation. It's an incredibly deep and pure connection."

"It's absolutely beautiful," Ella sighed in agreement.

It had been a few weeks since the dance, and Ella and Grayson seemed to have unintentionally fallen into a routine. Ella would train and follow him up to the rooftop during his breaks. They would have light banter, and she avoided asking him how she ended up back in her bed that night.

Today, he took the opportunity to ask her his own questions.

"You don't fly as in you don't know how? Or you choose not to?" Grayson pestered, plumes of smoke whisking into the air as he puffed on his smoking stick.

"What difference does that make? I don't fly," she murmured.

"You have wings. You're a flightless bird. Like a chicken," he said. By the smell of the smoke, Ella deduced it was Meraroot.

"What did you just call me?" she asked incredulously. He chuckled. Ella stared at him in disbelief.

"Cluck, cluck," he mocked out of character, his large frame towering over her.

"Whatever," she huffed, turning her back to him.

"Afraid of heights then?" he tried. She frowned. "Not in the slightest. I've been coming to this rooftop for months," she said.

"Yet you won't jump off?" he prompted.

"Someone could see me," she replied.

"So, you *can* fly. You just choose not to."

"You're infuriating!" she yelled.

He leaned over the stonework, peering below at the ground, and whistled. "Yeah. That would kill you. If you couldn't fly." He turned his head to her, his expression serious.

"Why do you care so much?" she asked, her tone defiant.

He shrugged. "You have massive wings, but don't fly. There's a story there." He stubbed out his smoking stick and leaned back against the parapet.

"It's a long story I wouldn't want to bore you with." Ella was fidgeting uncomfortably now.

His lips curled up. "Well. I do have time to kill for the next hour…"

"Don't tell me you actually want to get to know something about me?" She almost barked out a laugh.

"Don't get overly excited. I don't care all that much," his telltale sneer coming to the surface.

"So, then I won't tell you."

He was quiet for a moment. "If I pushed you off, would you just fall and die?" he asked.

"Get the hell away from me, you lunatic," Ella hissed.

"I didn't say I *would*. You could just tell me why you don't fly."

"I thought you didn't care?"

"You said it was a long story, and I'm bored," he reasoned.

"So, find something else to do besides pester me," she glowered.

"All these times I've asked for solace from you, and you never obliged. Allow me to return the favor," he said.

"You're impossible," Ella sighed. She plopped herself onto the floor, leaned back, and looked up at the sky. She eyed his snubbed smoking stick and bit her bottom lip.

"Why do you smoke that stuff?" she sighed finally.

"I thought I was the one asking you questions."

"It made me feel drunk—almost. How come it doesn't bother you much?" she asked, a little miffed.

"Prying into things that don't concern you. If you must know, I have an unusually high tolerance. Now, just tell me why you don't fly," he said with a hint of annoyance. He jumped onto the edge of the rooftop, walking back and forth along the stone. Ella became uneasy.

"Get down from there!" she snapped, the worry in her voice evident.

Grayson glanced at her. "What for?"

"Because! You need to come down now!" her voice betrayed her growing panic.

"Will you share your story with me then?" he bargained.

"If you get down, I'll tell you," she negotiated.

"No. Story first, then I'll get down," he countered.

"Fine."

Ella bit her bottom lip. She hadn't had to tell the story in years. It was common knowledge in Hellharth. This was the first time she would be telling an outsider about it. Grayson wasn't exactly the kind of person who would sympathize, and she was half worried he would make some sick joke out of it. "I had a friend who fell from a lighthouse, and I failed to save him. He died."

Ella had assumed he would say something, yet his silence caught her off guard. After a lengthy pause, she resumed the conversation. "When I was younger, I had this friend named Gideon. His family was among the few Nomaji left who found safety in Hellharth during the Purge. His parents were always cautious around me." Ella tried to gain their trust by cultivating vibrant flowers for them, offering delicious sweets, and demonstrating her magical prowess. However, nothing ever seemed enough. If anything, it scared them.

"Maybe they sensed the truth about me, but didn't dare to confront it, knowing who my father is now," she wondered out loud. She could hear his voice now—remembering the last time they had kissed.

"What's so funny?" He had mumbled, pulling his lips away from hers. He was easily embarrassed by the smallest things.

"Gideon was my first kiss... We were only younglings back then—he was a bit older. But his parents disapproved and even my own mother called our relationship 'inappropriate.'" Ella suspected her mother wanted to protect her from the negativity caused by her Elven lineage. "There aren't too many halfling elves around."

At her final remark, he let out a snort and Ella sensed that he completely understood, being a halfling himself.

"We would go to this lighthouse by my home and Gideon would draw. It was there that he told me he loved me for the first time. I told him I loved him back."

"When we marry, we will have a family, and our children will live in a world where they are free to be who they are. We will be safe, and they will grow up knowing nothing but happiness." She paused, remembering how happy he looked, telling her of all that.

"We were arguing. He wanted to find a way to leave Hellharth, and I wanted to stay."

"You sound ungrateful," Ella scoffed. "My mother gives land to the free people. No one starves or is without a home. Who would say that's what it would be like out there?"

"The salty air, over time, had caused the metal railings at the top of the lighthouse to corrode." Ella hesitated and took a deep breath.

"No one knows. That's the point. It takes away our choices," he shouted back.

"And what about the Elves? What place do they have out there?"

"I don't know! I've never been out there!" Gideon shouted angrily. His jaw clenched, the way it did when he was holding back from saying something.

Ella shuddered.

"This is your father talking—"

"Don't start that, Ella!" He pushed off the railing, set to walk away from her, but the railing gave out. The rusted metal split and Gideon fell backward, his brown eyes wide in shock.

"He leaned on the railing—it broke. I lunged for him, and our fingers grazed each other," she unconsciously mimicked the movement with her hand.

"GIDEON! GIDEON!" Ella cried out, her fingertips brushing against his. She shot forward, her body lurching downwards, arms outstretched for him.

"And a gust of wind caught me, spreading my wings further and preventing me from getting any closer," she finished softly.

She had stayed with his body for hours, holding onto the pieces that hadn't been torn away by the jetty and sea. She needed something to bring back—something for the pyre so that she could burn him and he would be greeted in the afterlife. She didn't need to share that part.

Grayson had remained silent. As the quiet grew too much for her to bear, she hesitantly turned to study his face. His arms were tightly crossed, and his green eyes intensely analyzed her. "Well?" she finally asked, breaking the silence.

"It's a ridiculous reason not to fly," he exclaimed.

"Excuse me?" she stammered indignantly. "It's far from ridiculous! His death is my fault!"

"Oh, really? So, you single-handedly shattered the railing and summoned the gale-force winds?" he asked sarcastically.

Caught off guard, her mouth moved as she searched for words to counteract his argument. "Regardless, the blame lies with me," she insisted weakly.

"It seems like you're eager to take the blame despite having no control over the situation. Death is an inevitable part of life, Miss Marks," he reminded her. "Your blame is misplaced. Forgive yourself."

Her eyes burned with fury as she stared at him. Time and time again, people had reassured her it wasn't her fault. Yet, no one had ever belittled her for it like this.

"Enough!" she demanded, her voice trembling. "Get down from there! The story is over."

He hesitated for a moment; his arms still crossed over his chest. Finally, he unfolded them and spread them wide. With her heart in her throat, Ella watched in terror as he fell backward off the roof.

"GRAYSON, NO!" she shrieked, her heart pounding as she vaulted off the rooftop. The adrenaline surged through her, fueling her desperate attempt to catch his rapidly vanishing form. "Please!"

⋙⟶

Grayson leaped into the air, embracing gravity's pull. Her desperate scream of his name echoed in his ears as his hair escaped its braid, flailing around his face. She appeared above him, plunging down with her ebony wings tucked tightly against her body to catch up to him. Her expression was frantic, her trembling hand outstretched.

Grayson's hand hesitated, searching for hers, and an overwhelming thought flooded his mind and surprised him. Her eyes were bright and wisps of light spiraled around her. She was using magic to go faster.

"Beautiful," he whispered.

The moment their hands clasped, she opened her wings, abruptly halting their descent. Their connection jolted from the sudden maneuver. Grayson instinctively pulled her close to him and rolled them into a controlled spiral. Her terrified scream rang out as he released a membrane-like skin from his back with an echoing crack. Bony finger-like structures stretched out between his shoulder blades, horned spines supporting the leathery wings that now stabilized their fall.

He soared through the air at an impossible speed, his green eyes glowing. "You can fly!" Ella shrieked at him. "You son of a—"

Her outburst came to a sudden halt, and silence took over. Grayson soared high above Morning Song, its majestic spires growing smaller with each ascending movement. He could hear her breath hitching, so he cautiously loosened his grip, carrying them past the clouds.

A vibrant palette of red and orange glinted off the cloud cover, the sun's warm embrace enveloping them. She let out a startled gasp; her face a whirlwind of surprise as he brought her to his side. He loosened his grasp, watching intently as she dipped a little before readjusting and hovering near him.

"Haven't you missed this?" Grayson whispered, his gaze fixed on her. She nodded silently, their wings flapping in unison while her eyes closed, embracing the thrilling sensation of flight again. Abruptly, she snarled and locked her amber eyes on him with intense fury. She launched herself at him, her fists swung wildly. "You! You made me think you were dying!"

Dodging her thrashing leg, Grayson swooped downward. "I never asked for your gratitude!" he retorted sarcastically. Her eyes widened as he dove straight into the clouds. He could feel her falling behind him, closing in on him. A stream of fire whizzed by his head and he whirled around to face her.

"You never mentioned having wings!" She hurled a fireball at him, but he caught it effortlessly and extinguished it in his hand. "And why should I? It's none of your concern," he snapped back, his voice tinged with irritation as he brushed his hair over one shoulder.

She had never seen his hair that way before, and it caught her attention. It wasn't straight but wavy and slightly curled at the ends, reaching down midway to his torso. His face was uncharacteristically flushed as he glared at her.

"Well, if I had known, I wouldn't have jumped after you like a reckless fool!" she shouted, her anger palpable. He tilted his head to the side and noticed her scrutinizing his large, dark wings. As her eyes roamed over the delicate membrane, he felt increasingly self-conscious. The way she was looking at him, he could almost feel her judgment.

His wings were so very different, and he was suddenly aware of the lack of beauty they had compared to hers. They were so large and bulky, and their texture was coarse and rough. Almost translucent where the membrane caught the sunlight and revealed rivers of dark veins.

Clearing his throat with a hint of annoyance, he declared, "I need to get to my classes. Find your way back on your own."

Ella stayed in disbelief, unable to grasp what had just happened. Grayson's silhouette vanished beneath the cloud cover, compounding her feelings of confusion and unease. "I haven't flown in ages," she whispered to herself, feeling the memory of flying ingrained within her very being as she took off into the sky.

Gideon's laughter echoed inside her head like a haunting melody, while the lingering sensation of Grayson's touch burned on her skin. "How could he do this?" she thought, frustration swelling within her. As Ella twisted and spun through the air, a tidal wave of relief and sorrow washed over her.

"I'm flying again...but nothing's changed," she murmured to herself. Gideon's absence remained permanent; he was still gone forever.

Grayson had leaped from the sky, mimicking the most traumatic moment Ella had ever experienced, making her heart feel like it would stop right there. Yet, when their hands finally clasped together midair, it brought forth a surge of relief Ella never knew existed.

"Forgive yourself," Ella whispered Grayson's words, feeling the weight of their meaning. He had held her, her back to his chest as he had taken her high in the air. It was the first physical touch they shared that *wasn't* violent. Ella began to grasp that Grayson, in his own twisted manner, was trying to help.

CHAPTER TWENTY-SEVEN

From her terrace, Kahlisenya observed the people of Hellharth gradually embrace the concept of change. Everything appeared the same, yet everything had transformed. As the world progressed, Kahlisenya found herself trapped in a realm where haunting visions and vivid dreams tormented her sleep.

Night after night, she witnessed Ellarhyssa being struck in the heart by an arrow and collapsing, with Idmodias towering above her. Each time she awoke from her nightmares, she felt an itch in her hand and saw faint pink scars on her palms.

As the days passed, Kahlisenya's dreams grew more intricate. Gradually, they connected like fragments of a puzzle until everything became clearer.

In the fourth month following Ella's disappearance, Kahlisenya's dreams unexpectedly fused together, revealing insights she had never considered before. That day, she screamed, cried, and laughed until a blood vessel burst in her eye. She drank herself into a stupor, and when she finally awoke, she knew that the nightmares had to come true.

Inevitable.

Unyielding.

Afterward, she forbade Hamlet from going to see Ellarhyssa.

"You can't do this!" he had screamed, inches from her face. "She's all alone out there!"

Kahlisenya's voice was ice cold as she retorted, "She needs to learn independence." He cursed her name and then stormed out of her chambers. In the days that followed, she felt alone and adrift. She had never been so isolated in her life.

Nattya had spiraled into a cycle of heavy drinking, constantly toying with the Lifestone on her wrist that Ella had given her. Highwing would boldly lock eyes with her, his disdain written plainly across his face.

She had become the most despised person in Hellharth.

Fighting to communicate her visions with those around her, Kahlisenya felt as though invisible hands had sewn her mouth shut and robbed her of speech. Sometimes it felt as if something had seized her spine, threatening to break it. The chilling realization struck her — she was undergoing a cosmic intervention, just as Kiandall had forewarned.

What Gods were bringing this hell upon her?

As she stood on the terrace, Kahlisenya gazed at the people below, completely unaware of the drastic shift in their world. Laughter escaped involuntarily from her lips, bewildered yet entranced by the mystifying power that enshrouded her existence.

A newfound determination coursed through her veins, and she started devising a plan. Hellharth would return to Arcadea once again — but this time, for eternity.

Her eyes were drawn to a mysterious, swirling mist materializing beside her. From within the haze, an ethereal young man emerged, glowing with a faint, captivating aura. His movements were smooth and otherworldly, as if floating.

"Hello, Gideon," she greeted.

⫸────▸

Once again, the visiting weekend arrived, and Ella sat in the High-master's office, tapping her foot impatiently.

They didn't show. Again.

As days turned into weeks, neither Hamlet nor Nattya appeared. By the third visiting weekend without them, Ella's mood turned unbearably sour. Anna and Ethan made every effort to lift her spirits, but nothing worked. Not even a single letter was received.

It felt like she had been completely abandoned.

"Don't worry, I'm sure something important just came up," Anna tried to reassure her, but even she began to sound unconvinced as the weekends rolled by.

During training sessions with Master Moore, Ella unleashed her bottled-up frustrations by hurling furniture across the room and setting it ablaze. Surprisingly, Master Moore didn't utter a word of complaint; instead, he silently conjured up replacements for her.

Four months had passed since Ella had joined Morning Song. The chilly winter gave way to the warmer embrace of spring, and students excitedly planned their vacations. Despite Anna and Ethan's insistence on staying back with Ella, she refused to let them miss out on their own plans.

"No," she had said firmly, "you two deserve a break as much as anyone else."

Anna and Ethan had promised to write, and as the school began to empty, Ella's stomach twisted in knots.

⫸────▸

"The girl is undeniably in a state of depression. She hasn't eaten at all. My attempts to contact Hamlet have been futile—the messages just linger before me. I worry she won't escape the dark abyss she's been pushed into," Gregor lamented as he poured Grayson a generous glass of wine. He had arrived unannounced at Grayson's quarters.

Grayson was seated at his desk, the soft tune of his music box playing as he hummed along, engrossed in paperwork. Ella had shown small improvements in her studies, but he found himself using an excessive amount of red ink for no apparent reason, causing the pages to appear as if they were bleeding.

Throughout the week, Gregor had persistently advised him to be more lenient with her. "She's making an effort," he reminded Grayson during one of their earlier private dinners. Grayson could only scoff and roll his eyes in reply.

As much as he hated to admit it, her determination was getting under his skin. "She'll feel better once Mister Isles and Miss Dox return from their vacations," Grayson conceded. "Regarding Hamlet, can you genuinely say you're shocked that he left her with you? Wasn't it you who told me he once abandoned you in some field?"

"I wouldn't exactly put it that way," Gregor muttered under his breath, feeling a sting of humiliation. "It was a long time ago, and we were drunk."

Grayson remarked with disinterest, "She's been incredibly intense during training. It's like the room has turned into her personal rage space. At least she's not directing it at Miss Rydelle—I can see that glint in her eyes."

Gregor hesitated before suggesting, "I was actually hoping you could spend some extra time with her."

Grayson glanced up from his paperwork, his expression a mix of annoyance and disbelief. "Really? As if training and having her trail me every break after third period aren't enough; now you want me to spend more time with her? I'm not here to be her buddy," he retorted.

"It seems you two have really bonded over the past few months," Gregor observed with a smile. "I wouldn't be surprised if you've become friends."

Grayson rolled his eyes and said, "You're reading too much into it. We're not throwing tea parties or anything."

"Oh? And the whole flying off the rooftop thing?" Gregor questioned playfully, raising an eyebrow. "Is that just part of her training?"

Grayson's gaze sharpened, and he responded in a fierce tone, "That's simply to help her overcome her emotional baggage and guilt so she can reach her true potential. Nothing else." He set his glass pen down and leaned back in his chair. "You've been watching us. I put a tight illusion on her so she isn't noticeable when she is with me."

"Nothing escapes my knowledge," Gregor answered with a smile. "Please, do me a favor. Let her escape these dreary four walls and explore the wonders of Calisan and Hildfree. It would surely brighten her spirits," Gregor earnestly urged. Grayson hesitated, his gaze falling upon the music box on the table, its delicate tune filling the room. The small, ornate mirror on the lid reflected his scowling face back at him.

Grayson raised an eyebrow suspiciously. "And why is it that I get the feeling you're trying to play matchmaker with us?"

Gregor feigned shock, holding a hand to his chest in mock offense. "I would never dare to intervene in such personal affairs," he insisted, though a mischievous glint in his eyes betrayed his true intentions.

Chapter Twenty-Eight

Hesitantly, Grayson knocked on Ella's door. As it creaked open, the refreshing scent of soap filled the air. She peered her head out the door, and her damp hair shimmered. "Master Moore," she said coolly, her annoyance evident. His recent aerial adventure clearly still bothered her.

A smug smile appeared on his face. "Get your coat. I've been assigned to escort you outside."

She swung the door open, wearing a fluffy white bathrobe, and crossed her arms defiantly. "I'm not in the mood for that."

He rolled his eyes. "Your mood is irrelevant," he replied sharply. "Just get dressed and meet me in the courtyard. Ten minutes."

Fifteen minutes later, she joined him in the courtyard wearing a simple blue dress decorated with white daisies, short sleeves, and a long hem. Her hair was braided with a bright yellow ribbon woven through it.

When he finally told her they were heading to Calisan Capital, her excitement was overwhelming. She was bouncing on her feet, and her eyes were sparkling. She was rambling on about all the things she would do and see.

"What have I gotten myself into?" he grumbled.

The Calisan market was a labyrinthine expanse of narrow, winding alleys, lined with stalls and carts overflowing with magical curiosities. Elaborate canopies and awnings, adorned with shimmering fabrics and embroidered symbols, stretch overhead, casting a dappled glow upon Grayson and Ella as they walked.

Grayson reluctantly followed behind Ella, who halted every ten steps to peer through window shops with the same look of amazement and curiosity. He sighed heavily when she dove into the tenth dress shop. She had been talking about someone named Nattya, and how much they'd kill to be in her shoes right now.

He didn't know if she was serious or not.

"There's so much here!" she exclaimed. She hadn't bought anything yet.

"It's a city. What did you expect?" he mumbled. "Typical girl."

When Ella caught sight of her first horse, she gasped and he ran into her back, almost knocking her over onto the cobblestone walkway.

"Seriously! Watch where you are going! Who stops like that?" he barked.

When she didn't say anything, he followed her gaze. "That's a horse," she said lamely, cutting people off as she walked across the street and to the horse-drawn carriage. A large chestnut mare with a white spot on its head huffed at her approach. She patted its neck and scratched its nose.

"Yes. It's a horse, and it fucking stinks," he said in annoyance, waving a hand in front of his face.

"I've never seen a horse before. Only pictures. It's so much larger than I had imagined," she breathed. She brushed her knuckle over the horse's spot.

The horse's owner—a fat, stout man with a bulbous nose and small eyes—came up to her and introduced himself.

"My name is Hawthorn," he said, "and this is Evangeline. Care for a ride?" He took off his hat and bowed to Ella, and her eye twitched.

Grayson looked at the carriage the horse was pulling. It looked clean, with decent coverings for seats. Evangeline started peeing right by his boot, and he jumped back while Hawthorn laughed.

"I've never ridden a horse..." Ella admitted.

"Don't worry. You wouldn't be riding her, just sit in the back and let her pull you. Or you can sit up front with me and I'll let you steer," Hawthorn said with a wink.

"She'll sit in the back with me," Grayson answered quickly. Ella steering a horse through a crowded street was not how he wanted to die. He held the small black door to the carriage open and nudged her inside. The space was cramped, far too small for his large frame, and he practically loomed over her lap.

"Is it going to be a fast ride?" Ella inquired with enthusiasm.

"No, this is more of a leisurely trip," he replied. She looked a bit disappointed at this.

As Hawthorn clicked his tongue, the carriage jolted forward, unexpectedly sending Grayson tumbling into Ella's lap. Her blue dress hitched up in the process. Swiftly recovering, he gripped the ceiling with his claws and peered out the window, cheeks burning from embarrassment.

"Back at home, we don't have horses," Ella mentioned after a brief pause. "We care for other creatures—Vilkri rams, spotted deer... Our Hyla cats are massive enough to ride, way larger than Pentarian felines. Oh! And there are even some Direwolves."

Intrigued, he asked, "Have you ever ridden any of them? A Hyla cat or Direwolf?"

"No, I haven't ridden a Direwolf," she began. "Nowadays, they're quite rare. Instead, people use Hyla cats for hunting and in battle. And then there are the Ferian Eagles, Cynian Owls, and Hylycyn Hawks that wingless warriors rely on."

"I've seen pictures of them," he interrupted. "Are they really that massive?"

"Well, I'd need to see the images for comparison, but they're definitely larger than this carriage and the horse combined." Noticing how closely Grayson was observing her, she felt compelled to change the subject. "And what about you? What kind of creatures reside in Direfell?"

Taken aback by her curiosity, Grayson fumbled for his response. "Um, well... Dragons and Direwolves, I suppose — given the name."

"You suppose?" she prodded.

"I've never been," he admitted quickly. "Dragon folk aren't too friendly with halflings like me."

Ella's eyes bore into him as she carefully chose her words. "Your parents must have loved you though..."

Grayson scoffed as memories washed over him like a crashing wave. "My mother dumped me on my father immediately after I was born. He was killed during the Purge in Idris when I was barely four."

Overwhelmed by his confession, Ella emitted a strangled noise. Grayson jerked his head in response and glared at her watery eyes.

"Don't you dare," he warned angrily as she tearfully followed the line of his crooked scar and back into his eyes.

"The blade was cursed," he explained, his voice tense. "When they killed him, they turned on me. If it wasn't for Gregor intervening and defeating them, I would have been next."

"You were raised by Gregor?" she asked, her eyes wide with disbelief. She remembered Ethan saying that Gregor had paid a large sum to get Grayson out of the Idris prison—but didn't know he was raised by him too.

She wondered if anyone else did.

He inhaled deeply through his nose, ignoring the foul stench from the streets. "Yes."

"And by 'they,' you mean…" She let the question hang in the air and it began to fester.

He hesitated, not wanting to answer it. Their journey had been enjoyable so far, and he wasn't sure why he had decided to open up to her at all.

Maybe it was because she had shared her own story about the boy she had loved, shifting his perception of her ever so slightly. As he glanced at her now, her eyes downcast and with a solemn frown etched upon her lips, he couldn't help but yearn to escape the confines of the carriage and breathe in even the foulest air outside.

"Elves," he finally replied, his voice emotionless.

An hour later, they found themselves back at the bustling central square, gratefully thanking Hawthorn for the ride. As Grayson placed a shiny silver coin in his hand, he couldn't help but feel relieved to escape the claustrophobic carriage. Within mere minutes, he was already approached by three bold women—one even daringly offered him money to sleep with her. Grayson's face twisted in revulsion.

As Ella stepped into a quaint pastry shop, Grayson grabbed her shoulder firmly. "Miss Marks, haven't you had enough? We've been roaming about for hours. I believe I've been sufficiently punished."

Her lips formed an exaggerated pout, making him briefly consider biting it away. "Just this one last stop," she pleaded. No sooner had she spoken, her stomach grumbled loudly, causing her cheeks to flush crimson. Grayson's gaze drifted toward her midsection, and she covered it with her hands.

"Fine," he snapped with impatience. "Make it quick."

Ella darted toward the counter where a delectable assortment of cakes and tarts lay temptingly displayed under sparkling glass. As she pointed at a delicate tart, the shopkeeper engaged her in cheerful banter.

"Anything for your husband?" The jovial man inquired, nodding toward Grayson, who loomed near the door with a sullen expression.

Ella's eyes widened in disbelief as she glanced at Grayson. For his part, Grayson merely shook his head.

"O—oh! He isn't—I mean, we're not, uh," Ella stammered awkwardly.

Grayson intervened curtly. "No, thank you."

The shopkeeper placed the tart inside a paper bag and eagerly waited for payment while Ella rummaged through her dress pockets. Disapproval clouded his face as he raised an eyebrow expectantly at Grayson.

Irritated, Grayson shoved Ella aside, snatched the pastry bag, and slammed a bronze coin onto the counter. Ignoring any change, he pulled Ella out of the shop with a firm grip on her arm.

"Hey!" she cried, yanking her arm back defiantly. "What the hell was that for?"

He plunged his hand into the bag, extracting the tiny lemon tart with a flourish. Forcefully gripping her jaw, he made her mouth open and unexpectedly shoved the pastry in. Her cheeks ballooned, tart jelly oozing down her chin. Eyes wide, she swallowed painfully and coughed.

"Never humiliate me like that again," he snapped. "Men are supposed to pay for things when accompanying ladies."

"Excuse me for not knowing the local customs! I'm fully capable of paying for my own things," she said between a fit of coughing.

"The impression it left was terrible for me."

"Do you really care about what others think?" she asked, wiping her mouth.

"He assumed I was your husband! I'd sooner crawl on this street than let anyone believe I'd allow *my wife* to pay in my presence." He shoved her down the street, dragging her along as she stumbled.

"Well, I'm not your wife!" she shot back pointedly.

"I know! Gods, you drive me mad!"

An awkward silence engulfed them as they returned to Morning Song. The day had turned to dusk, the sun vanishing behind the trees. The path was winding and lengthy, and Ella remained furious at his earlier display in front of the bakery.

As they neared the lake, Grayson suddenly felt a surge of heat traveling up his back and exploding between his shoulders. He halted in his tracks as the flaming remnants vanished from his skin.

"Really?" he chuckled bitterly. "Was that supposed to do something?"

"It's what you deserve," she replied, shoving past him to take the lead, nose in the air.

With a flick of his finger, he sent a root spiraling around Ella's ankle, causing her to trip. She fell to the ground, landing on her hands and knees.

Ella growled with frustration, rolling onto her back and flinging several stones at him. He towered over her, his broad figure casting a shadow. As one stone struck his nose, he recoiled in pain and shot her an intense glare. Ella's heart skipped a beat, but she quickly regained her composure, leaping to her feet and sprinting away. Silence filled the space behind her; Grayson wasn't following. She dared a quick glance over her shoulder, noticing the empty meadow.

Suddenly, his winged figure swooped down upon her, plunging her world into darkness. Grayson's strong hands pinned Ella's wrists as she struggled beneath him, her teeth clenched and elongating. Grayson whispered through gritted teeth, "Is this what you want?" Their eyes locked as their breaths mingled from panting, electrifying the air between them. Ella's heart pounded fiercely in her chest as an undeniable tension simmered just beneath the surface.

She didn't know what she wanted.

To hurt him

To bite him.

To—

Struggling beneath him, Ella fixed her fiery gaze on Grayson and let out a fierce hiss. His grip was so tight that her fingers began to tingle. No, it was more than that—a strange sensation emitting from her palms, causing her skin to burn. Suddenly, a flash of white electricity erupted from her fingertips, wrapping around Grayson's arms. Surprised, he released her with a gasp.

Sitting up and exchanging puzzled glances, neither Ella nor Grayson could comprehend what had just transpired.

"Did that... hurt?" she asked hesitantly.

With a dismissive scoff and an eye roll, he replied, "No, of course not. It was just... unexpected. I never knew you had that power."

"Neither did I," she admitted with a wince, rubbing her rune-covered foot.

Intrigued, Grayson's voice softened. "Let me see your foot."

But she resisted. "Honestly? I've had enough of this today. Just leave my feet alone."

As Ella stood up and brushed herself off, she stole a glance at Grayson's intense eyes. They seemed to glow. The remaining daylight gave way to the soft glow from the school windows. It was miraculous no one else had seen them.

"Let's hurry up, shall we? I'd prefer not to be seen like this." He gestured at his charred clothing and pink, exposed skin on his arm. Her dress was a disheveled mess, the yellow ribbon long gone. They rushed through the halls towards the intricate sigil-marked wooden door Ella and Hamlet had used on her first day.

"Master Moore's office," Grayson announced. A blue light enveloped them as he cautiously opened the door.

"Why are we going to your office?" she asked.

"Why do you ask so many questions?" Grayson retorted, pushing her inside before entering himself. The portal door led to his closet.

"Seriously, stop pushing me!" she cried out, stomping into the room.

"Well, maybe if you moved faster..." he taunted.

Ella glared at him and made a rude gesture. "Ugh, you always have to be so..." she paused when he lunged forward and grabbed her legs. She tried to break free, but Grayson was too strong.

"Hold still! Just—stay still!" he ordered with a low growl. Ella yelped when she felt his powerful limbs wrap around her midsection, and wrestled him to the office floor.

His hold left her confused, feeling both anxious and excited. She could feel the heat of his hands through her dress.

"Get off me, you irritating..." Ella said halfheartedly. He pulled her boots off and tossed them aside.

"Fading," he muttered under his breath, sliding a finger across her glowing runes, which now looked more like healed scars. Her toes flexed as he rubbed at her runes.

"What?" she asked breathlessly.

He let go of her for a moment and pointed at her foot. "Look here," he said. "The runes. They're fading."

"But I thought they were supposed to be permanent?" she asked, eyes wide.

"So did I," he replied honestly. "They are supposed to be."

She stared him down. "So why are they fading? Don't you know everything, *Master Moore*?" She was bordering on teasing.

Grayson raised an eyebrow, blinking slowly. Was she flirting with him?

He sighed, "Apparently not everything, Miss Marks."

Ella snorted in response. "Yet you sure love to act like it."

He motioned her towards the door. "Get out," he said flatly.

"You definitely have a knack for spoiling enjoyable moments," she grumbled as she headed for the exit.

"If I have to put up with your insufferable company any longer, I might just tear my own wings off!" Grayson deadpanned.

Ella couldn't help but smirk back at him. "Oh, don't worry. I'll see you in training bright and early tomorrow, *Gracie*." The room filled with an unspoken charge—before she disappeared out his door.

Grayson's eyes fell on her forgotten boots.

CHAPTER TWENTY-NINE

Ella couldn't help but notice the enticing tray of pastries Grayson had prepared the following day during their training session. She stole furtive glances at him from behind her steaming cup as he hesitantly reached for a raspberry tart before popping it in his mouth.

"You always squint your eyes suspiciously whenever you try new foods," she commented, amusement apparent in her voice.

Grayson responded with mock indignation, "I didn't realize I signed up for a culinary audition."

"I wasn't examining you," she lied unconvincingly, a smirk dancing on her lips.

It was Ella's turn to practice conjuring a sentient being from her flame. When she started, beads of sweat formed on her brow and she struggled to give it form. Grayson observed her efforts, contemplating how to offer guidance.

"Envision the form you want your flame to adopt," he suggested, demonstrating his skills by summoning a tiny fireball that danced gracefully in his palm. He captivated Ella's attention as the incandescent sphere morphed before her eyes.

Much to Ella's astonishment, a fiery blue miniature horse emerged from his hand. It galloped wildly around the room, growing larger and more majestic with each stride until it was the size of a live stallion.

"Show off," Ella muttered half-heartedly, yet her admiration was apparent. The powerful stallion charged towards her with thundering hooves, and she tried to dodge it. In an instant, Grayson's firm hands gripped her waist, lifting her into the air. "Ahh!" she exclaimed, suddenly finding herself on the wild horse's back as its mane danced with flames.

Clutching tightly to its back, Ella's heart hammered in her chest while the horse sped around the room. She had never experienced anything like this before. Remembering her conversation with Grayson, she called out over the loud hooves, "I told you I've never ridden a horse before!"

Grayson watched her with a stoic expression, puzzled by his own actions. Her melodious laughter echoed throughout the room like wind chimes. "Take control of it," he instructed.

Breathless, Ella gripped the fiery horse's mane. "What am I supposed to do?"

"It's a creature of flames," he replied. "Take control." Casually returning to his seat, he brushed lint from his pants.

"Take control?" she repeated in disbelief. "What does that even mean?" As the horse grew more agitated, it tossed her around wildly. Desperate and losing her grip, she pleaded, "Won't you help me?"

Without looking at her, Grayson simply responded, "Nope."

The stallion made a mighty leap, causing her to gasp sharply as she experienced a fleeting sensation of weightlessness. She felt a pull in her chest and her fingers clenched into the horse's hide.

The surrounding hues morphed dramatically from cerulean blue to shades of orange and yellow. Ella let out an exhilarating whoop, her hair wildly dancing around her as she leaned to the right, prompting the horse to make a swift right turn.

"Can you believe this?" Ella exclaimed with pure joy, coaxing the horse to rear up on its hind legs.

"You have successfully taken possession. Now turn it into something else," Grayson instructed. "Morph it."

"But I've only just got on!"

"Think of what you want it to be. You control it."

Ella wasn't sure what she wanted the horse to turn into next. She considered a dragon but feared it might pale in comparison to his creation. Suddenly, the horse reduced in size and she lost her balance, falling off its back and rolling along the cold, solid ground.

"Clearly, I didn't think that through," she chuckled, laying on her back. Grayson appeared above her, looking down at her. He reminded her of a feline—the way his eyes narrowed and the slight tilt of his head.

"A cat? Seriously?" he exclaimed, unimpressed. Ella shifted onto her stomach, her eyes following the fiery feline as it slinked away, leaping at unseen targets.

"Valla, my cat," Ella defended.

He rolled his eyes at the mention of the other thorn in his side. He had to figure out a way to keep that thing out of his rooms.

"And how exactly is that going to help you in battle?"

"I didn't realize I was being trained for combat. You told me to turn it into something. I did, and I succeeded in your little test!"

"Barely," he scoffed.

"You can't even let me enjoy this victory, can you?" she snapped back, frustration audible in her voice. An uneasy silence settled between them, punctuated by the soft growls and mewls of the vanishing fire cat.

"You didn't get this victory without me practically handing it to you. And it's because you're your own worst enemy," he said, wrapping his cloak around himself.

"What do you mean?"

"You doubt yourself when you shouldn't. I've witnessed you achieve incredible feats without even trying. But when you are asked to do something, you freeze up. You are good at these things. Allow yourself to be."

Her eyes widened in surprise. "Was that... a compliment from you just now?"

"Absolutely not," he retorted sharply. A muscle in his jaw fluttered.

"It was! You actually think I'm good!" she teased with triumph. She clapped her hands together.

"I think you're an insufferable thorn in my ass," he bit back before turning away from her and settling into a chair. "You'll let such praise go straight to your head when it's already inflated enough." As Ella watched the twitching veins on his forehead, she couldn't help but stifle a laugh.

"Thank you," she said finally. She saw his eyes widen a fraction, then his face returned to his signature scowl.

"Don't thank me for doing my job," he mocked.

⟫⟫⟶

"Grayson, I have to admit, whatever you did certainly made a difference," Gregor exclaimed with delight. "She seems much happier lately."

"Well, I only carried out what was requested of me," Grayson responded, sounding defensive.

"Fair enough. We have three more vacation days left, but there isn't much to entertain us here. Mistress Devoro approached me early this morning—more like barreled into me—claiming she saw

Ella wearing a crown in her dream. I had to sneak a Forget-it-now potion into her tea.”

“What else would you expect from someone who catches glimpses of the future?”

“It’s truly extraordinary. I feel constantly on edge by it all. Trying to persuade a Seer that her visions are merely dreams is a futile endeavor,” sighed Gregor. “She didn’t seem distraught, at least.”

“A good sign. Did she see anything else of note?” Grayson asked with interest.

“Not that she told me. I extracted the dream while she slept off the potion’s effects. When she awoke, I fed her some information about her just telling me all about her curriculum plans coming up.” He held up a tiny jar containing floating silver strands. “I need to add these to a drink and then sleep to view her vision.”

“But is that safe? Dream Jumps can trap you within the dream realm. It’s not like a Waking Nightmare—an illusion. If you perish in the dream world, your demise is real.”

“I’m aware of that. *I* taught *you* that,” Gregor grumbled, tapping the jar with his fingertip. “Why don’t you go see how Ellarhyssa is doing?”

“I’m not her babysitter!” Grayson shot back. “Being around her too much will give off the wrong impression.”

“Just like with Sienna?” Gregor said, his violet eyes locked onto Grayson’s.

“That’s not fair,” Grayson protested. “You dragged me to Desmouth Isle countless times, and both you and her mother practically forced us together.”

“Sienna is a lovely girl,” Gregor began.

“I’m not disputing that. But our connection was shallow and short-lived. Sifrrod sending her here was likely a desperate attempt to rekindle something fleeting.”

“I had hoped you two would have developed something more,” Gregor sighed in disappointment, “but it appears fate had other plans.” Sienna and Grayson had practically grown up together, during his trips between Idris and Desmouth. It had been ideal that that would have married. They were barely friends, both cold and elusive—selective.

Two people so similar could not possibly fit together.

"You're being absurd. My only consolation is that she didn't let it affect our school environment. I have to give her credit for that. Your continuous meddling in my love life has to stop. The impropriety of it alone..."

"Fine. I'll stop meddling." Gregor looked away from Grayson, a smile on his lips.

"Liar."

⟫⟫⟶

The next morning, Gregor wiped the sleep from his eyes and stretched, the enticing red silk sheets of his bed beckoning him to return to their warmth. His dream had unfolded just as Mistress Devoro had foretold: Ella held a crown in her hands.

"What a waste of time," he grumbled in frustration. His vacation was almost over, and there was still no message from Hamlet.

Suddenly, he heard a gentle knock on his closet door, and the familiar portal sigil began to glow.

"Trust you to show up at the break of dawn," Gregor teased lightheartedly as he slipped on a vibrant yellow robe.

Cautiously, Grayson cracked the door open before entering. "Well? Anything?"

"Nothing at all. That woman is nothing but theatrics," Gregor dismissed. "The dream offered nothing more—it was shrouded in darkness."

"And you don't find that ominous?" Grayson probed. "Ella clutching a crown while surrounded by shadows?"

Exasperated, Gregor buried his face in his hands. "If I thought it held any significance, I'd share it with you. It feels like I'm the only one here who's trying to untangle this confounding prophecy."

"Why not reassign her?" Grayson suggested. "Add her to someone else's daily task list instead of mine."

With purposeful strides, Gregor approached his elegant ivory vanity, extracting a fine-toothed comb from its drawer. Settling into the chair in front of the mirror, he kept his eyes locked on Grayson's reflection as he meticulously untangled his golden mane. "Who else could handle her? You've said so yourself. Her powers are growing inexplicably. Besides, I see you've reached some common ground with her. She's not alone anymore, and neither are you."

Grayson rolled his eyes, agitated by the interference. "Must you always meddle? This is all just an act. I'm merely doing as I've been instructed."

Gregor raised an eyebrow, smirking slightly. "Is it truly so terrible to think of her as a friend?"

Grayson gritted his teeth, steadfast in his reply. "Yes."

Perched atop the rooftop, Grayson savored a brief respite from the chaos, basking in the sun's gentle warmth as it ascended. Drawing a deep breath, billows of smoke escaped his nostrils. It was the only solace he could find amidst Gregor's unrelenting demands.

Grayson muttered to himself, "I'm just doing my duty." The acknowledgment resonated within him; after all, she would be worthless without the ability to fly and harness her magic.

He couldn't deny her allure. He had acknowledged her beauty. But he was determined not to be swayed by the close quarters that Gregor had orchestrated this time—not like he had been with Sienna.

"Keep it professional," he whispered to himself.

Suddenly, her melodic voice reached his ears from behind, causing his heartbeat to pause. Gradually, he pivoted and glanced down at her bare feet before slowly lifting his gaze to her face. The vibrant orange and crimson shades of the sunrise gently caressed her features.

A grin spread across her face, revealing tiny, sharp fangs as her dark, flowing hair danced in the breeze. Clad in a casual blue sweater and comfortable pants, she seemed at ease. He couldn't help but leap backward, an overwhelming sensation consuming him. It made his skin prickle.

"Hello, Grayson!" she exclaimed with joy. The sound of his name on her tongue irked him for reasons he couldn't quite fathom.

"I don't recall allowing you to call me by my first name," he replied gruffly. Her smile faltered momentarily, and he clenched his jaw, turning away from her.

"Isn't it stunning? My friends and I used to watch sunrises together," she murmured gently. "I have always loved sunsets more. There's something special about witnessing the sky transform and give way to the stars."

"Hm." His personal space was once again intruded upon, yet surprisingly, he didn't object. She moved past him, climbing onto the ledge with arms outstretched and face uplifted to the sky, eyes closed. He watched as the fabric on her shoulders seemingly opened on its own, revealing black wings that unfolded gracefully. The familiar sheen of an illusion enveloped her entire form. Glancing back at him with a widening smile, she beckoned, "Coming?" Without waiting for a reply, she dove downward, vanishing from view. Her exuberant laughter reverberated throughout the air.

It dawned on him that it was his choice; no one was forcing him. Gregor hadn't tasked him with this mission. He could simply return inside and abandon her presence, retreating back to his room and his peaceful life of isolation. He had told himself as such just moments ago.

So how had he found himself on the rooftop's edge, plunging down after her?

⫸⟶

They soared above the treetops, gliding effortlessly through the sky. The world below them appeared smaller, insignificant compared to the vastness of the open sky. A sense of freedom enveloped her, and the weight of her worries seemed to fade away.

Grayson led the way, flying at an altitude that allowed them to view the land below from a distance. He flew in a wide arc, taking them in a circle, the ground below a sea of lush green.

She could see the city of Calisan, the town of Hildfree, and the glittering waters of the sea. Her eyes focused on the ocean, hoping to catch a glimpse of Hellharth if it flickered. A gust of wind veered her to the left—her wings faltered for a moment, and she found herself lurching forward, flapping frantically.

She was falling.

She couldn't right herself—couldn't find a way to slow her descent. The ground was coming up too quickly. The trees below her blurred and she squeezed her eyes shut. She felt her body slam into something hard—the air knocked out of her. She opened her eyes—she was still falling—pressed against Grayson's chest.

He let out a low snarl, wings encasing her into darkness.

They crashed through branches—heard the sounds of snapping—and she felt his hand come up to cradle the back of her head and roll himself in the air. His back hit the ground first—a grunt and gasp from him—but he held her tight.

The impact was harsh and left him breathless. Her weight on his chest was not helping, but he could not move. Not yet.

She lifted her head, the light creeping through his wings. "Grayson?"

At the sound of his name, he released her, rolling her gently off of him. Sunlight filtered through the towering canopy of trees, casting dappled patterns on the forest floor below. The interplay of light and shadow created a mesmerizing dance—as if the forest itself was breathing with life.

It reminded him of his bedroom.

"Are you hurt?" he asked, wincing as he flexed his limbs. Nothing was broken, thankfully.

"N-no. I'm sorry. I started panicking and—I was trying to see—" her breath caught and her eyes welled with tears. "I'm sorry." She turned away, hiding her face. The movement made her braid fall to the side, revealing her neck.

Grayson felt sick.

Her neck was so delicate, now marked with bruises and scratches from where his hand had rested. He brushed her hair away, and she jerked back, flinching.

"You said you weren't hurt," he snapped, his voice cold and harsh. She pulled from his grasp, standing up and dusting off her pants. She looked him over—his black trousers and blue tunic had snags and rips throughout.

"I told you I am fine," she argued. Her neck just stung a bit. She could feel the blood pooling underneath. She wouldn't tell him that though, after she just made him nose-dive after her.

He took a step towards her, and she backed away. His eyes flashed at her and he snarled, baring his teeth. "Let me see it!" he demanded. His white teeth flashed—the canopy lights dancing along his face.

It was hard for Ella to take him seriously with a twig sticking out of his hair. She insisted again that she was fine, and suddenly she was pinned between a tree and his body. His leg was between hers, making her sit atop the front of his thigh, and lifted her up slightly so she was stuck on her tiptoes.

Ella let out a startled gasp and tried to wriggle away, but he clasped both her hands above her head—the tree bark was digging into her skin. "Let go!" she yelled. He tightened his grip on her, holding her in place. As she moved to squirm away, he pressed his face to hers, breathing hotly into her ear.

He whispered, "Let. Me. See." Every word was a caress that traveled down her spine and sent a jolt through her.

Angry. Commanding.

And Gods damn her—her body betrayed her. That wave of heat against her neck made her knees buckle and her hips rolled involuntarily.

Right over his thigh.

He stilled, and she was certain he could feel the warmth that was now radiating from between her legs.

On his thigh.

On his thigh! She internally screamed.

Grayson froze. His face went from angry to disbelieving. He stared down at her for a few seconds, not quite sure if he imagined such a thing.

But there—there was no denying it. Her scent spiked and her breath quickened. He released his hold on her hands, claws digging into the tree behind her head, momentarily sagging against her before righting himself. She yanked her hands free and grabbed the tree, kicking him away from her. He stumbled back, looking dazed and bewildered.

He swiped at his nose a few times, his feline eyes darting around—looking anywhere but her.

She hastily moved her braid aside and turned her back to him. "Look at it then," she said, her voice shaking.

It took Grayson a few seconds to regain his composure, chasing away her scent by covering his nose and mouth with his hand. Her neck had large purple finger marks along the skin, blood pricking where his nails had cut into her. He gently placed a hand on her neck—ignoring how she leaned into his touch and how she let out a shuttering gasp. A soft, radiant glow enveloped his fingertips. He gently placed the whole of his hand on the bruised area. His magic responded, weaving its ethereal strands into her skin. The bruising gradually began to fade, and he winced when he felt his own neck bearing the marks. The glow faded, and he lifted his hand.

A soothing sensation spreads through Ella's neck as if a gentle balm had been applied. "How did you do that?" she asked while rubbing her neck.

"Magic," he answered, his voice quiet and flat. "We should get back. Are you alright to fly? We are just before the Mountains of Frey."

"Yes. I'm fine," she answered.

Even though she had assured him a dozen times that she was okay to fly, he hovered above her all the way home, his shadow engulfing her.

That night she fought with herself. Grayson didn't say anything the whole way back to Morning Song, and when they finally arrived on the rooftop, he didn't spare her a backward glance.

She was mortified.

He was probably scrubbing his pant leg at that very moment. She let out a sigh of frustration and threw herself off the bed. Hamlet was right—she was a prude. Inexperienced. The only thing she had ever done beyond kissing was let Highwing fondle her.

On a tree.

"What the hell is with me and the trees?" she muttered.

Perhaps it was her age—she was going into birthing years now—maybe there was something wrong with her.

What if he didn't speak to her again? The thought of it made her heart ache. When did his presence become a balm for her?

"Just pretend it didn't happen. Act unfazed," she said aloud.

CHAPTER THIRTY

Grayson sat alone on the edge of the roof, his gaze fixed on the horizon. He exuded an air of aloofness, a shield protecting him from the world around him. The tranquility of the morning seemed incongruous with his somber demeanor. There were just a couple of days left until vacation was over—and then he would be bombarded with the meager task of teaching again.

As he stared into the distance, lost in his thoughts, Ella approached him, her eyes shimmering with a glimmer of hope. She was wearing a light green sundress, and it gently draped over her body, skimming the curves in a flattering way without being too form-fitting. Her hair was pulled back in a messy ponytail, and she was barefoot.

It dawned on him that he still had her boots.

She wore a warm smile and held a wicker basket in her hands. Valla was at her feet, the morning sun making her fur glow, her tail swishing back and forth.

"Master Moore," she said hopefully, her voice carrying a gentle warmth. "I thought you might like some company?"

Grayson glanced at Ella, a mix of skepticism and curiosity flickering in his eyes. He had grown accustomed to solitude, finding comfort in it—but she had slowly started integrating herself within his routine. The idea of sharing food seemed inconsequential to him.

It was apparent they were not going to mention the incident in the woods. He flexed his neck experimentally. The salves he had dressed on the bruises had done the job, and they were no longer painful.

Reluctantly, Grayson rose from the ledge, his movements slow and hesitant. He didn't speak a word, but Ella sensed his silent agreement. She smiled and settled herself on the stone floor, the basket in her lap. Valla was sniffing at it, smelling something she liked.

Ella spread out a vibrant red blanket on the floor in front of them, arranging an assortment of delectable treats from the basket with care.

Grayson watched her as she meticulously set the plates, her every movement deliberate and graceful. There was a gentle comfort to her presence that had begun to slowly chip away at the walls he had built around himself.

The memory of her rolling her hips against him assaulted his mind, and he clenched his teeth.

He scowled at the thought. This was a dangerous path to tread. He knew that. He knew better than to get too close to her.

Finally, Ella gestured for him to join her on the blanket. He hesitated, his eyes flickering from the blanket to her. Valla was patiently waiting for whatever it was that she had sniffed out.

With a sigh, he lowered himself onto the blanket, his posture guarded and his expression distant. He observed as Ella poured glasses of sparkling fruit juice, the bubbles rising and dancing in the sunlight.

As Ella extended a plate of bacon, she broke the silence. "I know you prefer your own company…"

Grayson remained quiet, his eyes locked on the plate before him. He reached out, taking a small bite. Valla impatiently swatted at the plate, and Ella giggled, handing her a slice of bacon.

Gradually, Grayson's guarded façade began to crumble. She would talk and he would answer stiffly, responding to her questions with a simple yes or no.

"I'm guessing that Valla has been staying with you at night?" she asked, her eyes crinkling.

"Not by my own choice. She walks right in," Grayson scoffed, his voice gruff.

"She doesn't usually take to people that readily. She seems to have taken a liking to you, though," Ella said.

"She's taken a liking to my bed," he corrected, his voice heavy with sarcasm. He took a bite of the bacon, offering his unfinished bite to Valla, who took it greedily.

"She is usually a great judge of character," Ella teased.

"I find that hard to believe," he scoffed.

"I noticed she's been getting a bit pudgy lately," she said, patting Valla's exposed belly. "Could it be she's been getting a bit pudgy because of you?"

"Why am I to blame?" he demanded, unconsciously offering Valla a bite of egg. Valla eagerly accepted, her eyes closing as she savored her treat. He realized what he did and quickly covered the plate with a napkin. "Oh," he said dumbly.

Ella laughed at his expression. It was a laugh that carried a melody of joy and genuine mirth. He looked up, drawn to the source of that beguiling sound. Her eyes sparkled with mischief, her smile radiant, and her laughter filled with an unapologetic vibrancy.

For a moment, Grayson forgot to breathe as he watched her, the corners of his lips twitching ever so slightly in response. It was as if her laughter had reached into the depths of his soul, stirring dormant emotions and awakening something within him that he had long forgotten.

It wasn't like her fit of laughter when she had consumed Meraroot—one that had been forced out of her by the plant's effects. As her laughter subsided, he found himself unable to tear his gaze away from her.

An uncomfortable silence fell over the two of them, the only sound the chirping of birds and Valla's snores. Eager to break the silence, Ella asked, "Did you always want to teach?"

"Hardly. That was forced upon me, like most things. I had no choice in the matter." He didn't elaborate further, his words tainted with a hint of bitterness.

"Well, what did you want to do?" Ella prompted.

"I never had the luxury of thinking about it." He paused, his eyes turning away from her, his shoulders slouching. "Being Fae—even a halfling Fae—out here, doesn't give you many choices."

"I suppose not," she replied, a hint of sadness in her voice. "Is that also because of—of what my father did?"

Grayson jerked his head, his eyes meeting hers. She blinked rapidly and bit her bottom lip, fiddling with her hair. She seemed uncomfortable with the direction of the conversation, despite having led it.

Grayson moved his hair behind his ear, revealing a slight point—much smaller compared to hers. "You haven't had to face the kind of persecution that comes with being Fae. Be grateful for that."

"I didn't mean anything by it... I wouldn't say I haven't had my share of persecution," she added pointedly. "You didn't exactly welcome me with open arms."

Grayson cleared his throat, his expression hardening. "No, I didn't. I wasn't sure what to think of you. You were different. I suppose I didn't expect you to be so different from what I had been told about Elves," he admitted. She gave a small smile.

Ella focused her thoughts. Slowly, the plates began to quiver, a gentle levitation lifting them from the blanket. The plates hovered gracefully in the air before neatly stacking themselves on top of each other and shifting themselves into the basket.

Her eyes changed from warm brown to glowing gold, and light stripes appeared on her hands and arms. She stretched and sighed, letting her wings spread out from her back with a low groan.

She turned to Grayson. "Honestly, you don't know how good that feels. Kills my back keeping them pinned in all the time." She gave a gentle flap and a black feather drifted over to him.

He reached out and plucked it, holding it gently, before letting it flutter away. "Don't I know it," he agreed.

He rolled his shoulders and his wings emerged from his broad back, their span and structure reminiscent of the mythical creatures that roamed ancient tales.

Dragons, Ella thought with a slight shiver. Covered in iridescent scales, his wings shimmered with an array of vibrant hues, ranging from deep emerald greens to fiery reds, as if catching the light of unseen flames. The edges of each wing were lined with razor-sharp spine—beautiful and deadly.

"They're beautiful," she breathed. She ran her hand along the length of his wing, marveling at the intricate structure. Like the veins in a dragonfly wing. "Beautiful," she repeated.

Grayson could feel the warmth of her fingertips tracing along the veins of his wing, sending jolts of electricity through him. He shivered at the sensation, his body reacting to the contact. No one had ever called his wings beautiful before. He certainly didn't think so. It was an unexpected sensation, and it made him feel oddly vulnerable. He moved his wing slightly, the edges of his wing flaring out and back in slowly.

"Sorry," she muttered, flushing. She stood then, beginning to gather her things. Valla stretched and yawned, her eyes blinking open.

"I'll leave you to your day. Um. Thank you for keeping me company," she added hurriedly, opening the door and letting Valla walk through first.

He didn't see her for the rest of the day.

"Assign her to someone else," Grayson said to Gregor. He was sitting at his desk, a stack of papers in front of him, and a blaring migraine forming in his head.

Gregor sat atop his desk, plucking a grape from a proffered bowl. "Why? Everything seems to be going quite well."

"Assign her to someone else," Grayson repeated, with clenched teeth.

Gregor popped another grape into his mouth. He chewed slowly; the juice running down his chin. He swallowed and smiled. "No."

Grayson slammed his fist down on the desk. "I told you not to do that. Not to meddle!"

"I'm not doing anything, Grayson," Gregor replied, his tone placid.

CHAPTER THIRTY-ONE

Sienna's grip tightened around Ella's ankle as she pulled her relentlessly into the water. Grayson observed from a distance, standing firmly in the middle of the field with his arms crossed over his chest. Today's activities involved affinity training, and everyone had been ushered outdoors to form groups based on their unique magical affinities. Not how everyone had planned to come back to school.

Ella found herself to be the only one in her unconventional category. Meanwhile, Anna had joined a cluster of individuals who were deeply attuned to nature's magic—oblivious and huddled together making random flowers bloom. Ethan was placed among a generic group, while Sienna stood side by side with a few Fae and Maji who shared her affinity toward water.

As they began to pair off for practice, Ella should have anticipated that she'd be matched against someone wielding water powers.

Bracing for the challenge, she couldn't help but let out a nervous laugh.

Glancing at Sienna, she had said, "Alright then, let's see what you've got."

That's how she found herself drowning. She had let her guard down, and Sienna had the advantage. Before she knew it, Ella was submerged beneath the lake's surface, gasping for breath as Sienna's golden tail shimmered and glinted in the murky depths below. Ella struggled for air and broke the surface. She caught sight of Sienna's webbed dorsal fin circling her like a shark—spiny and knobby and impossibly sharp.

"A precarious position you've found yourself in, Miss Marks!" Grayson yelled from the safety of the shore. "She might indeed have the advantage—you're in her domain. But victory is not yet hers."

Sienna emerged from the depths, her arms propelling a massive wave that engulfed Ella and pushed her beneath the surface again. She gasped and sputtered, managing to swim back up.

"Fire doesn't beat water!" Ella retorted; her voice strained. Curious onlookers, including fellow teachers, had amassed on the shoreline, hooting and hollering as they witnessed the spectacle. "What kind of twisted school—" she was cut off again by another wave.

Grayson's unmistakable laughter echoed in Ella's ears. Her anger surged. She wanted nothing more than to yank him up by his long braid and choke him with it. Suddenly, Sienna reappeared before her, eyes dilated and predatory. That pretty blue color that usually showed in her eyes was now replaced entirely by black. Her skin glistened with iridescent scales that shimmered beneath the water's surface. Sienna let out a high-pitched trill—a sound so resonant it coursed through the water and sent vibrations through Ella's very core.

Focus, Ella, focus! she urged herself internally. Just then, she felt Sienna's tail fin forcefully collide with her back, and a flurry of air bubbles rushed out of her mouth. She plummeted deeper into the ominous abyss, her gaze upward, dizzily watching the light refract above her.

Her foot emitted a faint burning sensation, while her hands radiated an eerie orange glow. The surrounding water's temperature began to rise rapidly and Ella caught a glimpse of Sienna's menacing siren form hurtling towards her. Mustering all her strength from within, she unleashed a fierce wave of heat that caused the surrounding water to boil relentlessly. Suddenly, Sienna let out an agonizing screech as the searing liquid engulfed her.

Ella took the opportunity and took off, clawing for the surface and paddling for the shore. She pulled herself up, her uniform sopping wet and weighing her down. Grayson had a hand over his mouth and Ella realized he was trying to suppress a laugh.

When Sienna finally joined the rest of them, Grayson reiterated the importance of never underestimating your opponents. Sienna blushed her blue coloring, her arms a darker hue from being burned.

Grayson couldn't help but chuckle when he deliberately teamed up Ella with Sienna. To him, it was a perfect opportunity to teach a valuable lesson. However, his decision to pair her with Gertrude Rydelle was nothing short of pure spitefulness. Throughout the entire training session, Ella shot disdainful glares in his direction.

Gertrude wasted no time taking advantage of the situation, sending numerous cheap shots at Ella. Grayson watched her struggle, mentally noting that she was learning another vital lesson in patience.

"Hold still and take it!" Gertrude shouted between sparks of light, blonde hair whipping about furiously.

She was dodging blast after blast, rolling around in the dirt. He could tell she was reluctant to use offensive tactics, but she had to learn.

"You can't always run from an opponent," Grayson said, sucking his teeth.

The tipping point came when Gertrude unleashed a relentless torrent of light attacks that made direct contact with Ella's chest and sent her sprawling onto the feild. Gertrude was smug with herself, flicking at invisible dirt on her clothes with a bored stance.

Grayson hesitated, almost ready to halt the whole exercise, but miraculously, Ella managed to rise back to her feet. She was covered in filth, spitting out grass and mud, clutching her sides with her hands.

"Come on, Ella!" Armand cheered from the sidelines, surprising Grayson. He was under the impression that Miss Rydelle and Mister Tyren were an item.

Gertude let out an indignant noise, her mouth agape and face going red. She sent a bolt of light toward Armand, who managed to dodge it. In place where he had been standing, was smoldering grass.

With the distraction, Ella sprang towards Gertrude—and much to Grayson's mixed feelings of shock and perhaps fury, her fist connected with Gertrude's face, sending her sprawling onto the ground. Gertrude let out a gasping wail. He couldn't let this slide. She was rolling around on the ground clutching her nose, the tang of blood spiking the air. Her blonde hair was matted to her head with dirt. The rest of the group gasped in unison.

"Detention for you, Miss Marks! Miss Rydelle, I suggest you head to the infirmary."

Ella protested vehemently, "You've got to be joking! That was not a foul!"

Grayson shook his head and reminded her, "The objective was to counter magic with *magic*, Miss Marks. This wasn't meant to be a physical brawl. Detention after lunch."

Ella popped another grape into her mouth while Grayson looked over some more papers. He had been becoming increasingly agitated by the number of mistakes the Seniors were making. It wasn't much of a detention if he were being honest.

"Who showed you how to fly?" she asked unexpectedly.

"Huh?" He set aside his glass pen, visibly exhausted from grading papers.

"Who taught you to fly?" she insisted.

His brows knitted in confusion. "When I was five, Gregor threw me off a building."

"Are you SERIOUS?" Her mouth was hung open, enchanted brown eyes wide.

He casually shrugged. "He had tried everything else—like having me trail a flock of geese. Honestly, it's a miracle I reached adulthood with him as my guardian."

"You can't just hurl a kid off a rooftop!" No sane person would do that.

He let out a soft laugh. "So, how do they teach your kind to fly?"

"They support us until we grasp it, then let us loose. Never high enough to hurt," she answered with a shrug.

He recalled the fear and adrenaline he felt plunging from the sky when he was thrown. Gregor had assured him they'd reunite on the ground. As Grayson's tiny wings caught an air current and he soared, he could hear Gregor cheering: "That's it! Keep going! You've got this!"

Grayson's throat tightened with nostalgia, and he cleared his throat. "Well, it sure was effective—I caught on quickly." He hadn't thought about that in years.

He noticed her face take on a sullen expression and asked her what was wrong.

"I can't help but miss them. I just can't fathom how they could leave me behind without any explanation or even a note."

Ah. She was thinking of her own family, he thought.

"I'd offer you words of comfort, but I am unsure of what to say," he answered truthfully. He pushed the bowl of grapes closer to her. She seemed more content when there was food in her mouth.

Her gaze drifted towards the elegant music box resting on his desk. Biting her lower lip, she boldly traced her fingers along the top. She raised the lid, and light danced off the tiny mirror affixed inside it while a gentle tune filled the air. Subconsciously, she could feel Grayson's eyes on her, watching her while she traced the floral designs.

"It's beautiful," she said, captivated by the light thrum of music. It was a light cacophony that ended in rolling notes repetitively. She hummed it absentmindedly.

"It was all that remained from the ruins of my childhood home. Used to have this in it," he gestured to the worn leather cord encircling his neck, from which dangled a silver oval medallion. "It's a necklace that belonged to my father."

She glanced at it curiously, then apologized. "I didn't mean to be nosy."

"You tend to be impulsive," he said, allowing a small smile. "Honestly, I don't mind sharing." As he spoke, she gently closed the box with a soft click, her eyes never leaving his face.

"Can you recall him?" she asked.

"Do you mean my father?" he replied, shifting nervously in his chair. "I remember bits and pieces. The memory was vivid when you unintentionally dragged me into that horrific world."

"I'm not sure how that happened," she admitted.

He examined her carefully before asking, "Can you recall the specific event?"

"Yes, but it's hard to put into words."

"What emotions were you feeling when it occurred?"

Her cheeks reddened as she looked away. "Certainly nothing positive." She cleared her throat, appearing embarrassed.

"Do you think you could recreate it if you tried?" He was examining her.

She grimaced and crossed her arms defensively. "I don't want to go through that ever again."

"Just try it on me," he insisted, adjusting his position in the chair. He leaned closer, and she backed away. She felt the warmth of his breath on her face. She sniffed, her nostrils flaring, and the smell of his minty breath tickled her nose.

Her eyes widened. "Don't you remember what happened last time? We didn't talk for weeks. It was traumatic."

"You caught me off guard. It won't happen again," he reassured her.

"I don't even know how I did it in the first place," she objected, toying with a strand of her hair anxiously. Hamlet had always claimed that the mind was fragile.

"If the magic can only be activated by negative emotions, its results will always be detrimental. Emotions play a role in magic, but they can also lead to disaster," he explained.

"Is this another one of your teachings, Master Moore?" she asked. When she addressed him in this manner, it just didn't feel right anymore—not like it used to.

"Every moment is an opportunity for learning, Miss Marks."

She was quiet, chewing on her bottom lip in thought. He cocked his head at her. "Well?"

Slowly, she nodded her agreement. "Okay. But only if you promise not to fault me should anything happen." If he began seizing and screaming again, she would have to get Gregor.

"Reasonable enough," he said. If anything, Gregor would fault *him*.

Ella struggled to recreate the moment she had first grasped the concept of shadow work. Waking nightmares.

However, with Grayson's intense green eyes staring at her so intently, concentrating was impossible. She glanced at his lips and caught herself.

"Stop staring! How am I supposed to focus?" she huffed.

Grayson deliberately averted his gaze, fixing his eyes on a tiny speck on his wooden desk. "We don't have all day," he reminded her.

Frustration bubbled up inside Ella, mixed with anger at being abandoned by those she called family. Feelings of inadequacy, depression, and anxiety swirled within her. She wondered if anyone truly loved her or if their love was just superficial.

And there it was—the swirling storm inside her that morphed into raw anger.

"Hold on to that emotion," Grayson advised, watching her carefully.

Ella could feel the magic building at her fingertips, and she slowly let it go. It felt as if she were a spectator within her own body.

"Can you hear me?" Grayson asked as her eyes began to glaze over.

His voice sounded muffled—as if she was underwater. She nodded in response.

"Now, imagine something that brings you joy," he suggested. If negative emotions led to dire consequences, maybe happiness could make a difference.

A sarcastic smile appeared on her face. "Nothing makes me happy right now." Dark matter began to swirl around her, moving closer to him. His jaw tightened, but his expression remained unchanged.

"Do you recall pushing me into that table during the winter formal?" His voice was steady. She found herself laughing, the memory becoming clearer. She pictured his annoyed face as he wiped away desserts and frosting from his cheek.

"What about your first kiss?" he proposed. She almost felt it: Gideon's lips meeting hers awkwardly and eagerly. However, the vision of Gideon's lifeless body overpowered her thoughts.

"I can't," she whispered. "I can't." She was on the verge of losing control—her sight blurred and her ears rang.

"Tell me about the first time you learned to fly," he said soothingly. She sensed his breath on her cheek and found herself drifting away, enveloped by the scent of mint.

Then she saw Grayson; her anger started to dissipate. The dark tendrils encircled Grayson's limbs as he became more distinct. His eyes closed, and he exhaled sharply, the last of his breath escaping him before he was taken in his mind.

CHAPTER THIRTY-TWO

Perched atop a roof, Grayson gazed down at the bustling city of Idris. Green and white flags fluttered triumphantly in the sky, accompanied by dancing kites and dazzling fireworks that crackled and boomed in the twilight. Market stalls were overflowed with exotic wares, their merchants beckoning passersby with tales of far-off lands and treasures from distant eras.

The air was alive with the mingling scents of fragrant spices, freshly baked bread, and the sweet aroma of incense wafting from temples. Music drifted through the night—cut off by the occasional boom of a firework as musicians played haunting melodies, their melancholic notes echoing through the cobblestone streets.

As his heart pounded in his chest, he found himself face to face with Gregor, his blond hair styled in a high bun. Adorned in festive robes embellished with green and gold sashes, Gregor knelt before a five-year-old Grayson. His shoulder-length hair framed a vivid pink scar across his nose and cheek. Dressed in matching robes, young Grayson clutched an enchanted paper crane that flitted its wings. His own small leathery appendages drooped behind him.

Ella had inadvertently transported him back to this memory. One filled with details unknown to him, seen from every perspective simultaneously. He was just a spectator. He wondered if this was something akin to Dream Jumping.

"I'm scared," little Grayson whimpered, causing his older self to wince at the shrill tone. He didn't remember ever sounding like that or looking so pitiful. His youngling self was a scrawny thing, barely enough meat if birds were to pick at him.

"I don't remember not having my fangs," he added softly. The boy had gaps in his mouth where his teeth should have been.

"Grayson, don't worry. I'm here for you and will be waiting at the bottom," Gregor said soothingly, and he affectionately tousled the young boy's hair. "Just like we practiced."

Grayson didn't remember practicing at all. He raised his brows.

"But what if I fall?" cried little Grayson, tears brimming in his eyes.

"Then I'll catch you. I promise — I will always be there to catch you." With that, Gregor carefully took the paper crane from the child's grip and released it over the ledge so they could see its flight together.

"It's too high up!" protested little Grayson.

Lifting Grayson on his hip, Gregor asked gently, "Are you truly afraid?" The young boy nodded emphatically. "Okay. Let's go home," Gregor sighed. Little Grayson looked relieved at this.

Older Grayson couldn't help but let out a chuckle as Gregor unexpectedly hurled his miniature self off of the rooftop. Panicked, the young Grayson shrieked, but Gregor rolled up his sleeves, runes gleaming, and summoned the wind. Suddenly, little Grayson's airborne figure reappeared before them, his small wings extended and flapping vigorously.

"You're doing it!" Gregor cheered. "Keep going!" He clapped his hands and bounced with excitement as the older Grayson stood beside him—invisible. He watched as Gregor expertly manipulated the wind to guide little Grayson's first flight.

Grayson murmured, "So that's what happened." He always assumed he was just a prodigy flier.

Young Grayson chased the paper crane with euphoric laughter ringing through the firework explosions.

"That's it, son," Gregor whispered to himself, a proud smile tugging at his lips. "That's my boy. You did it."

Taken aback by this tender revelation, Grayson stared at Gregor as he continued to clap and holler in celebration.

Grayson was abruptly ripped from the scene, jolting in his chair. Ella was clutching his head in her hands, her face frantic.

"Hey, hey. Are you alright?" she asked, her brow creased in concern.

It took Grayson a moment to catch his bearings. "I'm fine," he answered dismissively. She released her hold on his face, and he cleared his throat. "Nothing happened," he declared. Her face scrunched up in confusion.

"I don't believe you," she said, arms crossing. She was sufficiently dry now—a bit of mud still clinging to her tattered uniform.

He waved his hand at her, cleaning her in an instant, and then his chair where she had been sitting. It was punishment enough to have her sit in her own filth—his poor chair didn't deserve it though.

"Nothing *bad* happened," he promised. "But I have a meeting I need to get to. Thank you. You did...well." He didn't know what to say. He felt vulnerable and raw.

"Are you sure you are alright?" she asked again. She gathered her bag, and the dried outer uniform cloak from the chaise, preparing to leave.

"Yes. Everything is fine," he said again, clearing his throat repeatedly.

It wasn't until after she slipped out of his room, giving him one last glance of disbelieving, that he let himself sag in his chair.

⟶

A knock resounded on Gregor's door as he shuffled through stacks of papers. "Come in," he called out, eyes still focused on his task. To his surprise, Grayson quietly entered and sat down across from him, a distant look in his eyes.

"Is something bothering you?" Gregor asked, putting down his papers.

Grayson shook his head, rubbing his eyes. "Nah, just exhausted."

Gregor's eyebrow quirked up. "Been smoking those Meraroot sticks again?"

Grayson scoffed in response, waving a hand to magically summon two glasses and a bottle of wine. "Can I stick around for some conversation?" he asked. A grin stretched across Gregor's face, and Grayson returned the smile awkwardly.

"To what do I owe the pleasure?" Gregor asked sarcastically, taking the glass and helping himself.

Grayson was silent for a moment, and it caught Gregor's attention. He cocked his head at him questioningly, a look of guilt flickering upon Grayson's face.

"No reason," Grayson answered.

⟶

Nattya had given in, passionately embracing Highwing, grinding atop him. With every month that passed without Ella, their frustrations grew stronger, and her Lifestone now lay between them.

He held her firmly, guiding her movements along his shaft, while she held a wineglass that splashed about, spilling on his chest. At the pitch of her moaning, she stopped moving abruptly.

She was dry, and he was tired.

"This isn't working," Nattya sighed. Highwing stopped and gently pushed her off.

"Thank Gods," he agreed.

Nattya laid her head on his pillow, the Lifestone shimmering in her hand. "Highwing, can't you fly us out there the next time the veil lifts? I've heard people have been gathering by the shores lately."

He played with a curl of her hair. "But how would we even find Ella if the veil lifts?" Highwing asked. "I've never been to Arcadea. Do you expect me to carry you across the sea?"

"I guess not," Nattya mumbled. She investigated Highwing's eyes and said, "I do know that she's at Morning Song."

"So, we reach wherever that is, and start asking people about Ella? That's our plan?" Highwing questioned skeptically.

"Well, do you have any better ideas?" Nattya snapped back.

Highwing had been pestering his mother and father about what they knew — and they assured him that they knew nothing. Hamlet was actively avoiding them and had even set up charms in his rooms in order to keep them out.

Finally, Highwing sighed, "It's as if she's privy to some secret we're unaware of."

"Who?" his Nattya asked.

"The Queen," he replied. "She seems to be preparing for something. Making my mom her heir, dismissing Ella's claim, ending our courtship, and even banning any communication with her." He paused, deep in thought. "She just doesn't want Ella involved in whatever is going on."

She handed Highwing the Lifestone, and they observed it in silence.

CHAPTER THIRTY-THREE

Grayson angrily tossed the freshly printed newspaper onto Gregor's cluttered desk. The ink was barely dry, as it had come straight from the midnight press, and the student body had yet to catch wind of the explosive news.

"They're trying to incite chaos!" Grayson spat furiously, motioning to the paper. "This should never have seen the light of day."

Gregor took a deep breath and rubbed his temples. "I need to figure out their motives. Perhaps I can reason with Aiden—he's levelheaded, at least. I'll reach out to Sifrrod, too; she could serve as a mediator in this situation."

Grayson paced anxiously across the room. "And what about the students? You know their parents will lose their minds over this news," he said, his voice rising in pitch. "Hellharth's return? 'The people haven't forgotten'—that's what they cry at every gathering!"

"I'm fully conscious of the impact this will have on all parties involved," Gregor replied, exhaling a weary sigh. He rummaged through his desk drawer in search of a comforting bottle of brandy, only to find emptiness greeting him time and time again. "Damn it!" he grumbled.

"You ought to cut back on that habit, old man," chided Grayson.

Gregor leaned back into his chair with frustration, knitting his brow. He hadn't thought that he had gone through his private stores so quickly. "There's an overwhelming amount to accomplish and such little time." Determined, he picked up his elegant glass pen and dipped it into the inkwell, carefully crafting his missive on a fresh parchment. Upon finishing, he held the message close to his lips, whispered the intended recipient's name, and watched in satisfaction as it disappeared into thin air.

"Are you certain Ellarhyssa will hear about this before anyone else?" Grayson asked, feigning nonchalance.

Gregor waved a dismissive hand, a smirk tugging at the corner of his mouth. "Ah, so it's Ellarhyssa now, is it?" he teased, raising an eyebrow in amusement.

"Quit fooling around," Grayson retorted defensively, running a hand down his velvet green frock. As if on cue, a letter materialized before them, gracefully fluttering onto the ancient oak desk. Gregor snatched it up and pored over the pages. His violet eyes narrowed as his lips formed a troubled frown.

"What's it say?" Grayson pressed impatiently.

Eyes still fixed on the parchment, Gregor rose from his chair and donned an ornate, vivid purple cloak. "I must meet with them at once. They're planning a visit to Hellharth," he said solemnly.

Grayson threw his hands up in exasperation. "For God's sake! Well then, I'm coming with you."

Gregor shook his head firmly. "No, you'll remain here. The intent is for this meeting to be diplomatic and civil."

"I am more than capable of being civil," Grayson scoffed, with an indignant glare.

Gregor's skeptical gaze revealed just how unconvinced he was by that statement.

"Fine," Grayson sighed in defeat. It was probably for the best being that these particular humans didn't trust much of anyone who wasn't human themselves.

Morning Song was alive with noise; people were running through the halls in excitement and fear. Ella was abruptly jolted awake by a hand placed over her mouth. Her eyes flew open in surprise. Ella felt disoriented, her claws instinctively coming out.

Seeing Ethan looming over her and Annabeth at the foot of her bed, she gave them a quizzical look. Annabeth was holding a large piece of paper in her hands.

"What are you guys doing?" she grumbled sleepily, batting Ethan's hand away from her mouth.

"You're the only one still in bed. Have you seen the paper?" Anna shoved the newspaper into Ella's chest.

"You just said so yourself that I'm the only one still in bed. How would I have seen it?" Ella grumbled, her claws retracting. She looked over at Ethan, who was still hovering over her.

"You're never going to believe this!" Ethan exclaimed excitedly.

Ella sat up, acutely aware that her nightgown was sheer, and rustled through the pages of the newspaper. Her eyes honed in on the big bold print on the front; ***HELLHARTH HAS RETURNED!***

Ella shot to her feet; her nose pressed to the pages.

In a bold and unprecedented turn of events, the mysterious and mythical Hellharth, Isle of Elves, has made a shocking return to the world of Arcadea this morning. Its speculated disappearance and reappearance have been a topic of intrigue to hundreds of thousands around the Known World.

Aiden Mormant commented on the situation, stating, "Hellharth's reappearance is both awe-inspiring and ominous. It has been twenty years since its lands were anchored down in place of our world. My colleagues and I will be immersing ourselves fully into gauging the threat—if there is one."

The sudden presence of Hellharth on Calisan's border raises important questions about its intentions for returning, and with it comes an unease within the people who must now wait for answers.

Ella threw the paper down, unable to finish. Her heart was hammering in her chest, anxiety threatening to swallow her. Her outburst took Ethan aback.

"Everything alright?"

Annabeth nudged him with her elbow. "She could be scared like the rest of them." She turned her attention to Ella. "Don't worry, I'm sure everything will be fine. It could be nothing."

Ella's determination to escape was unyielding; she bolted out of her room without a word, her friends' calls fading behind her. Taking a sharp right turn, she didn't even spare a glance at the threatening stone dragon guarding the doorway before pushing open Grayson's door and slipping through. The door swung shut, the sound of its lock falling into place echoing in the air.

There was a loud bang and cursing before Grayson appeared in the doorway, wearing nothing but a towel wrapped around his waist, his exposed torso dripping with water. His hair was wet and slicked back from the shower. Grayson's chest heaved as he surveyed the room, his eyes fierce and falling on Ella.

Grayson growled, his face a mask of shock and annoyance as he clutched his towel firmly around himself. "The hell are you doing bombarding in my room?" he demanded, incredulously.

Why did the damned dragon guardian let her through again? He thought to himself.

Ella stammered, her expression fearful and her breathing heavy. She finally managed to get out, "The paper! The paper!" Her voice shook as she tried to explain the situation, her hands waving about her.

Highmaster Gregor had promised Grayson he would update Ella on it, but obviously hadn't gotten around to it yet. Grayson huffed in frustration. Here he was, standing in the middle of his office, with no clothes on, while a terrified Ella stood before him. Not quite how he'd imagined this morning going. For a moment, they both stood there until Grayson broke the silence with a sigh, the tension in the air slowly dissipating. He wondered if she realized he could see through her nightdress. "Miss Marks?"

Ella clutched her hair, pulling it tight. Suddenly, her heart raced and a wave of dizziness washed over her. She clawed at her chest, feeling like it might burst open, while her palms grew sweaty and her legs weak. Taking deep breaths became difficult—like a weight compressed her chest.

The room spun, and her vision blackened. She attempted to walk towards the leather chair nestled among towering bookshelves, but stumbled. Her body tilted—on the verge of collapse. Just before hitting the ground, strong arms enfolded her, keeping her upright.

Her ears rang, and she was unaware of the tears streaming down her cheeks until they dampened Grayson's bare chest. His soothing voice reached her in a murmur, no louder than a delicate whisper that sent shivers down her spine.

"It's alright. Everything is alright, Ella."

"You really had us freaked out, running off like that!" Annabeth scolded. Ethan was offering up his biscuit, placing it on Ella's plate. She hadn't eaten at all, and he was persistent about her at least having something for dinner.

"They canceled classes for the next couple of days, reckon loads of people want to pull their kids out of school and go into hiding," Ethan said.

Ella remained silent as she pondered the implications of the news for her homeland and people. She couldn't help but be aware of how Grayson had softly embraced her in comfort, without any judgment or snide remarks. Their relationship had unmistakably evolved since she'd arrived at Morning Song.

Sienna plopped down next to her, biting into a raspberry pastry. "I knew it was only a matter of time. This will be enough to convince my mother to let me go back to Desmouth," she said happily.

"Will you be less lonely there?" Ella asked numbly.

Sienna looked confused by her question. "I'm not lonely," she said.

Ella turned to her fully, looking her in the eyes. "Yes, you are."

Sienna cleared her throat, sniffing the air a few times, her ears turning a bright blue. "Whatever," she scoffed, getting up and leaving.

Annabeth shifted uncomfortably. "I think she is the most afraid. Her aura is all muddy."

"Her mother was part of the Original Council. She's probably thinking about her," Ethan agreed. "Sifrrod will be one of the people to go to Hellharth…"

Ella pushed her plate away. "I'm really not hungry," she said. Ethan pushed her plate back, and she sighed. "Really, I'm not hungry." If she ate anything, she was sure it was going to come right back up.

"Ella, if there's something going on, you can tell us. We won't judge you," Ethan insisted. He looked to Annabeth to back him up, and she nodded her head vigorously.

Ella glanced around the room nervously, that feeling of hopelessness creeping up on her. She wanted to tell them. To tell them everything. Who her father was, who her mother was, who she was.

"I think I know what this is about," Annabeth said carefully.

Ella's eyes widened a fraction. "You do?" she asked quietly. Annabeth nodded.

"I've suspected it for a while now. Ethan and I—well—we've talked. *Just us.* But you know, it's gone the rounds in school. We aren't the only people who've noticed," Anna said with a grimace. Ella sat up straighter, her heart pounding.

Do they know? She thought to herself.

"And your reaction today—it kind of confirmed our suspicions," Ethan said slowly. Their eyes were on her, analyzing her as if she were about to get up and bolt out of the room again. She bit at the skin of her nails anxiously.

"Is it that obvious? Why haven't you said anything before?" she prompted, leaning over the table to Annabeth across from her. "You have no idea how it's been killing me keeping this from the two of you."

Annabeth grinned from ear to ear. "We stayed silent because it wasn't our place to interfere; we knew you'd tell us when the time was right. Also, I didn't think Master Moore would appreciate it becoming common knowledge." The last part made Ella pause.

"What about Gra—Master Moore?" she asked.

Annabeth and Ethan leaned in closer to her, their foreheads practically touching. "It's not like it's against the rules. You both are adults—and he hasn't given you any advantages academically that you didn't earn. He's been having Mistress Ased grade your essays."

Ella scrunched up her face in confusion, and Annabeth giggled. "Didn't you know that? Mistress Ased started taking over your grading a few weeks ago. I heard her talking about it to Mistress Devoro while returning books."

Why would he do that? Ella wondered.

"You ran into his room and the ward didn't even stop you," Ethan smirked slyly. "You were in there a while and came out all *sweaty* and breathing heavily."

Anna nodded. "You *reeked* of him, too. Anyone else here with a good sense of smell has picked up on how you two smell like each other."

"We get it though. You both are Dracaenean. It must be daunting hearing that Hellharth came back after all these years—with the history and all that," Ethan added flippantly.

Ella deadpanned. All this time, people were speculating that she and Gray—*Master Moore* had been sleeping together.

"How the hell did I not know that this was being said about me?" she asked in shock.

Ethan shrugged. "It's not the first time a rumor sprung up about Master Moore dating someone."

"Remember the whole Sienna thing? I still don't believe it. It was never acknowledged, and she never denied or confirmed anything," Annabeth said.

Ella remembered them talking about Sienna and Grayson possibly having been *together* a while back, but it hadn't had the same effect on her then as it did now. Just the thought of them together made a lump form in her throat that she seemed unable to swallow away.

Anna noticed the change in Ella's demeanor immediately. "Hey, I'm sure it was nothing. Trust me, I never noticed anything the way I notice it with you."

"That's because you're around me all the time," Ella grumbled. She was surprised at herself for feeling this way. For feeling jealous.

"Whatever happened to your boyfriend? I thought you two were an item?" Anna inquired; her tone laced with curiosity. Ella's heart plummeted at the mention of Highwing. She couldn't comprehend why she felt an unwarranted surge of guilt washing over her.

Ella hesitated before replying, giving herself time to collect her thoughts. She recalled the numerous conversations she had had with Highwing about their relationship. He had made it abundantly clear there would be no room for jealousy, and that they were free to explore other romantic connections. He was hoping to find his mate one day.

Why am I even entertaining this thought? Ella mentally chastised herself, her pulse quickening. She forced out a response: "There's nothing happening between us. Highwing and I are... We are...fine."

Yet, as the memory of Grayson tenderly whispering her name—not as Miss Marks, but as Ella—rushed back to her, her stomach churned uncomfortably. The skeptical glances exchanged between Ethan and Anna only heightened Ella's unease further, making her question the validity of her own words.

»»»———➤

"You said you'd talk to her before the whole world knew about it!" Grayson fumed, his face flushed with anger. Gregor reclined in his ornate high-back chair, leisurely sipping his glass of shimmering amber liquid. Grayson had a nagging suspicion he'd been drinking since the previous night.

"They're all set to storm over there—Aiden Mormant and his cronies," Gregor slurred, his words punctuated by a hiccup. "I never got the chance to inform Ellarhyssa, since I've been trying my darndest to persuade Aiden against going there."

Grayson raised an eyebrow. "And what was his response?"

Gregor burst into raucous laughter, the sound echoing across the room. "He claimed that my—*devotion*—to the Fae of this world has clouded my judgment, preventing me from seeing the grander scheme of things." He lifted his fingers up and made air quotes.

Grayson understood exactly what Aiden meant. After all, it was Gregor's soft spot for the Fae that had led him to have them admitted into a school originally intended for Maji only. It was also why he had taken in Grayson as an orphan.

"Ellarhyssa stormed into my chambers in a frenzied panic," Grayson said, shaking his head. "It was downright improper."

A peculiar glint appeared in Gregor's eyes as he studied Grayson. "Seems I'm not the only one with a soft spot for someone," he chuckled, hinting at an unspoken secret simmering beneath the surface.

"Don't you even suggest that I—" Grayson protested, his voice trembling with indignation.

"I'm not suggesting anything, merely observing," Gregor retorted smugly. "She's quite the spirited firecracker, isn't she? Always keeping you on your toes."

"Your excessive drinking has scrambled your brains," Grayson snapped back, disgusted. "I harbor no feelings for that girl."

"And how is that training going?" Gregor asked sarcastically, a sly grin revealing a hidden motive.

"Go to hell," Grayson snarled through clenched teeth.

When night came, Ella found herself anxiously pacing back and forth outside his door, feeling the stone dragon's irritated gaze follow her every move. She had politely declined Anna's offer to share her dorm for the night, fearing that her distress might cause her to make a mistake.

But being alone was even more worrisome.

As if sensing her inner turmoil, the door creaked open on its own accord. The dragon eyed her expectantly from the archway.

"Thanks," she whispered to the creature, and cautiously entered. The haunting melody of a music box filled the dimly lit room. There he was, engrossed in a book with his back partially turned to her, his lips mouthing the words as he read along.

Her stomach did an odd flip as she watched him, not want-ing to ruin the tranquil scene. It smelled like cinnamon and herbs—lavender and so undeniably him.

What the hell am I doing? She thought to herself. Since when had Grayson become her safety blanket?

Feeling eyes on him, his head slowly turned to her, eyes widening a fraction. Her breath caught in her throat.

"Miss Marks? I didn't hear you come in." He looked at the door in confusion.

"I—the dragon. It let me in," she answered.

"Looks like he's used to your presence," he said with a hint of annoyance. He put his book down, marking the page. Valla was asleep at his feet and hadn't even bothered to greet her. "Is there something you needed?"

His voice was colder than it had been earlier. He was back to calling her by her false name, and Ella needed him to call her by her real name. She needed it again.

"No. I just. Uhm." she fumbled over the words. Silence hung between them, and Ella fiddled with her fingers, avoiding his gaze. "Thank you."

"For what?"

Ella blushed. Was he pretending nothing had happened? "Never mind," she stammered, turning to leave as her nerves got the best of her.

"Tea?" his voice called out a bit loudly.

She stopped. "What?"

He sighed. "Would you care for some tea?" What had he said to Gregor all those weeks ago? *It's not like we are having tea parties,* he remembered himself saying.

Oh, the irony.

She smiled in relief. "Yes, thank you."

"Please stop thanking me." He motioned for her to sit at one of the leather seats by the fire while he conjured a tea set.

"It isn't laced, is it?" she joked.

He tapped the teapot, and it started steaming. "Truth syrup or Meraroot. Perhaps poison." he poured her cup, and she looked down at the brown liquid with narrowed eyes. "Oh, come off it! Drink it," he said with a chuckle.

Chapter Thirty-Four

The ships bellowed in the sea, surrounding Hylycyn's shore. Kahlisenya and members of the Court were apprehensive and on high alert, gathered at the shoreline. There were more ships than expected, but the Queensguard was ready for anything. As a single rowboat slinked its way onto the shores, holding a handful of humans, Althane was clearly agitated.

"Easy," Kahlisenya whispered quietly as she straightened her back, reminding him that this meeting was imperative for Hellharth's future. "There isn't much to be done," she said as Hamlet scanned the shores for anything suspicious.

"We have the Queensguard lining the shores, just in case," he added reassuringly. "They will light the Northern sky of Irefana City if anything happens."

Althane didn't seem convinced. "You put Lady Rayne as heir and now the humans are flocking to our doors. Your daughter is nowhere in sight, and we are on the cusp of war again."

"Are you accusing me of something, Althane? Hold your tongue during this meeting, or I'll have it cut out. You mention my daughter—and it will be your head," she threatened. She had barely moved her mouth when she spoke.

Lady Tanyl grasped her husband's hand in hers, the movement catching Lady Rayne's eye.

The boat settled on the shore, four figures adjusting themselves and making their way toward Kahlisenya and her company.

A man Kahlisenya presumed to be the leader stayed twelve feet back, forming a line with his comrades. One of them she recognized immediately.

"Sifrrod," she greeted warmly, "how lovely to see you again."

Sifrrod was an undeniably alluring sight—her striking blue eyes, pale skin, and cascading black hair gave her a classic beauty that was only accented by the revealingly embroidered satin dress in white she wore. The dress had pearls fashioned into seashells adorning it, adding a sophisticated yet sultry look to her attire.

"Queen Kahlisenya," Sifrrod said, "it has been a long time, has it not?"

Kahlisenya was no fool; she had seen enough to know Sifrrod Whitefish and knew all too well what it meant when she made an appearance: sirens lurked beneath the waves, their hypnotic songs waiting for the perfect moment to ensnare an unsuspecting victim. She could feel the eerie stillness in the air, a looming sense of danger that seemed to fill her with dread. Yet despite this, Kahlisenya stood bravely on shore, determined not to let these visitors become aware of her uneasiness.

She knew that the time wasn't on her side.

"Too long. I am curious as to what I owe this unannounced visit, and who are your companions?"

"I am Aiden Mormont," the man on the left of Sifrrod spoke gruffly. His eyes were sharp and piercing, reflecting intense focus and mistrust. There was a scar from his top lip that radiated down over the cleft in his chin.

"Ivy Denford," a woman with a large, round face and chubby cheeks said. Her gray hair was cut into a short bob, with a few stray hairs sticking out here and there. She wore a pair of large glasses that magnified her eyes, giving her a comical appearance.

"Hesta Braveheart," the last woman said. She had a sharp, angular face with a pointed chin and thin lips that were twisted into an unfriendly scowl. Her eyes were small and beady, and they darted around constantly.

Kahlisenya held her chin up, looking down at them from her nose. "Charming."

Hamlet cleared his throat, and the Court introduced themselves with an air of haughtiness. It was very clear this was not a welcome visit.

Kahlisenya's voice was stern and unyielding as she probed Sifrrod, "You've evaded my question long enough. What brings you here with an entire fleet in tow?"

Sifrrod, after a deep inhale, finally revealed her purpose. "You are aware of our motive. We have several inquiries for your attention."

Althane's sarcasm dripped from his words. "A simple letter would have sufficed."

Aiden couldn't resist a snide remark. "But then you could vanish on us just as easily, right?"

The tension amplified as Althane lunged forward, snarling. Quick as a whip, Rayne seized him by the shoulder, halting his advance. His surprise was palpable when he realized she had made physical contact with him after all these years. Tanyl immediately shifted positions to stand between the two ex-lovers with an exasperated huff, eyes locked on Rayne.

With cheeks quivering from anger, Ivy snapped, "Control your mongrels!"

Hamlet spoke with a chilling calmness that cut through the air, "I must remind you—you trespass upon our land without invitation or welcome. Either address this Court with due respect or return to your vessel at once."

Sifrrod raised her hands to demonstrate her peaceful intent. "I concede our approach is unorthodox, and I apologize for that. However, we needed to ascertain if there was a threat at hand."

"Exactly what constituted the threat?" Lady Rayne inquired. Her voice was laced with suspicion.

"Well, Hellharth vanished two decades ago. The Arcadean Council has sent forth a warrant to investigate Hellharth for un-apprehended supporters of The Son of Bashet–" Aiden began to explain but was abruptly interrupted by Cida's burst of laughter.

"The Arcadean Council? What audacity they have! They don't even have jurisdiction in our Court to issue warrants for our lands," Cida scoffed, furrowing his brow. Kahlisenya shot him an irritated glance.

"Do you truly believe," Kahlisenya retorted, "that I'd go through the colossal effort of eradicating The Son of Bashet, only to shel-ter his remaining acolytes?" Aiden shifted uncomfortably on his feet, his gaze drifting towards the horizon before quickly snapping back. Kahlisenya's eyes narrowed at him. "Fear not, your reinforce-ments are still there."

Lady Rayne interjected with a sharp tone, her magnificent wings twitching with frustration, "Pray tell us how you planned to dis-tinguish loyalists of The Son of Bashet from innocent civilians?"

Ivy folded her arms tightly across her chest, her eyes narrowing. "Naturally, we'd interrogate them. If they appear older than twen-ty—"

At that, Kahlisenya released a sharp, derisive laugh that rippled through the other Court members. The tension in the air thick-ened as they exchanged knowing glances. "Have you any idea how long Fae can live? And I don't just mean lower Fae like Orcs or

Sirens. I'm talking about High Fae! If that's truly your plan, it's nothing short of ludicrous."

Ivy was flustered with embarrassment.

"Truth Syrup!" Hesta shouted. Kahlisenya had to stop herself from rolling her eyes. The ships blared their horns and Kahlisenya breathed in deeply. She reminded herself to practice patience with their foolishness, as it was necessary to achieve her grand vision. "Just stick to the plan," she muttered under her breath. "Everything must align as it was meant to."

"How about we bargain a deal? Do this civilly," Kahlisenya reasoned. "You are welcome to visit, so long as it is peaceful, and see for yourself that there is nothing nefarious going on."

"You cannot be serious—" Cida shouted.

"They are hostiles!" Althane bellowed, "They come with a fleet behind them!"

Sifrrod and Aiden weighed the suggestion as the other two appeared to have swallowed something bitter. "Calisan seeks proof of The Son of Bashet," Sifrrod stated cautiously.

"I assure you; you won't find any," Kahlisenya confidently replied.

"Can't you see? There must be at least a dozen ships filled with their soldiers!" Althane exclaimed, his voice dripping with bitterness. "How can you simply allow them to set foot on our land, patrolling our beaches and cities?"

"I chose to take the initiative, offering them a token of trust," Kahlisenya answered. The Court had reconvened in the grand Hylycyn throne room, and the atmosphere was tense with heated debates.

"They would never extend the same trust to us!" Cida cried out indignantly.

Kahlisenya sighed wearily and replied, "That's precisely why we must be the ones to act first, don't you understand?"

I need you to understand, she thought desperately.

As the days passed by, it became more and more apparent that they didn't.

⟫⟫⟩———▶

HELLHARTH—FRIEND OR FOE?

In a shocking turn of events, Aiden Mormant has come with news that has left Arcadea in a whirlwind of chaos.

"Queen Kahlisenya has offered us free range in the Isle of Elves, as an act of solidarity. They greeted us on the shores of Hellharth, and for the last week, they emersed us in their culture and traditions," Aiden Mormant commented.

Sifrrod Whitefish was more than happy to share with us her experience. "Queen Kahlisenya showed us kindness in a very tense situation. There has been no indication of rebellion at all."

Ivy Denford and Hesta Braveheart note their reluctance to believe that Hellharth does not pose a threat to The Known World.

"Fae have the potential for danger—these Fae in particular. I'll never trust them," Ivy commented.

"Darkness comes out in the light," Hesta commented. "We will see just how far their generosity goes."

As for the people of Arcadea, the reactions are mixed. Some are delighted and willing to put the past behind them, while others are calling for emergency action. All in all, it is only a matter of time before the Elves are walking on the lands of Arcadea once more.

Gregor's eyes scanned the large print paper. He had already received dozens of missives from Maji families explaining that they wanted to pull their children from the school. He had spent the better part of the morning assuring them that there was no need for such drastic measures. It was noon now, and he had already lost a third of the student body, mostly the younglings.

Gregor could feel the unsettling darkness that surrounded Ella. Though Ethan, Anna, and even Grayson stood by her side, Gregor's gut told him that Ella was close to the breaking point. Her emotional state had been nothing but fragile lately, and with the looming threat of Hellharth's uncertainty, he feared it wouldn't be long before everything spiraled out of control.

"Take it one day at a time," Gregor had said to her every morning since the news first broke out, trying to offer some comfort.

Unexpectedly, Grayson seemed to glow with a renewed sense of positivity in recent days. Gregor secretly prayed that his uplifting demeanor would prove infectious, steering Ella back toward stability.

He pondered on the prophecy once again, desperately seeking a hidden understanding that all others had overlooked. As the day wore on, he found himself increasingly intoxicated. It was amidst this haze of inebriation that an idea struck him like a bolt of lightning. "Traitor," he murmured to himself, repeating it with growing intensity. The realization washed over him in a powerful wave. "To first make right, you must do wrong."

CHAPTER THIRTY-FIVE

Kahlisenya clutched her head tightly, wincing as the voices grew louder and more insistent. She felt an oppressive sense of doom as if her haunted and cursed existence was closing in on her.

"Kahlisenya, you can't just cut Ella off like this!" Gideon's anguished outcry echoed through the room. His ghostly form hovered over her, shimmering like a mirage.

"Why won't you just leave me alone and find peace?" Kahlisenya yelled back, her voice trembling with frustration. She stormed into the washroom, the scent of lavender filling her nostrils. She tore off her dress and practically threw herself into the smooth marble tub. Desperate to drown out his words, she turned the water on and plunged her ears beneath the surface.

Gideon's ethereal figure persisted above her; a deep scowl etched on his face. "Why don't you try visiting Ella instead? I'm positive she would appreciate your company far more than I do," Kahlisenya snapped sarcastically, sitting up with water dripping down her face.

"You know full well that nobody else can see me, Kahlisenya. You were touched by death and that venom is inside you; only you can see through this veil." Gideon's voice was tinged with sadness as his once-curly hair swirled around him like a watery halo. "Why haven't you told Ella about me?" He sounded sad.

"Because she would never have moved on! Just think about how she would have reacted if she knew your spirit was trapped between Olesa and Earth," Kahlisenya retorted defensively.

"I am not trapped; I choose to stay," Gideon corrected sternly. "I've seen her. She's so miserable at that school."

Kahlisenya hesitated before replying softly, "You know why I had to separate myself from her, Gideon. You know why." Kahlisenya was tired of hearing him complaining.

"But she doesn't, Kahlisenya. She cried, all alone in her room. She grieved for you." Gideon's ghostly voice broke with sadness. "There will be fire..."

Exasperation and pain coursed through Kahlisenya's voice. "You think I don't care? That I'm heartless? Everything I do is for Ellarhyssa! My life is dedicated to her! I'm burdened with this knowledge of what must be done—like a pawn in some grand game. It's all for a purpose, and I'm doing everything I can!"

Gideon extended his hand into the tub of water and Kahlisenya shuddered as an icy chill spread through her. "I am not confined by this world or its passage of time, Kahlisenya. I have seen the past, present, and glimpses of the future. I understand just as much as you do—if not more."

"Why do you keep hounding me? If you're aware, then you understand the importance of going through with this. It secures Ella's future," she exclaimed with frustration.

"I know. I truly loved her. I would've knelt before the Court just to marry her. But fate never intended for us to be together. She has found solace in her current situation. The Healer—Eros—"

"Enough!" she interrupted. "We're not discussing Eros in any way, shape, or form. I won't talk about it. Never!" The thought of the handsome Anaferian healer made her stomach lurch. He had worked diligently to heal Dasyra, and she had wondered if the girl's uplifted spirits were because of that man. She could only hope it was a fleeting thing. "I cannot think of him," she whispered sadly. "I can't."

Gideon's lower body slowly dissolved into the ground; his voice tinged with warning. "What do you think she'll do when she realizes you've betrayed her in the most unimaginable way?" He disappeared into the floor completely, leaving an unsettling silence.

Kahlisenya reheated the water again and again, but couldn't rid herself of the icy shiver that Gideon had brought along with him. She was blanketed in the silence she had asked for, but no longer craved. Although it was tough to admit, he was right–Ella would never forgive her once she discovered the truth.

But it was a burden Kahlisenya had accepted to carry.

Aware of Hamlet's persistent attempts to converse with her, she found it challenging to keep her distance. As she cleaned herself, taking extra care to prep herself, she tried to remember the way it felt to have a man's hips between hers. Slipping into her nightgown, this thought lingered in her mind. Standing before the mirror, she lifted her hand to trace the curve of one of her impressive antlers. She couldn't help but wonder if they would play a significant role in her plans for the evening with Hamlet.

Hamlet opened his bedroom door to find Kahlisenya standing there, her hand hovering in the air. He blinked several times.

"Sorry, I was just coming to speak to you," she said.

He crossed his arms over his chest. "About what?" he asked tersely. He hadn't given her much time since her announcement and had made it clear he wasn't going to be advising her. Not that she listened to his advice anymore, anyway.

"Don't take such a flippant tone with me," she huffed. He made to shut the door in her face, but her foot caught the door frame. "Ham. Please." She just needed a moment. Just long enough to ensnare him.

He cautiously opened the door once more, revealing her standing there in nothing but a delicate nightgown. Its sheer fabric left little to the imagination. "So now you want to talk?" he questioned, noting the weeks of silence between them.

Her eyes narrowed in response. "That's hardly fair," she retorted, crossing the threshold into his simple yet tastefully decorated chamber. "You've been avoiding everyone just as much as I have." She took in the soft blue and white hues of his bed linens, her gaze shifting upward to admire the enchanting, star-studded ceiling. "Love what you've done with the place."

Avoiding eye contact, Hamlet shifted his gaze to the wall. "It's rare to see you here. What brings you?" He could feel her piercing eyes on him, making him squirm in unease.

After a moment's silence, she spoke up, "I apologize. I know my presence has been inconsistent lately."

"Is that what we're calling it now?" Hamlet snarked, marching over to her and pointing an accusing finger right at her face. "You thought it was okay to disown Ella without even talking to me first? Announcing that news for everyone to hear! Forbidding Nattya and me from visiting her. Informing Highwing that his engagement is off? That's your idea of 'sporadic'?"

Kahlisenya's eyes widened ever so slightly, taken aback by Hamlet's sudden aggression—a stance he had never assumed before. With a softened tone, she asked, "You don't trust my judgment?"

"It's not just about trust!" Hamlet snapped back. "It's about the damage you've caused to everyone around you!"

To his dismay, her eyes began to shimmer, and her nose turned a shade of red. "Hey, hey, don't cry. I didn't mean to shout," Hamlet uttered gently. He had only ever seen her cry twice in all the years he had known her.

She nestled her face into his palm. "I'm doing my best, I really am." Her sudden embrace took him by surprise, and she buried her face in the curve of his neck. He could feel her unsteady breath traveling along his collarbone, causing goosebumps to rise on his skin.

Wrapping his arms around her, he traced comforting circles on her back, reassuring her, "It's going to be okay."

She lifted her head and pressed a delicate kiss on his jawline. He froze momentarily before she grazed the same spot with a bolder kiss. She repeated this twice more, inching closer to the corner of his mouth before moving back down his neck. She took several long breaths by his ear, feeling his skin prickle beneath her fingertips.

Her hand traveled up his back, clutching the base of his neck, kissing at the juncture there and biting it with her teeth. Hamlet pulled away from her slightly, his eyes darkening.

He grazed his fingers along Kahlisenya's quivering lip, clasping her jaw in his forefingers and forcing her to look at him.

She peered up at him, taking his thumb in between her teeth in a sensuous act, letting her tongue taste the saltiness of his skin. He inhaled a sharp breath, his pupils blown wide.

"Kahlisenya," he breathed, grasping the back of her neck roughly and pulling her face to his. "Don't tease me."

"Or what?" she challenged, swirling her tongue over his thumb and closing her lips around it. She sucked. Hard. Hamlet pulled his finger out of her mouth, pinching her chin between his fingers. He regarded her for a moment, eyes darkening.

She didn't know what she expected—gentleness was far from what she was experiencing from him.

He shoved her forcefully until her back met his dresser and lifted her up by the legs, seating her atop it. Picture frames crashed to the floor and shattered. His fingers were clenching her thighs tightly as if he were afraid she would break away. Her skin was pricked where his fingernails dug in, the small lick of pain igniting something inside of her.

"Do not start what you cannot finish," he threatened her. His voice was thick, nostrils flaring. If Kahlisenya couldn't smell the spike of arousal from him, she would have thought he was enraged.

"I plan on finishing, Hamlet," she breathed out, clasping her heels to the back of his knees and undulating her hips, rubbing herself against him. He bucked against her, rocking his lower half.

"Make me finish," she hissed.

She could feel him, warm and hard, grazing over her swollen flesh repeatedly.

Kahlisenya felt encouraged by the fact that her plan to seduce Hamlet was proving successful; she couldn't believe how ready and aroused he already was. She ran her hand over his firm erection, delighted with its size and eagerness. Her touch had an immediate effect, and he groaned in her ear.

Twisting off the dresser, she dragged him towards her by his shirt, bringing him to his bed—the scene of what she had seen in her vision. Her untouched body ached for his and when his mouth draped over her neck's pulse point, her fangs elongated. Taking charge, she forcefully pushed him onto the mattress, where she straddled him with legs on either side of his waist. She brought her lips down on his as his hands traveled beneath her dress skirt. He felt her with each stroke of his finger up and down the smooth skin, then at the apex of her thighs, making her arch atop him. He swiped over her clit through the fabric of her undergarments. Once. Twice.

"Fuck," she exhaled.

With each gentle stroke, he brought her closer to the peak of desire until finally moving her garment out of the way. The skin-on-skin contact made her jolt. Hamlet moved her to a seated position, his fingers pulling the fabric to the side as far as it would go.

"Look at me," he commanded. No one ever talked to her that way—with authority. It sent a thrill through her.

He swiped gently over her bud once, and she closed her eyes. He stopped and she whined.

"I said *look at me*," he rasped.

Her cerulean eyes locked on his and she started grinding over his still-covered length. He forced her up by the thighs, making her hover over him.

"What-" she cried indignantly.

Positioning his finger at her entrance, he slowly stroked the outside. He felt the warmth of her flutter around his fingers.

"Now, Hamlet," she snapped as he moved a digit in small circles at her entrance.

"Ask me nicely," he sighed.

"Hamlet!" she barked, trying to impale herself.

"Say please," he said with a raised brow. "Spoiled brat can't even ask nicely."

"Spoiled-I-Gods!" she could feel herself starting to drip over him and was becoming increasingly embarrassed. What kind of torture was this? "Please!" she shouted.

He released his hold on her and gravity brought her down around his finger. Then two were in her—pumping fast and curving upward.

"So wet," he groaned.

With sudden fervor, she moved her body up and down against his grip. They went on like that, kissing and panting and grinding with urgency. He felt her start to spasm around him and quickly removed his fingers, pushing himself on top of her despite her protests.

"I said please!" she cried.

He laughed lowly, his hands moving swiftly as he tore apart her dress, baring the curves of her pale-skinned figure. Her breasts were soft and firm in his touch. He wanted this moment to last forever, right here with his Kahlisenya.

Hadn't he earned her love?

Kahlisenya pleaded for him to go back to their position, but he ignored her plea as he slowly lifted one of her legs up onto his shoulder. With a skill she could not have been prepared for, he carefully coaxed her apart, lowering his face between her legs. She felt the heat of his breath blow over her slick and she tried to arch up to reach it. He held her steady, hovering.

He was looking up at her, eyes pools of black. She clutched his hair, twisting it as she tried to find her release in the open air.

"Tell me where you want me," he said.

Her face flushed. "You know exactly where I—"

He blew on her again and she bit her lip so hard she tasted blood. "There. I need you there."

"Show me."

Kahlisenya could have lived another hundred years and never would have guessed that Hamlet was a commander in bed. She released his hair, fumbling messily between her legs, and started rubbing herself.

Two can play this game, she thought.

His eyes followed her every movement as she rubbed circles over herself. Faster. Harder. Her toes started curling—moans got louder. She never took her eyes off of him. When she was about to teeter over the edge he swatted her hand away and dove, settling his tongue where she needed it. Languid, long strokes that teased her at the edge but wouldn't take her over. With each flick of his tongue, Kahlisenya's moans grew louder and more desperate before finally, he sucked. Hard. Her cries reached their crescendo as she gripped tightly onto the back of Hamlet's head.

She released him, her legs shaking on either side of his head, feeling a mix of sadness, joy, and anger as she watched her Lifestone dangle from his heaving chest. Wrapping her legs around his waist and fumbling beneath his waistband for her prize, she felt his hands rushing over her back as he kissed her again.

Taking control of the moment, he stood up with her in his arms and leaned against the wall, and positioned himself between her legs. He wanted the moment to last, but she didn't care about that. Pushing himself deep inside her with one hard thrust, he swallowed her gasp in his mouth. His lower half moved like the rocking of waves, sending new sensations coursing through her body each time, tingling right down to her toes. She clung to him tightly, wrapping her arms around him as she cried out his name in pleasure.

He slipped out of her and she bit down on his shoulder, drawing blood. Her blue eyes were puts of black and she was baring her white teeth at him—lips painted red.

He turned her around, pushing her down against the dresser, and lifted one of her legs, cupping her behind the knee and spreading her leg out on top of the dresser. His shoulder throbbed, and he could feel his blood dripping down his chest.

Grasping the smooth points of her left antler, he forced her neck to snap back and held her there while he pushed himself back into her.

All the lust and passion that was inside Hamlet was unleashed upon her as he drove into her over and over until he finally felt her pulse in her most sacred place. His face was buried in her neck as he let out a long, low groan. His back tightened, his muscles quivering with the strain.

"I love you," he whispered.

Kahlisenya's eyes shot open, her forehead hitting the wall, fingernails digging into the wood of the dresser. Her body was quaking—thrumming and she felt a pang of guilt for doing this to him. She couldn't say it back. She loved him, truly.

But it was only going to make things harder.

⋙———————→

They lay there in his bed languidly, both breathing heavily and intertwined in each other's arms. Kahlisenya fiddled with the Lifestone wrapped around Hamlet's neck, a sense of dread and sorrow threatening to pull her under. She swallowed thickly, a tear falling onto his chest. He raised his head and peered down at her.

"Did I—did I do something wrong?" he asked carefully, his voice quite small.

She smiled, wiping her eyes. "No, Ham. You were perfect. This is perfect. I just wish we had—" She didn't finish the sentence, the words catching in her throat.

She wanted to say; *I wish we had more time.*

But here Hamlet was, in her embrace, unaware that she lay there scheming, and knowing how things would end.

He deserved so much better than her. He deserved the moon and stars, and she was nothing but cloud and doom.

She sat up and conjured a pitcher of water and a glass, poured the drink, knowing very well there wasn't just water in it. She handed it to him, watching him gulp down some before offering it to her, but she shook her head and placed the glass on his night table.

Their heads jerked to the sound of blaring ships on the sea, reminding them that the veil was truly gone.

"I'm tired," she yawned, resting her head against him once more. He seemed unsure of himself before reaching for his comforter and tucking her beneath it with him.

"Stay here," he grumbled sleepily.

She nestled into his side, letting herself drift with him.

CHAPTER THIRTY-SIX

"I hate The Shires," Dasyra groaned. "Why do we have to come along?" she asked her father with a pout. Cida had gathered his four daughters and wife to spend the night in Tanyl's countryside estate.

"Because the Queen requested our presence in the morrow—and I have some things to discuss with your uncle Althane." He gave her a sidelong glance.

She cocked her brow. "What kind of discussion?" she asked suspiciously.

"Perhaps to see about you and Highwing getting married," Oryann grumbled. She had fastened her golden hair into a bun, packing a satchel of fruit. Oryann didn't like to eat at other people's homes or use their restrooms. She was peculiar in that way—always mindful of where she sat, counting windows, and separating her peas by size to eat from smallest to largest. She had routines that she didn't like to break and whenever they needed to stay overnight somewhere, she would bring a blanket to sleep on.

Dasyra tilted her head at her. "What do you mean, me and Highwing?" Her heartbeat had quickened. Was it because Ella was now gone—to wherever she was—and that left Highwing an heir without a betrothed? "Highwing made it abundantly clear he does not want me. He didn't even visit me when I was injured."

"Things change, Das," Cida said while hauling a pack over his shoulders. They would take a carriage, pulled by large cats, due to her wings still healing. "Your Uncle and I will be discussing it tonight."

"Am I to have no say?" she huffed. The gilded carriage pulled up, decorated with golden leaflets and painted white, each one taking a seat on red velvet cushions. Two large black felines with iridescent spots of turquoise and deep blues were mounted at the front, pulling the carriage with low growls. "Mysera would have a better time with Highwing than I would," she added.

At the sound of her name, Mysera's head snapped to her sister, blue eyes narrowed. "I would rather not taste where you have been." Arysta giggled and ducked her face into her blouse.

"Girls!" Gielda snapped, "Ladies do not talk about such things." She fiddled at her neck poof, looking offended and disgusted. Cida covered Arysta's ears. "This is the opportunity of a lifetime. You would be Queen by marriage. Our family would rise above the ilk that is Hylycyn."

Dasyra let her head fall back slightly, hitting the wall of the carriage. She had just started gathering herself together—breaking away from feeling like a man would complete her. She had been building her own confidence back up and the thought of being saddled with Highwing now would break it.

"Don't pout," her mother said, fanning herself. "Marrying up is the goal. You are doing this family a great service."

Mysera snorted and folded her arms. "You're trying to marry us off to Althane's brood. I don't even like Elmon." She looked at

Oryann and swatted her knee. "Aren't you going to say anything?" Oryann crunched into an apple thoughtfully.

"If Father wishes it, I'll marry Ruvane," she said wistfully. It was clear Oryann liked the idea.

"That's right. Because you are a sensible person," Cida said to Oryann. He scrutinized Dasyra, his gaze lingering on her short hair. At least she wore something tight, and the blue chiffon of the dress brought out the green in her eyes. He reached out and adjusted the silver circlet on her head. "Couldn't that healer Eros do something about your hair?" He tugged on a lock right by her ears and it bounced slightly.

"I like it," Arysta said. "She looks like a painting."

"A painting of a peasant. Only peasants cut their hair," Gielda said, clicking her tongue. Dasyra wanted to fade into the red velvet of her seat—disappear from them all.

"Warriors cut their hair," Oryann added gently, offering her a small smile. "It looks regal on her."

"We can say she won when she is Queen," Cida laughed, breaking into a fit of coughing. "We would have to find a suitable match for my baby, Arysta," he added slyly. Arysta looked mortified.

"Bastian is a nice boy," Gielda mused behind her fan.

"The cripple?" Cida asked incredulously. "The boy's wings were broken at birth. He's useless. Never mind that Safrina's line is muddled with humans. Petra has just enough Fae in her to keep producing those wretches. We want to marry high—not low."

Dasyra rested her elbow on her knee, her chin in her hand. Bastian was a perfectly good boy. Even if his wings were odd—so were hers now. His mother, Petra, had only been joined by the Court because she was a descendant of Safrina. Safrina, though she was the sister of Anaferi and Hylycyn, was considered of low status because of her choice to copulate with her human Lifestone partner. A majority of her line was saturated with humans—Nomaji and Maji alike. Petra was a halfling herself—and while her children were not considered halflings—their blood was tainted.

At least in the eyes of Cida.

"There is nothing wrong with Bastian," Dasyra said aloud, looking out her window into the night. Everything was shrouded in darkness, save for the stars that splattered the sky, and the ship lanterns that floated about on the sea. Her skin prickled at the sight of them. Cida leaned over her, his beard scratching her bare shoulder.

"They shouldn't be here. The lot of them. More humans than our kind out there. It's like they are sharks. The Queen is a fool," he hissed. Gielda shushed him, giving him a pointed look. He mumbled an apology and retreated back to his seat. Dasyra sighed. Perhaps if she persisted enough—annoyed her mother enough—she could spend the night in the Hylycyn gardens. She glanced over at her mother, who was staring out the window with a blank expression. She turned back to the window, watching the lanterns float by that lit the road paths.

The first hour with them all crammed into the receiving room was rough. Oryann and Ruvane had stared awkwardly at one another, while Mysera would bare her teeth at Elmon. Gielda had quickly made herself comfortable in the rocking chair outside on the porch. It only took a few complaints from Dasyra for her to get her way. "We would have such a time! The weather is perfect for it," Dasyra said, badgering her mother into letting them go spend the night outside. Gielda peered at her with one eye open. "Not privy to hear what they have to say about a marriage?" she asked. Not that they would hear anything. Althane and Cida had locked themselves up in his studies and the rest of them had retreated to the common room.

"No," Dasyra responded.

Gielda smiled. "We will see you in the morning. Get some rest. Enjoy yourselves." She waved them goodbye, and the four of them were off—skipping down the cobblestones and squealing excitedly.

>>>———————➤

Hours had passed since then, with Althane and Cida still holed up in the study. Tanyl had taken to drinking herself into a stupor—sprawled on the couch. Ruvane and Elmon were miffed that they had not been invited to the garden sleepover.

Gielda's attention was suddenly drawn to the blaring horns and a dazzling firework display lighting up the night sky. The vast expanse of the shires' rolling hills provided an unobstructed view, and her heart raced as another firework splintered the darkness. "Cida! Cida! There's something happening on the shores!" Gielda exclaimed, her fan slipping from her grasp. Like a shadow, Cida materialized by her side, with Althane and Tanyl following close behind.

"By the gods! Sound the bells!" commanded Althane, sending a servant sprinting along the cobblestone streets to raise the alarm. As more and more people emerged from their homes, their fingers pointed towards the spectacle in the sky. In any other situation, they may have marveled at its beauty—but this time, it was nothing short of ominous.

"Where are the girls?" Cida asked. Gielda had gone pale, her eyes widening. Cida clutched her shoulders. "Where are the girls?" he repeated.

"They went to the gardens. I said they could go to Hylycyn Castle. They were restless!" she stammered. Gielda shook her head. "Cida—the shores—"

"I'll worry about that. You get to the girls first." He pressed his lips against her forehead. "Get them inside the castle. Whatever you do. I'll come for you after, I promise." Althane grabbed him by his forearm and pulled him away.

Gielda stared at him with glassy eyes. Her head swayed back and forth, her mouth open. She was muttering something, but Cida couldn't make it out. The wind had picked up, whipping the trees around them, and Cida felt his blood freezing as he stared at Gielda's pale face.

"They will be alright," Althane said to Cida. "She'll take a Hyla cat and get there in no time. She will be fine."

Cida nodded silently, bracing himself for flight. He could see the outlines of Ferian hawks soaring in the sky, their white wings streaking in the darkness.

Gielda rushed to their carriage, two of the Hyla cats scampering beside her. Their hairs were standing on end, their spots glowing red and gold in the moonlight from their original blue tones. Something horrible was happening. Gielda had to get her girls. She had to.

Dasyra rested under a willow tree in the gardens of the palace, a blanket over her lap, staring blankly at the stars. She had been sitting there for hours, watching the light of the moon fade and the stars twinkle as the night grew darker. She was trying to tell herself that she was fine, but there was something swelling in her chest. Something that made her want to scream. She didn't understand it. Arysta had been running around squealing, laughing. Mysera and Oryann were contently reading a story about a princess and her dragon. Everything seemed tranquil.

Then the sky lit up, and horns sounded in the distance. The palace guards had been called to the shores of the sea.

Oryann lifted her head from the book she was reading, and the dim candle she had been using for light quickly snuffed out. "What was that?" she asked. She reached for Arysta, who huddled under her blanket with her. Mysera raised a finger to her lips to silence them, bringing her golden hair behind her ear and cocking her head to listen. After a moment, a loud boom that shook the ground reverberated through the gardens.

Dasyra jolted to her feet, and her sisters scrambled to do the same. The horns sounded again. There was a long wail of a siren, and then a roar of thunder. Dasyra's heart pounded in her chest. She could feel the blood pumping through her veins, and smell the fear in the air. She could hear her sisters' quick breaths. "They are invading!" she shrieked.

There was a cacophony of cries and shouts—roaring and screeching. Swords were clashing just beyond the garden walls. Arysta was hysterical, screaming. Oryann was crying. Mysera was frozen. Dasyra grabbed her small dagger from her side. It was a gift from Mysera—a joke even—she had never used a weapon in her life, but she took it tonight simply because the jewel on its end matched her dress. She held it in her hand, trying to calm herself—the hilt was cold and unfamiliar to her. Clamoring got closer and closer—she could feel the sweat on her brow. The screams and shouts were getting louder. Her hands shook. The roar of a Hyla cat and the sound of steel meeting flesh. Barking dogs. The smell of smoke.

The smell of blood.

The smell of fear.

Three Calisan guards burst through the gate, their snarling hounds yipping around them. The dogs were frenzied, their mouths soaked with blood. Arysta whimpered and clung to Oryann's chest. Dasyra looked at her sisters; only Mysera could fly, her mottled wings quivering anxiously. Mysera stared at the sky, wide-eyed. "Go!" Dasyra urged, pushing Arysta towards Mysera's chest. Mysera nodded and spread her wings, but a dog lunged, knocking her down and causing Arysta to fall, sobbing.

Dasyra leaped onto the dog's back and plunged the dagger into its neck, twisting it. The dog howled in pain before a sudden silence filled the air, followed by a roar. Dasyra released the dog and saw her mother charging on the back of a Hyla cat. Her face contorted in fury as she screeched and attacked the nearest Calisan guard, tearing him apart in seconds. Another guard lifted his hands, glowing brightly. He released a burst of light at Arysta, who fell to the ground. Dasyra landed on her chest, shielding her face. The last thing she heard was her mother's anguished scream as another blast shattered the wall behind them. Then everything went dark.

Chapter Thirty-Seven

Hamlet awoke drowsily to the blaring sound of horns. Someone was hammering on his door. Groggily sitting up, he felt the throbbing ache in his head and noticed the emptiness beside him in the bed. He ran his hand over the sheets, which felt cold.

"Hamlet! Hamlet!" Nattya shrieked just outside his door. In a hurry, he jumped out of bed, wrapped the sheet around his torso, and flung the door wide open. "What's wrong?"

Nattya's face was unnaturally pale, with Highwing standing beside her, his blue tunic covered in blood.

"Were you seriously asleep?" Nattya screamed. "Hellharth is under siege! Calisan soldiers are attacking!"

Hearing swords clashing outside, Hamlet swiftly conjured a uniform onto himself and sprinted down the corridors with the two accompanying him.

"Where's the Queen?" he inquired. Both Highwing and Nattya abruptly halted. He slowed down as the Queensguards rushed past him. Highwing stared at him with an odd expression that sent shivers down Hamlet's spine. "Where is she? Where is Kahlisenya?"

"She... she was on the beach," Highwing uttered hesitantly.

"Where on the beach?" Hamlet pressed. Highwing shook his head, his eyes darting to Nattya.

"Hamlet—she's not there anymore," Nattya intervened. The booming sound of explosions echoed throughout the castle, causing them to brace themselves.

Suddenly, Lady Rayne appeared before them, clutching her shoulder. "Hamlet! We need you!" As Highwing moved to help her, she brushed him off. "It's just dislocated," she muttered before slamming her shoulder against the wall.

"Where is the Queen?" Hamlet asked intensely. Her gaze darted to Highwing before returning to him, pausing on his chest. Several Queensguards emerged around the corner, urgently addressing her.

"Queen Rayne! Sirens are attacking civilian vessels trying to escape out at sea!" one exclaimed. "We're completely encircled."

Hamlet stared at her, perplexed. "Queen? But I thought—Kahl is..." His fingers fumbled for the cord around his neck, hoisting his Lifestone for closer inspection.

Instead of the once shimmering blue gem, a charred and blackened stone lay in his hand. He held his breath, as did everyone nearby.

"She perished on the shores not long ago," Highwing murmured somberly.

"No, that's not true," Hamlet insisted, trembling. "You're wrong. I would have known. She would have woken me." He blew on the stone as if that would somehow get rid of the darkness that had swallowed it.

He felt someone's hand rest on his shoulder and knew it was Nattya. Another explosion thundered through the castle and Rayne was throwing orders around.

"I have to see her," he demanded.

"Hamlet, that isn't a good idea," Highwing insisted.

"I don't give a flying fuck what you think is a good idea!" Hamlet seethed, spit flying about. His eyes were practically bulging out of his head, a vein throbbing angrily above his brow. "Please," he said in a softer tone. "Please."

Rayne's body visibly sagged. "She's in the room of the Ancestry tree. It was just until we could give her a proper send-off."

"Ella isn't here. How are we supposed to get inside?" Hamlet asked. He met Rayne's gaze and then Highwing's. "Oh," he sighed. "Oh."

"Highwing can escort you through the door," Rayne assured him. "You must hurry. They are relentless out there."

The trio stood before the grand stone door adorned with an intricately engraved tree. Hamlet had remained quiet the whole time, unfazed even by the castle-shaking explosions. Highwing paused and looked at Hamlet with concern. "Are you certain about this?" he asked, his tunic gradually losing its wetness. Hamlet couldn't help but think about the blood it had been soaked in—the metallic tang of it wafted around them.

Was it her blood? He thought to himself.

"Please," Hamlet uttered, his tone emotionless. Nattya gently placed her petite hand into his grasp, and he returned a comforting squeeze. With a sigh, Highwing pushed the door open, leading them inside.

The majestic tree from Hamlet's memories stood proudly in the center of the hidden atrium. Its bark was inscribed with enigmatic symbols standing for royal lineages and an ancient language filled with untold stories. Approaching the tree, they could feel the weight of the intense magical energy in the air surrounding them. When they neared, its branches swayed tenderly, as if whispering secrets. The Carver at its base shifted their gaze to the newcomers and groaned—eyes empty.

Surrounding a massive table nearby were Elder scribes—long white hair peeking out from between their huddled bodies.

Releasing Nattya's hand, Hamlet rushed forward and forcefully moved an elder aside. His eyes widened in shock, mouth agape at what lay before him.

Kahlisenya lay motionless on the wooden table, her silvery-white hair spread around her head like a shattered halo. Her eyes were half-closed, their once brilliant cerulean hue replaced with a lifeless white. Her parched, bluish lips bore no resemblance to the ones he had kissed merely hours before.

Overwhelmed with grief, he fell to his knees with a heart-wrenching cry, his hands trembling as they hovered above her. One of her antlers had been torn away, and her abdomen was drenched in blood. As the runes on his arms glowed and burned, a luminous aura radiated from his palms. He whispered through tears, "I'll save you, Kahlisenya... I promise."

An Elder forcefully pulled him away from her, casting him to the ground. The hairless man glowered at him. "How dare you introduce dark magic in this holiest of sanctuaries!"

"I must save her!" Hamlet countered, lunging desperately towards the table.

"Be aware that magic demands an equal trade," another Elder interjected. "Such acts are strictly forbidden here!"

"So, you'll stand idly by while your Queen lies lifeless?" Hamlet bellowed.

"Countless queens and kings have met their demise before her. It is the natural order of things!"

A female Elder stepped closer. "Even if you attempted it, the outcome would be futile. She was marked by death from the moment she took her first breath." She tenderly raised a lock of Kahlisenya's glistening white hair. "Upon birth, her hair was a pale blonde. This ethereal shade is a result of returning from the void."

"Kahlisenya was a sleeping child?" Nattya exclaimed in disbelief. The extremely rare phenomenon of a child born dead was virtually unknown. Historically, there were cases where mothers perished during labor, reviving their children who didn't come to the world awake, resulting in children born with white hair.

Kahlisenya's hair wouldn't have been questioned on the account that the light shade was seemingly inherited by her mother.

"Kahlisenya's mother survived childbirth," Hamlet retorted.

"But her father passed away," the woman added.

"No, he suffered from illness," Hamlet countered as he shook his head. "He met his end one week *after* her birth."

"That's nothing but a cover-up. He died that very night. Kahlisenya was revived through his life force. The late Lady Daliena's womb had been injured during the birth. Kahlisenya's little antler had torn through when she was inside of her. The Hylycyn line would have ended."

"Why reveal this now? Aren't the Elder scribes meant to guard such secrets eternally?" Highwing questioned.

The woman looked at him curiously. "The late Queen Kahlisenya had made this request. In the event that her loyal subject attempts to resurrect her following her demise, she instructed us to unveil that aspect of her existence and prevent him from acting."

"She knew I would come for her," Hamlet murmured. "She had meticulously prepared for this moment." Step by step, he approached the table where her lifeless form lay. His gaze shifted from his Lifestone to her unseeing eyes.

"Promise me you'll wait for me there, alright?" he choked out in a quivering voice. "You'll wait for me in Olesa..."

His mind returned to their first encounter when he modestly offered her a river rock during her coming-of-age celebration. While others showered her with lavish gold and gemstones, she favored the rock. She had said that while everyone had thoughtlessly planned their gifts; he had chosen to give her the one that was most meaningful because he gave her all he could offer her.

Over time, he followed her devotedly, reading stories to her and becoming her trusted confidant. They shared their lives, with each becoming an unwavering pillar of support for the other.

"I can't fathom how to navigate this existence without you," he admitted quietly, as tears finally found their way down his cheeks.

Much to his comfort, they granted him this brief instant before it was time to part ways. "We have to find a quicker exit from Hellharth. I can create a portal door; I would just need a moment," uttered Hamlet, his voice chilly and distant.

"The Throne Room offers the most protection," added Highwing urgently. "We must move quickly."

Nattya, frustrated, questioned, "Where on earth are we supposed to go?"

Hamlet faced her and said, "We need to reach Ella."

CHAPTER THIRTY-EIGHT

Grayson didn't need to turn around to know who had just opened the door to the rooftop. He was seated at the ledge, inhaling plumes of his smoking stick. Ella sat quietly beside him. The sun was just setting over the treetops. It was an unusually calm and peaceful evening.

"You're not ready for bed," Grayson commented. Ella shrugged, not looking at him. He flicked the burning end of his stick, sending a puff of smoke in the air.

"I find it difficult to sleep these days," she answered, her eyes fixed on the horizon.

She stretched and let her wings come out of hiding. Grayson watched her, his eyes following the arch of her back. He reached out and brushed the feathers gently with his thumb, before catching himself and setting his hand back on his lap.

"Don't you want to let them out?" she asked, tapping at his shoulder.

Slowly, the dark membranes of his wings unfurled. He looked at her; the fading light casting a shadow on her face.

Tentatively, she reached out and ran her hand over his wing. He held still, worried she would find the leathery feel of them repulsive. She smiled and stroked his wing, her fingers lingering over the ridges, examining the spines and bone. She placed her hand underneath the skin and began to gently massage it.

A low groan slipped out of his throat, and she stilled. Her hand slipped off the wing and her eyes darted to his. He was frozen, his breathing heavy. Her eyes fell to his lips, and he watched as her lips parted. A blush spread over her cheeks and her scent changed.

She slowly leaned forward, her head tilting to the side as her lips hovered over his. He took a deep breath and let his eyes close, his heart pounding.

A loud crash from down below made them both jump and pull away from each other.

Without another word, she stood and scrambled through the roof door.

For the next several hours, Grayson sat in the darkness, thinking about how he had just let her run off, and how he almost crossed a line with her.

Ella was pacing back and forth in her room. She threw her arms up in the air and then slammed them down on the mattress.

"How could I be so stupid?" she asked herself, her voice echoing through the empty room. "I almost kissed him!"

She wanted to run right into his room, to stand before him and demand to know what was going on between them. To shove him against his desk and press her mouth against his.

A jolt of electricity surged through her body, and she let out a small scream of frustration. "A cold bath," she ordered herself.

What if he never spoke to her again? What if she had been misinterpreting everything, and he was mortified?

She wanted to know what his tongue tasted like. What it felt like against her own. She wanted to know how he would feel pressed between her—

With that thought, she threw herself into her tub with her clothes on, clenching her teeth and fighting the urge to barge into his room and strip herself bare.

"What the hell is wrong with me?" She never had urges this strong before. She had never wanted someone so badly. Her eyes closed, and she concentrated on the sting of the cold water against her skin.

It did nothing to ease the ache that had been slowly building inside her.

⋙———→

Sienna dove into the river just off of Hildfree. She could have gone swimming in the lake by the school, but lakes do not connect to the ocean—and siren calls could only be carried through the connectivity of water.

Beneath the shimmering surface of the river, where moonlight danced upon the ripples, she gracefully swam through the crystal-clear waters. Her tail, a captivating hue of luminous gold, caught the light, casting a radiant glow that illuminated the water. Gliding past moss-covered stones and vibrant underwater foliage, she was soon at the far end of the river.

As she swam, her enchanting voice rose above the gentle lapping of the water. Her melodic calls resonate through the river, calling to the other sirens of her pod.

A series of high-pitched cries and low-pitched moans, their voices rising and falling in harmony.

It was frantic—too frantic. Sienna could hear the calls of her pod mates and their calls were becoming more frenzied. Out of the shrieking came her mother's call. Sienna dove deeper into the river, listening, the gills at her ribcage flexing.

Hellharth is attacking. Stay at Morning Song. Do not come here. The Queen is dead. The Queensguards found her impaled by her own antler—they say Calisan Soldiers did it—that they saw them hit her with their swords. Do not come here.

Sienna propelled herself through the water, her tail fanning, trying to get to the ocean. She was not far. She could make it.

Her body halted as if she had hit an invisible wall—her mother's Queen Spell working over her to command her to stay. She could not go forward—only back.

She needed to warn everyone.

Ella was abruptly stirred from her slumber by the forceful banging on her door. "Ella, wake up! Wake up!" Anna's voice called out. Valla flashed an angry red, disappearing under Ella's bed. In a flash, Ella leaped from her bed and flung the door open, revealing a chaotic hallway filled with panicked students.

"What's happening, Anna?" Ella asked fearfully, noticing the terror in her friend's expression. Grayson appeared behind Anna, his tense demeanor causing Ella's anxiety to escalate.

"Miss Dox, please exit the building using the portal doors! Everyone, exit using the doors and wait in the courtyard for your parents!" Grayson commanded loudly, but his words were drowned out by the commotion.

Ella seized his arm, forcing him to meet her gaze. "Grayson, please tell me... what on earth is going on?"

"We're under attack!" Sienna cried out hysterically, her face flushed with fear. "My mother was in Hellharth!"

An icy chill coursed through Ella's veins at this revelation. "What are you saying about Hellharth?" she demanded as students around them continued to throw their belongings and flee.

"Ella! Get inside your room!" Grayson pleaded with a touch of protectiveness and desperation in his voice, pushing Sienna aside. Sensing the subtle tension between them only reinforced the gravity of the situation for Ella; something horrific had happened.

"Hellharth is at war," Sienna gasped for air and continued frantically, "The Queen...The Queen of Hellharth is dead—Calisan troops have invaded!"

Ella's surroundings abruptly shifted, her vision blurred, and the surrounding noise faded. She felt Anna's hands firmly gripping her shoulders, shaking her while frantically asking about Ella's family.

"Hamlet... Nattya..." Ella whispered with difficulty. "Highwing... Mother..."

"We need to rush home!" Anna cried out, panic clear in her voice. Grayson pushed students aside to create a passage.

"Ella!" he shouted once more. "Go to your room and stay there!"

"You can't just send her back to her room! Everyone needs to leave!" Sienna countered. Turning to Ella, she revealed, "My mother ordered sirens to surround Hellharth to prevent their warriors from attacking us. We will be okay."

As Ella's consciousness started slipping away, she experienced an odd sensation. It felt as if she were watching the events unfold from within herself, like a detached observer. With Sienna's disclosure echoing in her mind, she found herself speaking up, but her voice seemed unfamiliar.

"Your mother has them trapped?" she inquired softly. Her eyes met Grayson's, causing him to flinch.

He detected a subtle hint of danger beneath her seemingly frail tone. Sienna nodded firmly, and Grayson stepped in front of her, shielding her from Ella's view. "Ella, listen to me—"

Ella's gaze pierced him from beneath her heavy bangs, her head tilted in unsettling curiosity. "The Queen is dead. Who did it?"

Grayson hesitated, his mouth opening and closing without a word as a shiver ran up his spine. Her eyes seemed to lose their warm brown color, turning into a threatening shade of crimson.

"The details are unclear," Sienna interjected nervously. "Queensguards found the Queen on the beach, impaled by her own antler. My mother said they claimed to have seen a Calisan soldier strike her down with his sword hilt."

"Ella, where's your family?" Anna asked with a shaky voice. "Come with me. Ethan's waiting downstairs already. Don't worry, you can stay with us until your family comes." She tried to sound comforting amidst the chaos.

"I'll stay with Miss Marks," Grayson added urgently. "Miss Dox, I urge you to head to the courtyard."

"But—"

"Go! Now!" he insisted.

Anna glanced between Grayson's stern expression and Ella's blank stare, tears welling in her eyes. The once-crowded halls were now empty, with panicked cries and screams having moved outside. A faint, ominous scent of smoke and iron lingered in the air. With a shaky nod, Anna said, "Please write to me once things have settled down."

Ella didn't even look at her. Her gaze was fixed intently on Sienna, something clearly amiss. Reluctantly, Anna left them and ran. Grayson turned to Sienna. "You need to get out of here too."

"And escape to where, exactly? My mother is caught in a perilous siege, and the Idris Sea is far from secure—my pod is with her at Hellharth!"

Grayson's voice was firm and urgent. "I implore you, to leave this place. Just go somewhere—anywhere but here."

Sienna sneered in response. "Oh, how convenient? Yet you insist on Ella remaining."

Ella slowly turned to face them; her piercing gaze locked onto Sienna's eyes. The air grew heavy with tension, as if an unseen storm of magic was brewing at their doorstep. With a final glare, Ella stormed into Grayson's room, slamming the door shut behind her.

"Oh, really? Alone time, now of all times?" Sienna scoffed bitterly. "In the heat of battle, and you two can't resist—"

"Shut it!" Grayson hissed sharply before rushing to where Ella had disappeared. As he flung open the door, there was no sign of Ella. Instead, an eerie blue light seeped out from beneath the closet door.

Muttering a curse, Grayson chased after her. "Repeat destination," he commanded. As the blue light enveloped him, he flung open the door to reveal the library—an inferno of destruction.

Ella stood at its epicenter, fire erupting from her body like a malevolent force, seeking out and devouring the airborne books and bookshelves around her with ruthless intent. Panic gripped Grayson as his breath halted in his lungs, his mind playing a cruel trick on him—making him feel like he was back in his own burning home once more.

The deafening crackle of wood and hissing flames filled the air. Ella stood there, a fiery beacon, unyielding even as the ceiling threatened to collapse. Dense smoke choked the room.

"Ella! Ella, snap out of it!" he cried out desperately, terrified that she wouldn't hear him.

Without hesitation, he lunged forward, flames climbing his body without causing pain. Standing before her, he peered into her pitch-black eyes. "Ella," he whispered gently, "I'm here."

"My mother is dead. My home was ransacked. My lands were desecrated. I know Nattya still lives, but what of Hamlet and Highwing?" Her voice broke as the flames raged around her. His anxiety heightened, imagining a small bed in the corner with his music box's melody playing.

Grayson realized that if the runes remained intact, Ella couldn't be causing such havoc. "Don't let these emotions consume you," he warned.

"This feeling... It's all I have left," she snapped back, raising her arms as swirling flames spiraled around her like a sinister serpent, growing more menacing and alive each moment.

"You're not alone; I'm still here," he promised. He needed to break her trance and bring her back before anyone else tried to help.

Tears glistened in her eyes as amber hues returned to her irises briefly. She offered him her hand, flames dancing on her skin like a deadly ballet.

He locked his gaze onto her fiery hand before cautiously taking it in his own. Instantly, his hand became engulfed in flames as their fingers intertwined tightly. The blaze enveloped them both completely, yet all he felt was warmth. The flames dance with an insatiable hunger, devouring row upon row of meticulously arranged books. Embers floated like fiery butterflies, twirling in the air, as shelves crumble under the relentless assault of the inferno. The symphony of cracking wood and crumbling pages echoed through the once-silent hall.

As the library fell apart around them, he pulled her closer until their bodies pressed firmly together.

"Grayson?" she whispered shakily, sadness lacing her voice. "Will you stay with me?"

He tenderly lifted her chin, his thumb gently stroking the curve of her lower lip. He knew he shouldn't do it, but he brought his other hand to cradle the back of her head, placing it on his shoulder and pressing his lips to the top of her head. She let out a strangled cry, her fingers gripping his back as she pulled him closer. "Grayson," she gasped breathlessly, his name escaping her lips like a broken sob.

The heavy beam above them groaned and splintered, crashing to the floor and breaking a table in the process. Slowly, the flames subsided, leaving behind the soft crackles of dying embers and the delicate dance of ash throughout the room. He pulled back slightly, biting his bottom lip. Time seemed to stand still as she wept, her grief pouring out in a torrent of disjointed phrases and barely comprehensible screams. Between her cries, he heard the word "mother."

Grayson sensed Gregor's presence behind them, his distinct aroma mingling with the acrid scent of charred papers. Gently, he pressed his lips to her forehead, wrapping her in a final embrace. His heart raced in anticipation of when Gregor would shatter their fragile peace.

Grayson hadn't done anything wrong; he hadn't crossed that line and had done everything right. Yet, he was overwhelmed by guilt and shame—an indescribable sense of loss and regret. His heart ached, his stomach churned, and his mind filled with questions. He had seen the darkness within her—the violence lurking beneath the surface, the shadows in her eyes, and felt the heat of the raging inferno threatening to engulf everything it touched. He had glimpsed the truth of her soul and its demons.

He saw the war raging within her.

Now she traced her nose along his jaw, her breath warm and soft against his skin. Her lips brushed his neck, and her hands tenderly caressed his chest. If he turned his head just slightly, he would feel her lips against his, finally.

"Ellarhyssa," Gregor spoke, his voice steady through the swirling smoke. Immediately, they separated, and Ella felt the sudden absence of Grayson's presence. Her eyes scanned the room, her mind clearing as embarrassment set in upon realizing she had lost control of her magic.

"I'm... unsure what's happening to me," she admitted.

"You're in shock," Gregor empathized. He exchanged a silent understanding with Grayson just before Ella fell unconscious to the floor. Grayson's hand lingered where her head had been, emitting a faint, captivating glow.

"She'll be out for a while," he said calmly.

"Are you really okay with that? She trusted you, you know," Gregor challenged, helping Grayson levitate Ella while surveying the room and frowning at the scattered flying books.

"Her trust wasn't something I asked for," Grayson retorted.

"Isn't that so? I recall being around for quite some time," Gregor raised a slim brow, daring him to lie to his face.

"Did you enjoy watching? It doesn't matter either way to me, Deacon." They cautiously stepped across the debris-laden floor, bearing Ella through the portal door into Grayson's candlelit chamber. The warmth of the fireplace greeted them—Grayson promptly extinguished it; he'd had enough fire for one day.

Gregor's tone softened as he placed Ella on pillows by the hearth. "Can you not see what's right in front of you? Are you truly dedicated to repressing your feelings?"

"How does any of this end?" Grayson erupted in fury, casting potions off their shelves to break against the cold stone floor. The pungent smell of spilled concoctions filled the air. With a quick motion, he cleared his desk and sent items crashing down. He seized his music box and nearly threw it as well when it sprung open to play its soothing melody. His breaths heaved as his throat constricted.

Holding the music box up, his reflection caught his attention. He handed it to Gregor, "This is all that remains from the first war. What will I lose this time?"

Gregor ran his fingers through his golden hair, deep in thought. "You're afraid of losing her," he said carefully.

A bitter laugh escaped Grayson's lips. "No, I'm terrified of losing myself."

Puzzled, Gregor furrowed his brow. "What do you mean by that?"

Grayson fidgeted with his pendant, anxiety in his movements. "When she set fire to everything in the library, my first instinct wasn't to extinguish the flames. When she reached out to me— at that moment, all I could think was: let it all burn."

CHAPTER THIRTY-NINE

Townsend was up in flames, the sky breaking into a fury of orange and red. Hylycyn castle remained a white pillar beyond the blackened smoke. Calisan guards swarmed in from their boats—Anaferian eagles and Hylycyn Hawks tearing at the sails.

The Queensguards without wings pummeled through on foot and feline back, breaking through the barrage of spells the opposing Maji had thrown at them. Hellharth's humans flanked the shores. Some of them stood their ground and fought back, but others ran, seizing boats and trying to row away.

Althane and Cida were on the shores, sand flying everywhere as bodies started piling up. Althane brought down his scythe—an Anaferian blade made with a malicious poison that if touched led to certain death. Cida, out of shape as he was, managed to hold off a dozen men on his own, but his leg had been badly smashed.

He looked down, seeing blood seeping out of his leg and the bone sticking out. He couldn't stop.

The invading humans kept coming. They were endless, and the sea was vaster and more dangerous.

The echoing call came up on the winds from the sea, the terrifying songs of the sirens that caused riders and their birds to plummet into the dark depths of the water. The deafening siren song filled the air, and Cida and Althane resorted to the extreme measure of repeatedly pricking their eardrums to induce deafness. The Calisan soldiers must have been using some spell to deflect the siren song.

A symphony of splashing and thrashing filled the air as the sirens converged upon their prey. Agile and swift, they darted through the water, their movements synchronized and precise. With a mesmerizing grace, they encircled their target, cutting off any escape route.

It was a massacre.

Althane was tired.

"There's too many of them!" Cida warned. "The call is drowning the birds and riders!" The birds struggled to no avail—trapped in a desperate frenzy of escape as they spiraled out of the sky helplessly. Amid the turbulent waves, they witnessed frantic fighting, as scaly fins thrashed wildly, mercilessly dragging down both beasts and riders into the watery abyss. "We need to evacuate the children!" Cida called out desperately, clutching his leg. Althane hesitated, his heart in his throat. Retreating wasn't an option for him.

"Go! Find your children—find mine—and get them the hell out of here!" Althane yelled to Cida.

As Cida soared above the treetops, his broken leg served as a constant reminder of his vulnerability. He spied the inner gardens of Hylycyn Castle below, a sight that should have filled him with hope but only heightened his desperation. Even from this height, the signs of battle were unmistakable, the once-tranquil garden now an overgrown, magically-enhanced war zone. Plant roots snaked around their unfortunate victims, crushing them until their last breath. Cida was determined to reclaim his family, injury be damned, and the sight of devastation only fueled his resolve.

The plants were a nightmarish sight, twisted and gnarled, seemingly alive with dark energy. As Cida flew overhead, he heard the screams of Petra's children, and his heart sank. He knew he was too late and what awaited him beyond the ravaged garden wall. Upon arrival, he found lifeless bodies in a pool of blood. Among them was Petra's youngest daughter, Alynn, just fourteen summers old, clutching her throat as life faded away.

The attacker—a human Calisan soldier—looked at him fiercely and silently mocked him, licking the dagger he used on Alynn. Cida felt rage overwhelm him and he nose-dived into the man, crushing every bone in his body on impact. The man was still and Cida roared out his frustration and heartache. His heavy fist came down again and again, onto the man's skull, until his head was caved in and he was dead.

He heard crying just beyond the wall and swiftly climbed over the rubble. There, beneath piles of rock and shattered timber, his daughter Mysera lay broken and deformed – lifeless.

"NO! MYSERA! My baby! My girl!" He wailed. He rushed to her and cradled her in his arms, her body stiff and cold. Her hand was caught on something, pulling it from beneath the debris. A hand was clutched tightly in hers, a signet ring around the pinky finger – his wife, his Gielda.

"Papa?" came Arysta's feeble voice from behind another mound. He gently laid Mysera down and scrambled to reach his youngest daughter. Arysta was filthy, covered from head to toe in dirt and grime, but fortunately, none of the blood was hers.

"Papa," she sobbed into his arms. "Mysera is – is gone. Mama and Oryann tried to stop them, but their dogs dragged Oryann away."

"Dasyra?" he forced himself to ask.

"She's breathing, but she won't wake up," Arysta cried. She pulled on his arm, leading him to a mound of dirt, where she started digging. Dasyra's face emerged, and he joined in, frantically uncovering her. She groaned and opened her eyes slightly.

"Father... Father—the dogs... Oryann!" Her attempt to scream came out hoarse.

"I know, I know. I'm here. I need to get both of you inside the castle." He hoisted each daughter onto his hip and let out a scream, his anguish reverberating through the eerie silence.

⇛⟶

Tanyl struggled valiantly, her boys bravely standing their ground against soldiers clad in powerful runic armor. Though mere fledglings at seventeen, their father's teachings had lent them strength. Elmon and Ruvanc skillfully coordinated their assaults, beams of intense light searing the faces of the approaching Maji. Tanyl appeared almost unrecognizable, her once—flowing hair reduced to nothing.

Cida set the girls down gently, enveloping them in his most convincing illusion. "Remain still and silent," he commanded softly.

With a flash, he charged into battle, slamming into a nearby Maji with tremendous force, his hands tearing through the man's jaw. He turned to the next Maji and sent him flying through the air, his body crashing into the next. His leg was heavy and he began to tire. He began to lose focus. He needed to rest.

"Uncle!" cried the boys, both relief and terror in their voices. Cida unleashed a whirlwind of destruction upon the remaining foes, taking a spear to his abdomen before snapping its shaft and repurposing it as his own weapon. Grief fueled him—the pain of losing his loved ones was thinly veiled beneath an unwavering fury that would stop at nothing to keep the family he had left safe.

As the ordeal concluded, he crumpled to his knees, the magical radiance of Illusion dissipating from his daughters. Tanyl winced in agony and attempted to regain her footing, her boys supporting her trembling frame.

"Al... Althane?" she uttered through gritted teeth, her voice strained by pain.

"He summoned you. The children must be escorted to safety," came the response.

A frenzied panic laced Tanyl's gasping breath as she demanded, "Where is he? Tell me, where?"

"Althane remains on the shores..." Cida informed her, urgency swelling in his voice. "We must get the children indoors, Tanyl. We must. Petra's children— my children...Gielda... They are dead..."

Tanyl gasped and clutched her chest, her eyes falling on Arysta and Dasyra. "The shores are filled with sirens—the land is full of Maji. They put this—dome of magic over us. How are we going to escape?"

"Hamlet is devising an escape route for Highwing and Nattya!" Rayne's voice came from behind them. Her face was a canvas of soot and blood. She was barely recognizable.

"Hurry! We don't have much time!" The air crackled with the sound of her wings unfurling as she prepared to take flight.

Chapter Forty

"We need more time—can you stall them?" Hamlet asked Nattya.

Nattya didn't waste any time, stripping off her shirt and revealing her breasts in a bid to distract the approaching soldiers and buy them more time. She ran off in the direction the invading soldiers were coming without a word.

"That'll do it," Hamlet mumbled.

"We can't just leave her here!" Highwing said from his side.

"We aren't. Get your head out of your ass and focus! We must get to Ella. She's at an Arcane school in Calisan called Morning Song." Hamlet had his palms outstretched in front of him, fingers splayed. The surrounding air was vibrating, a hum that filled the room. A dark portal appeared in the middle of the floor, a black hole that looked as though it would swallow him whole. He was about to step through it when the portal disappeared.

"It's not enough," he yelled at Highwing, his voice strained. The portal flickered in and out of existence, and he knew that he was running out of time.

The earth trembled violently beneath their feet, forcing them to make a choice as the encroaching inferno threatened to engulf them all.

"I can't just leave my mother!" Highwing argued.

"You keep going down that list of people you can't leave behind, and you'll be here forever!" Hamlet snarled. Again, the swirl of magic spiraled to life around him, but wouldn't hold.

"But—"

"My job is to keep *Ella* safe. That will *always* be my job. Yours is to protect the Queen— your mother. But you have a choice right now. Either you stay behind and get the hell out of my way so I can get where I need to be, or you come with me. Your choice." Hamlet waited for the inevitable argument to ensue.

Highwing gazed upon the relentless flames outside, captivated by their intensity as they rose like crashing waves, consuming everything in their path.

"Highwing," a gentle female voice urged him from behind, "go."

It was his mother, standing in all her glory. An invader's head, with his helm still attached, was dangling from her hand, a mace in the other. Her beautiful feline eyes were soft, misty, and hopeful. Her face was splattered in blood, the metallic scent soiling the air. The stench of death hung heavy around her.

The rustle of armor and distant clashes of swords filled the background as she spoke, her voice trembling. "Find Ella. She is... she's the rightful heir and has always been." She shifted her gaze toward Hamlet and studied his blackened Lifestone. "You must take the Court children with you. I beg you," she implored, desperation evident in her tone.

"I don't have time—"

"I will give you time. They are just behind me."

"I'm not a brood mother Rayne! I can't care for—" he started counting on his fingers, "*nine* children!" he finished, his voice rising to a shout.

Rayne knelt, coming face-to-face with Hamlet, their eyes locking with intensity. "We only have Dasyra, Arysta, Ruvane, and Elmon left," she said softly, choking back tears. "That's it. All gone." The scent of blood hung heavy in the air as she continued. "Cida lost Oryann and Mysera. Gielda is dead." With a painful grimace, she lifted the bloodied head. "But mark my words, this is just the beginning; it won't mean the end for the Anaferi and the Hylycyn lineage. Only the strong survive. Do you understand me?"

Hamlet nodded slowly; his heart wrenching with each shared memory of the innocent lives lost. He had known these children and watched them grow – never expecting such an unbearable fate. But there was no time to indulge his all-consuming grief. That could be reserved for a later date.

"Where are they?" Hamlet demanded urgently. "I can't stand waiting."

"Here!" Cida's labored voice resounded from the terrace as he stumbled into view – clearly exhausted. Arysta and Dasyra clung to his sides, their expressions etched with raw horror. Tanyl appeared next, her once long red hair reduced to a scorched fuzz on her scalp. Ruvane and Elmon were holding her up.

"Highwing!" Their cries harmonized into a desperate plea. Ruvane's voice wavered as he spoke up, "Father's still trapped in the battle down there!"

"Everything's burning! Please help!" Elmon interjected with a teary-eyed cry.

The danger tightened around them like a noose.

"Come on then!" Hamlet waved them to him. The portal was almost ready, and it was taking everything out of him. He could feel his runes igniting on his skin and the fatigue was starting to take over. "I need help," he rasped, his body shaking.

Cida knelt, his arm snaking around Hamlet's waist to steady him. In all the years they had known each other, this was the first time they weren't at each other's throats. Cida raised his hand, his eyes closed. He shook his head. "They must have magic in place to keep us from leaving." He glanced at the portal. It was fading away.

"We saw people trying to fly away, but they couldn't go past a certain point—," Arysta whimpered.

"Like a dome," Tanyl rasped.

"You'll need blood magic to break through. That's the only way," Cida said.

Rayne looked aghast. "The amount of blood we would need to break through their barrier would be deadly. It must be given *willingly*—"

Cida raised his hand to stop her. He stared intently into Hamlet's eyes, his face darkening. Tanyl embraced her sons and pushed them toward Hamlet.

"Be good," she told them.

"You take care of my girls," Cida instructed Hamlet.

Highwing suddenly stood up, alarmed by the sound of approaching footsteps. Nattya appeared from around the corner in a full sprint, completely disheveled and unclothed, her thighs marred with streaks of blood.

"MOVE YOUR ASS THEY ARE COMING!" She screamed.

Lady Rayne's eyes widened as she realized what was about to happen. She grabbed Tanyl's sleeve, forcing the woman to face her. "You can't do this, Tanyl. Think about Althane. Think about your boys!"

Tanyl offered a steady smile, tears brimming in her eyes. "I am thinking about them," she said, gently patting Rayne's hand.

Time seemed to slow down; Cida and Tanyl exchanged small smiles before Ruvane and Elmon noticed their intentions and lunged forward. Tanyl raised her hand, immobilizing them while Dasyra and Arysta shrieked in terror. In a single smooth motion, Cida slashed a sharp claw across Tanyl's throat while she mirrored his action. Blood spurted onto the floor, causing Rayne to hastily draw sigils in their blood on the stone surface, which glowed gold before the air snapped. The portal surged to life, its energy renewed as Hamlet pushed Ruvane and Elmon through first. Arysta frantically tried to claw her way back to her father, but Dasyra yanked a handful of her hair and forced her through as well. Finally, Cida collapsed to the ground, still clutching Tanyl's lifeless body until he drew his last breath.

Nattya jumped into Highwing's open arms, and he flung them through. He dropped her on the hard ground and turned, holding his hand out to his mother.

"COME ON!" He shouted desperately, his arm outstretched.

The stampede became deafening as the invading soldiers appeared in the throne room, surrounding Lady Rayne. She smiled at Highwing, and he knew.

"NO! NO! YOU HAVE TO JUMP THROUGH!" he pleaded.

She raised the mace above her head, screeching with determination to protect her son from the dozen soldiers wielding magic and spears. The portal swirled, closing rapidly, while Highwing pounded on it, realizing it was a one-way passage with no return. In a desperate attempt to save them, his mother's mace shattered against a soldier's armor just before the portal closed. Highwing was left in utter despair as his mother and the soldiers vanished into nothing.

Some time had passed, and the world outside went eerily quiet. Althane trekked up the steps of the castle, following the trail of bodies like breadcrumbs. Rayne was crouched on the floor in the throne room, the once grandeur room now suffering from the stale stench of death. He approached her slowly. Her wings were broken at odd angles, and a mess of human Nomaji and Maji lay in heaps on the ground.

"Rayne?" He called out in a soft voice. She was shuddering, stroking the head of someone in her lap.

Althane was filled with dread as he got closer, and the sight before him confirmed his worst fears. It was Tanyl's head, sliced apart at the throat, her eyes wide and empty. He stood frozen in shock, unable to comprehend what he was witnessing. He wanted to scream, but no sound came from his lips. His mind flooded with a sense of confusion and sorrow as reality slowly sank in. All that remained now were questions for which he didn't think he was prepared.

He vomited.

Althane collapsed to the floor. "Tan-Tanyl! TANYL!" He cried out, the words echoing off the walls and bouncing back to him with ferocity.

Rayne slowly turned to him, her face streaked with tears and soot. Her face was ashen, a gash along the side of her temple.

"I told her not to," she said weakly. "The portal—it was closing. The blood—the blood!" She lifted her hands, coated in it, now dried down and brown. "I wrote the sigils in their blood."

Althane was heaving air into his lungs, the room spinning. Cida was in a crumpled heap just a foot away. It looked as if Tanyl and he had died together, and Rayne dragged away her body to cradle it in her embrace.

"She saved them. Her and Cida—they saved them," she sniffed. "She loved you. She loved you *so* much," she said in a whisper. "I'm so sorry. I'm s-s-so sorry." She was sobbing.

Althane couldn't understand what had happened. He couldn't fathom how his wife and friend were now dead. His mind was a tangled mess of confusion and grief.

"The children?" He managed out.

"They went with Hamlet—wherever Ella is. The boys are fine," she answered. Althane watched her as she ran her fingers over Tanyl's eyelids to close them.

Tanyl's hair had been completely burnt off, with her scalp and flesh charred beyond recognition. Her skin was peeling away to reveal raw and tender flesh underneath. Her hair had been her crowning glory.

Althane asked shakily, "Did she suffer?" trying to hold back his tears as he awaited the answer. Rayne paused for a moment before taking a shuddering breath and responding, "It was quick. Cida was quick. They both died smiling." The bittersweet news settled into the atmosphere like a heavy blanket, as Althane painfully acknowledged that even in death there could be solace—Tanyl didn't die alone.

But he hadn't been there.

"I wasn't here. I was fighting. I was—I—" he couldn't speak anymore.

Rayne let out a mechanical laugh, her voice stark and emotionless. "She loved you," she said solemnly. "*More* than I did." He was taken aback by her words, and she scrutinized him with an intense gaze. She had urged Tanyl to think of him and their children before anything else, no matter what the cost. "I told her to preserve herself and to think of you and the children," Rayne explained harshly, "and she said she was...and then she died for you." It was clear from her tone that she admired her courage but at the same time felt deeply regretful.

Self-sacrifice wasn't something that Rayne herself would ever do—not for him at least.

For Highwing, she fought to the death. The countless bodies that lay in their decay were a mere testament to her commitment to her son. She had no intention of dying for what she held so dear but instead carried out massive slaughter in order to protect it. Unyielding in her conviction, she was relentless in defending what mattered most: Highwing.

Seeing her in this new light, Althane finally understood why Kahlisenya had chosen Rayne as her successor. Rayne now reigned as Queen of Hellharth—albeit a battered and war-weary realm, but a queen nonetheless. Inheriting a shattered throne beset by conflict did not diminish her achievements; on the contrary, it showcased Rayne's strength. She possessed the power to resurrect Hellharth from destruction, unlike the reclusive Kahlisenya.

With one last tender kiss upon Tanyl's lips, Althane withdrew. Tanyl offered him a kind of compassion that he had never received from Rayne, filling him with remorse for lost opportunities. Biting his cheek to suppress an emotional torrent, he tasted blood as tears welled up in the corners of his eyes, but refused to fall.

"Kahlisenya is dead. Petra's daughter... Bastian is unaccounted for. Cida, Tanyl. They ran our people out of their homes and set everything on fire. We cannot just let this go," Althane pressed.

"Are we really repeating history, Althane?" Rayne chuckled darkly. "The humans won't stop—"

"Then neither can we!" He shouted angrily, his mottled wings flapping in agitation.

"What has your visceral hatred for humans ever accomplished?" she spat out, her voice trembling with raw anger. "Need I remind you of the real reason we were torn apart? Tanyl and the others believed it was all because of *her*. If only they were privy to the truth..."

He quickly lifted a hand to silence her. "Stop! You can't use that against me. I was right all along! Just look around us, Rayne! This chaos... There's no Court left! No order, no respect! These humans brought this upon us!"

"And what would have happened if I exposed you as a disciple of The Son of Bashet?" Her voice cracked as she locked eyes with him. "Do you think they would have taken you to Bris Forest, bound to a tree—like a lamb to the slaughter? Left for wolves and cats to feast upon like many before?" Her eyes blazed with betrayal and resentment; years of suppressed rage finally escaped from behind her stoic facade. "I was painted as the cold-hearted partner who abandoned you. I was vilified, marked as the villain all along. Yet, here I stood, bearing your darkest secrets so your life could be spared!"

"What exactly do you want from me, Rayne?" he exclaimed, his voice strained with frustration. "Tell me! What am I supposed to do? I can't change the past. You're just fighting old ghosts." He paused, attempting to calm himself. "He had the right intentions; the execution was just flawed."

Rayne scoffed bitterly, her eyes cold and unyielding. "Oh, right? You needed someone else to be the public face of your cause because you lacked the courage to take responsibility if it went wrong. I should've spoken up when you told him about—"

"Enough!" he roared, desperation evident on his face as he interrupted her. "I'm not the villain here, Rayne! Our real enemy is still out there! Now ask yourself," he insisted, his voice laced with venom, "what are you going to do about this?"

Silent at first, she absentmindedly stroked Tanyl's head in her lap. "I never thought I'd be queen, and now I don't know what to do," she admitted honestly. "All this death and destruction. What am I the queen of? A battleground."

"Our son is out there—my sons are out there. If we don't do something, this will be their fate," Althane said. "My question to you is, what is your next move?"

Rayne fell silent, her breath caught in her throat as the piercing sound of ship horns echoed in her ears. Her eyes flickered with a powerful blend of magic and fury, churning like a deadly storm.

CHAPTER FORTY-ONE

Hours had passed by. They all stared up at the sky in silence, blanketed in darkness and smoke that had traveled from Hellharth to Calisan.

They all had taken turns reassuring one another that everything would be alright. But the pain was raw, and the air felt heavy. Occasionally, one of them would break.

Nattya lay peacefully sleeping beside Highwing, his wing tenderly enveloping her body. He had been doing his utmost to prevent Elmon and Ruvane from succumbing to anger. The twins' fiery red hair now served as the sole memento of their departed mother. Every so often, Ruvane would impatiently pace to and fro, while Elmon rocked himself, hands pressed tightly against his ears.

"You know, your mother was incredibly brave," Highwing said softly.

Ruvane's bright yellow eyes locked onto Highwing's, a fresh wound slicing down his jaw. "What do you care? Our mothers never got along."

But Highwing replied earnestly, "Ruvane, if there was ever a moment when my mother appreciated yours, it was tonight."

Elmon gratefully accepted a sliver of cheese from Highwing, which then distracted him from the haunting sounds. He sighed dejectedly. "We've been trained for battle since our childhood, but these screams... I can't shake them."

Highwing affectionately ruffled Elmon's hair. "I heard you fought admirably."

Elmon looked upward wistfully. "I just wish Father had been there to witness it. We might have made him proud," he added.

"Do you suppose Father is still alive?" Ruvane's question hung in the air.

Highwing managed a chuckle despite the heaviness in his heart. "That old bat? He's far too stubborn to die," he joked. The twins burst into laughter. For a moment, Highwing tried to push away the memory of his own mother's final moments as they shared this fleeting respite from their sorrows. The night went on and Nattya had finally awoken, giving quiet advice to the twins.

"Why the hell were you naked?" Hamlet finally asked her. He had long relinquished his cloak to her.

She gave him a snarky look. "Three of them I could handle fine. When the fourth and fifth showed up, I ran out of holes and distractions." She winced and turned her head away. Hamlet choked on his spit and Highwing slapped a hand over his face.

"There is a child present," Hamlet said gruffly, eyes darting to little Arysta who cocked her head in confusion.

"Are we just supposed to sit here?" Dasyra managed to speak. Her voice was hoarse and weak. Her blonde hair curled about her ears, but it was tinged orange from her father's blood spraying onto it.

"I've sent word to a friend at the school. But you all will need to disguise yourselves one way or another. I'm tapped out so I cannot do it for you." Hamlet grimaced.

Highwing snorted as his twin brothers morphed into small birds that flitted around them. Hamlet nodded his head in approval.

"Both of you, cover your ears," he instructed, pointing at Dasyra and Arysta. Arysta deftly braided her hair over her ears and tucked her head beneath the hood of her coat.

Dasyra frowned. "I don't have enough hair to do that," she said bitterly, flexing her imperfect wings that were just beginning to heal. Fresh feathers sprouted from them, making her resemble a young hatchling.

"Then just hide your wings and put on a hat," he snapped.

"But I'll look like a boy!" she protested.

"I don't care! Put it on!" Hamlet shouted, his voice bouncing off the tall trees surrounding them.

Nattya chimed in hesitantly, "Hamlet, is this the forest where you fought that beast? Grothong or something like that?"

"Grothorn," he corrected her. "And yes." He realized he should have been quieter.

Dasyra, growing more impatient by the minute, asked, "So we're just waiting around in a circle to be eaten? Where the hell is your friend?"

Elysium's voice emerged from behind them unexpectedly. "I'm here. Grothorn isn't happy that you're venturing off the path—again." Hamlet turned around to see Elysium, dressed in her same flowing robes and holding a gold staff in one hand.

"There's a path?" Dasyra mumbled feebly.

Sighing audibly, Hamlet got to his feet. "Took you long enough to get here," he said to Elysium. "In case you haven't heard, Hellharth is under siege."

"Oh, I know," Elysium replied solemnly. "All of Calisan is in turmoil. They're evacuating students from the school as we speak."

Hamlet's face tightened with concern for Ella. "And what about her?"

"The Highmaster and Master Moore are taking care of her right now."

Nattya interjected, her voice sharp with worry. "What does that even mean? Where is she?"

Elysium spoke cautiously, her gaze landing on Nattya for a moment. "She's safe. Stick close to me and follow my lead. The school is nearly empty."

She then turned to Dasyra, curiosity in her eyes: "Are you unable to perform illusions? Or do you share Ella's peculiar traits?" She was, of course, referring to Ella's strange talent for repelling illusions and certain magical spells. However, Dasyra bristled at the mere suggestion.

"I am nothing like Ella," Dasyra replied indignantly.

Elysium hummed thoughtfully, her eyes drifting towards the two small birds spinning and chirping around her head. She aimed a finger at Dasyra, who recoiled with a hiss. Suddenly, Dasyra's body contorted, and in her place appeared an offended little orange house cat.

"Don't worry, it's just temporary—enough to navigate past everyone," Elysium reassured her. She then turned towards Arysta, who stumbled back nervously. "The hair covering the ears—I appreciate the effort, but previous experience with Ella suggests this won't be effective." Without hesitation, she pointed her finger at Arysta, who screamed as her body shrank rapidly. The newly transformed mouse emitted frightened squeaks while Dasyra quickly scooped her up in her feline jaws.

Nattya hid behind Hamlet, stating, "I'm a Nomaji, so I think I should be safe."

Elysium tilted her head, her eyes narrowed at her. She then turned to Highwing, her finger hovering in front of her.

Highwing adjusted himself uncomfortably as his ears rounded. "Don't point that thing at me." Rolling her eyes in impatience, Elysium urged them all to hurry and follow closely behind her.

The tall spires of the castle loomed over them, billows of smoke coming out of a certain point of it. Students were evacuating and disappearing with a *pop!* Elysium held her hand up, signaling for them to wait at the tree line while the remaining people left.

Hamlet glanced around nervously. Grothorn was surely close by and watching them with his hundred eyes.

"Come," Elysium motioned. Dasyra's cat form darted into the field, dropping her sister-mouse onto the grass and shaking her head. She yowled angrily, orange eyes glaring up at Elysium.

"This is the school? It's massive," Highwing said. Nattya nodded her head. Thousands of glowing windows reflected against the lake's still surface. They varied in size, shape, and design, some with graceful arches while others boast intricately decorated stained glass artwork. "Ella's here..." he said quietly, his eyes scanning the building.

"Highmaster promises to come down and clear things up," Elysium shared, glancing at the slow-moving teachers ambling across the Courtyard.

Nattya, taking Highwing's hand in her own, led him nearer to the shimmering lake. "It's nice to see your ears rounded out," she commented with a smirk. She seated herself, sitting directly in the cool water. "I'm so nervous," she admitted.

"For whatever reason?" he asked.

"Everything that has happened. I don't expect Ella is going to greet us with a warm welcome," her eyes drifted to the smoking portion of the castle that had calmed some. Teachers were pointing at it and rushing around stupidly. "Or maybe she will," she muttered.

"Real warm," Highwing said sarcastically. He sat there quietly, flicking stones onto the water's surface.

"I don't suppose she will want to go back to Hellharth?" Nattya asked.

"If there is even a way to get back to Hellharth," he said. "There isn't much to be done right now."

Nattya was thoughtful for a moment and cautiously said, "If your mother... It means you are the King of Hellharth."

Highwing stopped skipping rocks and let her words sink in. "I don't think I'm much of a King," he responded bitterly.

The water's surface broke and a hauntingly beautiful sound escaped. A young woman's head bobbed on the surface a mere foot from them. Her piercing blue eyes, filled with fury, seemed to glow in stark contrast to the darkness of her hair. A golden tail fused seamlessly up her body, her dorsal fin flaring angrily.

"Siren!" Highwing exclaimed, his eyes widening as he scrambled backward.

The siren glared at them, her dark, webbed hand raised accusingly. "Elves!" she spat out with contempt before releasing a series of chilling chirps and a bone-rattling wail that left Highwing stunned.

With adrenaline surging, Nattya leaped to her feet, desperately hurling rocks and shouting for help. The hostile siren responded with a piercing shriek before breaking into an enchanting melody. Her gaze locked on her prey. Under the spell of the siren's song, Highwing helplessly drifted toward the water's edge. Nattya dove, plunging into the icy water, and grappled with the siren, who began dragging her deeper into the depths. The siren emitted a faint glow, patterns on her tail dancing furiously and signaling to Nattya her whereabouts. In desperation, the siren let out another piercing shriek, attempting to bewitch Nattya with her melodic call. However, Nattya fiercely sank her dull teeth into the siren's arm and scrambled toward the surface.

"Help!" she shouted, before being dragged under again by her ankle.

There was a light, bright and blinding and cold. The siren had stopped her descent and Nattya was pulled from the water, the heavy cloak weighing her down.

Elysium and Highmaster Gregor were peering over her, both with the same curious expression. They had a shimmering orb about their head that then vanished.

"The siren song didn't affect you," Elysium observed. Nattya was panting, searching for Highwing, who had been dragged away into the field. She noticed both Dasyra and Arysta were casually swimming along the water's surface, still in animal forms. Hamlet was rubbing his head, talking to Highwing.

She struggled to get up, chancing a glance at the siren who attacked them. The siren was now in human form, stumbling along with shaking legs and glaring at them. She pointed at Nattya and hissed, causing her to jump back.

"Sienna," Highmaster Gregor said calmly, "these are our guests."

Sienna's face twisted into a mix of fury and confusion. "They are from Hellharth! I heard everything!" She waved toward the teachers who had huddled around in the Courtyard, yelling for their attention.

"They cannot see us, I've illusioned this area," Elysium explained.

"You're assisting them!" Sienna shouted in disbelief. "My pod suffers out there because of their actions, and yet you help them! What about my mother?"

Highwing, finally regaining composure, retorted, "I witnessed hundreds of my kind plunge to their death from those Siren Songs!"

"After all this time, Ella has been one of them!" Sienna shouted furiously, charging towards Gregor with water surging behind her, forming sharp spirals that danced around. "I'll put an end to every one of you!" she screamed, commanding the lake water to swirl ominously around them.

Gregor raised his hand calmly, and a brilliant light burst from his palm, striking Sienna in the chest. She crumpled to the floor, losing control over the water's movements.

"I don't have time for this. I've already dealt with a fire outbreak in the library. Managing *two* agitated girls was not in my plans tonight," he sighed. "Take her to the infirmary. We'll deal with her later," he instructed Elysium. He then turned to Hamlet, his stance cold and unwavering. "And *you*. You *bastard*."

》》》————————▶

Grayson paced back and forth in her room. He knew she would wake up, but when she did, she was going to have questions he didn't have the answers to. Or maybe she would become irate that he had knocked her out. She was sound asleep, tucked beneath blankets and elevated on pillows.

It reminded him of that night he had to carry her back to her room after she fell asleep in his chamber.

He fidgeted with his necklace, glancing around her room. She was tidier than most others when he did weekly room inspections. Something caught his eye—a box that peeked from beneath the bed. He knew he shouldn't go through her things, but hadn't she done this to him countless times?

He lifted the lid on the box, a large gray feather and a letter nestled at the bottom. He opened the letter, letting his eyes scan it.

It must have been a letter from her friends. Nattya, he knew of. She had come on a visit before. He didn't know anything about this Highwing person. He lifted the large gray feather and sniffed it. It was a man's. He opened the other letter, one that Nattya didn't participate in. As his eyes scanned the paper, he became increasingly agitated.

Ella, it has been incredibly frustrating with you not around. Home does not feel like home. I hope this letter brings you comfort. I tried to plead my case with Hamlet on letting me come with them on this visit, but he was a foul bastard, and you can tell him I said so. I want you to know that even though our circumstances have changed, I still plan to marry you, and you are in my thoughts.
All my love, Highwing

Frustrated, Grayson tossed the items back into the box and hastily shoved them beneath the bed. "Marry," he uttered the word, allowing it to fill the room. The thought of her having a life beyond these confining walls didn't truly shock him. What astounded him was that she had never breathed a word about being engaged.

The door creaked open, interrupting his thoughts, as a peculiar group entered her chamber. "Hamlet? Nattya?" he murmured, recognizing them at once. With a flutter of wings, two birds swooped in and transformed before him, their vibrant red hair and fresh battle scars impossible to miss. The air filled with the scent of smoke and blood. Valla's hair stood on end before she became relaxed and greeted them excitedly.

An orange cat and a tiny mouse shifted into female forms, exchanging words with each other. Meanwhile, a towering man with pronounced ears unfolded his gray wings. "Those feathers...," Grayson noted aloud, studying the man more intently. His hair was a striking silvery gray, woven intricately around his head, complemented by tattoos that spiraled down his arms—large black cats painted in black on his biceps. The man's jaw was firm, squared, and unyielding as his steel-colored eyes locked onto Grayson's gaze.

Highwing couldn't help but scrutinize the enigmatic figure standing before him. "Who is this guy?" he wondered aloud, taking note of the man's untamed black hair cascading down his back. The man loomed over Highwing, appearing a head taller. Highwing's eyes were drawn to a striking scar etched into the man's face, a silent reminder of a battle once fought. They were each sizing up the other.

"I'm Master Moore," Grayson said with a partial introduction. "You must be Highwing."

Highwing nodded slightly and looked to Nattya, who was looking at the bed. His steel eyes followed hers and he lurched to the bed. "Ella! What the hell—why is she sleeping?"

"Rest assured, she's absolutely fine," Gregor said, leaning on the door frame. He was rubbing his reddened knuckles.

"Indeed. She'll wake up any second now," Grayson remarked calmly, observing Highwing rearranging himself on her bed, tenderly pulling Ella's slumbering figure closer to his. The closeness ignited a bitter feeling deep in Grayson's gut.

"Rouse her from her sleep!" the blonde woman demanded, her throaty voice betraying irritation. A young girl, hardly twelve years old, dangled wearily in her embrace. Dressed in tattered garments, remnants of a life that has been upended, the girl looked more than a little worn out. Her eyes—like precious amethyst—were blank. Valla rubbed herself against the small girl, and she unconsciously snuggled closer.

"We shouldn't startle her, Dasyra," Hamlet intervened gently, displaying a freshly bruised eye that shined. Grayson couldn't help but wonder what had happened to give him that bruise.

"I don't care about startling her! Wake her up!" Dasyra screeched, her feet thumping the floor.

Grayson cleared his throat with great emphasis, deliberately directing his gaze away from Highwing's tender embrace with Ella. He gestured subtly with his hand, anxiously waiting for the unmistakable cues of Ella's awakening.

Her gentle, whispered voice broke the silence, "Highwing?"

Highwing chuckled deeply, his laughter laced with both relief and a hint of madness. "Ella. By the Gods, I've missed you so much," he murmured, pressing a tender kiss to her forehead. She threw her arms around his neck, inhaling his scent. Ella's eyes darted around the room as she rubbed her throbbing head.

"What happened?" she asked hesitantly. "The library—I was..." Her voice faltered as her gaze locked onto Grayson's tense posture. "Grayson," she called out, but he remained motionless.

Elmon and Ruvane leaped onto her bed, their expressions mirroring each other's deep concern. "You've been absent for ages. We presumed you dead," Ruvane confessed bluntly.

"We? You owe me eight silver coins," Elmon snickered under his breath to Ruvane.

"Fuck off!" Highwing bellowed, sweeping his colossal wing to shoo his brothers from the bed.

Ella's teary eyes took in each familiar face she'd never thought she would see again. A choked sob rose in her throat as Nattya arrived at her bedside. "You're here," Ella uttered shakily. Nattya gave a slight nod. "Of course I am." She rubbed her forehead against Ella's—an old Elvish greeting.

"Get this lovey-dovey reunion over with," Dasyra snapped. "We have more pressing matters. We were attacked by a siren just outside here."

Grayson raised a brow and Gregor sighed. "That was a student. Sienna Whitefish seems to have heard a conversation that was amongst your friends, Ella. She is incapacitated now, but I am afraid I do not know what to do with her."

"Her mother is Sifrrod Whitefish—the one who summoned the sirens," Ella said to Dasyra, feeling the familiar darkness encroaching upon her once more. She shuddered involuntarily.

"What?" Dasyra's incredulous shout rang out, disturbing Arysta from her embrace. "You can't be serious! Get that thing back here and flay her!"

Ella beheld Dasyra—it had been months since they'd last met. Dasyra's blonde hair seemed to have grown slightly, while her wings appeared rather pitiful. An uneasy silence settled among them before Ella confirmed softly, "Yes... it was her mother."

"These chaotic times breed confusion," Gregor chimed in. "Sienna is inherently a good person."

"She tried to *drown* me!" Highwing retorted, his feathers ruffling with disdain.

"Me too!" chimed Nattya.

"Sienna believed her actions were for the greater good," Gregor explained, cocking his head towards Nattya curiously. "It's rather intriguing how her Siren Song didn't affect you."

Nattya huffed indignantly before burrowing herself beneath the blankets, pressing into Ella's side for comfort. Grayson offered his thoughts. "The only beings we know of who can resist a Siren's Song are fellow sirens."

Barely suppressing a laugh, Nattya responded, "If I had a tail sprouting from my backside, I'd know! Don't be ridiculous. Her song just wasn't as powerful as all of you thought."

"On the contrary," Gregor interjected sagely, "Sienna possesses what's known as a 'Queen Spell.' Her enchantment spreads wider and stronger than an average siren's. Most of us were entranced before Elysium could even shield our minds."

"I'm not a siren! Can we get back to the point at hand? What are we going to do about all of this? Hellharth is our home. We can't just lay down and take it," Nattya snapped.

"Interesting choice of words coming from a whore," Dasyra snorted.

"Mad that I've taken Highwing for a ride more times than you?" Nattya snarked back. Ella glanced between the two, and Highwing ran a hand down his face.

"Where is Sienna now? We should talk to her. Find out what she knows. Maybe we can get her to get them to stop," Ella offered.

"There's no reasoning with those sirens," Dasyra exclaimed, her eyes reflecting the fear she felt. "Their screams still haunt me, echoing in my ears. You didn't witness the horror—people clawing at their ears, and creatures plummeting from the sky!"

"Which is exactly why we need them to stop," Ella countered, her determination etched on her face.

Gregor took a deep breath before speaking. "We can't do anything tonight. First, we must restore the library and gather the staff for an urgent meeting." His voice resonated with authority as he continued, "All of you are to stay inside."

A scoff escaped Dasyra. "You can't seriously expect us all to remain cooped up in here?"

Gregor looked firmly at everyone. "That's precisely what I expect. I have been kind and empathetic to your situation, and now I ask this favor in return." His gaze fell sharply upon Hamlet.

With a reluctant nod, Hamlet conceded, "We'll stay put." A somber silence filled the room as everyone agreed.

Grayson began walking to leave the bedroom, feeling Ella's eyes on him. He turned slowly, giving her a slight nod. Highwing leaned in, his nose nuzzling her neck, and Grayson sharply averted his eyes.

"I trust you will find some semblance of relief, being reunited with your beloved," Grayson said numbly to her as he closed the door behind him.

 For two days they had all been there, never leaving the school grounds—taking up residency in Ella's bedroom. The news from Arcadea swirled around like a whirlwind – no one could separate truth from fiction when it came to the papers. Sienna was sedated for now, but Gregor was bombarded with letters from Sifrrod asking about her daughter.

He struggled to find the right words to respond.

Pouring himself a glass of wine, Gregor's hand wavered, and he chose instead to chug directly from the bottle. He was utterly drained from the non-stop meetings. Acting swiftly, he had persuaded the teachers to pack up and leave, effectively shutting down the school. Annabeth and Ethan's four unanswered letters weighed heavily on his mind.

As he reached the bottom of the bottle, a laugh escaped his lips, only for it to crumble into gut-wrenching sobs. In a fit of anger, he hurled the empty bottle against the bricks of his office wall, causing it to shatter into countless pieces.

He knew he had to act fast. Sienna couldn't just stay under suspended animation for much longer.

CHAPTER FORTY-TWO

Ella strolled down the dimly lit corridor late at night, pausing to gaze at the moonlit paintings on the walls. Over the past few days, she had been rekindling relationships with her old friends and sharing stories over warm tea. Ella had observed Nattya and Highwing appearing more relaxed than before—their shoulders eased, and laughter frequently punctuated the conversations. However, upon asking them about their experiences in detail, their expressions turned stone cold, and their words quickly vanished, leaving an awkward silence behind.

Hamlet was withdrawn, avoiding her gaze, a faraway look constantly in his eyes. The only thing he managed to say was; "I never realized how much you look like her."

Nattya and Highwing refused to leave her side. She had conceded to letting them into her washroom while she bathed or relieved herself.

It started to suffocate her.

Dasyra's presence felt akin to sharing a room with Gertrude Rydelle—her seemingly permanent sour mood drained any joy from their gatherings. Despite this, the mischievous twins did their best to keep everyone entertained by shape-shifting into various animals and engaging one another in frivolous mock battles.

Nights were different.

The soft sniffles of suppressed crying had started to keep her up at night. Dasyra would awaken abruptly, thrashing about violently screaming how she couldn't breathe. Arysta would jump at every sound, eyes wide and frantic. The twins kept to themselves, though, they spent more time caring for their hair, taking turns brushing each other's. All the while, Hamlet moved with mechanical precision, his gaze empty and distant, as if operating against his will. He didn't eat—only drank water. Arysta would ask him how he was doing and he would respond with a half-hearted, "fine" or "good" and then return to his books. Ella would lay next to him in the dark, watching the rise and fall of his chest, and gently stroke his hair.

Everyone around her was suffering, and she felt helpless. She wanted to fall apart—wanted to grieve with them, but she had to be strong. She had to be the rock. She had to be the anchor.

Because it was ultimately her fault.

This particular night, Dasyra had startled awake, running water in the washroom to stifle her crying. Ella had meandered into the room—not having fallen asleep like the others. Grayson had been providing them sleeping potions that unfortunately didn't work for Dasyra or her. Quietly she entered and closed the door behind her. She expected Dasyra to flinch—to recoil from her touch—but she stayed still, face buried in her hands.

"Was it a dream?" she asked gently, settling herself beside Dasyra.

Dasyra's eyes were red, and skin blotchy. "I can hear the dogs barking. I can hear my sisters screaming. I can't get it out of my head," Dasyra gasped, putting a hand over her mouth to stifle her hiccups. "They were *chewing* on my mother. I was buried under-under the wall rubble. The dogs were chewing on Mysera and my mother." she kept repeating it over and over again, tears streaking down her face. "I couldn't fly. My wings—"

Ella listened while she relayed the events that had unfolded—the horrors she hadn't been present for. She listened while Dasyra told her how the Calisan Guards *laughed* while their magically perverted dogs tore her family apart. That feeling inside of Ella started to creep up again—visions of headless Calisan soldiers beneath her bare feet. Thoughts of filling the landfills with their bodies—burning their bodies in her fire pit. The thought of torturing them, making them beg for their lives. It was a horrifying thought, yet it had been growing inside of her for the past few days. Festering. She couldn't let it out. She couldn't let the feeling out.

Her stomach roiled and she exhaled, standing up. "I'm sorry," she muttered before bolting out of the washroom and silently creeping over everyone's sleeping forms. They had opted out of sleeping on a bigger bed—a tangled mess of arms and legs gathered on piles of blankets and pillows. Her mind warped them into figures of gore—heads and detached arms painted red.

She needed to get out of there.

That's how she found herself in the corridor, wandering aimlessly. She pushed through the door of the training room and marveled at the mesmerizing faux starlit ceiling. It reminded her of the nights in Hellharth—only there were no cool breezes, no fireflies. No lighthouse or the sound of waves against rocks. She climbed onto the platform and lay down.

Grayson had barely spoken to her, his terse words insisting she should be with her family instead. The term "betrothed" had not been uttered again, at least. His stone dragon had been especially cold and distant, keeping his door tightly shut.

Could it be that she hadn't told Grayson about her predicament with Highwing? She couldn't remember. The sting of Grayson's absence had grown more painful, and she longed for a heated argument, simply as an excuse to talk again.

"What is this place?" Highwing's voice startled her out of her thoughts.

"For Olesa's sake! You scared the hell out of me!" she hissed, sitting up.

With a sly grin, he sauntered over to the platform, donning the traditional Calisan robes of deep purple and midnight black. He hated their clothes and made mention of it every day so far. He settled down beside her, leaning in to inhale the sweet scent of her hair.

"You know, we haven't had much time alone together lately. Perhaps I owe you an explanation," he murmured. His lips feathered over the top of her head. He was scenting her, rubbing his face against her hair.

"Are you finally going to tell me what happened?" she asked.

He paused, stiffening momentarily. "To be honest, I'm still grappling with it all myself."

Her voice barely audible, Ella whispered, "You were there, weren't you? You were there when she died." Highwing's flinch confirmed her suspicions. "How did she die?"

Tenderly taking her hand in his, he said, "I'm not entirely certain. While on patrol, I crested a dune to find her there, impaled by one of her own antlers. A Calisan soldier struck her with the hilt of his sword, and she crumpled to the ground. That moment was when everything spiraled out of control."

There wasn't any time in between then that he could stop and assess what had happened. Just an immediate clang of swords and sparks of magic.

Ella let his words sink in, imagining what her mother's final moments must have been like. "Do you know why she was there?"

"No one knows why. Hamlet said she had been with him, and when he woke up, Hellharth was under attack."

"Hamlet was with my mother, as in...?" Did she even want to think about that?

"Yes. Her scent was all over him," he smirked slightly. "It was a long time coming." He realized what he said and the somber expression on her face revealed that she was thinking the same thing

"They never stood a chance. He waited an eternity for her," she whispered, her voice catching in her throat.

"He tried to bring her back. The Elder scribes stopped him. They said your mother was born a sleeping child and could not be brought back."

"Why am I not surprised she held more secrets to her grave?" If she could have reacted to the news, she would have. Nothing surprised her now.

Gently, he lifted her hand to his lips and kissed her knuckles. "You need to understand that my intentions for you remain strong. Hellharth may claim me as their King, but you, my dear, are the one true Queen." She was sure he had thought it was something romantic to say.

"We can't be certain that your mother is gone," she said to him. "What would there be to rule over? Ashes."

"Our people adore you, Ella," he added, his eyes shining with sincerity.

It was at that moment she grasped the fact that Highwing and Nattya were oblivious to her father's true identity and why she found herself in this situation in the first place. They all believed it was merely a tactic to prevent Ella from taking the throne—which was only half the story. She reluctantly withdrew her hand from his grasp. He was utterly unaware that she was the catalyst for all this mayhem.

The truth weighed heavily on her—she was Idmodias' daughter.

Daughter of The Son of Bashet. Daughter of Hellharth, torn in all directions.

In a bitter tone, she asserted, "I am not fit to be Queen."

He refused to accept it. He took hold of her chin, guiding her face to meet his gaze. "Ella," he declared with conviction, "*You* are *my* Queen." And with those words, he pressed his lips against hers.

Someone cleared their throat and they pulled apart. Ella's heart lurched when she saw Grayson standing there with his arms crossed. "If you two would kindly finish this merry little chat in your own room, and not in my training area," he said monotonously.

"Grayson," Ella started, "I-I wanted to talk to you."

Grayson's fluorescent green eyes scanned over them. "I can tell you, you won't find me in his mouth," he quipped with the same emotionless tone.

Highwing's feathers ruffled in annoyance, snapping back, "You have no right to speak to her that way."

Grayson's gaze turned icy, his pearly fangs glinting as he snarled menacingly, "Leave, now." He pointed to the door with a flick of his finger.

Unfazed, Highwing rose to his impressive full height, challenging him. "Got a problem with us?" The Rune on his palm glowed slightly and Ella could have sworn he got bigger.

Grayson let out a cold, dangerous laugh. "Not yet. But you're about to." He took a step forward and Ella sprang up and quickly positioned herself between the two men.

"Highwing, we're leaving! Grayson, that's enough," she demanded with urgency in her voice. Grayson halted abruptly, sizing her up with a lingering sneer before finally scoffing at Highwing. "Fine, just go."

Reluctantly allowing Ella to guide him from the training room, Highwing couldn't help but glance back as Grayson unleashed an otherworldly burst of blue fire at the closing door with an animalistic snarl.

"Is there something I ought to be aware of?" Highwing inquired, an eyebrow arching as the sound of furniture being smashed reached his ears from behind the door. Ella's gaze fell to the floor, her lip quivering between her teeth. "You can confide in me," he said.

"Well, there was an... incident. A couple of them actually," she confessed. It was hard to pinpoint what exactly. They hadn't actually done anything—but everything *felt* intimate.

"You look like you feel guilty about something," he observed, gently pulling her away from the training room entrance. "Did you sleep with him?"

"No, we didn't," Ella stammered. They hadn't even come close to that.

"He's causing all that commotion over nothing?" Highwing asked in disbelief.

"I never mentioned you to him," she admitted. "Not that I intended to keep it a secret. It just slipped my mind." She gave him a pathetic shrug.

A skeptical eyebrow rose on his face. "You forgot about our *engagement*?"

"You were the one who said it wouldn't matter if I—if *we*—found pleasure elsewhere," Ella retorted with a huff.

"It doesn't matter to me. I've been with Nattya," he revealed nonchalantly.

Ella rolled her eyes in exasperation. "If you end up getting my Lifestone partner pregnant, that's *your* problem." She could picture it now; Highwing in the middle of the throne room, seated in his chair, with a daughter that looked just like Nattya.

It made her laugh warmly out loud. Highwing frowned in confusion and studied her for a moment before continuing. "Nattya had her gaze locked on Master Moore earlier. You know how she is when she sees something—or someone—she desires."

His words brought Ella to a standstill, her mouth falling open in surprise. She could feel the heat rising in her cheeks as she looked away. There was that pang of jealousy in her chest.

"By the gods! You've fallen for him!" Highwing whooped. "For the record, I fabricated the bit about Nattya being interested in him—I just wanted to gauge your reaction."

"I'm not in love with him," Ella scoffed defensively.

"If you say so," Highwing snorted. "Judging by his behavior, he's clearly not too pleased with my presence."

Once again, they found themselves at her door, and she couldn't help but glance at Grayson's intricately carved dragon door. "Grayson made me fly again, you know."

"What?" Highwing exclaimed in utter disbelief. "That's incredible!"

"Shush!" She whispered, shooting him a stern look. "I only managed it because he jumped off a roof first. I thought he was going to die."

"Is he insane?" Highwing murmured. His face scrunched up with genuine concern.

She chuckled softly and said, "Maybe." As she spoke, her fingers danced through her hair, twirling the silken strands absentmindedly.

"I adored Gideon. Adored him so deeply that my breath would catch simply by looking at him. I did not want to continue flying, because it felt unfair to enjoy his favorite thing—the very thing that caused his death. I wanted to remember Gideon's smile and laughter forever." She paused, gazing at a painting of an ocean, and grimaced. "But instead, the image of his broken body against the rocks, his blood merging with the sea, haunts me. I blamed myself incessantly. Words wouldn't have made a difference. Grayson forced me to fly again and, by doing so, he showed me that not everything had changed. The sun still rose and set each day while I tormented myself here. No amount of self-loathing could ever bring Gideon back. I do not know if that was his intention..."

Highwing listening intently, said, "Had I known that forcing you was all it would take, I would have pushed you off that lighthouse long ago." He sighed at her obvious infatuation. "So, does this mean... you don't want to marry me?" His shoulder sagged slightly as he asked.

"No, that's not what I'm saying," she clarified hastily. "It's just that marriage is the *last* thing on my mind at the moment. There has been so much happening..." If she was to be the next Queen again, she would *have* to marry Highwing. He could not just relinquish the title to her—the people wouldn't trust it—all the back and forth. It had always been the plan, but now something dark loomed over them. It didn't feel like a choice anymore. Not for either of them.

The question he asked next had an impish grin spreading across his face. "And what about... sex?" Before she could respond, he pulled her close into his embrace, burying his face in her hair. Her mind went back to the day he kissed her in the tree, and her hair stood on end. She could feel his lips against her cheek—her jaw and neck. She would let him have this moment, to make up for lost time. She wouldn't think about Grayson.

There is nothing between Grayson and me, she thought to herself while Highwing bit gently on her neck. It left a bitter taste in her mouth.

With a sarcastic smile, she teased and pulled away. "Oh yes, right here in this very hallway. Just have your way with me." Her tone turned playful as she added, "If you're looking to 'scratch an itch,' there are two other ladies in my room as we speak."

Ella observed the mischievous sparkle in his eyes as he mulled over the idea before playfully swatting him away.

As he gallantly opened the door for her, a surreal scene unfolded before them. It seemed as though time had stopped—everyone was sprawled across the floor at peculiar angles, deep in slumber. That wasn't what was unusual.

Amid it all stood Gregor, his hands cupped together, holding a mysterious powdery white substance, a black mask over his mouth and nose. He slowly lifted his head, his violet eyes focused on them.

Highwing attempted to push Ella out of harm's way, but Gregor swiftly blew the powder into his face. Highwing's eyes rolled back into his head as he stumbled and blinked furiously before ultimately collapsing to the floor.

Ella's scream pierced the air as she turned and sprinted through Grayson's door, the dragon conceding her entrance. He followed her through, immobilizing the stone guardian with a swipe of his hand. The door swung shut behind him.

Gregor pursued her relentlessly, closing the gap between them and cornering her against a wall. Gasping for breath, she shouted, "What have you done to them?"

The sharp scent of alcohol tainted his breath, his glistening eyes betraying his inebriation. "Fear not, they merely slumber. Grayson possesses the means to rouse them. As for *you*," he said, reaching into his pocket to produce more of the mysterious powder, "I thought a stronger dose would be required."

With a swift motion, she swatted his hand aside and buried her nose in her shirt to avoid the pungent odor. "Why are you doing this?"

Genuine remorse filled his voice as he shook his head. "Sometimes, we must do the wrong thing, in order to get the right result." The haunting tune from Grayson's music box drifted softly through the room. "Curious how prophecies can be so misinterpreted," he added distantly.

"You wish to kill me? Did Grayson forget to mention it? I've acquired new talents!" Her eyes narrowed dangerously, a surge of electrical energy crackling from her hands. Gregor's eyes betrayed a glimmer of surprise. Her arm thrust forward, releasing a lightning bolt that sent him flying across the chamber. He landed with feline grace—still retaining all the poise of a master sorcerer—and deftly weaved intricate patterns with his hands; a golden shield shimmered around him.

"I am not your enemy, Ella!" He shouted in despair.

A skeptical glare crossed her face as she retorted, "Really?" Another furious bolt of electricity slammed into Gregor's shield and disintegrated upon impact.

She tried another tactic, looking him in the eyes. She felt herself slip into his mind, and what she found there made her fall to her knees. Hamlet's voice echoed in her ears.

Some people's minds are dangerous.

Grayson's desire to chase after them consumed him. He visualized himself tearing the feathers out of the man who dared to hold Ella in his embrace. Overcome with fury, he ripped off his necklace and threw it violently at the ground. The metal broke apart upon impact with the tile floor, the jewel shattering.

Immediately, remorse filled Grayson as he scrambled to gather the broken pieces of his pendant. As he did so, his fingers brushed against a tiny object hidden within. Carefully picking it up, he found a small vial embedded inside the jewel of his pendant. Intrigued, he pried apart the remaining metal to investigate further.

"Is this... blood?"

CHAPTER FORTY-THREE

Grayson's eyes widened as he discerned the dark crimson liquid within the minuscule vial. The mere presence of such a substance in his necklace was unsettling.

Blood?

Fear and curiosity intermingled as he cautiously fiddled with the vial.

This trinket—joined with a meager collection of other belongings—was all that remained of his parents. Grayson struggled with the burden of his Dracaenean heritage, for his mother had abandoned him in infancy to his Maji father, who then perished in the Purge War. Grayson had longed for information about the enigmatic Dracaenean woman who had captivated his father—a woman whose name was forever lost to him.

Grayson learned from his studies with Gregor that the Dracaenean people considered blood most sacred. To them, it was the very essence of life and held memories deep within. Swallowing hard, Grayson realized that all this time, he had a fragment of his mother—her blood housed within this small container, and all this time it had been close to his heart.

Did she intend to leave him a message, or perhaps an explanation for departing so heartlessly? Clasped between trembling fingers was the truth, a key to unlocking the mysteries of his elusive past. Yet, why did it feel so incredibly difficult for him to raise the vial to his lips and revisit those memories that were hers? The scents and sights hidden in this minuscule capsule could either enlighten or break him—either way, that truth beckoned to be discovered.

"I don't require the details," Grayson uttered, his breath hitching. "She's made her decision. I don't need to know." He attempted to reassure himself while clutching the vessel tightly, as if it were his lifeline, anchoring him to reality. Leaning against the cold training room wall, he recalled countless nights spent wondering.

Annoyed, he moaned and placed the vial between his teeth, crushing it open. The metallic tang of his own blood merged with the stranger's. Disappointment enveloped him when nothing happened at first; he found his own desperation amusing.

Then it began.

A faint tingling sensation spread across his face like ripples in water. At first subtle, the sensations grew in intensity until they engulfed him entirely. His whole body trembled involuntarily as he coughed uncontrollably, ripping at his throat in sheer terror. Leathery wings burst forth from his back, accompanied by an echoing SNAP! The sudden release knocked him off balance. His head throbbed as curved horns sprouted from his skull and fangs extended past his lower lip. The pain was nearly unbearable; every vein was ablaze as if doused in oil and ignited by an invisible spark.

It's because I'm a Halfling. It's burning my Maji blood.

His face met unyielding marble flooring with a painful wince. Soft murmurs reached him through the din of pain; ears instinctively perking up to eavesdrop on an unhappy infant's wailing and the heated exchange between a man and woman that went with it.

"We must send him away! They will surely slay him as a potential rival!" implored a frantic woman.

"There must be another way! A child needs a mother's presence!" the man countered, his voice shrill.

"This is our only choice! Take him and this!" The urgency in the woman's voice was palpable. "What will happen when they come looking for him?" the man demanded.

"They won't," she replied coolly.

"Have you gone mad? What have you done?" he shouted, his fury abruptly silencing the infant's cries.

His eyes fluttered open, struggling to adjust to the enveloping darkness. Gradually, his surroundings came into focus—a vast chamber bathed in warm light, adorned with majestic tapestries depicting dragons entwined around a mysterious sphere. On the high-vaulted ceiling were the remnants of a dragon, its enormous skeletal form suspended in mid-air above an imposing throne. The skeletal wings, extended and spread wide, showcasing the intricate structure of interlocking bones and tattered membranes. Its tail curled protectively beneath its skeletal form, tapering off into a series of bony spines that went all the way down the throne steps.

Suddenly, a flicker of movement caught his attention. Two women stood nearby; their expressions tainted with melancholy.

"Excuse me," he called out hesitantly, his voice echoing eerily within the massive space. The women showed no signs of acknowledgment, engrossed in their animated conversation. Both were breathtakingly striking; one possessed long, flowing off-white hair while the other had raven-black hair with sharp cheekbones and emerald green eyes that seemed to pierce right through him. Her lips were painted in red, and her black eye makeup ran down her cheeks purposefully. She also had brown leathery wings that dragged along the cold stone floor—unmistakably a Dracaenean woman.

"I cannot be part of this, Lady Kahlisenya," the Dracaenean woman uttered fiercely.

Kahlisenya? Queen Kahlisenya? He wondered, curiosity piquing as he cautiously inched closer. He could feel his wings twitching with anticipation. Kahlisenya was supposed to be dead.

"Lady Lelot, I implore you!" Kahlisenya pleaded earnestly. "Our people need us to unite!"

Lelot? Princess Lelot?

"But the Treaty of Stagnation would be *shattered*," Lelot retorted somberly. "We cannot bear arms against our Elven brethren. That pact was sealed in our ancestors' blood."

"Excuse me!" he repeated louder and more gruffly, stepping into the light for them to notice him. However, their gazes remained fixed on one another, never swaying in his direction. It dawned on him; he was seeing a memory—merely an observer unable to intervene.

"You still refuse?" Queen Kahlisenya bemoaned incredulously. "Even while I stand before you as the Queen of Hellharth, and you, ruler of Direfell?"

"Queen Kahlisenya, my refusal is not an *unwillingness*," Lelot responded softly, a hint of sadness lacing her voice. "I simply cannot. You know I cannot." She paused, her gaze drifting towards Kahlisenya's stomach, a knowing glimmer in her eyes.

Instinctively, Kahlisenya's hand cradled her abdomen.

"Have they knowledge of your condition?" Lelot inquired tenderly. "Do they know you carry a child?"

"Ella…" he murmured under his breath, his heart seizing at the realization. Ella was within her, safely cradled in her womb.

"No one knows," Queen Kahlisenya answered defiantly.

"So, they are unaware both of the life you nurture and the demon blood coursing through its veins?" Lelot pursued cautiously. At this provocation, Kahlisenya's eyes flashed with anger as she assumed a defensive posture. Lelot simply tilted her head, unfazed.

"I bear you no malice," she reassured gently. "Your secret is safe with me. We each have our burdens to bear and those we love, to protect." She continued earnestly, "No one needs to know that this child was conceived *after* Idmodias became The Son of Bashet."

Oh, Ella, he thought desperately. It explained so much. They had assumed Ella had been conceived before Idmodias had turned demon, because of Kahlisenya's willingness to defeat him. The time had overlapped. Had Gregor guessed this? There was no way that Hamlet hadn't been privy to this information.

Ella's power developed unpredictably, changing constantly. As it did, her demeanor shifted towards a darker tone, causing her to appear unlike her usual self.

Ella was a *halfling*.

A halfling elf and demon spawn with Bashet's blood running through her veins.

"It only happened once. Shortly after he... you know," Kahlisenya said quietly.

Lelot let out a bark of laughter. "Once is enough."

As their voices faded, an unseen force whisked him away, leaving him kneeling in the somber glow of a dimly lit throne room. Lady Lelot sat regally upon a throne crafted from dragon bones, emanating an ominous presence as she gazed down at her two visitors. Her crimson dress flowed so extensively that it concealed the steps below. She was decorated down her front with a necklace made of bones that had been encased in gold. Both figures, unmistakably female, bowed their heads in reverence.

"Why have you come? I was informed that the Elven Queen and The Council have put Idmodias to rest," Lady Lelot's resonant voice echoed throughout the vast chamber.

"This is all that remains of The Council..." the first woman visitor replied solemnly. Lady Lelot's expression shifted to one of surprise.

"Mira and Froafna?" Lady Lelot inquired gently. Met with silence, she flinched and averted her gaze. After a heavy pause, she spoke again. "They were formidable warriors."

"Aye. They truly were," the second woman concurred.

"Sifrrod Whitefish. Wenda Ased," Lady Lelot addressed them resolutely. "I must ask once more. What brings you here? I presumed my absence from the war meant I was excluded from The Council."

Grayson recognized the names; this was Sienna Whitefish's mother and Amira Ased—Mistress Ased's grandmother—original Council Members. He observed intently, absorbing each word exchanged between them.

"With Queen Kahlisenya's assistance, we managed to imprison The Son of Bashet within this mirror," Wenda Ased declared, brandishing an object shrouded in white cloth that Grayson couldn't quite discern.

"And why did you bring it here?" Lady Lelot scoffed disdainfully.

"The Treaty of Stagnation," Sifrrod Whitefish explained. "No one besides us knows the mirror's location. Any remaining Elven followers of Idmodias wouldn't dare challenge you or your kind—and frankly, no others would either."

"Who claims I desire that burden?" Lelot retorted sharply. The two women appeared uncertain, but Wenda steeled her resolve.

"We all fought with valor and purpose. We've lost countless comrades in this war. You, too, have lost your friends—our friends. Accept the damned mirror!" Wenda cried out, waving the concealed artifact vehemently.

Lelot raised a gilded clawed finger to her lips, deep in contemplation. Unperturbed by Wenda's outburst, her emerald eyes seemed distant and glassy. Rising to her full stature, she strode gracefully towards the duo, her wings trailing along the cold stone steps behind her. Though Wenda stood firm, Sifrrod retreated nervously.

Lelot towered over Wenda by a foot and tilted her head down to meet the woman's gaze.

"Very well," she agreed at last.

The room spun and pulled him in all directions as if he were malleable. His vision warped and then he was in a darkened field. The grass beneath him tickled his face and he sat up, eyes homing in on two figures standing together in the tall grass. He recognized Lady Lelot instantly.

The man had his back turned to him, dark hair in a high bun, and wearing odd green garbs with gold embroidery on the back.

"Princess Lelot—sorry. *Queen* Lelot. I forgot you are *married* now," the man said bitterly.

Lelot's feline eyes softened, and her mouth turned down into a frown. "Don't be that way. Not with me. You know that I try my best—"

"Your best is a mockery," he shot back.

Lelot's arms trembled slightly as she clutched something gently in her hands. "I have brought presents for him," she said softly. With a sense of pride, she revealed a beautifully crafted wooden box adorned with intricate floral carvings along its sides. As she opened it, a mesmerizing melody emanated from within, casting a spell over the entire clearing.

He knew that tune.

Glancing inside, the shimmering reflection of starlight danced on a small, yet intricately designed mirror. The item caught Grayson's eye.

"Fucking hell!" Grayson exclaimed, quickly rushing toward her. He instantly recognized the melody from the music box and the necklace nestled delicately in its velvet lining. The man standing nearby—

Grayson's heart skipped a beat.

There stood Alfreid Moore, his expression weary and defeated. His arms hung across his chest defensively as he tried to decipher Lelot's intentions.

"Father," Grayson whispered.

Remarkably, everything began falling into place just like that.

The vial of blood hidden within his necklace and the mysterious old mirror concealed inside a music box.

The scene unfolded before him, revealing long-buried truths. "Safe inside a Morning Song—" Grayson gasped.

The prophecy hadn't been talking about *Ella*. It had been talking about the *mirror*.

"Answers found right near his heart..." The necklace had been held by his heart all these years.

It dawned on him then, that perhaps Gregor had known this truth all along.

The surroundings transformed abruptly, pulling him back to the familiar confines of the training room. He experienced a distinct throb, akin to his bedroom door creaking open, just behind his eye. As his vision intertwined with that of the dragon guardian stationed at his door, he stared in sheer terror as Gregor chased after Ella.

CHAPTER FORTY-FOUR

Grayson hurried down the chilly stone staircase, his footsteps echoing through the dimly lit corridor. He felt a mixture of rage and fear bubbling inside him. "How could I have been so blind?" he muttered angrily, his jaw clenched tight. "Please, Gods. Don't let it be too late."

The very idea made his heart seize up with dread. Bursting through the doors of his bed chamber, he caught the bewildered eyes of his door guardian, who looked down at him in alarm.

"Gregor!" Grayson shouted.

He found Ella on the floor, unconscious, tear stains streaming down her face. In the center of the chamber stood Highmaster Gregor, clutching a small wooden box tenderly in his hands.

"All this time, it was right here... Safely hidden within Morning Song," Gregor whispered, his voice quivering as he traced the intricate carvings adorning the box. Recalling the prophecy with a bitter smile, he added, "Answers found right near his heart."

"Gregor," Grayson pleaded, attempting to control the tremble in his voice, "Let her go. This doesn't have to happen."

Locking eyes with Grayson—violet meeting green in a duel of wills—Gregor continued unfazed, "Your mother was entrusted with this precious burden. Did you know that? She refused to take part in the war and yet she was given such a grave responsibility."

Grayson felt a muscle twitch near his eye as he responded coldly, "She was a fool."

Gregor let out a heavy sigh. "We both know that isn't true. Deep within your heart, you must have harbored some suspicion about your past. Are you going to pretend you knew nothing all this time?"

"I've been an orphan for many years—"

"Ah," Gregor cut in, "So you choose ignorance. Then why do you tremble at what lies inside this box?" He challenged Grayson, "You know, don't you? You know that Lelot is your mother."

Grayson gritted his teeth, growling in denial. "What does it matter? She abandoned me!"

Gregor shook his head solemnly, "No, she didn't. The Dracaenean are among the eldest beings alive—kin to the Elves themselves—and bound by ancient traditions. Princess Lelot dared to fall in love with a Maji named Alfreid Moore—your father. Your existence spelled a threat to the Dracaenean's old ways since no half-blood had ever claimed power."

Gregor continued, "In the midst of Alfreid's destroyed home, I discovered a bundle of letters. It was Lelot who secretly gave birth to you and placed you in your father's care, promising never to lay eyes on you again. Alas, your father met his end during the Purge, leaving you unprotected and alone as a young child. By pure chance, I was at the right place and time to rescue you. As I took you under my care and sifted through the charred remains of your former life, it dawned upon me that the paintings of the

Dracaenean woman were crafted not out of simple admiration, but deep love. In those heartfelt letters, she emphasized the significance of two cherished relics—an ancient necklace and this music box holding a golden mirror..." He lifted the lid, and the mirror reflected the candlelight hauntingly. "I didn't know it was the Mirror of Shadows."

"What do you hope to achieve with this?" Grayson asked him, inching forward. "Where are the others?"

"Ella's companions are sleeping in her room. You'll have to wake them when this is over. I honestly don't know," Gregor admitted. "I've deduced I won't be around to see what happens."

"You're speaking nonsense. You are drunk. Give me the box," Grayson demanded, holding out his hand.

"*Blood of the Lady*. Lady Lelot," Gregor hummed, putting the box down on Grayson's desk. "I only need to make a small cut." His hands were shaking.

A dagger materialized in mid-air, slicing a vicious gash on Grayson's arm before swiftly returning to Gregor's outstretched hand. Grayson lunged toward him, only to be stopped by an impenetrable golden barrier. With fists pounding against the unyielding wall, he cried out in despair, "Enough of this madness! Deacon! Gregor! Father!"

At the mention of 'father,' Gregor's eyes sparkled, misting over with unshed tears. An authentic smile crossed his face, turning into an open-mouthed grin. "I've never heard you call me that before."

His words hit Grayson like Ella's lightning bolt. In all his life that he had shared with Gregor, he had never allowed himself to call him father—not even when others referred to him as such. Grayson implored him, voice hitching with anxiety, "Please, please... This doesn't have to happen."

There was so much to do. So much to make up for. He would be a good and proper son. He would be kinder, and he would spend every night meeting the end of a bottle with his father if it made him happy. He would play music with him, and not grumble in the corner when Gregor invited him to dance with him. He would never push him away again. Never. "Father. Please." He needed him to know of all the promises he planned to make.

Ignoring his pleas, Gregor allowed the dagger's blood to drip languidly onto the mirror's gleaming surface before pricking his own palm. Grayson's screams reached a fever pitch as he hurled spells in desperation at the impenetrable barrier separating them.

"Blood of the Traitor," Gregor mumbled, his voice breaking. Then he pressed the dagger deeper into his palm, the blood welling and falling onto the mirror.

Gregor turned to Ella's unconscious form, and with deliberate precision, he sliced along Ella's thumb. "Blood of the Daughter." The mirror shimmered and distorted. A crimson haze danced in its depth, and a figure materialized in the mirror.

He held the bloodied dagger above the enchanted mirror. Meeting Grayson's terror-filled gaze, he uttered softly, "You will *always* be my son."

As the scarlet droplets collided with the mirror, and it gleamed vibrantly, reflecting a multitude of colors. The sound of shattering glass reverberated throughout the room as delicate cracks spread like a spiderweb across the mirror's surface.

Eerie tendrils seeped through the cracks, coiling around Gregor like sinister serpents.

From the smoky tendrils appeared a towering figure with majestic ebony horns that curved gracefully, framing his handsome face like crowns of onyx. Dark stripes, varying in width and intensity, traversed his face with artistic precision. They curved gently along his forehead, tracing the elegant contours of his cheekbones, and accentuating the sharpness of his jaw. Tanned skin stretched tightly over large muscles, a dark webbing of scars marked across his forearms.

The darkness of his obsidian-black wings stretched behind him, an ethereal extension of his being. Each feather was a reflection of the night sky, glistening with a hint of iridescence, as if touched by stardust.

Grayson's gaze darted anxiously towards Ella's limp figure, sprawled behind his desk. The air in the room was heavy with miasma, making it difficult to breathe. He looked up at the shadowy figure, recoiling when he met the man's eyes—pools of molten gold, flecked with hints of fiery ember.

Ella's eyes.

"Son of Bashet rises once more,
War upon us,
As twice before."

CHAPTER FORTY-FIVE

Kiandall grasped Kahlisenya's trembling hand, pulling her to safety through the portal. Her tail quickly wrapped around Kahlisenya, drawing her nearer to the soothing warmth of the flames Amaris had carefully maintained. "You've seen what was necessary," Kiandall whispered softly. "Now everything makesss sense." Exhausted, Kahlisenya let her head rest on Kiandall's shoulder as if they were lifelong friends. In reality, perhaps they always had been. Kiandall had known about the impending events throughout. Kahlisenya's venom gave her an enhanced perception.

"They believe I'm gone for good," murmured Kahlisenya, her eyes filled with both fear and determination. "I've started a war."

Gideon appeared beside her, frowning at her words. "I hope you know what you're doing."

Amaris scoffed with contempt, her ghostly white orbs whirling chaotically. "It was bound to happen. The grand tapestry of fate weaves intricate patterns that elude even our grasp." She handed Kahlisenya a warm, crusty loaf of bread and a metal flask filled with refreshing water. "Welcome to our secret group. You won't find joy here."

Kiandall rolled his eyes and said sarcastically, "At least there's someone else as sssane as me now. I'd prefer it if the apparition left." She motioned her head at Gideon, who was floating above them.

"You won't see much of me; I have tasks to accomplish," Gideon replied before disappearing in a haze of light.

Amaris retorted sharply, "That's hardly comforting. After three centuries, even sanity starts to fade."

Grateful for the provisions, Kahlisenya solemnly recited a line from the prophecy. "Blackened stone, and she shall part." Their gazes met in a shared understanding for a moment. Kahlisenya extended her arm, revealing Hamlet's genuine Lifestone, its bright electric blue glow pulsating fiercely. She knew that upon waking to the heartbreaking revelation of her demise, he would instinctively reach for the Lifestone around his neck, seeking comfort in its connection to her life force.

"Hamlet," she whispered, "I'm so sorry."

What he would ultimately discover was nothing more than a scorched, lifeless stone.

When Kahlisenya was sure that Hamlet had been sufficiently asleep, she unclasped the Lifestone from his neck. It glowed proudly in the moonlight, and she could feel the familiar pull of her magic. There was a creaking sound and the terrace windows opened ajar.

"He's asleep. Hurry up," she commanded monotonously. Two shadows slinked into the room. Verik and Asher—two of the Silent Soldiers.

"Did you find someone?" She asked. She didn't expect an answer, just waited for them to nod. "I need them on the shore within an hour. They need to be seen." They both nodded their heads vigorously.

Kahlisenya pulled on a bedsheet, conjuring it into a nightdress, and put it on. She held out her hand to Verik, his face covered by a black mask. He dug into a small pocket at his side and produced an exact replica of Hamlet's necklace and Lifestone, only this stone was black and void of any magic. Carefully, she placed the replica around Hamlet's neck, kissing him softly on the lips.

This was going to be her goodbye, and hopefully one day, he would be able to forgive her.

"We need to move quickly," she urged. She allowed Asher to pick her up, guiding her onto the terrace and casting an illusion on her. "Those human monocles are enchanted to see magic. We cannot be seen by them." Asher nodded his head, pulling a black cloak over her.

They escaped over the garden wall, past the cobblestone bridge, and neared the Vilis Lighthouse unseen. On the beach, near the waves, two Calisan Maji paced back and forth. When Kahlisenya had agreed to allow Calisan soldiers to stay in Hellharth, she didn't do it as an act of good faith.

No. She had seen what needed to be done in her visions, and her soul would be damned for it.

There, a drunken man slouched against its base, his slurred words barely audible over the sea winds.

"This is what you brought me?" she said in disbelief. "He can barely stand."

Verik slapped the man across the face, and he jumped up with a start. "Damnit! What the hell was that for?" the man snipped. Verik punched him in the gut, and he vomited onto the ground.

"He will have to do. Can't wait anymore. The potion will wear off soon and Hamlet will wake up," she said.

"Who do you think you are? The Queen?" the man snorted.

Kahlisenya contemplated for a moment, steadying her resolve. "No," she said, "but you are." She held her hand up, focusing all her strength on this one task. The ships drifted in the sea, occasionally shining a blaring light onto the sandy beaches.

She was running out of time.

The man's face contorted in pain as he clutched his stomach. His hair morphed from mousy brown to lengthy white tendrils while twisting antlers sprouted from his skull. Kahlisenya's power flowed through her fingertips, and she began to shake, her brow sweating.

Kahlisenya watched in morbid fascination as she turned this man—now a woman—into herself. This person was now her—down to her very core. It wasn't an illusion.

"What on earth did you do to me?" gasped the imposter Kahlisenya, her face contorted in pain. She opened her mouth, attempting to let out a scream, but Asher's fist smashed against her cheek, leaving her dazed and disoriented.

"We must be patient and wait for one of those Calisan ships to cast their light upon the beach—it must be timed just right. We need the Queensguards to witness them," Queen Kahlisenya said. "Look, there are four approaching along the dunes as we speak."

The sound of waves crashing nearby filled the air as Verik and Asher firmly gripped the imposter by her arms. They could feel her body trembling with fear as they dragged her toward the beach. The salty sea breeze mixed with the scent of adrenaline as they neared their destination.

Once they were at an adequate distance, Verik and Asher flung the imposter down the sandy slope, sending her tumbling with a cacophony of thuds and grunts. They quickly ducked out of sight behind a nearby dune, holding their breaths as they heard the Calisan soldiers run toward the direction of the commotion.

Perched atop the lighthouse, Kahlisenya observed intently as her imposter clumsily struggled to regain balance. The curious Calisan Soldiers soon broke into frantic shouts. Clutched in the imposter's hands was her broken antler. As the Queensguards heard the commotion, they hurriedly approached the scene, their silhouettes visible against the dunes. The glow of ships' lights focused on them from the sea.

"Don't come any fucking closer!" the imposter yelled, brandishing her antler at the soldiers. She swiped at them with it viciously.

One soldier, driven by panic, struck her with his sword hilt. She spun from the impact and fell on her stomach. The scent of blood wafted to Kahlisenya on the breeze.

The Queensguards raced forward with their swords drawn, barking orders. Among them was Highwing.

"No! Don't move! Oh—oh Gods!" gasped Highwing as he reached out for the imposter, who struggled to stand.

The antler had impaled her abdomen on impact, causing an alarming amount of blood to drench her white nightdress. The rampant sounds of struggle intensified; swords clashing and angry voices echoing in the frenzy.

The Queensguards charged at the soldiers while lights from ships illuminated flares into the sky. Hellharth came alive with panic as Kahlisenya turned away from the mayhem she had unleashed. With a final surge of magic, she conjured a portal leading to the Highlands.

As she stepped into the portal, Kahlisenya knew with a heavy heart she had just single-handedly ignited yet another war.

Her only thought; Ellaryhssa.

To be continued...

About the Author

Genesis started writing stories and poetry at the age of twelve. Her love for writing only grew as she did. She enjoys the quiet life in upstate New York, with her small family, and her dog, a Boston terrier named Loki.

Follow on TikTok @gigixbat

Goodreads: Genesis Batista

For updates on the next installment in the Tales of Arcadea Series.

Queen of Ash, Book two.